# A HIDDEN GIRL

# GIRL

by D.K. BOHLMAN

bp

# THE HOTEL CRISTAL

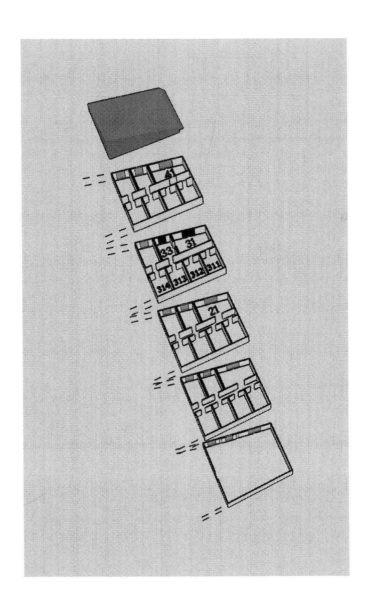

# In Memory

Dedicated to my dad Ken Bohlman.
Even in ill health,
he was making his usual meticulous corrections.

# Prologue

---

The thin, dark-haired girl opened her eyes and the air pressed in on her straight away.

It starts again.

She felt like she'd slept longer than usual. There was more light in the room than she was accustomed to on waking, enough to make out the outline of her alarm clock.

She rolled onto her back and stared at the ceiling. A thin strip of daylight illuminated a ghostly constellation of dust motes. They danced to a rhythm of endless *ennui*. It was hard to get up each day when every one was more or less the same.

Peeling herself from the sheets, she walked across the worn carpet to the opposite wall, where thick laths of wood were nailed across the window recess. Between the middle two was a crack. Not big. But enough to let a slice of light through and, more importantly, enough for her to see through.

Her spyhole onto the outside world.

She pressed her eye to the crack. She heard the tram before she saw it, like the rumble of thunder. A multi-coloured flick-book of tram slices sped past her eyes. She read the advert on the side "*Herpesz? Afta? Carbosan*". A cream for mouth ulcers: she'd seen it before. She sighed and leant her forehead against the wood. It would be good to see a new slogan on the tram. Something interesting to think about.

Once in a while, if there was some kind of hold-up, the tram stopped in her line of sight. She could watch people, holding the straps that hung from the ceiling of the tram. They stood talking to each other, reading newspapers or speaking into mobile phones.

She could watch TV for an hour or so each evening. But it wasn't the same as seeing real people through the crack in the wood. Like the difference between a CD and live music. *Sort* of similar, but wildly not.

She watched them, wondering where they were going, where they lived, who they went home to. Who they loved and whether they had children. When they might die … which struck her as an unusual thing for someone of her age to think.

One day recently, she saw a young mother struggling to get her pushchair down from the tram. It was raining and the mother was trying to pull a hood up on the buggy whilst getting drenched herself. Someone stepped forward to help her and she smiled at them, thanking them for their kindness. You could make out the baby's face, asleep with almost a grin throughout the whole episode. She'd wondered how she would feel about having her own child. About having that kindness offered to her. She'd felt a strong maternal urge at that moment, an urge smothered by her own situation.

She'd tried yelling at them, to attract attention. But the window was glazed with triple panes. No one could hear her from up here.

Right now though, it was the second-class performance, the tram sprinting across the crack's field of vision, the show she got most of the time.

However, *something* was different. She'd heard noises upstairs the previous evening. Banging, a faint raised voice.

And what sounded like a scream.

It'd been hard to hear, more like a squeak, she hardly heard anything through the walls or floor. She supposed they were soundproofed somehow. But there was definitely something, however muffled, last night. Not at all like him. And what's more, breakfast was late. It hadn't been delivered yet and she always heard it arriving.

The thought of breakfast made her stomach growl. Bread, jam, eggs, and coffee every morning – the menu never changed - but somehow she always looked forward to it. Partly because she was hungry by then. Probably, she thought, because it was the signal for the interminable boredom of night time to end, for the world outside to crank itself up and for her day of spying through the crack to begin.

She turned away from the window and switched on the small gas fire on the opposite wall. He'd had it installed a few weeks after she came here. It was the only heating she had but it was adequate. There was a faint smell of gas around the fireplace. She'd noticed it yesterday too. The fire came on fine though. She'd need to mention it to him. It would be something to do.

# NOVEMBER 2018

# Barlinnie jail, Glasgow

He stopped jogging, leant against the damp bricks of the nearest wall, gasping from his run, breath misting in the air. A bead of sweat trickled down the side of his brow, cooled. He flicked it off.

Staring out beyond the wall of the exercise area was frustrating.

The real world was so damn close. And the one person who used to keep his spirits anywhere near alive in this place was dead now. *Double whammy.* It screwed him up and there was nothing he could do about it, no outlet for his smouldering fury or his need for a soulmate. Or a *real* lover.

He'd been thinking a lot in the last few weeks. Thinking about what might help him. In the end, there was only one thing he'd ever been able to come up with. Revenge. But what did that actually mean, what would *really* make him feel better about his miserable existence?

Recently, his thoughts had settled on a new target.

The girl.

The one who'd dug under Glenda Muir's deceptions and caused the whole set of events leading up to her death. Precocious little thing. She'd been too cocky in the trial as far as he was concerned. He'd taken a dislike to her clever nice-girl-next-door image. Somehow she'd overtaken Calum Neuman on his list of people to get back at. Neuman had played his own part in one of his earlier convictions, but his little girl assistant … well, she'd been the nosey little bitch who'd actually caused Glenda's demise. Not to mention his own incarceration. And Glenda had been the *only* love of his life.

It was all about working out his first move. The question was how. How to get to her. He needed to find out a bit more about her first. Where she lived, who she loved, that kind of thing. He also needed really good prep on this and no more misses like the one with Neuman, unlucky as that was. How the hell was he to have predicted the guy's surfboard would tip as he pulled the trigger? Anyway, this was a job for one of the old crew. He still had plenty of money. And a few favours to call in. The thing he'd needed most had been a phone, but that problem was solved. Drone drops, who'd have imagined that when he'd started his prison "career"? The biggest issue now was keeping the phone hidden.

Alan Burton pushed himself from the wall and continued to pound around the rectangle. His renewed movement spurred him on to decide to make a call that night. To start the process. To get his revenge. A dish best served cold apparently. And he was bloody freezing.

*Just fucking do it.*

# A funeral

---

Private investigator Calum Neuman stared ahead into a glade of fir trees. Thin spheres of mist clung to the trunks, a drizzle slewing across the ground.

As the first spades of soil sprayed and clattered across his daughter's coffin, he looked down at the burnished wooden box and dissolved into tears. Lungs tight, hard to exhale.

Cassie, his ex-wife, was slumped against his tall frame, arms taut to her chest. Her slight figure looked down with him, raising a pale hand towards the freshly dug hole.

'Bye, little one.' The sobbing came again.

Her grief fuelled Calum's. He pulled her tightly into the cover of his raincoat, as the drizzle speckled their faces.

It still made no sense to him. Sure, she'd been ill with the cystic fibrosis for a number of years now … but it'd always been pretty much under control. Until Saturday 27th October.

He'd had a call from Cassie that evening. Ellie was bad, worse than previous episodes. The doctors were concerned.

By the time he'd got to the hospital in Inverness, his daughter was dead. Walking into the room where she lay, peering into the eyes of those around the bed, seeing their hurt and their unspoken message for him … that was a scene driven hard into his memory, hurting forever.

She'd been fine during the day, been to the local cinema with one of her friends, Ally. Then, after the walk home, she'd started with laboured breathing, just like when she had an occasional poorly period. An ambulance whisked her to Raigmore hospital. It didn't take long for her to go critical. And not much longer to die.

The doctors had seemed genuinely shocked. One of the consultant's team, who'd seen her during a previous episode, had struggled to explain why it had happened so suddenly and so quickly.

Calum cast a glance to his right where his old assistant Jenna stood, arms linked with Gregor, her one-time boyfriend from their home village. Tears streamed down her face. She mirrored Calum's gaze, twisting her lips into an attempt at a comforting grimace.

He turned his gaze back towards the coffin, feeling Cassie's warmth seep into his side.

So he and Cassie stood in silence, together with Jenna and Gregor, two sets of ex-lovers, reassembled by the events of ten days earlier.

Calum half-turned into Cassie, motioning his head towards the row of cars lined up at the entrance to the cemetery. She resisted his movement, her eyes on the casket quickly disappearing under the damp earth.

She whispered a final, throaty goodbye before giving way to Calum's lead and walking back to the funeral car, through the group of black-clad mourners.

Calum opened the rear door, as they moved like zombies into their seats. Peering ahead through the windscreen, all they could see was the empty space in the hearse ahead, the carpeted floor scattered with broken white carnations.

# A wake

In her house in Inverness, Cassie's gaze drifted between the remaining faces. She couldn't clear her eyes of their soft-focus, caused by a steady trickle of tears as she'd spoken to everyone. The worst were Ellie's friends … young girls … all plaintive sobs and comforting huddles with each other.

Paper cups, drained of cheap wine, had fallen flimsy onto the tired-looking sandwiches remaining on a large oval serving plate.

People stood talking, slowly, earnestly, endlessly. It felt like a video played at half speed. They'd been here three hours, Cassie was done in now. She ran her hands through her fine blonde hair, sweeping it back from her forehead to the nape of her neck. She wanted them all to go. She needed to be alone.

Almost.

Calum stood talking to Cassie's mother as the last two teenage mourners slipped out of the back door from the kitchen. Not really wanting to say goodbye, not really wanting to stay either.

'I'll clear these few things up, make us a cup of tea, eh love?' Cassie's mum played the role she thought was expected.

Cassie stared at her ex-husband. She suddenly wanted to wind the clock back. Wanted to have Ellie in her arms as a baby again, Calum stooping over her, stroking her flyaway hair and cooing in that ridiculously over the top way he used to. Wishing for the past wasn't going to help, though, was it?

'You want one?' her mum asked again.

She did. But she also wanted her mother to leave her alone with Calum.

Calum looked at her, seemingly interested in her reply.

'No thanks, Mum. You've done enough today, really, thanks. You must be tired. Why don't you go home and get some rest, I'll be OK now.'

Her mother looked torn between insisting she stay, wanting some company herself and giving in to the reality of a long, draining day.

'But I don't think you should be alone right now. I'm sure Calum would agree,' she said, glancing at Calum.

That was the opening she wanted and she took it.

'No, really, it's fine, Mum … I need to talk to Calum about a couple of things anyway, so I won't be alone just yet. I'll be ready for bed after that myself.'

She felt her heart beating very quickly all of a sudden, nervous of the likely responses from both of them. *What the hell was this all about?*

Calum leaned back against the kitchen doorframe, looking at his mother-in-law.

'OK. I'll be on my way then.' She picked up her woollen coat.

15

She walked over to her daughter and put one hand against her cheek, kissing her softly on the other one.

'I'll ring you later? Make sure you're OK?'

'No need, by the time you're home, I'm sure I'll be in bed. I'll ring you in the morning, first thing, OK, Mum?'

Her mother nodded, pursed her lips together into a faint smile and left, clutching a bag full of emptied Tupperware boxes she'd brought the sandwiches in.

As the door clattered shut, Cassie decided she would move quickly, or else she might lose the courage. She looked at Calum, taking in his blue eyes, looking for some trace of how he might react.

He smiled. Nervously, she thought. But not without some warmth. Maybe she could still read him like she used to.

She took three quick paces forward, hooking her fingers into his belt loops. *Was she really doing this?*

Peering at his chest. Waiting for a response, not wanting to look up at his face and see retreat.

*Be positive.*

She pulled on the belt loops, felt a momentary resistance then a relaxation as his hips bumped clumsily against her.

Now there were warm hands sliding, tentatively, around her back, releasing her held breath.

She dared to snatch a glance upwards. Saw enough to look again.

'Look, I … can you stay? I don't want to be on my own and, well, you know … it's just that you …'

Now her eyes were moistening and she needed him to help her with this, quickly, before she felt very stupid.

He coughed and cleared his throat of his own insecurity.

'Sure, I know … well, maybe it's a good idea … I don't know.'

She remembered he struggled to move his emotions into words and just went for broke.

'Come on, upstairs, I want to curl up with you.' *Did she really say that?*

She pulled away from him, leaving one finger in a belt loop and guided him gently towards the staircase.

## After the wake ...

---

Gregor and Jenna had left the wake early.

Gregor felt he had to take this chance. There hadn't been one for a while now. And, well, she *had* left the gathering with him when he'd suggested it.

They'd walked down the street from Cassie's house in the Drakies area, to where he'd parked his Fiat.

'Shall I drop you back at your place then?'

Jenna dropped her eyes a touch, pulled her lips into a faint wry smile.

'Yep, thanks, that would be nice.'

Gregor's heart skipped a little as he squeezed the remote and popped the door locks open.

Jenna had a shared flat in Inverness now, close to the University of the Highlands and Islands, where she'd started her degree last summer. It was only a few minutes' drive. A few short minutes during which his mind would be buzzing feverishly, planning how to play out the scenario of her jumping out of his car. He would want her to stay in the car awhile and talk … or to follow her into the flat …

As he pulled away from the kerbside, she peered out of the window. 'So you'll be needing to get back on the road to Plockton now then.' A statement, not a question.

'Err, well, not a big rush. Roads are clear right now. I checked the forecast. Why?'

She kept her gaze out of the window. 'Well, you know how the weather changes quickly on that road this time of year. Don't want you to get stuck.'

He fell silent for a moment. Not like Gregor. But he knew he had to get this right and it was stifling his normal chirpiness. And making him nervous.

'Left just here. Only a minute down this road, on the left, number 173. It's got a bright red door, you can't miss it.'

Gregor nodded, still trying to find the right words. The road tore past him and clawed at his mind, rendering him mute. He was running out of thinking time.

'Here, just here Greg!'

As he pulled to a slow stop, Jenna pushed the door open before he had a chance to turn the engine off. She slung one leg onto the pavement.

'Nice to see you … thanks for the lift.' Then she was out of the car, flinging a brief smile at him before heading onto the short path to her front door.

Gregor looked swiftly over his shoulder and threw his door ajar, pulling himself up via a hand on the doorframe. He spoke to her across the car roof.

'Got time for a chat, Jen?'

She turned, still walking, fumbling for her key. 'Mmm … not now eh? Not really in the mood after today. It's been too sad, hasn't it? Maybe I'll call you in a couple of days?'

He grunted, silently disagreeing. Within seconds she was through her door and out of sight.

He slumped back into his seat, cursing his slowness of thought. With a sigh, he turned the ignition key, staring blankly up the road at a couple taking an early evening stroll. He crawled off towards the A9 and the long drive home, feeling more downbeat than he had for a while.

*

The automatic light in the shared entrance hall was slow to trigger. When it did eventually flicker, it grew from a dim glow very slowly. Energy saver bulb, the old type. The landlord was too skimpy with his maintenance to change it for the newer, faster ones. Jenna stopped in the hallway, waiting for enough light to see clearly. She'd already tripped over someone's bicycle pedal in the hallway one night and bruised her shin; she didn't want to risk another stumble.

The gloominess sent her primary senses into overdrive, overwhelmed by smells: damp carpet, a faint aroma of food, probably trodden-in chips from a late snack brought back by an inebriated resident. Oiled bicycle chains. Something else. Sweat maybe. But she couldn't *feel* anyone there.

Eventually, the light was bright enough to move safely. Only a few seconds had passed but it always felt longer. She hurried up the bare staircase and slipped through her door.

She threw her keys onto the table in the centre of the lounge. She shared the flat with Amy, a second-year psychology student. No one home right now.

Stepping across the painted floorboards, she sat on the large window ledge, facing back into the room. She arched her back and breathed out. She would call Gregor soon. How that would work she wasn't sure, but it felt worth doing.

She felt a slight pressure on her back. Nothing really physical, more a *sense* of pressure.

Turning towards the windowpane, she half-expected to see Gregor still there, sat in his old Fiat.

He was gone, though. Nothing there, except a passer-by trudging up the darkening, winter-bound street. There was a slight crack between the window frame and wall where it hadn't quite been latched properly. The lightest draught of air moved through it, brushing her nose.

She shivered, pushed the latch closed and pulled the curtains firmly shut. The half bottle of red standing on the tiny kitchenette worktop looked attractive … and she started to hope that Amy would be home soon.

# A new case

Calum had disentangled himself from Cassie the following morning with some awkwardness and not without a little worry. She'd clung to him for half the morning. Even brought them breakfast in bed and insisted on staying there for a while after the toast and cereals were long gone. He had an afternoon meeting with a client back home in his office in Plockton and it was a good long drive to the west coast.

The appointment was at 2:30, a new piece of work. Without Jenna to help with things like this now, he had to arrange bookings himself and so he'd spoken to this prospective client two days ago. She'd seemed frantic to see him, but with Ellie's funeral ahead of him, he'd had to put her off for a couple of days. She'd even offered to come to his office the same day. So better not be late today.

After a quick shower, he came back into the bedroom to dress.

'You still look good Mr Neuman.'

22

Calum cringed a little, tried not to show it, smiled back and took the compliment. But he quickly shrugged his clothes on to stop the conversation developing in that direction. Still felt good to be told that though.

'Thanks for ignoring my little belly, Cass. Well, time to go now, else I really might be late for my new customer.'

'Hehe, still tall, dark and handsome. Mr Blue Eyes.'

He hadn't a clue what to say next. He wanted to say … it had been good to sleep together, that it was a one-off, that he didn't regret it, that there shouldn't be another time …

Somehow, that all seemed wrong to say aloud. Maybe leave it unspoken. But that could leave doubt, couldn't it? It could.

'OK. I'm off. So, thanks and, well, you know, be in touch.'

Cassie smiled and looked as if she was about to reply but he waved and stepped outside the bedroom smartly and closed the door.

'Let myself out,' he shouted back over his shoulder.

He blew out a long sigh as he strode down the front path to his car. So he'd blown the parting scene again. He tried to put any consequences out of his mind and gunned the engine, pulling out from the kerbside with gusto twinned with relief.

Back in the house, Cassie lay on her back with a flat feeling and a resigned expression. Whatever she'd had in mind when they came upstairs last night, it probably wasn't going to end in a good place. But those thoughts were simply tiny pieces of leaf, strewn aside by the gale of Ellie's death. Tears dripped slowly onto her pillow, as visions of the hospital room flooded her senses. She wished it was time to sleep again.

*

It was an easy drive back for once. No tractors, no cattle on the road. Just open skies and the highland scenery, which he softly sucked in. It gave him quiet time to think about his daughter, not that he could think of anything else for more than a moment. Driving down the last bit of coastline towards the small village of Plockton, the cabbage-palms along the harbour front coming into view, he reminded himself how lucky he was to live in such a peaceful part of the west coast.

He parked on Harbour Street and made his way up the passageway to the office, followed by a light spray of rain.

He shook his coat and smoothed his hair down, flicking the kettle on and raiding the small fridge for the pork pie that had been occupying his mind for the last ten minutes of the drive. He hadn't had one of these cholesterol binges for a few weeks, so that was OK. His latest bloods showed his LDL was under control. He deserved a treat now and then didn't he?

Susan McTeer rang the office doorbell ten minutes early. Calum cursed softly and swallowed as much of his freshly made cup of tea as its temperature would allow, before hurrying across to the hallway. If Jenna hadn't left, she could have entertained the client till he'd finished his drink.

He opened the door to a short, dark-haired woman, late forties maybe. She threw him a tight grin and cocked her head to one side, like a large sparrow.

'Good afternoon. Mr Neuman?'

'Indeed. I'm Calum Neuman. Call me Calum, please … and come in.'

Calum squeezed out his best new-client smile and ushered her across the hallway threshold.

'Door to the right … come and have a seat.'

He pointed her towards Jenna's old desk, positioned six feet away, parallel to his own. He preferred to interview clients this way, without a desk in between them. He could observe all their body language this way.

She surveyed the seating arrangement and took her seat somewhat cautiously, as people often seemed to. Odd things human beings, creatures of habit, funny how a small deviation from the expected norm could send them out of kilter.

'Thanks.'

'Tea? Coffee? I have a real Italian machine if you'd prefer the latter … or latte.'

Susan smiled at his weak joke. 'Tea will be fine, thank you.'

Calum busied himself with the tea making. While it was brewing, he gazed into the large mirror in the entrance hall, via which he could see the corner of the room where Susan was sat. Except she wasn't.

He debated with himself over whether to return to the office, then decided to wait. After a couple of minutes, with a steaming mug of tea in hand, he re-entered the room.

Susan was stood next to the window near his desk, gazing out onto the street fronting Plockton harbour. He glanced down at his desk, checking all was in order before he announced the arrival of the tea.

Susan promptly took the mug from his hand.

'Beautiful view here. Not sure I'd get much work done next to this window.'

'Don't worry, your fees are safe with me. I'm immune to the view, born up here, lived here a lot of my life. It's great, but to be honest I like to look at something different every now and then.'

He mentally bit his tongue for his defensiveness, but she seemed to have ignored it.

They both sat down and Calum gazed at her face for a moment before speaking.

'So, I understand your daughter is missing?'

'Yes. It's been over a week now.'

Susan stared out of the window again. Her eyes welled up as she spoke.

'Sarah's a post-grad at the university in Inverness. She's been doing research towards her Master's. She just disappeared from contact, beginning of last week. She said she might be going on a trip, but didn't say where. Now she isn't at her flat or answering her phone. We reported her missing after a day or so. The police have been making enquiries but nothing so far.'

'So why do you need my help? It does sound like a job for the police force. What do you think I could do that they can't?'

'I'm not sure to be fair. I just want to try everything I can. It's so out of character for Sarah not to be in touch, we're really close you know? It just feels all wrong. Just wrong.'

'OK. I can understand that. So let's get some basic details down. Then we can see how I can possibly help.'

She nodded meekly. 'She's twenty-four. She did her degree at Aberdeen. Politics, specialised in eastern Europe. Took a year off travelling after that, had a couple of temporary jobs then before starting her Master's degree. I'm not really sure, to be honest, what that's all about, something concerning Hungary, I think. She hasn't told me much about it. I know she's been learning Hungarian for the last few months, though.'

Calum considered his words carefully for his next question.

'So, does Sarah tell you about most things or ...?'

Susan curled her mouth sideways, making a cynical expression. 'Depends if she's in the mood, to be honest. She's got a bubbly character, but she sometimes keeps things to herself. Anyway, she's not told me much about this degree. Nor her dad.'

'How often do you speak to her or see her?'

'Well, she shares a flat in town with another girl. Name of Niamh. Sarah comes to see us most weeks, or calls every few days. Not a clingy child, you know, just normal. She's grown up now, isn't she?'

Calum heard some sadness in the last few words. Was that the normal resignation of a parent whose child had not long left home? Or something else? He scribbled down a few more personal details. It took a while. Susan seemed to be one of those people who told you a story about everything before giving you the one-liner you were really after. Calum had learnt over the years, though, that the preamble sometimes provided him with some useful information. So he listened intently.

'Any idea what she'd been doing in the few days before you last heard from her?'

'Nothing unusual as far as I can think. She came round for Sunday lunch last week. Didn't mention anything other than day to day stuff, you know?'

'Boyfriend?'

Susan hesitated fractionally. 'Not sure. Maybe you'd better ask her flatmate that one.'

Calum looked harder at Susan. She turned her head away.

'I think it may be useful for me to talk to her flatmate anyway. Let me get the address from you. I'll make that the first step and then let you know what we might do next.'

'Thank you. Do you think you can talk to me tomorrow, update me?'

'All depends on her flatmate being willing to talk to us, and when she's free. I'll try and do that tomorrow, though, no problem. Might get an associate in Inverness to do that to speed it up.'

'An associate?'

'Yes. She works for me from time to time.'

Bit of a lie. Jenna hadn't worked for him since last summer since she went to Inverness to study. But a white lie sometimes helped impress an eager client.

Calum wondered whether he was letting himself in for a frantic progress chaser. Wouldn't be unreasonable in the circumstances though.

'Any recent pictures? Height and build would be useful too, photos can be a bit misleading.'

She fished an envelope out of her bag.

'Here, a couple of her this year. She's medium build and height I'd say. Black hair, shortish but sometimes gets onto her shoulders.'

Calum thanked her, said he would be in touch.

She nodded acceptance and stood up, remaining still for a moment, staring out of the window, contemplating something.

She looked back to Calum.

'I may as well tell you this, in case it makes a difference, maybe when you talk to her flatmate. Sarah's gay.'

'She's her lover?'

'I don't know. But maybe. So, you might want to bear that in mind?'

Susan moved towards the hallway, clearly wanting to leave the conversation.

'OK, so I'll be in touch, let me get the door for you.'

He didn't get the chance. She was through it before he could pass her in the hallway. She muttered a goodbye and thanks, as she hurried towards the loch-side road.

Closing the door, he wondered if there was a reason why those last dregs of the conversation had been so painful for her. Was it just she perceived her daughter's sexuality as a stigma? Or something else?

He thought another cup of tea might tell him the answer.

A few minutes later he sat down with it and started to re-read his interview notes.

*

The tea didn't work any magic this time. His mind kept springing back to Ellie like the snooze buzzer on an evil alarm clock.

He slumped back into his chair, wondering how to start. The assignment definitely interested him. Since the Muir job a year or so back, he hadn't had much excitement in his case-load. Mundane, local stuff mostly, often things the police weren't interested in but the client wouldn't let drop.

He had a case recently, trying to establish whether the crew of a local fishing boat had been pilfering a share of the daily catch of prawns. Spending time with a telescope on the top of the brae behind the village, for hours on end, in all sorts of weather, had been a depressing experience. And not a stolen prawn in sight. Sometimes he did think his law degree might be used more productively. But this case … maybe it was more like what he needed.

On the other hand, it might need an amount of travel and some research: and those two things weren't always done easily in parallel. If only he had Jenna with him still.

It'd been harder since she left. Harder on Gregor too, for sure. But Calum missed her, and not just because she was an extra pair of hands. It was fun having her in the office and the room felt dead without her banter.

But Jenna was at university in *Inverness*, wasn't she? Maybe there was a way in there … and maybe a bit of extra money would go down well with her for some part-time work? After all, she'd been pleading poverty when they were chatting at Ellie's wake.

So, a call or an email? Or a WhatsApp? He pondered on the best way to get Jenna interested.

He needed to *persuade*. So he would write an email. If he felt brave enough he'd call her with it to hand. If not, he could send it.

He started to type. Fifteen thoughtful minutes later he had a draft.

*So, Jenna-ration more switched on than me. Since you were saying you might need a bit of cash for that high-tech lifestyle you live now, I've been thinking (I know - it's been tough :)). So … here's a thought. I've got a new case. A girl's gone missing. Needs a bit of research. And since she's living and studying in Inverness, I thought it might be up your street, so to speak? You could start by talking to her flatmate and finding out about her colleagues at the university. Easy for you over there. Not for me over here. And you know how lazy I'm getting. What d'you think?*

*Oh, and I thought you might like us working together again. Be like old times. Batman and Robinette. Just don't know how I'd get you to make the morning coffees from over there :)*

*Well, let me know.*

*Calum/ alternate father figure/ wannabe uncle.*

He sat back and re-read it again. Nice bit of flattery: not too much, she'd known him since she was small and understood him very well to boot. It was good enough. But not *quite* good enough to spur him to actually call her. He clicked the send button and let his thoughts drift towards what he might have for his dinner. And Ellie.

# An invite

Her flatmate, Amy, had been late back, well after Jenna had gotten herself into bed, still a bit spooked by something unseen in the street. She'd heard her come in, though, that was the trigger for her to finally fall off to sleep herself.

She'd no lectures until the afternoon on the following day, so she overslept without a care and roused herself out of bed around ten. She stood in the kitchenette, waiting for the kettle to boil, a digestive biscuit half-crammed into her mouth and her mobile phone already lit up with the morning's tweets and posts.

With the tea brewing, she decided it was a dull social media day. Even Gregor had been silent. She'd expected some kind of message from him this morning.

It was kind of annoying to admit it but she felt irritated that he'd been mute. But it was she who'd paused their relationship last summer, wasn't it?

It seemed the right thing to do then, to give herself the space to start university without any expectations, personal or otherwise. Decisions weren't easy, though, or always right. Relationships less so.

She flicked over to her emails.

One from Calum. Likely to be wanting something then.

She read it. His *sad* humour made her laugh, as usual. How could such corny lines make her giggle and smile?

It had her attention, so she read it again.

She clicked the email shut and absentmindedly finished making the tea, spilling the milk over the edge of the mug as she thought about his offer.

It had her interested, of course. She'd loved working with him, especially on the more unusual stuff, although the Glenda Muir case had definitely been more than she'd bargained for.

But a missing girl, helping investigate the background here in Inverness?

It was an easy decision. Of course she would, she was sure she could work it around lectures and study.

The only real question was how hard to play hardball in agreeing to it … especially knowing she could wind him up a bit over it. This could be fun.

So, the first step would be to … not reply for a day. Let him fret over whether to chase her again. Her betting was weighted towards him doing just that. He'd probably put a read receipt on it too. So he'd know she'd seen it.

With a smile on her face, she took the cup of tea back to bed with her, plus a couple more digestives as a light breakfast, and promised herself she would get up and shower by eleven.

# Calum waits

It had been nearly twenty-four hours now and no reply. But she'd definitely seen the email. The day had dragged because it was full of drudgery and because he was waiting for her answer. He chided himself for having nothing more important to chase down, to fret over. But he knew they had a special relationship and it actually hurt a little to be ignored.

If she didn't reply by breakfast the next day, he'd have to think up a spiky chaser, something to make her laugh *and* say yes. He reluctantly shut down his laptop and locked up the office, making for home.

He stopped on the way at the village store. He needed something for his evening meal and didn't fancy the pub tonight. He picked out some fish and veg. He had potatoes already. That would do. He handed them to Jackie, the shop assistant and pulled out his wallet. Overtaken by a sudden desire to allow himself something indulgent with his healthy dinner, he called a halt.

'One second.'

He returned with two cans of full-fat lemonade. One for tonight. *Only* one, he promised. At least so far, he wasn't showing any signs of his blood sugars getting to too high. He could afford to give himself a treat.

Jackie smiled as he put the cans on the counter. He knew why. She was aware he tried to eat healthily. And she knew he was weak sometimes, but she never said anything, just smiled at his bashful indiscretions. He paid her and left the shop, the doorbell tinkling gently behind him as he strode off up the loch-side.

Ten yards into his walk home, a hand grabbed his shoulder, with a gruff 'Hey Calum' behind it. He spun around. Gregor.

'Hey, Greg. How're things?'

'Not bad, you know, for this place.' He looked across the harbour.

Calum knew what he meant. An idyllic place to live, on a loch, on the north-west coast of Scotland, but an existence which could get tedious if you worked here all the time: like Gregor did.

'But I did have a good chat with Jenna after the wake. It went OK, by the way, didn't it? I don't know what else to say, Calum. Sorry.'

Calum smiled thinly back. 'Yeah, I know. But it was great so many people came along. It's done now. We've just got to move on, haven't we? Even though there's something about it all that bugs me.'

'What d'you mean?'

'Well, not sure there's any point going over it. It just makes me tense when I think about it. But it all happened so quickly, not expected, you know? And she'd been loads better the past year. I don't know what I'm saying really, but I just think there's something more to know, about why it happened the way it did. That's it really.'

Gregor lowered his eyes, obviously unsure what to say.

'I see. Yeah.'

Gregor's awkwardness was saved by Calum's phone warbling.

Cassie's name was flashing on the display. He'd thought she might call. He wasn't sure what he'd do if she did. In the event, he looked at the screen for two seconds and panicked a bit, clicking off the call, delaying the inevitable tricky conversation. He couldn't face it right now.

Calum shook his head to clear his thoughts, then remembered Gregor had mentioned Jenna.

'Anyway. Enough of that. You said you'd talked to Jenna. Any good come of it?'

An enigmatic smile and a twinkle in Gregor's eyes told Calum maybe.

'Yeah, could be. We'll see. Going to talk to her again soon.'

Calum mock punched Gregor's shoulder. 'Hey, that's good news, buddy. Hope it goes well.'

His brain made a quick connection and threw a proposal to his mouth, which he opened again.

'Actually, I just sent Jenna an offer to do a little work for me.'

Gregor's eyes lit up.

'What, here? In Plockton? But how could she do that, what with her studies?'

'No, not really, like you say that wouldn't really work but, well, I can't give away any of the case details, of course, but the work would be research, mostly in Inverness itself, I think. So it kind of works. Anyway, I was going to say, I need an answer from her. So if you speak to her before I do, use your charms on her, eh?'

Gregor gave him a rueful smile. 'Wish it were that easy, mate. My charm doesn't seem to work as well as it used to. But yeah, I'll try if I get a chance. No problem. Got to go anyway, pick up my fiddle. I'm playing down the pub tonight and there's a good few tourists in for this time of year, so better be on time.'

Gregor walked on down the street, with a back-handed wave. Calum looked on after him for a moment. They both missed Jenna, it was a little bond between them. Maybe together, their persuasion would be strong enough to get her back into both their lives.

With a hopeful sigh, Calum walked on home up the damp street, wondering whether he'd bake or grill his fish. He took a glance at his new Apple watch. His heart traces all looked fine. He promised himself he'd try *not* to check every day. Maybe every other day to start with.

# A reply

*OK, maybe I've kept him hanging on long enough,* she thought.

Jenna was staring out of her bedroom window, which had a side view of the street. Grey skies and a steady drizzle confronted her this morning. A damp runner wearing a beanie hat and a small dog in tow pounded across her vista.

She had an hour before lectures, so with a slice of toast in hand, she flipped open her laptop and started to type. Play hard to get? That would be a bit obvious with Calum. He knew her too well.

The brown painted chip wallpaper ahead of her wasn't inspiring her. It wasn't only Calum who was on her mind. Gregor. Gregor of the fast fiddle and easy smile. Gregor with *her* sense of humour and *his* lack of adventure. Should she stay or should she go (now)? That song lyric stuck in her head. She was sure she was doing what she wanted, starting her degree course here, on the opposite side of Scotland to her two male 'problems'. Well, she was when she started a month or so back.

She fidgeted around, made a coffee and came back to her seat, with half a reply in mind, for Calum at least.

*Hmm sorry, this went into my spam mail for some reason. Must be telling me something? Anyway, a something I'm going to ignore. I'd love/jump at the chance/be ecstatic to work with you again. Great idea. Fantastic. When can I get started?? What's her flatmate's address?? Tell me her course at the uni too?? I'll need paying a fortune, of course. And no dressing up as Robinette. Or coffee service. Or admin. And I want some juicy bits on this one.*

*Jenna x*

Well, that would make him read it twice for sure.

A few seconds after she'd pressed the send key, she thought about Calum's daughter, Ellie. Maybe the tone of that email had been a bit too bright right now. Or maybe that was what he needed. No point worrying about it now, though. And she had to get moving to her first lecture. And as for Gregor, well, that needed some thought before she got around to talking to him. She needed to think through that one a bit more carefully.

She brushed her teeth, stuffed a couple of texts she'd been reading last night into her rucksack and pulled on her orange cagoule as she locked the flat door behind her.

\*

Calum almost spat out a whole mouthful of his coffee in a mirthful fit. A fleck or two of froth did escape onto the screen and he wiped it off with his shirt cuff.

Well, well, she never failed to surprise him. She'd made his morning, afternoon and week.

*Wonderful! I'll call with all the details tonight so you can get started. Great to have you back on board.*

He didn't click *send*. He thought he'd wait an hour or so …

# Sarah McTeer

Sarah McTeer felt a bit crowded by the busy departures lounge, squashed into a seat between a hen-party group on one side and an overweight businessman with coffee-breath on the other.

She pulled out her iPhone in an attempt to leave that unpleasant reality and scanned Facebook and Twitter for something interesting. There wasn't anything in that category. It took a few minutes of flicking through the usual dross her feeds threw up each day before she admitted the truth she'd known for a while. Social media was really quite dull. When did you ever get an intense experience, a job offer, a pay rise, a hot date through Twitter?

Yet every day she read her feeds. Many times a day. It was just a more modern version of leafing through the post every day, all the fliers, junk mail and rubbish, hoping for the letter that said you'd won a prize in a raffle you'd forgotten you'd entered. It never happened. Maybe on this trip, she'd give it up … when was Lent?

She was hoping there'd be more diversions to keep her amused when she got to her destination. She felt that warm pulse of excitement that rose up whenever she was researching something new, something interesting. In this case, it might just be publishable too. It all depended on finding people who'd had some involvement. Without them, it would most likely be hard going.

Finally, her flight was called to board. She picked up her canvas rucksack and set off for gate ten, hoping the hen party and the businessman were on a different flight.

\*

She had one wish granted. The businessman, unfortunately, had a seat allocated right next to her. She thought business types flew in business class. Maybe this guy was a cheapskate or not making much money. Either way, his left arm was taking up the armrest between them, forcing her to lean into the window recess. She pushed a pillow into it and resigned herself to an uncomfortable few hours.

Once drinks were served, her unwanted companion decided to start a conversation. She'd avoided eye contact up to that point, but when the flight attendant asked her if she wanted a drink, she had to turn her head that way: and that was his opportunity. He smiled and helped pass her Diet Coke over.

His name was Stephen. Seemed he was exporting some kind of electrical products and visiting a new customer. Sarah feigned only the slightest interest and gave away as little as possible when questioned about her own plans.

It was tiresome, but she finally managed to create a break in the chat and get on to eat her meal when it arrived, pretending to get involved in reading an article in the flight magazine. A couple of small bottles of red wine helped her escape to a more soporific state, which turned into a post-prandial doze.

It was some unknown amount of time later when she felt something fluttering around her ankles.

She opened her right eye, her eyelid sticking slightly and presenting her with a blurred image. Not an image she wanted to see. Her neighbour had his head hovering over her lap and his hands somewhere lower. She froze momentarily, then in a decisive explosion, thrust her left hand upwards and pressed the attendant call button whilst grabbing the man's head under her right arm, locking it tightly, elbow curled around his neck.

Pandemonium broke out.

He sort of snorted and gasped simultaneously, creating an unnaturally good impression of a boar in rut. The passengers across the aisle turned their gaze at the flurry of activity and elbowed and poked their neighbours, encouraging them to have a look.

Meanwhile, the flight attendant was moving slowly down the gangway towards them until she realised what was going on, at which point she broke into a wobbly gallop.

'What the hell are you doing?' the man squawked hoarsely through his grunts, still unable, despite his considerable size, to get enough leverage to free himself from the perfumery of Sarah's armpit.

'That's what I want to know, matey.'

The attendant perused the scene: a middle-aged man with his head locked against his neighbour's breast, and his hands all over her, squawking loudly, whilst the woman looked calmly determined to hold onto him.

'Maybe it would be better if you let him go, madam, then we can sort this out.'

Sarah released her hold, leaning away from him, locking him with a suspicious glare instead.

For his part, he went quiet for a moment, composing his body, clothes and mind.

'I was trying to pick my napkin up. It fell down near your feet. I did say excuse me.'

Damn.

His eyes told her he was telling the truth.

'Really? I didn't hear you.'

'Well, I said it twice and then went ahead to pick it up when you didn't answer. Maybe you'd dozed off.'

He spoke in a clipped voice but a remarkably calm one, given what she'd just put him through.

'I guess I *was* dozing a bit.' She felt an unwelcome surge of blood flush into her face.

'Yeah. Maybe so. I guess it must have looked odd if you woke up to see me doing that.'

She couldn't resist a little laugh at that. It was comical really, now she was fully awake and realised he wasn't actually trying to grope her.

'So did you get the napkin?'

'With that headlock on? No chance.'

She looked down at the floor, couldn't see any napkin, leant further forward and down, so she could see under the seats a bit. There it was, further back, in between them. She plucked it out from its resting place and offered it to him.

'I guess this is a white flag too. Sorry. My mistake.'

'No problem. You can buy me a beer to make up for it.'

She nodded, without a sign of the exasperation that he'd just inflicted on her. Stretching back into her seat, she looked out the window and wondered how she was going to be simultaneously apologetic and stand-offish for the rest of the flight.

\*

A few strained hours later, Sarah fell backwards, arms out wide, caught by the welcoming 'oomph' of a soft mattress topped by a thick quilt. The curtains were still open, dusk settling around the old capital's streets. She turned her head sideways.

From the fifth floor of the Grand Danubius hotel, she could see the river, coursing strongly through the heart of Budapest. Tourist boats lit with strings of bulbs stretched down both sides of their length, drifted past her vantage point, sparsely filled with diners on a routine circuit up and down the main sights. The vast illuminated bulk of Buda castle looked down over it all, a reminder of the city's occupied past.

She was too weary from the flight and the strain of being pleasant to her temporary travelling companion, to go out to eat. She picked up the room service menu, scanning for comfort food. A hamburger and fries sounded just right. She dialled the number and got a thirty-minute wait time. That would be perfect. Time to laze and have a quick wash.

An hour and a half later she put the dirty plates outside her door and went back into her room, wondering what to do with the rest of the evening. Read or walk were the choices. Nothing arranged on the research until tomorrow. She took a look out of the tall window. The hotel had a faded charm about it, an imposing building, probably very grand a while back, but not so upmarket anymore. If it had been, she wouldn't have been able to afford it.

Outside, she could see a few people walking along the riverside, thick coats on. It turned cool quite quickly at this time of the year in Budapest.

A good brisk walk was quite appealing. She grabbed her coat and made her way out to the riverside. The tables outside the cafes on the elevated walkway next to the river were mostly deserted, too cold for the diners and drinkers. She skipped down some steps onto the waterfront and started to walk, sucking in the fresh air and exhaling slowly, relaxing.

There were a few boats moored along here, some were music bars and restaurants, some looked like river dwellings, large modern houseboats. She loved seeing how people in other countries lived. Twenty minutes was enough, though. She looked at her watch, turned around and headed back to the hotel. It was fully dark now and this stretch of the road wasn't well lit. She shivered against the cold and the occasional person loitering against the dull brick and steelwork that held up the tram line beside the river. Something … and nothing … suddenly spooked her and she quickened her step.

Ten minutes later, she arrived back in the hotel lobby and headed to the bar, ready to sink a good slug of whatever passed for the local spirit in Hungary.

The swarthy and very friendly barman suggested cherry palinka. A strong fruit brandy. After half an hour and a couple of what looked like pretty liberal measures, she realised he wasn't joking about its strength. The barman had suddenly become worryingly attractive in her soft-focus vision. That wasn't really her scene.

Dropping her frame carefully down from the barstool, she made her way slowly to the lift, hit the fifth-floor button heavily and didn't really remember getting into bed.

# Ervin Szabo

Sarah's breakfast was a slow affair, her metabolism shockingly dulled by the palinka from the night before. Three cups of coffee and a pile of fried eggs and local sausage later, she felt she could brave the day.

She had an appointment at the central library with a local academic at eleven o'clock. Eszter Borbely had promised to help her with article retrievals and some questions today, given her own poor knowledge of the Hungarian language. A week's crash course in the university languages department had only just got her to the point of making basic requests, never mind understanding natively-fast responses. Sarah's university tutor, Professor Robertson had arranged for Eszter to help, through his contacts in academia. With a bit of luck, Eszter might be free to assist her for most of the week or so that she intended to be here.

With a final gulp of coffee, she rose from the table, picked up her rucksack and headed out along the riverside path.

It was chilly again but perfectly still, and the crisp air felt really good inside her lungs.

She went as far as Elisabeth Bridge and turned away from the river, taking a Google map-led route through quieter streets, past the colonnades of the Magyar Nemzeti museum. The forty-minute walk woke her up and she was feeling quite bright by the time she entered the Ervin Szabo library through the ornate wrought iron and glass doors on Revicky Street.

She checked her phone for the photo of Eszter and headed straight into the cafe where they'd arranged to meet.

She spotted her contact straight away, seated at a small table directly opposite the entrance.

It seemed she'd been checking her photos too, as she smiled broadly and waved at Sarah, beckoning her to sit. She offered her hand to Sarah. A bit formal, Sarah thought, but OK, they hadn't met before, only spoken a couple of times on the phone.

She was small and wiry, blonde hair cut short with curly tendrils dropping across her forehead. Maybe forty-five, Sarah thought. They ordered two americanos with milk.

'So, how do you find Budapest so far?'

'It's a lot colder than I expected. But the drink I had in the hotel last night warmed me up. Pal... something, I think it was.'

'Palinka! Oh yes, that's very strong. Well, it sounds like you had a real Hungarian welcome. I hope I can give you some more of that, Sarah.'

The accompanying smile felt warm and genuine. Sarah was already beginning to feel like they could get along. That would really help. She brought Eszter up to speed with the latest position on her research and Eszter nodded her understanding at appropriate intervals.

'So, yes, let's get started then. I'll show you to the best section, to begin with. As I've said, most are in the Hungarian language, but there are some German and English texts too.'

They made their way out of the cafe and into a wide lobby area before taking the lift up to the fourth floor. As they exited the lift, Sarah was struck by the stained-glass window on the landing.

Eszter noticed. 'Lovely, isn't it? Let me show you around here first Sarah, before we start work.'

Eszter led her across the floor and into a side room. It was very elegant and led into a network of other, even grander areas. The decoration made Sarah gasp. In one room, two ornately carved spiral staircases led up to panelled galleries. Beautifully formed and painted plasterwork lined the ceiling, and old wooden panels adorned the walls. Antique oak study tables around the room were topped with green glass and brass reading lamps. It took Sarah by surprise. She hadn't expected the library to be this gorgeous. Filled from floor to landing with books, the grandeur lent it the air of a place of seriously civilised learning.

She felt hushed by it all.

'This part of the library was an old Baroque palace. And this was the smoking room.'

'Amazing. How great to be able to work amongst all this.'

Eszter smiled, then guided her to a small alcove at one end of the room, stopping close to one particular bookcase. She pointed at the third shelf down, which was easy to access with a stool.

'There's much of the material in this section, Sarah. And the two shelves below. These are mixed-language texts. So maybe best you have a look through yourself, to try to get a feel for what you want to look into. I'll try and make a list of a few items in Hungarian which I think are essential, from what I know of your research outline. Then you can look at the English content cross-reference index and pick out any you think too? After that, we can draw up a list and work out what help you need from me?'

Sarah nodded quickly. 'Perfect. I'll give you a shout when I'm ready to exchange ideas, then we can go back down to the cafe to chat about what we've got.'

Sarah turned to the book-lined wall and started the process of choosing where to begin.

\*

Ninety minutes later, Sarah was sat stooped over the English cross-reference index, feeling overwhelmed. It was always like this when she started a new piece of work. So much to read … just getting started was the best way, the first few things you thought about or read had a way of leading you on to other pieces that eventually started to take some shape. But it was still hard getting moving, especially with the shadow of a palinka hangover tailing her mind and body, tugging at her, slowing her down.

She stared out of the window framed with wooden shutters, looking for some inspiration.

The title of her research piece was: "Arrow Cross: an examination of the motivation and thinking behind its leadership."

It had been her professor's suggestion, based on her interest in the treatment of the Jews in the Second World War. And for a master's topic, it seemed to fit the bill on lots of counts, one of which was to do a bit of travel as part of the research. So here she was.

Arrow Cross had been a neo-Nazi movement in Hungary in the 1930s and 40s, led by Ferenc Szalasi. When Regent Horthy had tried to pull Hungary out of the war in 1944, Arrow Cross won the support of the Nazis to take power and continue protection of Germany's southern flanks against the Soviet army. At first Arrow Cross had run riot on the streets of Budapest, gangs of supporters, often as young as 15 or 16 years old terrorising the city into obedience. And killing a lot of people, especially Jews, in the process.

They didn't last long. At the end of the war, the party was shut down and Szalasi executed. But they had a strange blend of ideas, which had fascinated her. A unique mixture of nationalism, socialism and Jesus worship, which, in Szalasi's view had global worth. Deluded or what?

There was a lot of material on the formation of the party in 1935 and the early rallies and meetings. That seemed a good place to start. The other thing she wanted to dig into was Szalasi's family and upbringing. What had driven and formed him to be the apparent monster he became? There were other key people in the leadership besides Szalasi though. She wanted to look at all of them.

With a scribbled list of texts to start working through, she looked over at Eszter and caught her attention with a silent wave. After a mute imitation of eating something, the two women set off back down to the cafe to compare notes and work out their plan of action.

Settled at a table, they ordered open salami sandwiches with some grape sodas which Eszter recommended. Sarah picked up the bill. She was hoping to somehow claim it against her research grant but wasn't sure if she could. Best keep the receipts for now anyway.

After a quick lunch during which they discussed progress, they went back upstairs and continued before retiring yet again to the cafe around five-thirty. They'd both had enough reading and needed some downtime.

'So, what have we got so far?' Eszter said.

'Loads of background articles to read. Some I've scanned through and made a note to copy. Others seem less useful. Probably got about twenty per cent through what I've noted down. And there's more added to my list for you to read for me … with some pointers on what I need. Maybe you can double-check if there are translations available too, it will save us time if I can help with your list of Hungarian texts?' Sarah was feeling tired. The first day after a flight and new faces and places had taken their toll.

'Sounds fine Sarah. I made some notes from my readings. I think I just need to go through those with you tomorrow, make sure I'm getting what you need?'

'Yep, let's do that. To be honest I'm a bit tired now. Probably best call it a day, I'll maybe think through a few things after I've eaten in the hotel.'

'Suits me. The family will be expecting some food tonight so I need to go anyway really.'

'Who's at home then?' Sarah enquired out of politeness.

'Just Richard, my husband and Janos our son. He's fifteen now. The Xbox generation, you know.' Sarah didn't really *know* but could guess. She smiled sympathetically.

They bade each other goodbye with a brief hug and agreed to meet the following morning at nine-thirty.

*

Later that evening, when most visitors to the library had left and dusk had settled around the capital's streets, Beata Sandor sat down on the large comfortable chair in her office. She looked up at the ceiling, wondering whether to call or not. She always wondered what the implications might be if she did. She'd heard things. Stories that might or might not be true. Hard to think they could be accurate, but some people were evil and would go to great lengths to protect whatever they had.

Still, she was bound up with the need to protect, wasn't she? Even if she had her personal limits on how far she would go in that respect. In the end, though, she had to do this.

She always kept a close eye on that section. Today, there had been interest in it. Two women, for most of the day and they had been asking at the desk for further references. She couldn't ignore this.

The head librarian picked up her desk telephone and dialled the Bucharest number. Five hundred miles away, a phone rang.

# Peter Kovacs

Dr Peter Kovacs had a sense of fateful bad timing.

His father, Marton, was very ill now. It might not be long at all before he had to do his duty with his father's estate. Now he'd had a call suggesting someone else might be nosing around in their affairs. He didn't need any more complications than he was already facing. Maybe it would all come to nothing, though. A few people over the years had sniffed around. None of them had delved beyond the recorded history. None of them had had the imagination, it seemed.

Beata had always kept him informed from the library, though that wasn't the only source of threat. The world was full of self-righteous people, digging, scouring, wanting to find people with different ideas to themselves, so they could denounce them and pillory them for their beliefs. Social media hadn't helped, it was full of left-wingers terrorising their keyboards into weary submission. Funny how people with right of centre political views seemed almost afraid to express their views in those channels. Facebook, the left-leaning tower of Menlo Park.

But, for some reason, this call unnerved him more than most. He'd keep a close eye on this one. Maybe he needed to have someone in Budapest keep a watch on their movements. He resolved to call one of the group there and put it in place. First, though, he needed to get more of a trace on who they actually were and where these women came from. Beata had suggested one was American and the other a local. But he needed to know more than that.

He'd seen his last patient out of the door ten minutes ago: the receptionist had gone early, something about her child's concert. So he was alone in his Bucharest surgery with time to think, without interruption. He placed his large head in his even larger hands, planted his elbows on his desk and sighed.

After some deliberation he made two phone calls, the first back to his favourite librarian. She was probably still there, doing some paperwork after the busy part of the day had passed.

He ran his index finger up and down the ridge of a long scar on his left cheek until Beata answered. 'Hello, Beata. It's Peter. I've been thinking about what you told me earlier. I'm going to have these two watched. But I'd like you to find out a bit more about them if you can. Where they're from, what exactly they're looking for. As discreetly as you can. Maybe offer to help them with something? Assuming they come back, of course.'

Beata hesitated for a moment. Sniffed. Then remembered her duty.

'OK. Of course. I'll look out for them tomorrow and see what I can find out. I'll let you know, Peter, as soon as I can understand what they're here for. It's probably nothing to worry about, as usual.'

'Thank you, Beata. I know I can rely on you. It's a great help. And maybe you're right. But with Father so ill at the moment, somehow the timing seems like fate. Let's keep a close eye, OK?'

*

Beata replaced the handset and looked around at the walls of books in her office. Some were her own, built up over the years, as her small house started to overflow with her reads. She couldn't throw any out or even give a book to someone else. Loaning was OK, but she kept a list, in case she forgot who she'd lent to. Others were the library's. There were one or two which really ought to be set out on the public shelves, but ... well, at least one of them would tempt fate, wouldn't it? So it was here, under her safe control, so she could know if anyone asked for it.

Keeping those particular texts at home had previously been a very bad move. It had caused her so much personal grief back then. Anyway, now they were safer here in her office. Maybe getting rid of one of them would be better. Safer ... more logical. But she *was* a librarian. Somehow, destroying the only copy of a book, even for the *best* of reasons, was against all her lifelong held interests and principles. She'd done a damn good job of tracking down and destroying all the copies that she understood to exist, bar this one. Her position as a librarian had been a great help in that quest. But no, she should keep this one. Just make sure it was very safe.

She also needed to keep an eye on the two women. Maybe she'd check if they needed any help tomorrow, assuming they turned up again. In her experience, an offer of personal help from the head librarian was usually met with appreciation. She'd gauge their reaction carefully. In the meantime, she had a late meeting to go to.

# Jenna starts work

In the end, Calum didn't wait very long to send his email reply, but kept it short and called Jenna soon after.

'So, basically, she went off on a research trip and hasn't come back?'

'Seems so. At least that's what her mother implied. So like I said, can you start with her flatmate? I've emailed the address over, name of Niamh Sampson. There's time left tonight, can you pop over and see if you can make a start? I told her mother I'd, well, *we'd*, try to update her today. Tomorrow morning would be OK, though, I think.'

Jenna sighed. 'Any other deadlines you haven't told me about? I guess I can get over there in the next hour. I'll let you know how I get on.'

'Nope. But Sarah's mum says her daughter is gay. Not clear to me whether she thinks Niamh is more than a flatmate, so soft-pedal around that one. OK?'

'OK. Talk later then. Do I get a pay rise by the way?'

Calum was ready for this.

'Yep, of course. Since you've been headhunted back to my employ. Ten per cent on your old rate.'

'Can't hear you.'

'Ten.'

'Fifteen,' spat back down the line.

'Ten and no coffee service required,' he said.

A pause.

'Fifteen and *no* coffee service? Done!'

'Haha, cheeky. Ten.'

Another pause.

'OK. For now.'

\*

Jenna was on her way to Sarah's flat within fifteen minutes, having already called to check her flatmate was in and willing to talk to her. Double tick.

It was thirty minutes' walk, no more. The nights were drawing in early now and besides being inky black dark, it was pretty cold for November too. Jenna was bundled up warmly, with a thick coat, scarf and woolly hat. The leaves underfoot had started to coalesce into the annual mushy sludge that came once the rain had spoilt their crisp autumn colours. She skidded a couple of times on slippery piles of them, cursing loudly.

The flat was in the centre of town, part of a converted old 30's style semi-detached. Jenna was there sooner than she'd expected.

She strode up the two front steps and picked out the nameplate for McTeer/Sampson and plunged her thumb into the bell recess.

The door release buzzer sounded without pause and so she pushed her way in and across the hallway to flat 1a. The front door opened briskly, leaving her to knock on fresh air as she was presented with her first view of Niamh Sampson. Shortish, well-built rather than plump. A round face and red hair. A lot older than she expected. This woman looked like she might be approaching forty.

'Hi. Better come in.' Not a sniff of a question as to who Jenna was. Niamh showed her through a tiny hallway to a combined lounge and kitchenette. It was decorated to try to separate the two uses of the room. A big leather sofa split the lounge area off from the kitchen space. Jenna sat down on it, opposite an old coal fireplace, now filled with a fiercely glowing gas fire. Above it hung a large picture mirror and in front a thick woollen rug. Nice and cosy.

'Drink? Tea, coffee?' asked Niamh. Jenna thought she sounded nervous.

'Mmm, yes please, a coffee. Black, thanks.'

Niamh turned into the kitchenette and started to busy herself with making it.

'So, have you lived here long?'

'Err, a couple of years.'

'And Sarah?'

'Yeah, the same.'

'Ah, so you shared as undergraduates, same course?'

'Yeah, that's right.'

Jenna looked over her shoulder at her host. She was turned away from Jenna. Judging by the short answers so far, this might be tough going.

Niamh came over with a mug of coffee and placed it on the table in front of Jenna.

'You not having one?'

'No. Biscuit?'

'I'm fine thanks, just had something to eat.' She smiled at Niamh, somewhat apologetically.

'I'll get some anyway, might change your mind later.'

Niamh went back to the kitchenette and started making rustling noises.

Jenna thought she *might* fancy a custard cream if that's what she came back with. She took a sip of coffee and settled back into the sofa, readying her notebook and pen.

Whether it was some movement in her peripheral vision or a sixth sense awakened by Niamh's abruptness, Jenna couldn't be sure. But as she heard Niamh move close to her and say in a broken voice 'Here you are, some Jammie Dodgers,' she leant quickly forward and to the right, looking back over her left shoulder again. A plate of biscuits dropped past her, scattering its contents to the floor, as a knife blade slashed the air where Jenna's neck had been a split second before.

Instinctively she grabbed at the arm carrying the knife. Lucky timing helped her lock a grip around Niamh's wrist and yank it across her face. She had no idea what she was going to do next, as Niamh's body started to recover from the shock of missing her target. Jenna opened her mouth and sank her teeth into the forearm in front of her. Hard.

The bite, and the effort of the lung-bursting scream that ensued, forced the knife to tumble to the rug. By now, though, Niamh was beating at Jenna's head with her free fist, trying to get a handle on her hair. Jenna ducked a couple of times, managing to avoid the grasping fingers.

She fell forward onto the rug, half facing the fireplace. To the left side stood an ornamental fire-tending kit with a shovel and poker hung on it. It was low enough to swing her hand at and grasp the poker. She had hold of the wrong end but a good enough grip to roll upwards and bring the iron handle swinging around at Niamh. It struck the side of her face with a crack and a squelchy crunching sound.

Niamh yelled loudly and grabbed the side of her face, wincing as she touched it, tears welling up in her eyes.

Jenna looked at her eyes, saw indecision and despite Niamh's grip on her hair, swung again. This time she hit the fingers protecting the obviously fractured cheek. That was enough for Niamh. She wailed like a banshee and rolled away from Jenna, stumbled to her feet and scrambled for the front door.

Jenna jumped up. As she got to the hallway, Niamh snatched a glance over her disappearing shoulder. 'I'll get you, bitch. I'm not done yet.' She vanished through the door, leaving it swinging behind her. Jenna launched herself at it, pressing it closed and pulling the bolt across the top.

She leant her back against the door and slid to the floor, gasping, feeling a trickle of blood dribbling down her brow from a cut on her scalp.

She shook her head, heart pounding, trying to collect her thoughts. What the hell had she done to get that reaction? And why would Niamh want to attack her anyway? And where was Niamh going to go now, having attacked someone in her own flat?

In her own flat. That wasn't right. Had she got the wrong address … no, of course not, that had come from Sarah's mother. It didn't make sense.

She was about to call Calum before deciding whether to ring the police when it dawned on her.

Maybe that wasn't Niamh.

In which case, where the hell was she?

Jenna pushed herself up, looked around the hallway. Three more doors, presumably two bedrooms and a bathroom. They were all closed.

She tried the first. Opened the door slowly. White and blue tiles, a small bathroom with a shower. Empty.

The second was a bedroom. She looked through the crack between door and frame before stepping into it. A second-hand set of wooden drawers with a mirror and some makeup bottles on top. A few items of clothing on the bed. She spotted a small multi-photo frame by the side of the bed. It had pictures of a young woman, what looked like some friends and also one of an older couple. Parents, perhaps. The top edge of the frame was engraved with the words *Niamh's Closests*. Nothing untoward at first sight.

The next room was much less normal.

# A discovery

Jenna looked at the body on the bed in front of her. A woman. A young woman. Probably Niamh. But she wasn't taking anything for granted, after the attack on herself two minutes earlier.

She stepped forward cautiously. A little blood was glistening on the side of the face, which was facing away from her. Jenna walked around the bed to get a better look. Definitely younger than the person who'd attacked her, more like the age she'd expected. Eyes shut, but her chest was moving to a slow rhythm. Her mouth was taped and probably stuffed with something. Her wrists and ankles were bound with the cheap plastic tape too.

Jenna put her arm out and rocked the body gently by the shoulder. A muted moan. Then a slight flicker of the eyes, a slither of eyeball shuttering in and out of view.

'Hey. Are you OK? Who are you?' She peeled the tape away and pulled a rolled-up sock out of the woman's mouth.

No answer. She repeated the question a few times before finally, the girl opened her eyes for more than a split second. She jerked her head back violently from Jenna's direction.

'What the fuck. Who are you?'

The girl pressed herself back against the bed, cowering.

'Are you Jenna?' Scared of the answer.

'Yeah, yeah I am … it's OK, are you Niamh?'

The girl nodded. She started to cry.

'Someone was just here, they attacked me!'

Jenna sighed. 'Me too, it must have been the same woman. What happened?'

Jenna pulled a tissue out of her pocket and handed it to Niamh. She took it hesitantly and proceeded to mop her eyes with it.

'Well, it happened fast. She called up to the flat, said she was you. I buzzed her in and when I opened the door I thought she looked older than I expected, but she just hit me in the face … it happened so fast. Then she pushed something into my face after I fell down. It smelt like petrol or something and I passed out.'

'Did she say anything?'

'Not after I opened the door, no. Next thing I know is you're waking me up. Who is she? And why is this happening to me? I, well, I want to see your ID please.'

Jenna thought quickly.

'Don't have a specific PI ID but I have a driving licence so you can tell it's me from the photo.' She dug in her bag and flashed it towards the bed.

Niamh peered at it and then Jenna. The blood on Jenna's face at least looked like some kind of proof she may have been a victim too.

'Seems OK, I suppose. But what was she doing here?'

Jenna threw her arms outward. 'I don't know. I've really no idea. Look, let's get you a cup of tea. Let's get us both a cup of tea. Then I'm going to ring my boss and then the police.'

'I don't know. I think I want to ring the police myself. Now.' She looked at Jenna, watching her reaction. Jenna understood and relented, not wanting to cause her any alarm.

'OK. But I'm calling Calum now.'

She picked up her mobile and dialled his number. Niamh lay still and watched her for the moment.

'Hey, Jen. Quick report back?'

'Bit more than that. I've been attacked in Sarah's flat. No idea who it was. I'm alright. But she got to her flatmate Niamh first. She's OK too, just a bit shaken. So what's this all about Calum, is there part of the story you're not telling me?'

'Jesus Jen, no way. If I thought there was a problem I would never have put you in that position. You should know that. You really should.'

She heard the heartfelt tone in his voice, knew he was being honest. Not that she ever really doubted him.

'OK. So I'll call the police.'

'Sure. Want me to come over?'

'No, no need. It's getting late and it's a long drive. I'll be fine. I'll handle it and call you later OK? Might be in the morning depending what time the police finish with us.'

'Just call me, Jen, if you need anything, OK? Shall I tell Gregor?'

'Nope. No need. Talk to you later. Bye.'

As she clicked off the call, Niamh propped herself up on one arm. 'OK, can you call the police then please?'

Jenna smiled. 'Sure.'

She dialled 999 and resigned herself to a long evening. As she sat and waited, she asked herself a question. Niamh had said the woman had pretended to be Jenna. So how the hell did she know Jenna's plans? And react so quickly to them?

# An offer of help

Sarah arrived a little early at the library on the second morning. She decided to skip coffee after a large breakfast in the hotel and went straight up the lift to where they'd been working the day before.

Sat at the desk next to the shelves where she intended to work, was a tall, grey-haired woman leafing through a text, with a small pile of tomes next to her.

She looked up, as Sarah set down her bag next to the desk and took a seat near her.

'Good morning,' the woman said.

Sarah smiled back. 'Jo reggelt.' Just about the only Hungarian phrase she didn't have to think about before opening her mouth.

'I'd wanted to catch you. I'm Beata Sandor, the head librarian here. I noticed yesterday you were reading a lot around the Arrow Cross history. I wondered if there was anything I could do to help you. Are you an academic?'

'Oh yes. I am. Sarah McTeer. I'm doing a Master's degree in Scotland. Inverness. I'm researching Arrow Cross. My colleague from the university here in Budapest is helping me. Well, that's very kind of you to offer. We're still reading around the first layer of references but if I need anything I'll ask you, for sure.'

'Ah, Scottish. I had thought you were American. No problem. Will you be in Hungary for long?'

'I expect a week or so for this trip. Not sure after that, it depends on where the research takes me, I suppose. It's my first time here in Hungary, so I'm hoping to look around a bit too, you know.'

Beata pushed her glasses slightly back up her nose and sniffed.

'Ah, that's nice, we have a beautiful country here. I hope you enjoy your stay. Anyway, here are a few texts I have looked out for you. They all have some references to Arrow Cross. Whether they are useful, well that depends on the angle of your research.'

It was a question rather than a statement.

Sarah filled her in on the detail of her research topic. Beata nodded. 'I'm sure there's some material in here that will help with that.'

She closed the book she had open, placed it on top of the pile next to her on the table and slid them all towards Sarah.

'Fantastic. I'll have a look through them.'

'Most are in Hungarian. Can you read our language?'

'Heh, well no, but my colleague is Hungarian and she does the research on those texts.'

Beata nodded again and slipped her hand into the brown woollen jacket she was wearing.

'Of course. Here's my card. Let me know if I can help you any further. It's no trouble. We especially like to help our foreign guests.'

Sarah took the business card. "Beata Sandor. Head Librarian. Ervin Szabo Library. Budapest." Together with two phone numbers.

'Call me anytime. I'm always working. Books are my life really.'

Sarah instantly believed her and beamed her a grateful smile.

Beata rose from the table and walked away, towards the door. At the same time, Eszter appeared at the door and crossed Beata's path as she walked to meet Sarah. Beata cast her a short, sharp sideways glance before disappearing from view.

'Hi, Eszter. Guess what? That was the head librarian. She offered to help with anything we need. How nice is that?'

Eszter sat down and smiled. 'Very! I thought I recognised her from my visits here. Mind you, I've never had any help like that in all the years I've been coming. You're lucky!'

'Oops, sorry! She said she liked to help foreigners. That's kind anyway, eh?'

Eszter flashed a sardonic smile across the table.

'Of course, of course. So what has she given you?'

Sarah explained as the two of them settled down into looking through Beata's selections and picking up on their work from yesterday. Soon, they were buried in it and time sped away from them.

\*

Sitting back in the cafe at the end of the day, Sarah stretched her arms outward, yawning, ready for some fresh air. She summarised their progress.

In short, a lot had been read, lots of references taken for future use. Eszter had a list of specific Hungarian text sections which Sarah had wanted translating and some for which she had just given Eszter questions to answer.

Sarah now had a collection of names she felt worth searching for, on the off chance they were still alive. It was likely most weren't, given their ages when they were active in Arrow Cross. But some first-hand interviewing would be a real bonus, so worth a shot. She could spend some time on that, while Eszter did work on the Hungarian texts.

She looked in the phone directories and eventually found just three names from her list of more than forty. It was possible that there may be some ex-directory, of course, but she'd start with these three.

A thought occurred to her.

'Eszter. If I call these people I'd like to interview, due to their association with Arrow Cross … what kind of reaction am I likely to get, do you think? I'm guessing any kind of link with it is probably frowned upon? I mean, given their track record of brutality and so on? What do most Hungarians know or think about it? I'm just wondering if I do find someone, whether they are likely to refuse me an interview anyway … or is there an angle that might work best?'

Eszter leaned forward a little, so they were closer. She tightened her lips and pulled a half-smile. 'Tricky. Many young Hungarians don't really know much about it. It's not like it's taught in schools, but the older generation does remember and yes it isn't looked upon well, of course. I think it depends upon the individual.

By the way … there has been a lot of new right-wing sentiment here in the last decade. Like in much of the rest of Europe. There has been lots of talk in the papers and cafes about a new Arrow Cross taking root. Maybe it never actually died in fact, but went underground for years. There are always those who can't give things up, aren't there? Not sure if this will make your potential interviewees more or less willing to discuss it, though?'

'Well, unless I'm going to pretend to be someone or something I'm not, I guess I'll just have to ring cold anyway. At least I can say it's for an academic paper, not the press. Maybe I just have to stress that. And keep my fingers crossed.'

'I think so. When will you call them?'

'Early tonight maybe. Before they go to bed since some are maybe going to be in their nineties.'

'Good idea,' Eszter said, 'Actually, I had found two quite interesting articles from the press from the last ten years or so. The searches only went back that far, must have been about the time they started storing it digitally. But they were talking about one of those resurgent Arrow Cross movements I just mentioned, as part of a wider right-wing renaissance in Europe. Might be useful to add that to your list? Maybe there are some younger people with links to the original party or who knew the old members. Maybe you can find them more easily and maybe they might be more willing to talk since they haven't been associated with any war atrocities?'

Sarah was interested. 'Any names?'

'Umm, well, now you say that I can't recall specifically whether there were or not. But one of them referenced a text, a more modern one. "Arrows From a Re-strung Bow" or something corny like that. I looked for it but couldn't see it on the shelves. Maybe it's currently lent out. Anyway, the articles and texts are here. The articles are in English so you can start with those yourself.'

She slid a piece of A4 paper across the desk, with the article names on it.

Sarah picked it up and stared at it intently.

'Yep, great, I'll look through these, see if I can get some names somehow. Thanks. I'll head off now then, see you tomorrow, usual time?'

# Dialling the dead?

---

Sarah walked back to the hotel, dumped her bag on the hotel bed and got undressed. She stared at herself in the full-length mirror. Pretty good. Good enough for a steak dinner anyway. Then some calls and a run later. She thought back to the waterfront and her first night here. Maybe running in the gym then.

She ordered room service. Steak, medium-rare. Fries, salad. Some cheese. A large glass of wine for later.

Forty minutes. Perfect. Time for a nice long shower.

*

An hour later, she pushed the food tray back across the desk and made some room for her note-pad. She pulled out the phone numbers for the three names she'd found earlier. This was her list:

*1. Peter Gera. Possibly the grandson of Josef Gera, Arrow Cross ideologist. Would be in his thirties now.*

*2. Marton Kovacs. A young group leader at the time of the party rule in 1944-45. Probably lucky not to have been arrested and tried. Early nineties if alive. A longshot.*

*3. Ivan Kasza. Son of a former junior minister. Late middle-aged.*

She decided to start, in age order, youngest first, probably in the expectation the youngest one would be more likely to be alive to talk.

She picked up the list and dialled Peter Gera's number. No answer. She decided not to leave a message.

Next was Kasza. Her anticipation made her jump when the phone was answered. It was a woman's voice though, one which said her husband Ivan had died of a heart attack only two months ago. Fuelled by her poor grasp of Hungarian, and the lack of English understanding at the other end of the line, the conversation became extremely awkward. Sarah decided not to ask to talk further to his widow and made a stilted excuse about having to take another call urgently.

On to Marton Kovacs then. She crossed the fingers on her left hand for good luck and punched out the number with her right.

After half a dozen rings, the call was answered. An old man's voice.

Her heart leapt. This *could* be the man.

'Is that Marton Kovacs?'

A pause. 'Yes. Who is this please?'

'My name is Sarah McTeer, Mr Kovacs. I'm Scottish, please excuse my lack of Hungarian. I wanted to tell you what I am doing and why I'm calling you.'

The response came back slowly.

'Oh. Well I speak some English, so I can try that, but first please tell me why you are calling.'

Sarah took a quick, deep breath. 'I'm a university researcher. I'm doing a Master's degree. The topic is around the Arrow Cross party in Hungary. I'm trying to understand more about what was behind it. Ideas. Motivation. Aims. I was hoping you might be able to help, as I understand you worked for the party when you were young?'

Fingers crossed again. She heard a soft sigh. Another pause, longer this time.

'It was a long time ago, young lady. I'm not sure how much I can remember. Also, I'm very sick now, I'm afraid. But I can see you for a little while if it helps, I suppose. Yes. OK.'

Sarah let out a breath of relief, tried to stifle it and it became a cough.

'That's wonderful. Maybe tomorrow? Are you in the city centre?'

'Sorry, not tomorrow, I'm busy and my doctor is coming to see me. The next day. At two in the afternoon? I am at the Hotel Cristal. Ask for me at reception. They will show you up. I am the owner. All the staff know me.'

'Ah, OK. Well, yes that would be lovely. Until then Mr Kovacs.'

A great start. Sarah turned her attention to the glass of wine. Sod the gym, she felt like celebrating now. Ninety-something-year-olds had a habit of intriguing her with the amount they knew and sometimes the surprises they held. She was already looking forward to the interview with some fascination.

# Marton Kovacs

The following morning, Marton Kovacs rubbed the top of his bald head with an unsteady hand. The skin moved loosely over his skull, somehow depressing him even more.

He knew it wouldn't be long now. The last few weeks had dragged so much and the pain was worse than it had ever been.

He was too old and sick to deal with this. But he couldn't say no. It might arouse more suspicion if he refused to talk to her. He always lived by the maxim "keep your friends close but your enemies closer". He didn't want to make a mistake now, so close to the end of his life. His son and the hotel were everything. So, he would see her tomorrow and he would need to be on his guard. Maybe he needed his son, Peter, to be here. But that might introduce other complications, of a type he didn't need right now.

First, though, it was time to leave his watch at the jewellers. He'd meant to go before now. If he wasn't careful, it would be too late. He wanted everything to be left as he'd planned. So many years and so much *deceit*. It had been a crushing load to carry all this time. At least his death would have the consolation of freeing him from that torment.

He called down to the office. Aliz picked up the phone. 'Yes, Marton?'

'I need a trip out, Aliz. To Dob Street. Can you get whoever is concierge today to take me, please? I won't keep him from you for long.'

'Of course. I'll have him come up and help you down in a few minutes. Is that OK for you?'

'Perfect.'

Marton replaced the receiver and wheeled himself round to his old wooden bureau. He pulled the hinged desktop down and opened one of the small side drawers inside. He lifted out a battered looking wristwatch, with a cracked and faded leather strap, placing it on the desktop whilst he looked around for an envelope.

Picking up his favourite fountain pen, he then withdrew a sheet of writing paper from the bottom of the stack in front of him and checked the pre-prepared note. All fine.

By the time he had sealed up the envelope with the watch and note inside, there was a knock at his door.

'One moment. I need to make a call. Give me a moment please.'

A gruff acceptance filtered through the door to his room.

He wheeled his way back to the telephone and dialled, giving his name and asking for Alfred.

A wheezing voice eventually came on. 'Yes, this is Alfred. How are you, my friend?'

'Worse. Dying. I need to come and see you. Will you be at the shop if I come now?'

'I'm sorry to hear that, Marton. But yes, I'll be here. I'll ask the shop to send you straight through.'

The concierge was a swarthy young man called Andris, who Marton hadn't really liked right from his first day at the hotel. That's what happened when you left the hiring to the sub-manager, it seemed. He helped Marton down into the adapted sedan he'd used for nearly twenty years now since his legs had started to be more troublesome. All that smoking he'd done had left him a deadly legacy. Now it was actually killing him. By the time he was in the car his breathing was markedly ragged, not helped by the cold air.

Travelling along Kiraly Street, he felt he was back in his old town, a street lined with traditional shops. No chain boutiques here, just a tree-shaded boulevard with booksellers, cafes and old-fashioned tailors. The car turned left into Dob Street, slowing down for a pedestrian crossing near the junction. Marton studied the young man in a thick, dark coat and a woollen scarf whipped up around his neck against the cold. He felt the man's youth stab at his spirit and wondered if this would be the last trip down the streets of his home city.

Once at the jewellers he was shown into the tiny back office, where Alfred Nemeth was waiting for him.

*

Alfred looked expectantly at his visitor.

'Good to see you, my friend. You look tired.'

Marton dipped his head, shaking it gently up and down in agreement, before turning to his driver. 'You can wait in the car.'

The driver nodded, with a mixture of acceptance and annoyance on his face, and left the room.

Marton looked back at Alfred. He withdrew the envelope from his coat pocket, placing it on the jeweller's workbench which doubled up as Alfred's desk.

'So, my friend. It is becoming close to the time we spoke about. My life does not have much longer to run, I fear. Here is the watch. As we know, the receipt has been with my solicitor for a long while now. He's called Pasztor, David Pasztor. Please keep the envelope with the watch safe until my son comes for it with the receipt. You must insist on the receipt. You may not recognise Peter now.'

Alfred sighed his agreement.

'My friend, we have been like brothers for so long, we have done some good and some bad things together. Some would say very bad ... but those sorts of people were not there with us back then, were they? And we have lived our lives since then, worrying each day about a knock on the door, or a telephone call, which would drag us back to those days. We have been very lucky, unlike some. Now we are old men and we don't need any more trouble in our lives. You can rely on me. I won't ask you any more about this matter ... but I hope it will end well.'

He looked sharply at Marton, who suddenly looked very weary. Alfred knew there was a risk that Peter Kovacs would not respond favourably to the watch and the note he assumed Marton had included in the envelope. A risk that could also draw himself into difficulty. He needed to think very carefully through how he would prepare for any unfavourable consequences. And in all of this, Marton was suffering. It was all so wrong. He wasn't sure how he could make it right though.

Whether it was his own sense of frailty and the keen understanding of how unimportant worldly things are when death approaches … or just the sight of his dying friend in front of him, which caused him to make a snap decision, he wasn't sure. But he made it. He needed to tell Marton what *really* happened on that fateful night in the winter of 1945.

'Marton, there is something I need to tell you now. I can't let myself keep this from you anymore. Listen to me, my friend, and try not to be angry.'

\*

As Alfred lowered his voice and began to tell, Marton leaned into him, to hear better. Their heads were close and their eyes locked tightly as the story unfolded.

Five minutes later, Marton felt that he had never had a friend in Alfred Nemeth.

# Burton receives some news

Alan Burton ran the last of his exercise yard laps and stopped his run conveniently in the corner farthest from the main block. The yard was shaped irregularly so he could squeeze himself out of view around a small pillar formed by a derelict external chimney breast. As far as he could make out, the CCTV didn't scan into this tiny area. It had become the ideal place for drops.

He pulled out his smuggled mobile and texted the contact number. Thirty seconds later a reply appeared on his screen.

*One minute hold tight.*

He listened for the telltale wasp-like buzzing, as his breath spumed upwards like smoke into the chilly air.

There it was. Faint but there. He readied himself. A couple of the prisoners were up this end of the yard, leaning against the wall, getting their breath back after their runs. Normally that wouldn't be a problem. Unless they were squealers. And they could be dealt with if they made themselves too obvious. The single warder was down the other end of the yard. The lack of staff had some benefits at least.

Then it was over him, a small web-like structure of eye-pod cameras, white struts and rotor blades. It hovered quietly above him and dropped down slightly until he could reach the small black plastic bag hooked to one of its struts. He pulled out a razor blade and quickly slashed it free. The drone's controller reacted and it spun upwards twenty feet or so before slipping back the way it had arrived.

He ripped a hole in the bag and looked at its contents. A folded note, a pack of cigarettes and a SIM card. He pushed the SIM and cigarettes into his pocket and opened the note quickly.

*First try failed. Will try again soon. Don't worry, she's a goner.*

He pulled his lips tight and spat out a reaction. 'Pah, dumb idiot.' Spittle sprayed over the note and his hand.

He turned back towards the yard, pushing the note into his pocket, heading back for a shower. The sweat had rapidly cooled on him and he was feeling distinctly chilly.

His mood became even colder as a warder walked across his path and stopped him with a firm hand on his shoulder.

'Need you to come with me, Alan Burton. This way please.'

Burton frowned.

'Why, what's up?'

Warder Stark didn't really ever show any emotion on his face. A hard-bitten prison service veteran, who just got on with the job and was too wise to get into "conversations" with inmates. He set his blank stare on Burton.

'Not here. Just follow me.'

Burton knew he'd get no further and wasn't in the mood to goad Stark. So he followed him into the main block and down a couple of short corridors into an interview room. A table, two chairs. Burton walked to the far side and stood. Stark sat down in front of him. Looked up with a deadpan face.

'We saw the drone. Turn your pockets out.'

Burton's heart lurched. Damn. That was his mobile gone for a while then. How the hell had they seen him? Maybe just the drone, when it was approaching the prison walls.

He sighed. There was no point arguing. He did as he was told. The note, SIM card, cigarettes, mobile phone and razor, together with a twenty-pound note were thrown onto the table. His pocket linings hung limply outside his trousers.

Stark gave a wry smile, picked up the items in front of him and looked thoughtful.

After a few seconds, he pulled the cellophane from around the cigarette packet and removed a single smoke.

'Here, to help you get over your loss.'

Burton's fight response was suddenly triggered dangerously high. He pursed his lips and looked away.

Maybe discretion was the better part of valour. And he needed a smoke now.

He turned his head back and drilled a tetchy glare at his captor.

'Thank you for your kindness.'

*

Twenty minutes later, Burton was in a different interview room with Stark and the prison governor.

The governor was running this session.

'So, again, who is the note referring to?'

Again, no comment from a bored looking Burton.

'Look, Alan, you know where this is headed, we'll let the local police know, they'll want to interview you. It will get bigger. We'll consider loss of privileges in the meantime too. It's bad enough you've all the other stuff and the drone visit. Come on man, spit it out.'

Burton looked up. 'It's a note. I don't know who wrote it. Nothing to do with me. Must have got put in the wrong bag. You know, it's like fucking Amazon these drone deliveries, mistakes happen sometimes.'

Stark looked askance at his governor. No response. Just an attempt to leave a gap for Burton to fill after that comment. But Burton wasn't biting.

Governor Walters leant forward.

'OK. Hardball it is then. Expect a visit from the constabulary shortly and in the meantime, you can think about your answers in solitary.'

Burton's already narrow eyes closed even further as he tightened his face muscles into a frozen grimace. He grunted acknowledgement. No more than that.

'Off you go then.'

Another warder at the back of the room who had been providing extra security escorted Burton out.

The governor looked at Stark.

'He's up to something. Knowing him, something bloody nasty. He's a devious bastard. We need to get on this smart-ish I reckon. I'll get the boys in blue involved today.'

Stark nodded his agreement, looking pleased with himself. 'OK, gov. Thought it worth bringing to you.'

# Coast or jail?

---

Governor Walters had faxed a copy of Burton's note over to D.I. John Gregg's office the same day. The Glasgow detective picked it up off his desk the following morning.

Gregg was a surly man at the best of times. And lazy whenever he could get away with it. His morning hadn't been going too well. The D.C.I. weekly debrief had led to a private kicking afterwards. His progress on a recent spate of acid attacks on one of the worst local housing estates hadn't made enough progress *apparently* and the residents' group had been getting vocal on social media. Bane of a policeman's life now, that thing. Full of people who don't understand how hard policing is, mouthing off without any restraint. And he had a hangover and a night's growth on his jaw which made him feel tired and washed out.

He rolled his short, stout frame back into the sofa by the coffee machine and sipped from a plastic cup of cappuccino.

His follow up call to Walters had been short. Question now was, was it worth going to see Burton?

Sounded like he wouldn't get anything much out of him. Still, procedure more or less required he run through the motions on it. In the meantime, he needed to find out who Burton might have a grudge against. And if anyone had been reported as attacked by persons unknown recently.

He felt like lighting a cigarette, remembered he couldn't in the office and decided against a trip outside to the shelter where groups of sad-looking individuals stood pulling fast drags on white sticks. Too cold out there to tempt him right now.

He slipped a fruit drop into his mouth and started to drill into Burton's records on his desktop terminal.

It didn't take too long. Sounded like he'd taken a pop a year or so back at a private investigator he'd had brushes with and been put inside for that. He was also suspected of involvement in a murder in Italy, a woman connected with the investigator, but it hadn't been nailed on him so far. The team in Inverness had been led by D.C.I. James Beerly … he made a note to call him.

The private eye seemed the obvious one to start with. A Calum Neuman, based in Plockton. Now that was a nice trip to make. He'd get onto that. Burton could wait until afterwards. Might be the right order to do it in anyway.

He picked up the phone and dialled Neuman's number.

No reply. He left a message and pondered on whether to make a speculative four-hour drive to Plockton or a short trip to Burton's prison. He resigned himself to the right answer. He set out for Barlinnie jail.

# D.I. Gregg follows through

D.I. Gregg sat opposite Alan Burton in a spartan interview room at Barlinnie. It wasn't going well. Not that he'd arrived with expectations of anything better than this.

'Look. Like I said to you more than once, I don't know what the note means, it wasn't for me, for sure.'

Just a roadblock. One that wasn't showing any weak spots.

'So, the drone just picked you out randomly, dropped on your head and you just had a razor handy and helped yourself to the contents?'

'That's about it, yeah. You guys should do more to stop these things flying in, they're dangerous, I could've got injured.'

Gregg smirked, his usual deadpan disposition slightly amused by the repartee.

'OK, have it your way. I'll let the governor know you haven't cooperated. We'll try and track the SIM purchase down too. And look at your past conflicts. So, whatever you're doing, just be aware we're onto you, Burton. We won't let go of it.'

He stood up from the table to leave.

'OK, officer.'

Gregg wheeled round. 'What?'

'OK, off you go is all. Byeee.'

Gregg grimaced. 'Let me know when you change your mind.' He shut the door quietly on the way out. No sense in showing how pissed off he was.

*

Burton, despite his outward indifference, was thinking about the exchange long after D.I. Gregg had gone. Not that he had much else to think about in his solitary cell.

That was bugging him. He really did not like being alone twenty-four hours a day, without knowing when it would end.

Gregg might find out where the SIM had been purchased, but that trail would be cold. The *real* worry was that he'd know soon, if not already, that Neuman and Jenna Strick would be obvious targets for him. And if an attempt had been made on Jenna already, well maybe it had been bungled rather missed. In other words, a miss that had become apparent to Jenna. And that little bitch would talk all about it, wouldn't she?

His mind whirred through tactics to deal with the outcome. Maybe he could co-operate, put them on the trail of those helping him … but only after he'd understood when the next attempt would be so that Gregg would be just too late. That might work to get him out of this piece of grief and Jenna Strick still dealt with. It was all he had anyway. The tricky bit now was getting another communication out to his little helper. He'd need to work on that fast, God knows how close her next try might be. He needed to know *exactly* when and where this time.

What's more, something he'd read in the newspaper the other day had given him an idea.

**89**

# Jenna & the real one

Jenna was thankful Niamh seemed to trust her enough to agree to see her the following day after they'd both caught up on some sleep. It'd turned out to be a long session with the police, filling in the details of the attack on them the previous evening. Jenna managed to catch an afternoon lecture before heading over to Niamh and Sarah's flat around five o'clock.

Niamh buzzed her in and made her coffee. Somehow it was difficult to start the conversation about Sarah, after all the events of the night before. After some mutual licking of their wounds, Jenna made a start.

'So what can you tell me about her course, her study, where she's been recently and any personal stuff? No particular order.'

Niamh looked tired and a little overwhelmed by the question.

'I know that's a lot of questions. Maybe tell me about her course first?' Jenna thought she'd better leave the personal angle to the end. And then only if she seemed to have opened up at that point. She'd make a judgement on that one.

'She's doing a Master's degree. I guess her parents told you that? It's something about the Jews in the Second World War. But not the Nazi thing, something else. I think it's what happened in Hungary or Romania. Or both. Not sure of the details. The uni will be able to tell you anyway.'

'OK, that matches what her mother told me. So have you come across anyone who she's been working with? Or know of them? Anyone associated with her study?'

'Nope. She has a professor guiding her work, of course, as per normal. But I've not heard anyone else mentioned. Or met anyone from her department.'

'OK. What's your work, Niamh, or are you a student too?'

'No, no I'm a dress designer. Finished college a year back. I work here in Inverness. Small company took me on to learn the ropes. Doesn't pay much, but it's a start, eh?'

'So that's why you share?'

Jenna knew she'd overstepped a bit with that question. She looked steadily at Niamh, waiting for a reaction.

There wasn't anything odd about her reply, though.

'Yeah, yeah, just can't afford my own place just yet. Sarah's fine anyway. Works OK.'

In for a penny, in for a pound. 'So, any boy or girlfriends for Sarah that you know of?'

Niamh's expression didn't alter. 'No, not that I know of. We've only shared this place since September. Well, I mean she talks to friends on the phone and goes out on the weekend sometimes. But no one came here. I think her friends were mostly from Aberdeen. She did her degree there.'

'Fair enough. So do you know why she's gone away?'

'Like I told the police in the first place after her mum reported her missing, she went off, well, it must be ten days or more now, she said to do research but I didn't ask her about it. She took a suitcase. I know, because I was here when the taxi came.'

'And no idea when she'd be coming back?'

'She said maybe a week, but not sure. We're not joined at the hip. I just don't know much about her life.'

The last statement rang oddly with Jenna. Not just that either. Would she *really* not have been told where Sarah was going? Or asked? She thought she might want to dig around Niamh too. But not for now.

'OK. Maybe we've both had enough today. Look, Calum will be keeping in touch with the police. You want me to tell you if anything comes up? Not sure they'll bother telling you, only her family probably?' Relationship-building: it was something Calum kept reminding her about, not that she wasn't good at it anyway.

Niamh looked unsure.

'OK.'

Jenna felt she wasn't going to get much more but still went back over the events of last night. Horse, dead, flogging, just in a different order.

She left ten minutes later, with the university professor and Niamh's past on her mind's list of the next things to follow up.

As she arrived back at her apartment, her mobile rang. Calum.

'Sorry, Jen, but the police are assigning someone to watch over you for the moment. I know you'll hate it but it's probably for the best. Expect a visit tonight I guess.'

'Okaaay. Well, since someone's been tapping my mobile somehow, or some other way to know where I was going to be last night, I'm glad, even if it is a bit spooky. I guess I'll just have to put up with it. If I can put up with you, I reckon anything's possible.'

Jenna actually felt pleased. She was glad of the protection … and interested to experience exactly how they would carry it out.

'And … I'll swap my SIM for an old pay-as-you-go one, just in case my mobile's still being monitored. I'll text you the number later.'

'OK. Smart thinking.'

'Always.'

# The professor

Jenna hurried out of her second marine science lecture of the day. She had to run across the campus to Professor Robertson's office, having managed to get thirty minutes with him at short notice. She'd not mentioned she was a student here at the university: she was worried that might water down his respect for her role. She'd dressed more smartly, brushed her hair and applied some make-up for the same reason.

She knocked on his door and was met with a brisk 'come in'.

The office was sparse and what basic furniture there was, was covered with untidy clumps of papers and open books. A soulless room in a new-ish building. It was hard to see where the comfortable base for academic study would come from in here.

'Miss Strick, hello.'

He looked her up and down.

'You look too young to be a private investigator, I'd say?'

John Robertson offered her a handshake with a set of sausage-like fingers, which she gripped and shook as firmly as her small hand allowed. A big man, ruddy-faced, thin wisps of reddish-silver hair crawling over a huge cranium.

Jenna sat down promptly in the hard, upright chair he proffered with a wave of his arm.

'Well, yes, I'm assisting Calum Neuman in this case as I mentioned. I've been working with him for three years now, though.' She silently cursed herself for trying to justify her position.

He nodded, turned away to look out of the window briefly, then looked back.

'So, how can I help? Been through it with the police, of course. She's not been in touch with me since before she left. Or since before she *said* she was leaving.'

'Leaving for where?'

'Oh, I thought you would have known. From the police I mean. Budapest. That's where she was starting I believe.'

'Well no the police don't share everything with us. We do liaise where we can help each other, but it's early days. Sometimes we'll synch up after a week or two. All depends on the case. I'd expect the police have checked if she was on a flight for Budapest around the period she went missing … unless she travelled some other way. So exactly what is she doing in Hungary?'

He raised his eyebrows and looked weary. He looked like he'd been reading for a while and rubbed his eyes under his glasses.

'Background research on her Master's subject. The Arrow Cross party. Know anything about it?'

Jenna knew that saying no was going to precipitate a lengthy explanation. And so it did.

After twenty minutes, Jenna was punch drunk with facts and opinions on Eastern Europe, the end of the Second World War and the persecution of the Jews and the Roma. She finally managed to get him away from his monologue, to wrap up with a few more questions she'd written down.

'Was she supposed to be in touch while on the trip?'

'Not especially, might have expected her to call if she had a query she needed help with. But she has Eszter as her first port of call for that anyway.'

'And who is Eszter?'

Robertson looked surprised again.

'Oh, she's our contact in Budapest, from the university. She agreed to help Sarah with local information, contacts, some help with any Hungarian texts.'

Jenna took some contact details for Eszter. By now, John was looking at his watch. She sensed her time was up.

'OK, well thanks for your help. I'll follow up with Eszter, see if the police have got far down that route.'

She dropped her card on his desk. She could feel a trip to Budapest coming soon: hard to see what else she could do in Scotland.

Smiling, she said her goodbyes, avoiding another handshake.

\*

Jenna dialled Calum after her lectures were done for the day.

'OK, so I need to go to Budapest. But I've no idea how I can fit that in at the moment. University breaks up for Christmas in a couple of weeks so *maybe* I can fit a weekend in before then, I don't know really.'

'Just to talk with Eszter? Maybe you can phone her first, see how you get on? Anyway, I should go to Budapest myself if it seems necessary.'

Jenna imagined Calum could hear her pouting down the phone line.

'Hmm, well, yeah I guess. OK, I'll try and see what she can give us first then. I'll call you when I've had the first chat.'

She clicked her mobile off sharply and expanded her pout. Sometimes, just sometimes, he could be a little bit too harsh with her. He was right though, so she pencilled in a call with Eszter that evening. Her inner adventurer was nonetheless still set on a trip to Budapest.

# Calum talks to D.I. Gregg

Calum was up late this morning. A quick breakfast of porridge and orange juice, then a shower. He looked at himself sideways on, in the full-length mirror in his bedroom. Paunch still small. Just. Check. Couldn't be bothered with a shave, no clients to see that day so no real need.

Out on the street to the office, the weather was rough. Winter was closing in fast, the harbour waters were grey and choppy and rain lashed down the street in fluid sweeps. He hurried through the office door, shaking his cagoule vigorously before throwing it over the wooden coat stand.

Coffee first, then his messages and emails. He still missed Jenna making him that first cup of the day.

Colombian as usual, steaming hot. He planted it on his Talisker drink coaster and yawned, clicking open his emails. Nothing much there. Disappointing. He turned to the phone which had a couple of messages flashing. Partway into the second one, he sat up straighter and listened more intently.

' … so, if you can shed any light, call me, OK?' From a D.I. Gregg in Glasgow. Left yesterday morning, how come he hadn't picked it up before then?

So. Alan Burton. Again. Last time, Burton had taken a pot shot at him, for his part in convicting him for a misdemeanour. He got a long sentence for that. This was too much of a habit. He made the link quickly. There was no doubt in his mind that the person who'd bundled Niamh Sampson into her bedroom and attacked Jenna had some link to this message. Proving it might be a different matter, though.

He called Gregg back straight away and told him about Niamh and Jenna's experience the other night.

'So tell me again, is Jenna your employee, Calum?'

'Yeah, loosely. She worked for me for a couple of years or so then went off to university this autumn. She just started the other day on a bit of work for me, some research on a new case. She was about to interview Niamh Sampson when she was attacked. The Sarah McTeer disappearance … your guys are on it, yeah?'

'Yep. Not my team, though. Did the interview throw anything up?'

'No, not really. But I think that's barking up the wrong tree, to be honest. I think this has to do with Burton and I can't see any linkage between Sarah McTeer and Burton.'

A thought crossed his mind. *Unless he set the whole disappearance case up as a scam. Doesn't feel likely, though.* But Calum started to think about that a little bit more whilst he listened to Gregg.

'What is worrying is this woman seems to have had advance notice of Jenna going to the flat. So either McTeer's flatmate is in on that or someone is leaking or intercepting phone conversations.'

Calum nodded. Burton had the contacts to do that kind of thing. It all pointed harder towards Burton. 'Yep, you're right.'

'And sorry to ask but do you have any kind of … personal relationship with Jenna Strick?'

Calum felt himself blushing. 'No, definitely not. Never. Why?'

'Just wondering why Burton would want to have a go at her, rather than you?'

'Well, not for that reason anyway, unless he *thinks* we've a relationship. More likely to be that Jenna got innocently involved in the death of his lover, Glenda Muir. It was all part of the same case that he got banged up for in the end.'

'Hmm. OK. Makes sense. So, keep me informed on any new thoughts from your side too eh, Calum?'

Calum's mobile buzzed with a text message.

'OK. Need to go … bye mate.'

He clicked the call off and the message open. Cassie.

*Hope you're OK. It was nice, our night after the wake. Hope you thought the same. What are you up to today?*

He closed the phone and sighed. He'd felt OK about their night together actually. It felt right.

It did then.

But he kept remembering what someone in his past had told him: you can never go back. It's never the same.

He hadn't felt the need to repeat that night and he'd been nervous that Cassie might feel differently. Texting him might be the closure of that episode or a need to extend it. He wasn't sure which right now. One thing he did know was he'd need to tread carefully. Cassie was a sensitive soul underneath that brisk manner of hers. He didn't want to cause her more grief right now, Ellie's death was enough for both of them to handle. He decided to reply later, the same day but not straight away. The middle ground ... what he usually chose.

# Jenna finds Eszter

---

'Hello? Yes, this is Eszter Borbely. Who is this please?'

'My name's Jenna Strick. I'm calling from Scotland. I'm helping Sarah McTeer's mother look for her daughter. You're aware she's missing?'

'Well, yes, I am. I was working with her when she disappeared.'

Eszter sounded a bit indignant. Jenna reset her tack.

'Yes, I understand that. It must have been a real shock. We're just helping her mother Susan understand more ... she's really worried as you might imagine.'

'Yeah, of course.'

'Do you mind telling me what you were doing with Sarah the day or two before she went missing?'

'You are police?'

'No, no a private investigator. Susan McTeer hired us. We can provide this evidence if you need?'

'Ermm, well OK. I can tell you something then I think, it's OK. But I don't know much anyway. We had been doing some research, mostly in the big library here in Budapest. A few days. I have been helping with this, there is contact between our two universities, you see. Well, it was going OK, Sarah was doing some work on her own too, we met a few times, discussed progress and next steps for the work. Then one morning she didn't arrive at the library as we planned. I called the hotel and they didn't really help, but after another day I rang again. They checked their records and her room but she wasn't there. And not since. I told this to the police, of course.'

'Of course Eszter. Did they say if there was anything missing from her room?'

'No. I believe her things were in the room mostly. Clothes, bathroom things, some of her papers. She had a blue leather notebook, they didn't find that in the room or her iPad or rucksack. So she must have gone out somewhere, I suppose to do some work.'

'Unless someone took them, of course. Colour of the rucksack?'

'Oh yes, I see what you mean. Grey. Light grey.'

'Did the police say if the room door had been forced?'

'The police didn't say, but the hotel manager told me he had to let himself in to check, and that nothing seemed wrong … just that she wasn't there.'

'OK. Thanks, that's helpful. One thing I'd like to know more about though … what exactly is the research around?'

Jenna got the full works on Arrow Cross, and it became clear after fifteen minutes or so of Eszter talking and Jenna squeezing a few directing questions in, just how knowledgeable Eszter was on the topic. It all checked out with what Sarah's professor had outlined.

'So you're saying she'd made some follow-ups, some interviews off the back of the work she did with you?'

'As far as I know only one visit to anyone … a man called Marton. Marton Kovacs.'

'You saw her after that?'

'Yes, we spoke about her visit to him. But I think she was planning on seeing him again. I don't know if that happened. I didn't see her after that.'

Jenna slowed down her questioning. It might be jumping to conclusions, but Marton Kovacs seemed like her likely next port of call.

'I assume you told the police this?'

There was a short silence.

'Actually no, I don't think I did. At least, I'm not sure. I don't think they asked that question like you did.'

'Well, that's odd. Or pretty useless of the police. I think you should tell them, Eszter. It may help a lot. In the meantime, I'll see what Mr Kovacs has to say.'

Eszter hesitated before she agreed. 'Yes, OK I'll call and tell them.'

Jenna nodded. 'I'll give you my number and email, let me know if there's anything else you can think of that's important. I might talk to you again. It's possible myself or my boss will be coming to Budapest soon to understand more. Thanks for your time, Eszter.'

Jenna clicked the call off and thought about what to suggest to Calum. Visiting or calling Marton Kovacs had to be the next step. Given the circumstances, it seemed looking him in the eye would be the better option.

She yawned and pulled herself a cider out of the fridge. It was pretty much all there *was* in the fridge, so she made some toast and jam to go with it.

It was getting late by the time she finished her snack. She peeked out through the drawn curtains. Yep, there was her protection, sat in an unmarked police car. He'd been with her for a couple of days now, they said they'd probably stick with it for a couple of weeks then review. Unless they felt they'd cracked what Burton was up to any earlier.

Sleep came fast. Alcohol just before bedtime always did that.

But, just as certainly, wakefulness came early too. Around five a.m. she stumbled out of bed into the bathroom, trying not to wake her flatmate. She peed with the light off and left the flush. Her mouth was dry so she ran half a tumbler of water in the kitchenette and sipped it down.

She heard rain against the front windowpanes, the sash frames rattling gently in their sockets as a brisk wind blew through the street. She wandered over to the window and pulled the curtains back a touch, expecting that warm feeling of being inside and snug against the wind and rain.

She did feel that. But the warmth faded as she saw her protection was gone. She pulled her face back into the shadows behind the curtains and squinted up and down the street, through the rain-splattered grime of the glass. Yep, totally gone as far as she could see. Maybe he'd gone to the 24-hour McD's for some coffee or an early breakfast. The street was deserted at least.

But there was a strange feeling of pressure on her face. Like the rays of sun you felt but couldn't touch. Except this felt less sunny. Like she'd felt before, after she'd last seen Gregor.

She snapped the curtains shut and turned back into the room. It was pitch black and her eyes hadn't adjusted to it after the glare of the street lights. She walked towards her bedroom door by memory.

Then she was flat on her front, her left shin stinging and her forehead reeling from a hard blow. She rolled onto her back, moaning, trying to suppress a scream.

Amy's room door opened and the room lights went on. Jenna screwed her eyes up at her flatmate as she came into the lounge.

'What on earth are you doing? You woke me up.'

'Ouch, my head hurts. Sorry, I got up and fell over something. Think it was the coffee table, it must have moved a bit. I think I hit my head on the doorframe.'

Amy smiled weakly. 'Yeah, sorry, think I moved it to put my legs up on, watching TV last night. Let's have a look at your head.'

# Time to travel

---

After a totally oversold pitch from Jenna, on why they needed to interview various individuals in Budapest, Calum agreed with Susan McTeer a visit was necessary and outlined a budget with her. Dull but necessary. In Calum's experience, clients all too easily got upset if costs weren't clearly agreed upfront, even if they brought great outcomes.

He booked a flight for himself and three nights in the hotel where Sarah had stayed. Staying there might prove useful later on, being "on location" as it were. He hoped that would be long enough to get around everybody and double back on interviews if he needed to.

He considered Jenna. He knew she wanted to come, probably mostly for the trip but once she got her mind into something, it was hard to keep her from it. He'd have to tell her *not this time*. That bit he was putting off. He smiled to himself and shook his head. It was hard to put into words … he was her boss and yet he had to answer to her sometimes. It suited him somehow, though.

Bugger it, he'd do it now. He picked up his phone and took a deep breath.

'Are we sorted for Budapest then, boss?'

No damn tact sometimes. 'Yep. Just me for now. We'll see how it goes.'

She was ready for that.

'OK.'

Calum smile-frowned. Too simple. 'Really? Good.'

'Yes. Once you're there on your own you'll realise why you need me. Waste of my time waiting for that process to happen. I've uni work to do. Take your time and call me when you need me. I've done a pile of research on Arrow Cross, by the way. I expect it'll be useful at some point. Hope Eszter opens up to you, though I got the feeling she might be more receptive to a woman.'

The phone clicked off at Jenna's end.

Calum shook his head. *Man*, could she be annoying when she wanted to. Annoying *and naggingly persuasive*. He turned his attention to his packing and wondered whether, if he slipped a couple of his favourite pork pies in the case, they might stay fresh for a couple of days.

# Beginning in Budapest

---

The air of calm civilisation was what struck Calum most about Budapest. Grand buildings and wide streets. People that know their city is beautiful. Something like Edinburgh. Not Glasgow or Aberdeen.

His interview list was: Marton Kovacs; Eszter Borbely; the library. Then take it from there. The local police he really wasn't sure about. He had no contacts or third-party network into that organisation. For now, he'd try to do without talking to them.

He arrived in the evening, to be disappointed by the lack of Talisker in the hotel bar. The Grand Danubius hotel seemed a bit dreary. A faded beauty, quiet. He congratulated himself on having brought a half-bottle of the wondrous stuff in his bag and retired to his room to enjoy a dram before turning in.

The next morning, an early breakfast of ham, eggs, and coffee spurred him on to get started immediately. He strolled to the central library, thankful for his warm overcoat. The air was stone cold and the sky grey. One of those days that chills the bones.

He walked up to the reception desk in the lobby. A long wooden bar, with the thick glass-like polish of decades protecting its surface. He headed for the younger of the two receptionists, gauging this would probably mean better English. His name badge announced him as Janos.

'Hello, I wonder if I can ask you a few questions about some researchers that have been here, a couple of weeks ago now. My name is Calum Neuman, I'm a private investigator helping the family of Sarah McTeer. Sarah has been reported missing since she last spent time in this library. Are you aware of this?'

The tall young man behind the desk blushed slightly. 'Yes, we have all heard this, of course. The police have been here asking about her.'

He paused for thought.

'I think I will have to ask my manager if it is OK to talk to you. Just a moment.'

He disappeared through a door behind reception and closed it. Within a minute he was back.

'Yes, she says it is OK. What do you want to know?'

Calum motioned for him to follow him to the end of the desk, away from the reception queue, so they could speak more discreetly.

The young man didn't play ball, though. He moved only slightly away from the door he'd passed through and silently insisted Calum start to talk by cocking his head to listen.

'OK. So do you know how long she was here, how often and what she was working on?

'Yes, we told the police all that. A few days, most days for a few hours, usually in the mornings but not always. With another academic, from Budapest. They were researching Arrow Cross.'

'Did they have any books or papers out on loan?'

'Not that we know. Not according to our records. Not unless they smuggled something out.'

Calum looked up from his notebook. The boy's eyes danced around a little.

'People do that here?'

'Well, yes like everywhere I think. Not all of our books have a security tag on them, so we can't be completely safe from thieves. But, I mean, I don't think these ladies stole anything, of course.'

Calum nodded. 'Sure. So, did they meet anyone else while they were here do you know?'

'Not in the library as far as we know. We don't watch our visitors all the time, of course. The police looked at our CCTV, maybe they can help you?'

Calum's instinct kindled his interest.

'Do you know if they found anything like that? Them talking to anyone else?'

'They didn't tell us.'

Calum took a deep breath.

'Would you mind if I had a look at the CCTV files too?'

'I'm sorry. I was told we can't let anyone else see those. It's our visitors' privacy, you see. Of course, the police had the right to see them. But not anyone else.'

A stonewall, final answer response.

Janos threw his eyes left, almost glancing over his shoulder at the open doorway behind him. No one came through.

Calum pushed him a bit further about their patterns of work and managed to get some idea of a few texts they'd been reading or interested in. It didn't feel like that would help at all, but he knew not to turn down information, however peripheral it seemed at first.

'Sir, I'm afraid I need to help the queue now.'

He nodded to the line of visitors at the desk and his colleague who was starting to look as if she was going to give him a piece of her mind at any moment.

'OK, thank you. I might come back after I've made some more checks. But thanks for now.'

'You're welcome.' He smiled and turned to the queue, encouraging Calum to move.

Calum swivelled to leave and stuffed his notebook back into his pocket. He looked back over his shoulder to nod goodbye. Janos was gone. *Not* helping with the queue.

*

Beata moved away from the doorframe as she heard Calum bid his farewell and sat down. Janos came through immediately.

'So what did he want to know? I heard a little of it.'

'Same sort of questions as the police, Miss Sandor. He seemed OK. I told him he couldn't look at our CCTV, that's right?'

Beata smiled. 'Well done. They're a nuisance with all these questions, nothing more. I suppose they have to ask them. The poor girl's family must be very worried.'

Janos looked aside and asked a question.

'Did the police say they had found anything on the CCTV?'

'No. Not that I know. I don't think a library could be involved in her disappearing, though, do you? I'm sure there was something else going on here. It'll all come clear when the police finish their investigations, I'm sure.'

Janos looked at her and shook his head. 'I don't know. Anyway, I'd better go, or else Hanna is going to murder me for the size of the queue.'

Beata smiled again as Janos turned and went back to the front desk.

Her smile faded like a dropped stone as he went through the door. They needed to cut this new threat off cleanly … but she wasn't sure how. She dialled Peter, then Marton's private numbers. Neither of them answered. That was odd. Especially Marton, he hardly went anywhere these days. She'd try them again later.

# TWO WEEKS EARLIER

## Sarah visits Marton

---

Sarah stepped out of the cab, toting her grey rucksack and looked up at the facade of Hotel Cristal. It was lovely, like all the building fronts along this road. She paid the driver and strode up the stone steps into the lobby. The floor was laid with gleaming tiles and narrow walkways of well-worn patterned carpet. Traditional, cared for, old-fashioned. She walked up to the wood-panelled front desk.

She was greeted by a young girl. Smartly dressed, she spoke in a pleasing, even tone. It felt welcoming.

'Hello, I'm here to see Mr Kovacs. I have an appointment at two o'clock.'

'Ah, OK. Just a moment please, I'll ask the manager to help with that.'

The girl disappeared around the back of a glass panel behind reception. Less than a minute later she reappeared, followed by a tall and much older woman. Well past retirement age by the look of her skin.

'Miss McTeer? I'm Aliz Gal, the manager of the hotel. I believe you are due to see Mr Kovacs at two o'clock?'

Sarah nodded, noticed she didn't use the term manageress. 'Hello.'

'Well. You are a few minutes early but I have just called Mr Kovacs. He can see you straight away. Please come with me.'

Obviously comfortable in her managerial skin.

Aliz ushered her down the main corridor with a small flourish of the hand. She walked slightly ahead of Sarah, with a sedate, almost cat-walk perfect stride. She had the air of a woman with long-held confidence.

The lift was open and they stepped in and stood on opposite sides. As she pressed the button for the 4th floor, Aliz stared at Sarah's face. Stared to the point where it was uncomfortable.

'Please remember Mr Kovacs is a very old man. He is frail. So I hope you will be gentle with him and leave as soon as he is tired please?'

Not really a question. Sarah was already feeling intimidated by this woman.

'Of course. I will.'

The lift bleeped as it reached the 4th floor. Aliz stepped out first and led Sarah to room 41. She knocked lightly on the door.

A frail, but somehow strong voice replied. '*Kerlek faradj be.*'

Aliz opened the door, announced the guest and withdrew, leaving Sarah stood in the room. She looked down at Marton Kovacs. Big head, rheumy blue eyes. A large but slim frame, clearly ravaged by time. Maybe illness. A man who would once have been quite imposing. He was sat in a wheelchair, his legs half-covered by a blanket.

'Welcome,' he said. 'Please sit down.' He indicated a pair of winged leather chairs close to where he was positioned.

'One of these used to be mine, but I can't easily use it now. So choose whichever you like.'

Sarah smiled, looked around the room as she walked over to one of the chairs and sat down.

'This is a lovely old room.' She meant it too. It was filled with old but expensive furniture. Obviously kept clean and tidy. There was an air of calm, faded luxury around it all.

'Thank you … may I call you Sarah?' he enquired with a faint smile. He looked a bit nervous to her eye.

'Of course. I don't want to take too much of your time up Mr Kovacs. Just to help me with my research. I'll take some notes if that's OK?' She pulled a blue leather notebook out of her rucksack.

Marton nodded his agreement. 'Let's begin. I often become tired after half an hour of talking. So I hope you'll forgive me if I call a stop when I've had enough.'

*

More than an hour later, they were still deep in conversation. It seemed Marton was enjoying describing the roots of the Arrow Cross movement, his part in it, his family, life in Hungary at that time. Doesn't everyone like to talk about when they were young, invincible, unfettered by a life that has mostly played out? His manner was tinged with unease, though.

*'Of course, it was really about being Hungarian. Being a strong nation, not subservient to another. Our motivation was a pure one, I think.'*

*'No, I don't think our leader, Szalasi, was like Hitler. Hitler … and Germany … were conveniently useful to Szalasi.'*

*'Well, yes, the party attacked the Jews. We are not proud of that. But it wasn't really about the Jews, it was about Hungary for Hungarians.'*

*'I'm not sure it actually went wrong, Sarah. But well, the war ended and Arrow Cross was shut down, as you know. Many of the leaders were executed. So we will never know how things would have turned out, will we?'*

*'Me? Well, I was young, some of my friends were with Arrow Cross before they took power, I joined them, I was fed up with the war pulling our people apart, of the foreigners in our midst. I wanted to help my country.'*

*'My father agreed with what I was doing actually. My mother, of course, was worried too!'*

*'Now? I feel a little ashamed about some of the bad things that were done. It is all so long ago now. But I think Hungarian people still feel they want to keep their country free of outside influence. These days, there are a lot of people coming to Hungary. I'm not sure that is a good thing. Perhaps one day, Arrow Cross will start again. In a different way, of course.'*

Sarah had sucked it all in and thrown it out into her notebook, balanced on the arm of the chair with her left hand as her right scribbled feverishly.

Marton's last comment triggered a thought that Eszter had voiced yesterday.

'So, do you think the Arrow Cross will reform, or as you say, take on a new, modern guise?'

She peered at Marton, searching for a reaction.

And there was something wrong about it. He looked away briefly. He hadn't done that so far, not that she could remember anyway.

He turned back with a faint smile on his face. 'I don't know, I leave that to the young people. It is their future now, not mine.'

She nodded.

'Well, Sarah, I'm afraid it's time for my nap, I'm a little tired now, I hope you understand. I hope I have been helpful to you?'

'Of course, of course. May I call again if there is anything I have forgotten or if my research throws up some extra questions?'

Marton looked thoughtful. 'If it is important, of course.'

She wasn't sure how well meant that was, but accepted it graciously, before making a prompt exit.

Aliz Gal was at the front desk when she made her way out through the hall. The manager flicked her head in acknowledgement at Sarah as she passed and said goodbye. Sarah felt her gaze follow her back, as she skipped down the entrance steps and out into the cold afternoon air.

Something about Marton didn't feel quite right. She couldn't put her finger on it. But a sixth sense told her she should go back: whether or not her research needed her to. Right now, though, she had some catching up to do with Eszter. She made her way back to the library, thinking she might manage a hot chocolate in the cafe first.

*

She bought two hot chocolates and sat down with Eszter to check where they were both up to.

'There was just something a bit edgy about him. For a very old man that seemed strange, you'd think he'd not be bothered about anything. Mostly old people get like that, think they can say what they want, upset anyone without any consequences. Like my grandmother. But Marton wasn't like that. He was careful and deliberate, courteous but edgy. Well, I can't put my finger on it *exactly* but I'd guess there was something he didn't want to talk about.'

'OK. So maybe go and see him again? Think up some more specific questions. What exactly was he nervous about?'

'Well, no one particular question, but he didn't really go into any detail about things he said the party should have been ashamed of … though I didn't press him too hard to be fair, and … well, what's going on right now with any kind of a re-birth of the ideas: that was a no go somehow.'

'Go for it then. Want me to come with you?'

'No, that's fine, I might make another appointment, I'll see. I'd rather you dragged through those other Hungarian texts, save my poor brain. He *is* an old man, I don't want to pressurise him with an extra person in the room, even if I do go again myself.'

Eszter smiled. 'Well, let me tell you about what I've found from *my* work today.'

Sarah took a deep sip from her hot chocolate, licked the foam from her lips and listened to what she had to say.

# Marton & Peter conspire

After some deliberation, Marton picked up the phone to his son. He felt his breath wheezing in and out of his lungs. It seemed worse today, he didn't want to speak for long.

'Father, I have already heard about this woman, from Beata. She is being watched, together with her friend. I suggest we do only that for now. They will probably do their research and then go away. They will know nothing. We should just be calm.'

'You're probably right, Peter. I just wanted you to know. You know I am close now. I don't want this kind of thing. I can't have stress. You know this, don't you?'

'Of course, Father. Trust me, I will keep an eye on her. Of course, we don't want to have to do anything drastic … but if it becomes necessary, I will take care of it. You mustn't worry.'

That was exactly what Marton was worried about. Peter taking care of it. But what could he say? He hadn't the energy anymore to deal with it and his old colleagues in Budapest were either dead or infirm to some degree. He pressed his lips together and cursed his age and his failing health.

'Alright, Peter. If she asks me more questions, I will agree to answer them, of course. I don't want to arouse any suspicions without need.'

'Yes, naturally. But tell me if she does start to dig too deeply or seems overly interested in certain aspects. You *must,* Father.'

Marton dipped his head, without saying anything.

He replaced the receiver. There wasn't anything else to say, really. So now he would have to wait to see if Sarah McTeer wished to talk to him again. That was too much to bear, though, waiting for it to happen … or not. And how long would he have to wait to be sure she wasn't going to come back? A week? A month? Until the day he died?

The more he thought about it, he developed the conviction that it would be best if he took matters into his own hands. Invite her over, give her the chance, then maybe she would go away happy. Yes, that seemed better to him, he could put an end to the uncertainty that way.

She'd told him where she was staying, so after a few moments composing himself, he telephoned the front desk of Sarah's hotel and left her a message.

# Eszter uncovers some history

'So, you're saying that you think Marton Kovacs might have been implicated in some kind of war crime?' said Sarah, staring hard at Eszter.

'I can't be sure. It's just this reference I found … but it isn't that detailed and it refers to another book. But when I looked for it, it didn't seem to be on the shelves. Maybe I'll ask at the desk tomorrow. To be honest, I'm not sure whether we want to be interested in this aspect, so I left it for the moment. Funny though, there was that book about the new Arrow Cross movement I read about the other day and that wasn't available either.'

'But was there any clue on what he may or may not have done?'

'Look, there were lots of articles I found that referred to Jews being hunted down across this city over 1944-45. There was stuff organised by Arrow Cross and there were also lots of unofficial groups running around, loosely attached to the party, doing pretty much what they liked.

So, well, you know, for the young men in these groups, it was probably exciting, an adventure almost. Some of them got carried away I expect. The author of the book I read suggests lists of people who may have been involved. I've no idea whether it is true, whether any of them were tried for crimes successfully or anything like that.'

'But Marton Kovacs's name was on these lists?'

Eszter straightened her face into a colder version of its usual self.

'Yes, in some, he was.'

Sarah leaned back into her chair to absorb the information.

'I don't know. I'm not sure this is worth the hassle and intrusion of following up. I got some good input from my interview with him. I haven't finished going over it and I may need to add to it later but for now … well, maybe let's just sleep on it until tomorrow?'

Eszter agreed. She seemed pleased with Sarah's conclusion and her face measurably brightened.

\*

When Sarah returned to her hotel to find an invite from Marton for a follow-up meeting, she felt her heart suddenly start to pound erratically. To add to the tension, he'd suggested the next day, which put her under an unpleasant pressure: if not to go, at least to decide whether to.

More importantly, she would have to decide whether to press him to talk in detail about the sorts of crimes that were committed under the Arrow Cross banner. Well, at least if she felt her research, rather than just her own curiosity, could benefit from it. Right now, she definitely wasn't sure about that.

She needed to make that decision with a full stomach and a glass of red inside her, to steady her racing thoughts. Flinging her books and papers onto the hotel room floor, she set out in search of somewhere she could find that sustenance. The hotel restaurant had already become routine, so she was trusting that a walk into the city's heart would offer up some possibilities along the way.

As she walked along the riverfront from the hotel front door, she tried to recall what she'd expected of this trip. Whatever it was, it was turning into something rather more challenging.

# Marton re-visited

Sarah tapped on Marton's room door the following afternoon at 5 p.m., as requested, with a nervousness that transmitted to her hands and turned an intended knock into a fluttering drumroll.

Marton shouted her through and she turned the large oak knob, entering as if under coercion. She took a deep breath as she came face to face with her host.

'Good afternoon, Sarah,' said Marton, in a voice that reminded her of daddy bear from the Goldilocks story. She shivered fleetingly, as that story scuttled through her head, unsettling her even more. Maybe those two glasses of red wine last night had given her unwarranted Dutch courage.

'Take a seat please, dear.' He motioned to the armchair next to his.

'Well, firstly, let me say I know we agreed you would call me if you had any further questions. Now I have invited you here myself. I think I should explain that I felt I should do this. I have told you I am unwell. Well, I fear that it is now a little more than that, I don't think I have long at all.

So, I thought I should give you the opportunity to talk again sooner rather than later. I want to make sure you have all the material you need for your research. So, I hope I can help you a little more today.'

Sarah dipped her head in acknowledgement, whilst blinking slowly and feeling bemused. Was that really the reason?

'Well, thank you for that, though it's not been long since we met and so we haven't done too much further work yet. But I really appreciate you wanting to help me like this.'

'I know. I know. But I have remembered some more about my family and friends which might be helpful background. It's hard to remember everything quickly when you are my age. One day you will find the same I expect. Shall I talk you through what I wrote down?'

Sarah felt some inner relief and nodded agreement.

As Marton wove his way slowly around various anecdotal clumps of his memories, interspersed with his views about the causes and beliefs of Arrow Cross, some of which he had covered on her first meeting, Sarah became more unsure as to why she was in the room. It just didn't seem that new or important. She was feeling vulnerable too, despite Marton's age and infirmity. As he rattled on, she was having a running discussion with herself, wrestling with whether she should raise the matter which Eszter had pointed out to her the previous evening.

A large mantle clock was ticking slowly in the background as Marton spoke. It drilled into her head. It felt as if time was running away from her, out of her control.

Marton stopped his discourse abruptly. He looked down then back up, fixing her with his rheumy, vein-ribbed eyes. 'So now your turn, my dear. Is there anything you'd like to ask me? I noticed you hadn't taken any notes while I was speaking?'

Sarah's heart leapt … then leapt again.

She decided to go for it.

Suddenly there was a loud knock on the door.

Sarah lurched sideways, almost fell out of her chair with the shock of it.

Marton shouted for the arrival to enter. The door opened slowly and creaked to a halt. Something metallic clanked against the door, then a maid carrying a coffee tray appeared and placed it on a table, before making a goodbye curtsy.

'Coffee, my dear?'

Sarah declined.

'Would you mind pouring me some, just a little milk please?'

She stood up and obliged him, handing him the cup with a slight tremble.

'Now, where were we?'

Sarah took a deep breath to recover.

'Well, you asked me if I had anything else to ask. So, yes and no. I think what you've just run through is a nice addition to our chat yesterday, thank you. There's also something I wanted to ask, about some research my colleague was doing yesterday in the background.'

Marton dropped his eyelids momentarily then looked more alert.

Sarah continued, 'Look, I know Jews were being hunted down across Budapest in 1944-45. We discussed this before. I suppose what would be interesting is to understand how those young men involved actually felt about it.'

Our research listed names of those in the loose groups that were involved in what went on in Budapest, in the final months before the Russians entered the city. And, well, your name came up on the lists. Well, we think it was your name unless it is a common one? Anyway … I was hoping if indeed it was yourself, that you could tell me how that all felt. Why you did it, what you did, how you felt. I'd like to understand the motives, just from an academic point of view?'

Marton coughed. It was a nervous cough. He looked distracted and started to move himself into his wheelchair.

'I understand. You'll have to excuse me, though. I need to use the bathroom. I'll only be a moment or two.'

He wheeled himself close to Sarah's chair, keeping his gaze away from her and then toward the bathroom door on the far side of the room.

'Of course.'

The door slid shut behind him and she heard a faint clink as it was locked.

She looked around the room. Was she feeling so nervous for no reason? The clock was still making her feel unsettled. Now, it was the only sound.

She began to scribble some notes onto her pad, to distract herself. The sound of running water started to tinkle from under the bathroom door.

*

Marton ran the tap at half-throttle, to mask any other noise he was or wasn't going to make. For all his infirmity, his wits were still sharp.

128

He leant forward from his chair and pulled open a small door fronting a tiny cabinet underneath his bath. He dialled his personal code number into the safe inside and pulled out a parcel wrapped in oiled cloth, together with a small, transparent plastic box. He unwrapped the parcel and assembled its contents with an item from the plastic box. He pushed the whole thing down by the side of his right thigh and then flushed the toilet, leaving a moment or two before pressing the open button on the bathroom's electronic lock.

*

Sarah registered the click of the opening lock. It resounded in her head like a pneumatic drill. She heard Marton's chair softly brush across the carpet as he wheeled his way back towards her. Then it stopped, still out of sight behind her.

She looked around quickly.

Marton was by his large desk, retrieving something from a pile of books spread untidily around one side of it.

He picked a book up and rolled back next to his original seat. He stayed in the wheelchair.

'I have something for you. It might be of interest.'

He handed Sarah the book. It was a thin text and had a title in Hungarian that she didn't understand. She opened it and flicked through the first few pages. There were some sections with photographs in. She stopped at one section. It was full of black and white photographs of bears and what appeared to be hunting parties and weapons. She looked at Marton quizzically.

'Carry on. A bit further. Around page twenty-five.'

Flicking the page once more, she found an image of a young man with a weapon in one hand and a fur pelt in the other. It was Marton, you couldn't mistake his head and facial features. She looked back at him … thought she half-understood.

Not quickly enough to react though.

Something flicked past her outer field of vision and was followed by a heavy thump in her left arm. Then it was painful. Her arm started to burn and she yelled loudly. She looked at the pistol Marton was holding in his right hand. Something was missing from the scene. There wasn't a loud bang. There wasn't any smoke. But her arm hurt like crazy. Now her head was hurting too. Aching. Her head drooped as she felt herself falling into a soft faint.

'My dear, I'm sorry, but you can't ask me these things,' he said as he rolled towards her, with a blanket in his other hand.

Sarah slumped forwards into her own lap, becoming aware of a darkness enveloping her head. She realised he'd pushed his chair blanket over her. She tried to yell again, but the volume didn't quite match her first scream. She felt dizzy. She was sinking, her senses spiralling down below the surface of consciousness.

'Shhh, shhh, my dear. You will be asleep soon. Don't struggle.'

She felt herself fall forwards, crashing onto the floor, shouting as her hand banged against the floor, sparking a pain that bounced endlessly around her head, twisting her face into agonies.

Her head thumped into Marton's right knee as she fell and he too yelled out, cursing and moving his wheelchair back, crashing into the wall behind him.

*

All the time he watched Sarah, though. Watched her wilt, slump, fall to the ground. She scrabbled at the floor as her body succumbed to the tranquiliser dart. He'd measured the dose the previous evening, so she should be just temporarily disabled.

He wheeled over to his desk and grabbed a roll of strong, wide tape and started to bind Sarah around her ankles, wrists and mouth once she had gone completely still. It was almost too hard for him. He did it step by step, taking a rest between each binding. Finally, he lay back in his wheelchair, wheezing heavily, feeling very faint himself and perspiring unnaturally.

The next step would be the problem. He knew there was only one way. To ask Aliz to help him. She was the only one he could trust with this.

He called her from her office behind reception and she appeared at his door two minutes later. As she walked into the room he put an unsteady finger to his lips and motioned for her to be silent.

'Shut the door quickly,' he whispered.

Aliz's face crumpled in horror as she surveyed the bound body of the young woman in front of her.

'Marton, what have you done?!' she hissed.

'Aliz, I know I have trusted you with a lot and it is much to bear. However, trust me please that this was unavoidable. I had to do this to prevent our shame and to protect our hotel and family. And you. Please help me hide her. It is all I need from you. Except then you must not speak of this incident.'

Aliz stared at him, with some hostility in her face. They both knew though, that she would do this. There was too much history that trapped them both together in this. She had no real choice. She let out a huge sigh.

'For my father, only, do I do this,' she said with real venom.

It was still difficult. Aliz was not so strong. It was only by clever use of Marton's wheelchair and a desk chair with castor wheels that they managed to move Sarah across the room and pour her limp body into the rectangular wooden receptacle that was to become her temporary tomb.

As Aliz pulled the cover shut, Marton let out a sharp cry. He said nothing but the tear rolling down his cheek told her how much he regretted this. He looked up at her from his chair.

'Please, make me a sandwich Aliz and get me a glass of water. Then I must sleep. And after that, I must think a lot.'

Aliz left the room, banging the door heavily. Marton sighed, with some considerable sympathy. He knew how their past had entangled them both, for different reasons. In Aliz's case, it was her father's name she was protecting, although he had known for years that she wasn't exactly unsympathetic herself with the party's original aims. Far from it, in fact.

He hauled himself over on to his bed and lay still, exhausted. It was an hour before he managed to drop off to sleep, but his sandwich still hadn't arrived by then.

# A chambermaid listens

Hanna Elek dawdled along the third-floor hotel corridor, trailing the cleaning cart behind her. She was tired, her daughter was suffering from a nasty sore throat and had kept her awake for a good part of the previous night. She'd had to leave her with her grandmother for the day since she'd seemed adamant she was too poorly to attend her primary school class. At least Hanna's mother was fit and well enough to look after a lively eight-year-old when she needed her to. Not that Lili was likely to be running around much today, by the look of her when Hanna left the apartment. She hated leaving her when she was ill, it just didn't seem right.

Still, she needed to keep this job, it paid OK and she could swap shifts around when she needed to. The managers were fair and old Mr Kovacs who owned the place had seemed kind when she'd cleaned his room sometimes. He seemed to eat an awful lot for an old man, there always seemed to be a pile of dirty dishes to clear up in there. Obviously, it hadn't done him any harm, he must be well into his nineties now.

Today was dragging already. She needed some more coffee. Maybe she'd pop a guest kettle on in the next room she cleaned and help herself to a free sachet. No one would know. Maybe one of those little packets of biscuits too.

She stopped the cart outside room 312 and looked at her daily room list. Number 312 was ticked as needing attention, so she pulled down her cleaning bucket and some disinfectant from the cart and reached for the master key in her overalls pocket. She leant against the wall opposite the room door and sighed, trying to energise herself for the next spurt of physical effort.

She didn't quite pull the key all the way out of her pocket though.

There was an odd noise, coming from somewhere behind her. Some thumping and a woman or a girl's shout?

It was very faint. Could have been a television. There were a lot of daytime soap dramas on the new cable channels. But there was something not quite television about this noise. It was a bit more dynamic than you'd get from a TV and the thumping was almost *felt*. But it was still very distant. She turned her head slightly and pressed her ear to the wall.

There wasn't much more definition of the sounds. She couldn't tell if it was a shout or a cry and couldn't make any words out. Hard to tell where it was really coming from as well. Maybe it was a room above or below. Except Mr Kovacs was pretty much above this spot, when she thought about it, and he didn't make much noise. So it must be below or to the side somewhere.

Anyway, she'd have a listen when she moved along and went down to the next floor. Right now, she needed that caffeine.

She pushed herself wearily off the wall and entered room 312, closing the door behind her so she could enjoy her secret coffee break in peace.

She filled the kettle, clicked it on and sat down on the small dressing chair in the corner, waiting for it to boil. There was a packet of chocolate chip cookies left unopened on the coffee tray so she ripped the cellophane off and started to munch one. It was good. Maybe she'd have another pack from her cart as well. She didn't earn that much and bringing up Lili on her own was a struggle. A few snaffled biscuits and the odd sachet of hot chocolate were just about her only perks in this place.

She couldn't hear any noises in here, except for some traffic outside. She pushed her mouth into a pout and shrugged her shoulders. All thoughts of the noises left her then, not to return for a while. She pulled out her mobile phone and dialled home, hoping for an update on Lili's sore throat.

# Sarah in a box

Sarah sensed her consciousness rise from a muddy mental swamp; her brain felt as if it was moving slowly in circles, with a miniature accordion lodged in her temples being squeezed in and out with a regular rhythm, a spiralling crescendo which hurt with a vengeance.

She opened her eyes gingerly, to be met with a blank view. Some kind of large flat surface inches from her nose, illuminated only by the merest hint of light. It looked like wood.

She made to stand up and was shocked to find no part of her really moved at all. Her heart rate shot upwards as she remembered the gun in Marton's hand. Had he paralysed her completely? She struggled with a massive effort and understood that her limbs were not exactly lifeless but very constrained somehow. Her neck could twist around a little and that was about the extent of her free movement.

Her panic made her gasp for air and then she realised she was gagged.

So, bound and muted in some kind of cupboard seemed to be her current reality. She loosened the tension in her limbs, as she began to cogitate more clearly about where she might be and what it meant.

She thought about Marton's room. There were some wardrobes she remembered, and a wall cupboard that stretched from floor to ceiling. Somehow they didn't fit with what she was experiencing. She couldn't see or feel any other items in her space. Surely there would have been something in a cupboard. Perhaps he had dragged a crate into the room. *Crate* rapidly turned into the most dreadful word she could think of right now.

*Coffin.*

She instantly perspired across her brow as her pulse soared again. Then she checked herself. It was the wrong shape for a coffin. The light was coming from the side, somewhere behind her. Maybe not even a crate, then?

Just as she recovered from the thought she might be nailed inside a coffin, a sudden loud whirring noise immediately above her would have made her jump out of her skin … if she had been able to move at all. Instead, she made to cower, as she imagined a circular saw bearing down on her, cutting through the wood like in a stage magician's stunt. There was a banging movement and she realised she was descending. Thirty seconds later, her body shook as the drop ended with a firm bump. Then silence.

She was feeling very drugged still. The light levels had dropped even further down here. The air smelt stuffy, dead, with a faint tang of food. Not fresh food. Had he lowered her into a cellar? A well? No option she could think of was sounding appealing right now.

**137**

# EIGHT YEARS EARLIER

## Katalin and the book

---

Katalin jumped out of bed with a flourish and pulled the curtains wide. It was a gorgeous late spring morning and the leaves were filling the gaps on the horse chestnut trees at the end of the small garden. Shafts of sun shot through the gaps in the branches and streaked across the lawn. The old rope garden swing moved gently in a light breeze, rocking to and fro an inch or two, the seat still glistening from some overnight dew.

She opened a window and smelled the air. Lavender and grass filled her nostrils.

She was looking forward to a full day of reading in peace. Mother was away until late evening and she'd been too busy recently to spend much time on her hobby.

She just *loved* reading. Almost anything worked. Long days of doing nothing but living inside another person's head, in another time and place. Yawning occasionally. Feeling peckish but finishing another chapter first. Then another. Then piling up some sandwiches and eating them slowly as she ploughed on and on. Stretching slowly, taking a quick pee and making a cup of tea. Then returning to the sofa and settling down for more.

Bliss.

She made herself some toast and coffee, ate quickly and dressed, eager to get started in the study.

She hadn't decided what to begin with, for once. She allowed herself that little excitement of scouring a room full of shelves which held, even now, plenty of titles she hadn't read, and then picking one or two out for that day. Mother always read so much, she had years' worth of delight stashed around that room.

She took the remains of the pot of coffee in with her and sat on the desk, peering around the hundreds of book spines for somewhere to start.

There were a lot of novels. They made up most of the room. Some of Mother's own interests and hobbies were part of the stacks too: pottery, wildflowers, some history - mostly about Hungary.

She pulled out one about flower-pressing. She loved to read about her mother, things she had been interested in as a girl. She imagined her collecting flowers on the shores of Lake Balaton, near the village of Tihany where she'd been brought up.

As she pulled the book down, a brown tome with a scruffy spine, its title almost illegible, came out too, the two books' covers stuck together with heat and time.

It fell to the floor, a section of its binding loosening, spilling a dozen or more chunks of pages around itself.

She swore under her breath and picked up the book and the spilt pages carefully.

She set the spine and the loose pages out on the desk and started to assemble them back into order. She wondered how to glue them back into position. Mother had some paper glue in the desk drawer that might be good enough for a quick repair. She slid the drawer open and rummaged around, finally picking out a cream bottle encrusted around the neck with old glue.

She pinned each section that had slipped out into position, after first giving the inside edges a thin smear of glue. Within a few minutes she'd almost finished and she picked up the last loose section.

She stared at it a fraction longer than she intended. Something on the visible page had caught her eye. She scanned it again, more slowly this time.

It was a name, which had somehow caught her attention. Marton Kovacs. It was a name she knew. A man who had visited Mother sometimes, for tea on a Sunday. Maybe once a year or so, though he hadn't been for a while now. Someone her mother knew through her work apparently. Katalin usually ate her tea politely and then went to play with her own things. The man had never really spoken to her much.

She read around that page. There was a photo too. It was part of a chronicle of the Arrow Cross activities in 1944-45. Marton's name appeared below the photo, with a number of others. She counted in from the start: he was the fifth name. She looked up at the fifth man in the picture, a group of them all lined up like a school class photograph.

He didn't look like Marton. It was an old photo, not exactly high definition. The book was published in 1951 too, so its own pages would have yellowed somewhat.

Most of the faces on the faded brownish picture looked very young. Teenagers. But that face was just the wrong shape. She let her eyes drift across the photo. Then snap back to a boy in the next row. Now *he* looked as if he could have grown up to be the man who had visited their house. A large round face and a big nose. Yes, possibly him. They must have printed the names underneath the photograph incorrectly, maybe screwed the rows up. In any case, if that was Marton, then what she read further down the page about those boys filled her with horror.

She knew the Arrow Cross had done some bad things in support of the Nazis. The group in this photograph had been linked to a number of war crimes, including the killing of children in their own houses, along with their parents. Some of the culprits had been caught after the war ended and tried successfully, others had disappeared.

She rubbed her temples and ran her fingers along her scalp, back through her hair. She didn't want to know about this. Not at all.

This man, if it was Marton, had been visiting her mother's house freely. Was he one of those who disappeared? Or was he innocent of anything, just a member of a group caught up in the weirdly distorted sense of righteousness that war breeds? And why did Mother have this book?

There was only one way to find out. She would have to talk to her when she returned that evening.

\*

It was a long day after that. Time dragged and she found it difficult to read for long without returning to the black feeling that was hanging around her thoughts, prodding her mind, asking her to worry about what it all meant. She took a long late lunch, went into the garden with a sandwich and sat on the swing down in the far corner. She idled there, swinging in a dozily warm shaft of light, feeling anything but sunny.

It was almost eleven p.m. when the latch clicked, as her mother came into the front hallway. Katalin was sitting in her bedroom and heard her drop her bag with a clunk onto the tiles.

'Hello?' she shouted from the hallway.

'Hi, I'm upstairs. I'll be down in a minute.'

Katalin took a deep breath, composed herself, walked out of her room and down the carpeted stairs. Mother had moved on by then, so she walked to the threshold of their small kitchen and stood against the doorframe, arms crossed.

Her mother was filling the kettle.

'Hi, Mum.'

Mother turned her head. 'Hello, darling. Coffee, or is it too late for you?'

'I'm fine thanks. It's been a long day, I might have some wine.'

Her mother looked at her, squinting her eyes, alerted by something in her voice. 'Are you OK? You sound ... I don't know ... tired?'

Katalin felt herself flush. She always did that when she was nervous.

'Huh, well, there was something I wanted to talk to you about. I found a book this morning ... dropped it actually. Some pages fell out and when I was trying to mend it ... well, I read some things that seemed weird.'

By now her mother was glaring at her. She turned to face Katalin, folding her arms and dropping her head to one side.

'Which book?'

Katalin gave an edgy little giggle and looked away from her mother. 'Mmm, I didn't really notice the title. I was too busy trying to fix the pages back. It was about Arrow Cross, though.'

She looked back, to gauge the reaction.

It stood out. Like a queen bee on a jam sandwich. This was something that her mother was most definitely not wanting to talk about. She turned away from Katalin and attempted to busy herself with the coffee machine. She was flustered, though, and her movements were jerky. She spilt some coffee grounds on the counter, cursing.

Katalin kept silent.

Then her mother cracked.

'So, what did you want to know, my darling?' She turned to face her daughter as she spoke, coffee in hand. 'Oh sorry, you wanted some wine.'

She got a glass for Katalin and filled it with white wine. She walked across the kitchen and handed it to her. She remained standing very close, looking her steadily in the eye.

'Is it him? Is it Marton who comes here sometimes?'

Katalin saw the tremor in her mother's eyes. Just a quiver in the pupils, a small dance.

Mother breathed in heavily, ready to exhale the truth.

'It is, yes.' Katalin looked away and back again.

'And you read about this, in this book, yes?'

'Yes. A long time ago … where is the book now Katalin?'

'It's in the study. And he still comes here? Is he guilty of this, what it says in the book?'

'I don't know. Maybe. It was a long time ago Katalin. Things were different then. People were at war. Everyone was scared for their lives. A lot of the people from that time are dead, killed by the war or old age since. Marton is just a friend. He has helped me a couple of times and well, you know, since your father died before you knew him, he has been kind to me. I don't judge him for what may or may not have happened in the war.'

'But he was in the Arrow Cross, you can see from the photos and everything. He should be investigated for this ... and the crimes they may have committed!'

Katalin's voice was ratcheting up the volume more than a few notches now and her hands were starting to tremble.

She had heard a little about Arrow Cross before, in school. The notion her mother might be somehow comfortable with someone who hadn't been tried for their crimes was just astonishing. Especially when this chronicle suggested there was actually something specific to answer to.

Her mother remained silent. Either unwilling to speak or unable to say anything that would help.

'You know what? I'm going to need to think about this, about what I should do about it!' Katalin blurted, pushing her head forward, shouting the words and spraying a fine mist of spittle in her mother's face.

Her mother recoiled from the verbal assault, taken aback by the emotion that came with it.

'I'm going to bed,' Katalin said, 'I'll let you know in the morning what I think we ... you, should do about it.'

She picked up her wine and slung it into the sink, before running out of the room and up the staircase.

*

**144**

Mother stood still for quite some time, propped against the countertop with one hand.

She pondered the truth, round and round in her head, like she hadn't done for many years now. And she also recognised how little of it she'd told Katalin.

How that was going to turn out tomorrow was anyone's guess. She wondered whether to warn Marton, but decided against it, for reasons best kept to herself.

*

In the event, the worry of what tomorrow would bring was taken away from Katalin's mother in an unexpected way.

Katalin had lain in bed for hours, unable to sleep, unable to believe her mother would have stayed quiet for so long.

What exactly had Marton done to 'help' her and why hadn't she *told* anyone? Or maybe she *had* and it had gone no further for some reason.

But Mother wasn't saying anything. She was holding back, she could see that much at least. So, if her mother wasn't going to tell her, maybe Marton would. But she'd need to find him first.

She left at dawn carrying a rucksack, full of clothes curled around a stash of banknotes she'd kept under her mattress and some bread for breakfast.

The thought of tolerating a Nazi sympathiser as her mother was making her feel physically sick.

She needed to know everything and that meant finding Marton Kovacs. She would find his address later.

What's more, she wasn't going to come back here until she knew something.

In fact, she nearly never came back.

## Marton receives a guest

Marton Kovacs was seated at his desk when Katalin was shown into his room at the Hotel Cristal three days later.

The girl nodded politely as she entered and had the door closed behind her by the bellboy who'd shown her to the room.

'Good morning. Mr Kovacs.'

'Hello, my dear. Please take a seat. There are a few to choose from.' He smiled as he swept an arm out across the spread of the room.

Katalin looked around and chose a comfortable looking armchair close to his desk.

'Well, you have grown up a lot since I last saw you at your mother's house. I remember you on a swing in the garden sometimes.'

Katalin pursed her lips into a forced smile.

'So, coffee?' He indicated a large pot, on a polished walnut side table behind her.

'No thanks. I'm OK. I just want a quick talk about my mother. And you.'

'Yes, so you said yesterday when you called me. So why don't you tell me what is on your mind, my dear?'

Marton stared at her. Looked at her posture, heard her voice. Felt the tension in the air.

'You see my mother sometimes, although I haven't seen you for a while now, I know. You are friends I assume?'

Marton looked thoughtful. After a moment, he replied.

'Yes. We are old friends. We keep in touch. Well, we used to. I haven't seen her or talked to her for a while. I'm not so well now, as you can see. You lose contact with people as you get older somehow. Except for a very few. But didn't your mother tell you that anyway?'

'Mmm, well yes I suppose she did, though when I was younger I didn't really think about who you were. I only thought about that recently. She has many friends, my mother.'

'Go on.'

'Well, I found out recently that you had something to do with Arrow Cross. Did you?'

'Yes, I did, Katalin. I was in the party when I was a boy. Why do you ask?'

His heart sank even as he asked that question. He was fearing the answer. Fearing what had been poking him in the back for a lifetime, shadowing his moves, always threatening to burst into the open and destroy his world.

Katalin cleared her throat and swallowed before speaking.

'Because I read a book. A book my mother had. There was a picture in it, a photo of a group of the Arrow Cross party. You were in it, though I think they got the names confused. Was it you?'

Marton's old mind raced in a way it hadn't done for years. Names confused … the term sprinted round in his head like a lizard in ever-decreasing circles until he had to squint.

'Well, it's hard to know. Do you have the book to show me?'

'No. My mother has it. I didn't think to bring it.'

She faltered, then recovered. 'But it was from January 1945. The picture I mean. It talked about some killings by this group of young men, in the Jewish ghetto. You know, in the war. Were you involved in that?'

The girl's directness and lack of any social niceties before she barked these questions out was astonishing Marton. He was stunned.

'My dear girl, no, of course not. The people that were responsible were punished after the war. It was all very thorough.'

'I read that some of those accused disappeared and weren't found though?'

Marton's age was beginning to tell. He was trying to answer her … at the same time as working out what to do with this situation … and he was struggling to cope. He held his face as best he could. He spoke slowly, trying to avoid any mistakes. He felt sure that she would notice.

'Well, yes, maybe some did leave the country. But not me. I have stayed here since the war. In fact, apart from some trips to Bucharest, to see my son, I have never left Hungary.'

'Oh, you have a son. May I ask … is your wife alive?'

Marton considered his stance on this question. 'In fact, she died ten years ago or more. Emphysema. But I'm not sure why I should be telling you about my family. What exactly is the point of your questions? Is this about Arrow Cross? Or your mother?'

She looked surprised at that.

**149**

'My mother is nothing to do with this really … although, of course, I was unhappy to find out she's been friends with an Arrow Cross member, however long ago that was. Even more so if he'd been guilty of a war crime. Especially where children were killed.' She stared long and hard at him as if trying to discern the truth in his face.

Marton was silently making a decision. One that would affect the rest of his life, in a way he couldn't understand yet.

He rose slowly from his chair. 'Look, I'm sorry, I need the toilet. You will need to excuse me for a moment.'

Katalin blushed. 'Of course. Of course.'

'Help yourself to coffee now maybe?' He motioned towards the coffee pot again.

'Yes … yes, I will, thank you.'

Marton moved slowly to the bathroom on the other side of the room, using a stick to steady himself. He slid the door open then back shut.

*

Marton was churning through his options as fast as his mental state would allow. Not that quickly. The pressure of time started as soon as the door lock slid into place and he felt it squeezing his heart and tensing his shoulders, clouding his brain.

He shook his head and pressed his eyes shut as his head dropped into his hands. There was a sandstorm going on inside his head. And a big problem at its centre. He needed time to think. To react properly. To plan how to deal with her. And he had no time, well, not if he was going to let her walk out of here with the freedom to talk to who she wanted, armed with whatever he told her or what she decided to assume.

**150**

That wasn't permissible. He had to stop that happening. Then decide what to do. He had only one, ugly, solution forming.

He stooped down and opened the small cupboard under his bath. He opened the safe inside and, pulling out the contents, unwrapped a number of components and assembled them quickly.

He pushed the result into his waistband, underneath his over-long cardigan.

Last time he used this gun it was on a bear in the Carpathians, during a hunt. He just hoped he'd judged the dose correctly. Otherwise, his target might not survive.

\*

Katalin heard the toilet flush and door lock open, turned to watch him return across the room to his desk. He remained standing behind it, both sets of fingers making a tent on the wooden top, his body leaning forward slightly.

He started to speak.

'I am afraid ...'

'Of what?' she interjected before he could finish. He stood silent for a moment.

'Just afraid. And I suppose of what you might do ... what you might *think*, no matter what I say to you, even if it is all the truth and all innocent.'

He pushed a big right hand under his cardigan and retrieved a gun. Katalin's terrified expression showed she understood she wasn't going to be able to decide her own fate now.

He stood up straight as a rod, looming over her like the giant over Jack. He extended his arm, pointing the pistol straight at her chest. It had a funny shaped thing stuck out the end of it, like a dart.

'I'm sorry, my dear, but …'

That was all he got to say to her. She screamed over the top of his words, crossing her arms tightly over her chest. He aimed slightly higher and right, pulling the trigger.

The dart hissed into Katalin's left shoulder, tearing the flesh, filling her body with pain and her eyes with tears. Marton lumbered around the desk and lunged at her, pressing a massive hand across her mouth, stifling her screaming. She bit at it, as hard as she could. He grunted then pulled his bloodied paw away before clamping her again, this time with his other hand pressing her jaw upwards, so she couldn't open her mouth.

Katalin tried to wriggle her face free, but her resistance was fading before his eyes and she gave way to his own poor strength. Her eyelids closed slowly and her body went limp.

*

Faced with a deadweight tranquilised body to deal with, Marton had panicked for a good few minutes, before managing to calm his nerves with his favourite Scotch whisky, the one he only drank on special occasions. This was definitely one.

Four fingers of whisky later, he thought unsteadily through his options. She would probably stay unconscious for a few hours if bears were anything to go by. He could always shoot her again, though the thought wasn't particularly appealing. No, he needed to sort this out in a couple of hours. But for that, he really needed some help.

There was only one person he could turn to easily, apart from Alfred. But Alfred was old and not here right now. Aliz Gal was. She was in the hotel today, his manageress. Aliz was the only person who knew the truth about himself and Alfred. What's more, her father had been in Arrow Cross too, so she had some sympathies. Sympathies without any of the internal moral tussles that it seemed to cause in other people, or at least that's the impression she gave.

He called her and asked her to come up straight away, to drop whatever she was doing.

She arrived at his room within a couple of minutes. She was a tall woman, always so elegant, even as she had become an old woman she was always impeccably dressed. Never lost her temper either, so calm. He admired her for that. She still had energy too, more than he had, for sure.

Even *her* cool manner was ruffled by what she saw on the floor as she entered Marton's room, though.

A young woman, sprawled awkwardly on the floor, as if she had fallen without restraint from the chair next to her. With a small arrow in her shoulder.

Aliz gently pressed a hand to her mouth and shut the door quickly behind her.

'What have you done, Marton?'

'Aliz, look, I need to trust you in this. She was asking me about Beata Sandor and a book Beata has at home. She is her daughter. She knows about the group Alfred and I were in. She was asking if I was implicated. I didn't know what to do. She could say the same thing to anyone Aliz, anyone. Then what might happen?'

Aliz stared fixedly at him. She didn't react. But her eyes gave away her sense of the danger this girl might pose.

'I'm sorry, I didn't know what else to do. So I stunned her with my shooting pistol. We have a little time to work out what to do.'

'How long, Marton?'

He looked timidly at her. 'Two hours, maybe a little more.'

She winced and looked thoughtful. 'Well, you don't really have too many options then. You let her go, you kill her, or you keep her. Simple as that.'

The emotionless ease with which she arrived at that clarity took Marton aback. He sat very still for a moment except for a soft nodding of the head, thinking through each of the paths she'd suggested.

His thinking became crystal clear at that moment. 'Keep her,' he almost shouted. He wanted the words out fast, then maybe they wouldn't be from him. And before he changed his mind.

'But where, Marton? It needs to be somewhere no one else will find her. Also … maybe someone knew she came here. There must be no trace of her left in this room.'

They both looked down, then up at the same time. They knew what each other was thinking.

Room 31.

Room 31 was their secret. They had reserved it for anything Arrow Cross. Books. Pictures. An occasional gathering of old survivors. More recently, for a new group of young people, who were interested in rekindling those old fires that they once burnt themselves.

They'd walled up the door from the corridor years ago and kept just a double-locked connecting door from Room 33, which was only sparingly let out to guests if the hotel was full to bursting. Almost never, in fact. It was heavily soundproofed as well, so no one could hear what was going on in there.

'We might need to make some changes? Block the window … maybe hide the door off inside the room … somehow. But yes. It could work. Certainly for now.'

He didn't discuss it much further. He had no immediate alternative. Within an hour, Aliz had brought up a large food trolley from the kitchens and they had pulled Katalin onto it and covered everything with a white dining tablecloth. She was taped up and gagged to give them time and space to work out how to manage the next steps.

'I'll check her in an hour or two, Marton. I need to sort out some things on the front desk. I'll block off any bookings for Room 33 completely. Tell everyone you need it as a store for a while. Then I'll be back.'

She shut Marton's door behind her, leaving him to contemplate the future.

# Katalin has a new home

When Katalin woke up from the dark, she felt as if she'd spent all day drinking palinka mixed with vodka. Her tongue was dry and sticky at the same time.

She was facing sideways, across the floor. Her eyes were stuck together with sleep mucus. She moved her hands to rub them but they wouldn't obey her brain. Her brain was slowed by the effects of the tranquiliser and didn't understand what was happening.

She moved her head upwards and sideways, to peer around the room. That part of her anatomy wasn't playing ball either. She could feel some resistance to flexing her neck muscles and twisted her head to try and work it out. Then she saw the tape on her ankles, felt it on her wrists and around her mouth. The best she could do was rock herself gently and stare ahead, which quickly made her feel sick.

Ahead of her was a wall, papered but scuffed. She sensed a big source of daylight behind her. Probably a window. It didn't feel like Marton's room, though. Where the hell had he put her?

The thought of that and the remaining effects of the drug made her retch and vomit, bursting the weak tape seal around her mouth. A thin veneer of bile slapped across the floor and splashed the wallpaper. She fell back into a doze, not to wake until night stole the room's light.

# NOVEMBER 2018

# A delivery

---

Yet another tram shuttered past the crack in the wood and Katalin's stomach grumbled. Breakfast was very late, it was lunchtime in fact. Food was hardly ever delayed and never as much as this. She started to pace the room in frustration and for something to do.

Mealtimes were a welcome interlude between the interminable blocks of dead time. Long hours that moved imperceptibly to the next clatter and scrape of the dumb waiter. She would often spend an hour or so on a meal, chewing each mouthful slowly and savouring every squelch of flavour, every swallow. It made her feel fuller and it minimised the time with nothing to do but stand at the crack. Sitting on the exercise bike didn't help pass the time in that way. It was an automatic process, pushing the pedals around and her brain trudging repetitively through her daily stimuli: the crack viewings that day, what she had seen on the television recently. Sometimes a new flavour in her food that she hadn't recognised.

Suddenly a bump or two on the ceiling, then a flurry of movements. After a moment of silence, the drone of the dumb waiter started.

It continually frustrated her that she seemed to be able to hear faint noises in the room above her, yet no one heard her when she screamed. It had been a long while since she'd tried.

Her digestive juices woke up with a vengeance, as the thought of imminent food flooded her thoughts. She turned expectantly to the closed hatch. The rustle of the rope and pulley mechanism stopped abruptly.

Normally a bell rang. This time it didn't. She hesitated, wondering if she was supposed to go and retrieve her food yet.

But she was really hungry now and she decided there was no point in waiting. She walked over to the hatch and put her hand on the wooden handle.

As she touched it, the bell rang out long and shrill. It startled her and her hand dropped away from the handle sharply. For a reason she couldn't put her finger on, she felt nervous.

'Stop it, why are you worried about eggs and coffee? Or lunch either, if it's all arriving together today,' she muttered at her own chest.

With a brisk movement, she grabbed the handle again, shoved the sliding door upwards to its full height and peered inside into a cubic space of about three feet each way.

Except there didn't seem to *be* a space today. She blinked. Her mind couldn't process the visual signals she was getting. There was no coffee jug, which was the first thing she always spotted. Usually smelt before she saw it too. So good in the morning, that delicious aroma. But now there was no jug.

In the milliseconds that followed, she saw no bread or eggs or any other kind of food or crockery of any sort. She shook her head, trying to clear the fog of confusion that was stopping her seeing what was in front of her.

But she could see no small items, just a fullness. The space inside the serving hatch was packed, full of a canvas of black fabric. And some blue material, like denim. She moved a step backwards and tried to get a wider perspective on the waiter's contents.

It was then that she saw the black fabric move. More exactly, it *swelled*. Like an inflating balloon.

Then the swollen area sank quickly. Then rose again just as fast. From somewhere inside the hatch, a strange noise made her jump and move further backwards.

Another noise. This time she heard it for what it was. A grunt.

Then came the realisation that froze her to the spot and stopped her breathing with the same instant iciness.

She was looking at a human frame. It was squeezed impossibly into the narrow dimensions of the hatch.

She realised it was the first time she had been so close to a real person for a long while. Now, she could smell the body odours, as her brain relaxed its pre-programmed anticipation of food and allowed her to deal with the reality sitting squarely in front of her.

Whatever was expected of her, she was unsure. But it was pretty clear the person in the chute was stuck and wouldn't get out without some help.

She put her hands out in front of her, towards the breathing black fabric, as she tried to work out how to start to help the person get out. She realised she was looking at the person's back, and the legs were pushed upwards into the hatch, on the far side, so she could only see the rear waistband of some denim jeans. Her movements were tentative and it was a few seconds before she placed her fingertips on either side of the person. It triggered a rapid inflation again and a higher-pitched grunt, followed by a sort of *wiggle* of the black material. The body had recognised another human's touch.

Katalin placed her hands more firmly on the body and tugged. Nothing moved. She pushed her hands further round and curled her fingers into the person's buttocks. They were soft. Felt like a woman's bum. She pulled again, moving things an inch or two but then felt resistance from the hatch frame.

She released her hands and stood back, looking around the room for some idea on how to get this person free.

*Free her … but into her room, though?* She hadn't thought of that. What was that going to mean? Did she want this person … woman … girl? … in her room? How could she be sure she wouldn't be a threat? She paused, uncertain what to do next.

More wiggling and grunting emanating from the hatch brought her thoughts back to the here and now.

So, she was grunting which probably meant her mouth was gagged. Which also implied she wasn't *his* friend. And being squeezed into that space wouldn't be a voluntary thing. Most likely it would be hurting too. And then the clincher. If she stayed in the hatch, how would any more food get delivered?

With that thought making her decision for her, she picked up a wooden chair and hammered the back against the floor. It was enough to break a couple of the more decrepit spindles and gave her leverage to twist and pull the top bar off the remaining ones.

She poked the smoothly curved bar of wood into the side of the hatch, between the frame and the body. There were a few inches of space either side of the person, so once she had the bar well inside the hatch she pulled against it hard, shoving the body sideways. It grunted and growled viscerally, with pain in its complaints.

Now there was space enough on one side to try to tilt the body that way, get the head a bit lower so it might be able to slip out of the hatch. Katalin grabbed the upper part of the back and yanked it sideways, keeping the bottom jammed down against the opposite corner. Now she could see most of a girl's head. Tangled hair, jet black, almost reaching her shoulders. She placed her hand up and around the head, feeling the heat of the skull and dragged it down and outward. There was a brief muffled yell and then a sudden, springing release, throwing Katalin backwards and the girl halfway out of the dumb waiter.

Katalin jumped back to her feet, ready to deal with whatever happened next.

The girl was writhing and growling violently, having banged her head against the floor as she poured the rest of herself out of the waiter. She lay in front of Katalin, bound and gagged tightly, clearly in a state of wild distress.

Katalin stared, wide-eyed and heart pounding with the closeness of this bundle of humanity lying in front of her. A few years younger than Katalin by the looks of the part of her face that was visible. Pretty, medium frame.

Now her food delivery route was open again, there was a choice to be made.

Driven mostly by a need to self-preserve, Katalin decided on a course of caution.

'*Nyugalom, ez OK,*' she said to the girl. She tried to smile softly at her, to try to calm her writhing, but the girl just continued to roll around, pulling at the bindings around her wrists.

She would wait an hour. See how the girl reacted. Then decide what to do. But maybe she could ungag her first, that couldn't do any harm, could it?

# First encounter

Katalin reached down towards the girl's face and tugged tentatively at the mouth gag. The girl pulled her head sideways a little, perhaps trying to help wrench the tough, sticky tape away from her face. There was no knife or pair of scissors in the room. Perhaps he'd thought she might buckle under the solitude and end it all with a piece of culinary steel. Even her food was delivered chopped up and with plastic cutlery. Whatever, it made this task too hard. All she could do was drag the layers of tape downward enough so that the girl's mouth was cleared and there was some movement possible with her jaw.

It meant she could speak. The first words that came out were surprising; because they were in English.

'Who the hell are you? And get this tape off my hands!'

Katalin's English was poor now. She'd learnt it at school and had used some in her career. Well, what there was of it before he'd kept her here. She watched some American TV shows occasionally too. But lack of practice had let it decay. This sudden outburst was hard to comprehend.

'Sorry. I not speak English very good. Hello, I am Katalin.'

The girl on the floor took a moment to consider this. 'Katalin who?'

'Katalin … Sandor.' She wasn't sure she wanted to mention her family name, but it just came out. 'And what is your name?'

The girl pursed her lips and hesitated before replying. 'Sarah. Sarah McTeer.'

'Why you here Sarah?' enquired Katalin, entirely unsure of what the response might be. All the more reason to keep her bound up for now.

Sarah looked around the room before she answered.

'I'm not sure. I came to see Marton. Now I'm here.'

At the sound of his name, Katalin visibly recoiled, drawing her arms more tightly across her chest. Her eyes were sad. No passion, no hope in them.

'Why? Why you see Marton?'

'I came to see him about … the war.'

At the mention of war, Katalin's attention clicked up a gear. The war was the reason she herself was being kept here. Maybe this girl could be trusted. She knelt down by Sarah's feet, tentatively grasped the layers of tape around her ankles and worked her fingers slowly under them, then pulled them laterally, trying to stretch the tape to free enough space for her feet to slip through.

It took Katalin a while, but the girl seemed to understand what she was trying to do and moved her ankles to try to help the process. After ten minutes of wrestling the tape, finally, there was enough room for a foot to slip out. Katalin pulled the trainer off Sarah's left foot and helped push her foot back up through the tape loops.

Katalin dragged the broken chair towards Sarah and then watched as, now able to at least spread her legs out, Sarah somehow pushed her body upwards into a standing position, then sat carefully on the chair-stool. She winced and straightened herself as one of the splintered spokes scraped against her back.

'So what about the war, Sarah? What you want to know about Marton?'

'I wanted to know what he did. You know … when Germany was in Hungary. With the Arrow Cross.'

Katalin felt shocked. She struggled to stop it turning into panic. It was a long time since she had talked about this. At first, it had been all she could think of, the reason she came here. And the reason she stayed here. But over time, she found she coped better by not thinking about it. So it had become stowed away, perched quietly on an innermost shelf in her memory.

Now, here was a mind librarian, plucking it back out again.

She moved away from Sarah, sat down on the bed and leant against the wall. She pulled her feet up under her. This was going to be a long conversation.

# Getting to know you

'So you are here to find out about Marton? How did you find out his name?'

'No, no. Not Marton specifically. Just the Arrow Cross party. We kind of stumbled across Marton along the way and went to meet him. That's where it all started to go wrong, I think.'

She nodded at Sarah, knowingly.

'Yes, I'm sure that may be problem. Marton is not be happy talking to you about Arrow Cross.'

'But he agreed to the request for a chat! He agreed to see me.'

Katalin looked thoughtful.

'Well, maybe he wanted to know more of you. Understand if you are dangerous for him. Sorry, my English correct?'

Sarah waved a hand at her, dismissing the apology. 'No, your English is good enough, I can understand no problem. Anyway, I'm Scottish myself.'

She wondered if that joke made any kind of sense to a Hungarian, but pressed on.

'I'm trying to understand the background to the Arrow Cross party. I came here to read about it and meet some people who can tell me more about it. It's my work, I'm researching … studying, at a university in Scotland.'

She peered into Katalin's eyes, 'How long have you been here Katalin?'

Katalin looked away. Sarah thought she looked … ashamed. She looked down at the floor as she answered.

'I think eight years.'

Sarah threw a hand up over her mouth, stifling a gasp of shock.

'Eight … years? God, you poor thing.' She leant forward towards Katalin, to try and embrace her, but Katalin backed away a little. Sarah's eyes started to tear up. Not just because of Katalin's plight either. She was beginning to worry about what that meant for her *own* future. She remembered her mobile phone and pushed her hand into her jeans pocket, searching for its comforting shape. Not there. It must have been taken from her in Marton's apartment.

'So haven't you tried to get out?'

Sarah immediately knew that wasn't the most sensitive thing to have said.

Katalin's reaction reinforced that thought. She threw her arms wide, pleading for understanding and common sense. 'Of course! But he is clever and there is no way out here!'

Sarah looked around the room. 'But there must be a door. Even if you can't see it, maybe it's boarded up?'

'No. No. I think was filled with stone. I can't see it.'

Sarah nodded. She felt herself break into a sweat as the reality of Katalin's situation became absolutely clear. There was no way out of this room. It really was a prison.

'I tried to get out in the lift. Where you came down. But it's very hard. No space, I am too big to get in and doesn't move.'

Sarah peered behind her at the dumb waiter. There was no obvious switch to launch it, for sure. As she continued to scan the area, though, the lift's motor started to operate and the bottom shelf slowly disappeared up into the shaft above the entry hatch.

'Maybe food. No food today,' exclaimed Katalin, looking brighter. The motor stopped.

Sarah realised she was hungry herself, a combination of nothing to eat for hours and now a subsiding adrenaline flow.

Sure enough, after a brief delay, the waiter motor restarted and the shelf frame returned into the hatchway.

Katalin skipped over, opened the hatch door and found the shelf loaded with two small trays, each carrying three covered dishes.

She pulled a tray out. 'Maybe this yours,' she indicated, pointing at the one remaining.

Sarah was interested in the food. But she was more interested in what had just happened. Clearly whoever had restarted the waiter had probably been aware she had got out of it. Because they'd heard her talking to Katalin? How else? So someone was listening to them in all probability. She needed to watch what she said. It struck her that Katalin wouldn't have had to worry about that, with no one to talk to.

She grabbed a piece of paper and a pen laying on a table near the boarded-up window and scribbled.

*I think Marton or someone can hear us. They know I am out of the lift. That's why they sent the food. We must be careful what we say. Understand?*

Sarah held the note in Katalin's line of sight. She studied it for a while and then nodded her understanding vigorously.

'Yes. You are right.'

Sarah went to retrieve her food tray. Katalin had uncovered her dishes by now; there was some soup, a meaty-looking dish and some fruit in the last bowl. They both ploughed into it with some relish, sat side-by-side on the edge of the single bed.

It was at that point that Sarah wondered where she would sleep in here, assuming this was not a fleeting visit. What's more, how could Katalin have survived down here with no access in or out, other than the waiter? It didn't make sense. If she was ill, how did she tell anyone, never mind get treated? And if something went wrong, like the lighting, how did it get fixed? There was something missing from her understanding of this situation: but for now, she resolved to keep her questions to herself.

'*Paprikas krumpli*,' Katalin said, pointing at the meat dish. 'Sausage, spicy.'

Sarah nodded and smiled. She was hungry and sausage sounded good.

After they'd eaten most of the food and were lazily attacking the fruit, the conversation picked up again.

Sarah had noticed the television. 'Does the television work?'

Katalin looked up. 'Yes. I watch television many times. Only way I can see world. Except for window.'

Sarah noticed the tiny crack in the boarded-up window for the first time and wandered across the room to inspect it. Through that sliver of visibility, she could see the street and the daytime traffic cruising along it. Frustratingly close for someone who'd been here for so long.

She turned back towards Katalin. 'So why did he imprison you? What did you do to make him do this?'

**171**

Katalin hesitated for a moment. Then spoke firmly.

'I find out something about him. By mistake really, well at beginning. But he found out I know. To do with the Arrow Cross. He had done some bad things.'

Sarah started to understand her own mistake. Letting Marton become aware of what she thought she might have uncovered, had led to her being dumped down here. She felt stupid and naive. How could she have got this so wrong? She should have been far more careful in the way she'd interviewed him the second time. But even so. To be this concerned after more than half a century ... it felt bizarre.

Sarah considered whether to ask the next question, then just went for it.

'So, what *exactly* did you find out about Marton?'

Katalin looked down and shook her head slowly. She was still for a moment or two.

'I can't say today. Maybe another time. I not know much about you. So, sorry, sorry but not now.'

She looked up with a plaintive ask on her face.

Sarah knew she was right. *Who was this woman who had dropped into her life after eight years, through a serving hatch?* She'd probably be just as wary herself if the roles were reversed. She needed to build some trust first. Then maybe she could get her to open up.

'OK. I understand, Katalin. I suppose we will get to know each other a bit better in time, unless he decides to let us both go anytime soon.'

Sarah threw a rueful smile at her. It was quickly reflected, with more than a little warmth. Maybe they would become bound by a common cause. She needed to build on that start. Katalin had been here a long time. Sure, she would be nervous with someone new in the room after so long alone. But she'd be lonely too, wouldn't she? She needed to become Katalin's new best friend.

# Reality bites

It was sometime after their meal that Katalin and Sarah began to think, separately, about the reality that there were now two of them in a room designed for one. The obvious upcoming issue was the sleeping arrangement. A single bed, albeit probably one of those halfway between a single and double size, looked a bit of a squeeze. In Sarah's mind, it was a risk too. She really had no idea how stable or trustworthy Katalin was, despite some promising early signs. And Katalin probably felt the same about her.

She looked around the room. There was a large wardrobe at one end. She wondered if it might hold something to sleep on.

'Is there any more bedding, Katalin?'

Katalin nodded at the wardrobe she was looking at. Sarah walked over and pulled a spare duvet and pillow from the top shelf.

She looked at Katalin for acceptance.

'Of course. You can put over there.'

She pointed to the space under the window, away from her own bed. Clearly, Katalin felt nervous about this first night too.

Sarah threw the bedding down. It was early really but she felt tired, the adrenalin had subsided and her body was ready for some rest … but her mind was still ticking along briskly so she knew she wouldn't sleep straight away.

'Shall we watch some TV?' she said, looking at Katalin. It would be an easy way of avoiding struggling for more conversation. That had become slower in the last hour and she sensed they both needed a break from the strain of learning about each other.

Katalin seemed to brighten at this, grabbed up the remote and switched the small set on.

As a Hungarian soap opera flashed onto the screen, Sarah's mood sank as she realised she wasn't going to be able to follow much of the action, given the lack of subtitles. She watched it as best she could, feeling a tension between them as they both stared at the screen … and thought about the night to come.

After the soap opera, news, weather forecast and half of a quiz show, Katalin looked like she had fallen asleep first. Sarah stood up and stepped over to her bed and reached for the remote. Katalin's hand snatched it back away from her and she glared at her with some hostility.

'OK, OK, I switch off TV. Go back in bed. Please.'

Sarah laid back down on the quilt and draped it around herself as best she could. No chance she was going to sleep tonight. The room was a bit cool. It smelt of body odour and cooking.

There was another smell too, it was familiar but she couldn't put her finger on it right now. She could smell Katalin too. A mixture of sweat and some cheap fragrance. She supposed that meant she did get some things she needed. As the night dragged on into the early hours, and dawn still seemed a long way off, Sarah had one thing circling endlessly in her mind. It led her down myriad gloomy tunnels, always ending at the same question.

*Eight years of this?*

# Marton has regrets

Marton was sat on his bed, thinking about the end of his life and what was to come.

He hadn't meant to keep her down there. Time had just passed. And he hadn't thought of another way. Murder had never been an option for him. But there it was. And now there was another girl. A complication he'd hoped would never happen. For so many years, it had seemed Katalin would be the only one. It had been a real worry. What if she got sick? Really sick? At least she couldn't get pregnant. And so far, he'd been able to treat her minor ailments via the pharmacy.

Now it had happened again and it had overwhelmed him. He was too old and sick to deal with this. But he couldn't say no. It might have aroused more suspicion if he'd refused to talk to her.

If only Katalin hadn't been to see him. But she had and so his life had been complicated for many years.

But the hotel, all he had worked for, to have a good life, a *fair* life, one he could be proud of: that was what had kept him going. The hotel. His family's name was still respected. He needed to make sure it stayed that way. That was going to be the hardest task of all.

What Alfred had told him after he deposited the envelope and the watch with him, didn't help now. What could he do with that revelation? It was too late, they were both too old and nobody would listen. It hadn't stopped him developing a wave of furious anger towards his friend … and that was a word he wasn't sure he could apply to Alfred anymore.

Aliz had sent some chicken sandwiches up to his room for lunch, delivered by a bell boy. He chewed his way slowly through the second one, feeling less hungry than he'd thought. But that was the norm now, he just didn't enjoy food the way he used to. Somehow, the poison being spread throughout his body by the tumours had made its way into his saliva. The familiar flavours just didn't taste too good anymore. Only stale, acidic.

He felt a little breathless and put the rest of the sandwich down.

He coughed sharply. Two globules of saliva flopped out of his slack mouth onto the bedcover. They looked like little silvery bags of deep red blood. There had been more of these in the last week or two and it was getting harder to recover from his breathlessness. A couple of days ago, he felt like he was suffocating, unable to ease his breathing at all. It had suddenly cleared after a coughing fit, but he lived in fear now, of that coming back and choking the life out of him. Dying wasn't going to be easy, he knew that for sure.

# A problem deepens

Marton was feeling particularly breathless the following morning.

Getting washed, he had help with that, but it took a while. He still insisted on getting himself dressed and that took him the best part of an hour. In fact, it took so long he was worried he wouldn't be ready to take Katalin's food in from the bell boy. He'd thought about getting more food for the new girl. It concerned him, though: maybe someone down in the kitchens would think that a bit odd. As far as they were concerned, Mr Kovacs already had a double helping of all his meals. Fortunately, his rapidly failing appetite meant he didn't need to bother. He just took an odd slice of toast or cut of meat and passed the rest down.

As usual, he had the bell boy put the trays on his wheeled meal trolley. He took a look at the food, then put a piece of toast on a small plate. He stared at it, wondered how many more times he would eat a piece of toast with warm butter melted onto it.

Something made him decide to treat himself and he picked a boiled egg from the serving dish and chopped it onto his toast. Then he sliced a wedge of butter from the block and smoothed it over the egg crumbles. He stared at it again. Maybe some fresh pepper. He ground a few twists onto the assembled dish.

Then he ate it with the most exquisite relish. Every single mouthful was chewed and swallowed slowly. For once, his senses seemed to come alive and he tasted the food like he was a teenager eating paprika beef for the first time.

He picked up a crisp white napkin and cleaned the butter from around his mouth, then leant back and burped with a satisfyingly loud noise. His heart was beating faster now, probably struggling to cope with digesting the food he had just taken in. He took quick, shallow breaths, like a dog panting on a warm summer's day. Tongue loose, not wanting to move at all.

But he did. He needed to get the breakfast into the waiter while it was still hot. Lukewarm food wasn't appealing to anyone.

He sat up and pushed the trolley with one hand whilst he wheeled his chair with the other hand. It was only a few yards but it exhausted him. When he got to the waiter, his heart was beating even faster and tripping into little beat runs that he felt in his mouth. He pressed the button to open the waiter's door and started to push the two trays onto the shelf. He got the first one in OK. Then he tried to pull the second one towards the shelf and curled himself forwards as his chest began to hurt. It hurt a lot. He moved back and forth to try to rid himself of it, but it got worse. With his vision blurring, he gave the tray one more push and pressed the down button, falling backwards from the effort.

Slumped in his chair, leaning sideways over his right arm, he felt very sick suddenly and spewed a thin brown liquid containing his breakfast onto the carpet. His arms felt like hot pokers as his blood seemed to pulse harder and harder in them. He spat a dreg of vomit out onto his arm as it dangled in front of him and he focused his failing vision on it. He couldn't move, nor avoid the rising sensations all over his body. Now he started to gasp as he couldn't get enough air in to satisfy his lungs. He struggled again to breathe in, his heart pounding with great weight as he panicked and fought what he realised now was inevitable. His heart spasmed with an electric mains shock of an impulse and stopped.

Marton's lifetime of shame and hiding was gone.

# Bad news day

---

It was the bell boy, returning to collect Marton's trays at the end of the morning who raised the alarm. He went downstairs to tell Aliz after he'd had no reply. He'd knocked and knocked again, waiting for five minutes before eventually deciding he'd better call for help. His own master pass key didn't work on Mr Kovacs' room.

Aliz rushed back upstairs with him and unlocked the door.

Marton was kneeling in front of his wheelchair, head towards the door and with his crown hard against the floor. There was vomit smeared around his hands which were propped under his bulk at a strange angle. He was absolutely still and silent. The clock ticked its relentless background rhythm as if counting down to something.

Aliz moved quickly and quietly towards him. She called his name softly under her breath.

'Marton. Marton.'

She put her hand on his midriff and spoke again. The slight pressure her hand exerted was enough. Marton rolled away from her, trapping a hand awkwardly underneath his weight and snapping a brittle finger joint with a dry cracking sound. It broke in time with the clock tick.

His body settled to a stop quickly and he lay on his side, facing her, eyes wide open, staring at her. His tongue protruded a little out of his mouth, falling to one side, saliva mixed with a brown gruel coalescing into a glutinous drop on the tongue tip, not quite ready to fall.

'He's dead, he's dead,' shouted the bell boy, stepping sharply back from the body.

Aliz nodded. 'I think so. Go and call an ambulance, please. Be quick.'

As the bell boy left on his errand, Aliz sat down cross-legged in front of Marton's cadaver. A welter of mixed emotions flooded over her and settled around her shoulders. The weight was unbearable. She slipped to the floor and rested her head on the carpet, staring at the body of the man she had worked with, helped, occasionally admired and sometimes detested, for decades.

Now, it was the unknown. It was not clear to her what would happen next. She would have to tell Peter. Marton had assured her that Peter would sort it all out. But Peter didn't know, did he? So how would that all work? Marton had always told her not to worry, that it was all arranged. But she did worry. Things that were cleverly planned could go wrong. Very wrong.

She should tell Peter straight away. At least then whatever Marton had planned could start, she assumed.

She stared a moment longer at Marton's face, recognising this might be their last private time together. She drew his face into hers and kissed his forehead. It was the sense of a shared burden that caused her affection, nothing more really. Taking a mental snapshot of his glaring eyes, she rolled herself upwards and stood up, walked over to Marton's desk and dialled Peter's number, which was scribbled on a reminder pad Marton kept by the phone.

It rang four times, then Peter answered.

'Father?'

'No, Peter, it's Aliz.'

'Oh, sorry, I recognised his private line number. Are you in his room?'

Peter's brain then caught up with the tone of Aliz's voice. He'd heard, but not registered, what it said to him.

'He's bad? Or dead?'

'Yes, Peter, I think he has just died. I'm with him. We are calling the ambulance, but I'm sure he's dead. I thought I should call you straight away.'

Peter took a deep breath and sighed quickly before his throat tightened. He ran a finger down the scar on his cheek.

'Well, we knew he hadn't long left, didn't we? But it seems to have been a long time coming. Now I don't know what to feel. I'm sorry you had to deal with this, Aliz. I'll be in Budapest as soon as I can get a flight. I'll call you back and let you know, OK?'

'Yes. It will be good if you can be here soon, Peter. I need your help now. I will tell Marton's solicitor. He asked me to do that when this finally happened.'

'Really? Well, I'm the executor … but fine, thank you, it will be one less thing for me to do. I need to ring the airline now. I will see you soon, Aliz.'

Aliz nodded and replaced the receiver on the phone. She wondered how easy this was going to be, once Peter knew *all* of the story.

# Girls get hungry

Breakfast time was long gone now and as the clock ticked toward five in the afternoon, Katalin and Sarah were feeling hungry and had started a conversation in broken English about the no show of lunch.

'He never does this. Well, it happen when you come Sarah, that day, but not another time.'

Sarah grimaced. It wasn't any help to her stomach to know this was unusual. In fact, it made her more worried than if it'd been a regular thing. Maybe he wasn't going to send them any more food. At all.

'You have no cakes or biscuits? Or fruit anywhere?'

'Hmm … some biscuits yes, in the cupboard.'

She pointed across the room. Sarah didn't need any second invitation. She found four large packets of biscuits, which seemed to calm her hunger pangs without even eating one.

She opened a packet and offered Katalin one,

'No, I wait now. See if dinner comes first.'

'OK. I'm not waiting.' She took five biscuits out and tied the packet up tightly for later. She started to nibble slowly on the first one, intending to make the experience last awhile. Not exactly any rush to do anything in this room.

'What time can we watch TV?'

'Seven. But dinner about six-thirty.'

Sarah sighed and swallowed a small mouthful of well-chewed biscuit. She wondered how to fill the time to the evening. She rolled onto the floor, on her back and raised all her limbs slightly off the floor.

'You done any Pilates, Katalin?'

'I don't think so … what is this, pirates?'

Sarah laughed. It had been a day or two since she was last able to do that.

'Get down on the floor, next to me … not too near, enough space to spread your arms out. I'm going to teach you some moves.'

Katalin dropped to the floor. Sarah rolled her head sideways and looked at her. There was some trust now, she felt it. She knew they'd need that in the days and weeks ahead.

'OK, we'll start with some abs warm-ups. Just as well we don't have full stomachs. Then I'll teach you the delights of the hundred.'

Katalin smiled, nodding.

An hour later they were still lying on the floor but by now somewhat more alert, their core muscles pleasantly warm with exertion and their minds relaxed after the bouts of giggles that had punctuated their attempts to teach and mimic.

They'd heard a little noise upstairs. But no food yet. It wasn't far from dinner delivery time and as it got closer to six-thirty their relaxation turned into tension again. They found themselves watching the hatch intently. Katalin took Sarah's hand and squeezed it. Six-thirty came and passed. So did seven.

Katalin got up and switched the TV on. To her dismay, there was no picture. She turned towards Sarah.

'Something is wrong. No food. No TV. Something is very wrong.'

Sarah looked up at her, narrowing her eyes, then rolling them upwards. Somehow she'd gone from being at home in Scotland to undertaking some innocent research, to being held captive in a foreign city with a stranger … and now there seemed to be an even darker twist. Not the November she'd planned for herself. For the first time since she'd entered the room, Sarah began to contemplate dying in a foreign land. It sent a cold shudder into her and blew a sense of dread through her thoughts. She looked around the room once more, wondering how she might escape its clutches.

# A visit to the solicitor

Peter was in Bucharest Henri Coanda airport when his father's solicitor, David Pasztor, called him.

'Yes, yes, it is very sad Peter. I offer you my condolences. I knew your father for a very long time. I need to tell you all about the will, of course, but also I have to tell you there is an envelope that you must collect straight away from me. Your father made it clear this would be very urgent.'

Peter had no idea what could be urgent now after his father was gone. Right now, nothing seemed urgent other than getting to the hotel and taking charge of things.

'Well, I suppose I could pick it up on the way in from the airport? Are you central?'

'Of course. We are on Aradi Street. You can collect it from me if you let me know when you will be here. I will keep the office open for you.'

'Very kind. I'd expect to be there about eight o'clock. I'll call you if I'm delayed … let me have your number.'

It was nearer ten when Peter's airport taxi pulled to a stop outside Pasztor's office. His bag had been held up in some kind of union go slow at baggage handling. He told the taxi to wait and wearily climbed the steps up to the front door and rang the bell. He was buzzed in and he walked through the unlocked door into an office that felt more like a home than a place of business. David Pasztor was sat in a comfortable looking armchair in a large room, off one side of the hallway. It was dominated by racks of books, together with cabinets and tables filled with antiques. Lamps, clocks, ornaments. Obviously a collector.

The solicitor rose to meet him. 'Good evening, Peter. I'm so sorry again. Please sit down.'

Peter nodded and took a seat.

'Can I offer you a drink? Scotch maybe?'

'That would be wonderful. Neat please.'

David rose and walked over to a carved wooden side-table, slugged a healthy measure of Chivas Regal into a tumbler. He handed it to Peter together with a large white envelope.

'Your father wished you to open this immediately, in my company, and to read it.'

Peter looked at David. The solicitor's eyes gave nothing away. Maybe he was unaware of the content.

He took a deep sip of the whisky, set it down and opened the envelope.

He read it to himself, taking increasingly deep breaths as he scanned each line.

*Dear Peter,*
*As you now know, I have finally had to leave you all.*

**190**

*It has been a hard goodbye to write. I feel so sad doing this, but now I am dead and no longer sad or anything else.*

*You have always been a good son. You have supported me when I needed you to. And I hope I have been a good father to you, Peter.*

*Of course, since your mother died, you have been the named executor of my will. David will tell you all about this. It is burden enough. But there is something else I need you to deal with. I'm so sorry this has to come to you, but I have lived with this for some years already and I don't know any other way. Please take the repair receipt in this envelope to the shop it was issued from. There you will find my watch. And something else in the envelope. It is for you only Peter. I hope you make the right decisions with it. You MUST do this today, even if the shop is closed. Just telephone the number on the receipt and Alfred will assist you. He is my very old comrade.*

*Please take good care of the hotel, especially Aliz, she has helped me so much over the years. I wish you and all the family a happy life, my son.*

*Your father,*

*Marton.*


Peter looked up, to be met by David's gaze.

'Anything I need to help you with, Peter?'

Peter grimaced. 'No thanks, David. I'll talk to you about the will tomorrow maybe. For now, I have something else to do for my father. I need to leave straight away. I'll be in touch.'

He rose with a weariness borne out of travelling and apprehension from what he'd just read.

Peter took his seat back in the waiting taxi. The driver raised an eyebrow, looking for his next instruction.

'I need to go to the hotel Idral to drop off the luggage then to Dob Street. You can leave me there.'

As the driver turned the wheel and swept out into the street, Peter dialled the number on the jeweller's receipt.

# Time for a watch

Alfred Nemeth had been expecting the call. The old network had kicked into life ... what there was left of it after all these years. He was nervous. Funny at his age, he thought. He asked himself why it mattered really. Same reasons as Marton thought he had, he supposed. Honour. Pride. The worry for his family left with the aftermath. And Peter was Marton's family. Even so, what came first was his *own* family. And the worst thing that could happen would be if Peter heard the truth.

He should have done it straight away when Marton gave him the envelope, but he'd steamed it open now and withdrawn the note he suspected would be within. It was risky. He didn't know what Peter might be expecting in the envelope ... but he'd needed to examine it, that was clear now he'd read the note. He put the envelope on a radiator to dry it out as quickly as he could. At least he'd put Peter off for an hour, saying he couldn't be at the shop so quickly. Peter didn't know he lived above his business, of course.

When Peter finally rang the door buzzer, Alfred's old heart gave a little jump. He went through from the back of the shop where he'd been waiting, wound the security screen up and opened the glass-panelled front door.

'Come in, Peter. Sorry to meet you for this reason. Come through to the back room.'

Peter shook Alfred's hand and followed him through, sitting in the same position opposite Alfred as his father had not many days beforehand.

Alfred cleared some phlegm from his windpipe, wiping his mouth with a handkerchief.

'I think you have a receipt for me, Peter? Sorry to ask but your father insisted.'

Peter harrumphed with some indignation, then produced the receipt from his jacket breast pocket.

'Thank you. Here is the watch.'

He passed Peter the white envelope. It was dry and he had sealed it with some red tape.

'It is as your father gave it to me.'

Peter pulled the tape off and emptied the watch onto the desk. He looked inside the envelope, shaking it gently upside down.

Alfred felt his pulse rise in ragged jumps. He was aware he probably looked unsettled. He wasn't sure he could trust his voice right then, so said nothing.

'Nothing else? Father said there was something else besides the watch.'

The air between them became thin. Alfred could suddenly smell his own anxiety. It was sour, like salt and old wine.

Alfred raised a wrinkled eyebrow, drawing upon decades of deceit in a struggle to appear calm. 'I don't know,' he croaked. 'I don't know what was in there, apart from the watch.'

He shrugged his shoulders to underline his innocence, but Peter didn't seem to be buying it.

'I think there's something wrong here Alfred. There should be something else. Something that father needed me to see urgently. Why would he want me to see an old watch with such haste that you opened the shop for me late at night? You're lying, old man.'

Alfred quickly realised he was losing the tussle of persuasion. He swallowed some phlegm and looked down at his hands, desperately trying to think of the best response.

Peter wouldn't hurt him, would he? Surely not, in a search for something he had no idea of the shape of? It was close by, though, he hadn't thought to hide it better. He'd chosen badly as it turned out.

'I have no idea, Peter. I'm an old man, like your father. I don't know why this was so urgent for him. He didn't tell me that. All I can do is give you the envelope.'

Peter stood up and backed away from the desk. He stopped, leant against the door into the room, well away from Alfred. He scanned the room carefully, side to side, keeping Alfred's face in his peripheral vision, watching for a reaction.

He got what he needed. As he looked left, Alfred threw a quick glance towards a metal filing cabinet.

'In the cabinet then?'

Alfred shook his head. 'I don't know what you mean, Peter.'

His voice was reedy, frightened, and Peter seemed to take some perverted energy from that. He took a couple of steps forward and wrapped one of his massive hands around Alfred's throat.

'Tell me, Alfred, or I'll wreck your office looking for it!'

A squeaky yelp came out of Alfred's throat, but he was still shaking his head in denial.

Peter's patience snapped and he threw Alfred against the wall with a hard shove and turned to the cabinet.

As his head banged against the stonework, Alfred knew he was in trouble, his head swam and waves of pressure rolled onto his brain, forcing him down.

He slipped sideways, the thin hair at the back of his head scraping against the rough wall. He was only barely aware of the pain the graze caused to his skin.

Sliding towards his end, he could only think of one thing. He shouldn't have hidden the note. Katalin needed to be freed. It didn't matter anymore now. Peter needed to get her out of there. He mustn't take any other course. It would all be for the wrong reasons. For the first time in his life, he started to feel real guilt about Marton's predicament. It was all his fault after all.

Too little, too late, though.

\*

The cabinet was locked. Peter turned back to the desk. No key visible there. Alfred was slumped against the wall, slid to a sitting position, still as stone. Peter crouched down and rifled the old man's pockets. A small bunch of keys jangled in one of them.

Peter looked up slowly, sensing a change in Alfred. He stared at his chest. He wasn't sure it was moving. It was hard to tell, though, what with his own heart pounding away like a jackhammer and his ageing muscles unable to hold him steady on his haunches. With one hand on the wall, he steadied himself and focused. Alfred's shirt was almost perfectly still. No mistake.

He leant forward and rested an ear on the bony chest. A desolate, raspy sigh, irregular pulse … weakening.

'Szar!' he cursed. This wasn't what he'd intended.

He stared at Alfred for a few long minutes before deciding not to try to help him. That dragged less heavily on his professional principles than it should have, but he let Alfred slide sideways to the floor and then stood up. He tried the keys one by one until he got the drawers open. He didn't need long to look. A small folded note in the front division of the first drawer. *Peter …* scrawled in his father's handwriting on the front fold. He unfolded it turn by turn.

It wasn't a long note. He read it once, then again, just to be sure he had grasped what it said. And to know that he *really* could have read such a thing.

His father was a monster. He knew his father had a secret. He'd sensed that in lots of different, sometimes quite subtle, ways over the years. But this was something more. A problem, a huge problem he didn't want. Within the matter of a minute, his father had become the most hated thing in his life.

He stared at it again, in disbelief, rubbing his eyes in frantic contemplation.

*Dear Peter,*

*This is the hardest part, I'm afraid. I'm sorry for this further note for you, but I needed to take precautions. Alfred is aware of what I am to tell you, but my solicitor David is not.*

*I don't know how to start. It's almost as much to bear to write this down, as it has been to deal with it for the last few years. Whatever you think of what I am going to tell you now, please consider I always thought of your dear mother, yourself and all your family when I chose to do what I have done. Peter, I am not a bad man. I truly believe that. What happened all those years ago … I can't understand it still. It does not feel like I did those things with Arrow Cross then, but I know I did and I've learnt to live with that part of it all.*

*You have stood by me despite that. I hope you can help me one final time. But you need to act fast. There is something else.*

*I have been holding a girl hostage for a number of years now, in our hotel. She is in the room below my apartment. The door from the next room is boarded up and hidden behind wardrobes, but there is another way in, via the dumb waiter in my own room. This girl, she found out a secret. Something from the war. I didn't know what else to do, to protect our family and business and, of course, our reputation. Also, our freedom may well have become threatened by the girl. I always intended to find another way. But over the years I could find none. I am not a bad man like I said. So I could not harm her. Or let her go.*

*You must decide what to do now. I was the cause of all of this, so it may not be a problem for you if you release her. Please go to the hotel quickly and speak to Aliz. She knows about the girl: she is called Katalin. She will need to be fed, Aliz will help organise this at first.*

*I can say no more. I can only hope you make the right choices for everyone. My love is with you.*

*Again, your father,*
*Marton.*

He sat down heavily on the desktop and closed his eyes. The room was full of silence. He couldn't move for a moment or two as it weighed him down and pressed against his chest.

He let out a breath, the first for five seconds or so. Suddenly he needed to get out of the room and find some fresh air. He had to think, hard and fast.

He checked through the scene in front of him. What had he left there for someone to find? He pocketed the watch, envelope, and the note before taking out a tissue and wiping the desk and cabinet around where he thought he may have left fingerprints. He locked the cabinet and put the keys back in Alfred's pocket. Except for one. He tried the bunch for the front door and left that one in the inside keyhole before switching all the lights out. Then he looked carefully up and down the street before breaking the upper door glass pane with his jacket spread roughly over it to muffle the noise. A quick rub of the key with his tissue again and he pulled the door shut.

He set off walking down the street. It was well past one a.m. the city deep in slumber, as he headed for the small hotel where he'd booked a room. He could have gone to his father's hotel and demanded a room … but for now, he wanted to be away from there, with space to think. It only took him ten minutes before he arrived and collected his key.

As he sat down on the wide bed, he felt like he continued sinking past the mattress, his head in his hands, glasses thrown aside. His head dropped lower, as he propped his elbows on his thighs, and his mind carried on falling to a depth he'd never felt before.

A choice lay before him. To carry on doing what his father had been doing for these years … to keep this girl captive, with all the risks that would carry. Or to free her. All manner of different issues would come with that option. As his thoughts bounced around those two choices, the stress it all generated was stopping him from thinking clearly. He supposed he could delay the decision for a little while, just feed her and let his thoughts settle.

Feeling comforted by that idea, he felt very weary too and pulled himself into bed, not bothering to undress. It was a while before he started to drift into sleep. As he did so a third, darker option started to appear in his mind's eye.

# A lie

Calum's follow-up call and visit with Eszter was
unremarkable, save for the mention she made of Beata Sandor's
helpfulness in the library. He did wonder how usual it was that a
head librarian would provide a personal service to two researchers.
He made a note to talk to Beata again at some point. Even after
his visit to the library and this talk with Eszter, he was feeling
pretty uninspired on how to progress his enquiries. He was
pinning his hopes on a visit to Marton Kovacs helping him get a
new perspective on events ... and maybe a fresh idea for his
investigation direction.

He called the hotel where Eszter had told him Marton
lived. The person who took his call asked him to wait a moment
while she called the manager. After a few moments, a woman who
sounded like she was at least in her seventies spoke to him.

'Mr Neuman? Yes, it's Aliz Gal here, I am the manager of
Mr Kovacs' hotel.'

'Oh, Marton Kovacs is the owner?'

'Yes, Mr Neuman. Well, he was. I am sad to tell you that Mr Kovacs passed away this week. He had been ill for a long time. So I'm sorry we can't help you with the investigation.'

Calum's spirits plunged.

'I'm so sorry to hear that. I was hoping to understand more about his discussions with Sarah McTeer, as I mentioned to your staff. I'm sorry to ask … but can you tell me anything about her visit? I believe she may have come for two appointments with Mr Kovacs around two weeks ago?'

There was a short silence before he had an answer.

'I know she visited, yes. They were short visits. Marton was an ill man so he couldn't talk for too long, you see?'

'Yes, I understand. So, on the second visit, do you know where she went after your hotel … did she call for a taxi or just walk out?'

A few moments of silence.

'Yes, I recall she did ask for a taxi. To her hotel, I think.'

'You have the taxi firm name?'

She gave him the name of a local company.

'OK, thanks. Well if there's nothing else you can tell me, I'll call the taxi firm and see what they have to say. I might call again if that's OK?'

'Of course, if it helps. Goodbye.'

The line went dead. Calum knew she was lying.

# Sarah's room

Calum made his hotel reception the next port of call.

The Grand Danubius looked like it had been grand once. Now it seemed it was in need of some loving renovation to help live up to its name. Calum walked down the worn carpet into an equally worn reception. The staff were pleasant and efficient enough, though. The manager happily filled him in on what he knew about Sarah and her disappearance. Her room had been left with most things in it, as Eszter had told Jenna. Calum asked if he could see her papers. He didn't exactly expect to be shown them. For one thing, he assumed the police would have taken them. But it seemed, for now, they'd been content to search the room and have the hotel lock it up.

He also didn't expect a foreign P.I. to be allowed a look. But a flash of his Scottish accreditation and a palmed 10,000 forint note was enough to get him ten minutes in the room, so long as he left his bag and jacket at reception.

Fair enough. He made a quick scan of the room to assess what was there and soon homed in on her papers as the items of most interest.

There were a lot of them. Photocopied material and pages of notes. To understand if there was anything in the piles that might help with why Sarah had gone missing, he needed more than ten minutes.

He scooped up the lot and got himself ready for some negotiating.

It turned out the equivalent of £200 would buy him the papers for a few days. Time enough to read them and copy anything he needed. He wondered about the deepness of Susan McTeer's pockets briefly, then agreed to go for it.

He shook the manager's hand and sat down in the lobby. He stared out of the window at the Danube flowing steadily past.

Time for some calls.

First up, the taxi company. The Grand Danubius hotel manager had said his staff didn't recall or have any record on her key card of her returning later on the day she disappeared. The timings looked like she'd gone to see Marton Kovacs and not come back.

The taxi firm confirmed that doubt.

'No, we have no record of a booking from the Hotel Cristal that afternoon, not in that name anyway, and no rides without a name. Sorry.'

So either Aliz Gal was mistaken … or lying. He stood up and wandered outside for some fresh air. He sat down on the steps outside the hotel and considered the implications of that train of thought.

Aliz was a relatively old woman. She sounded like part of the hotel furniture. Maybe he'd need to pay a personal visit. Or was that too obvious, to confront her with the mismatch of stories? Perhaps he needed a more subtle way to work out the truth.

He went back to his room and made a coffee, settling down to read through the papers he'd taken from Sarah's room.

The printed material was from texts. Some of it was in Hungarian but with hand-written notes in English in the margins. An awful lot about the origins of Arrow Cross and its key leaders. Some material on what happened to them after it had all been shut down at the end of the war. Items covering new right-wing groups in Hungary that likened themselves to the old party. Then there were what looked like two peoples' sets of hand-written thoughts, notes, questions. He guessed the two were Sarah and Eszter. He could check with Eszter later.

His mind was overloaded with detail now. He couldn't immediately think of a clear way to analyse this information, in a manner that might spawn something useful. Just reading it straight wasn't doing anything for him. It might need recourse to the library texts to cross-check references and go through with Eszter. That wasn't his bag really, he'd rather be talking to Aliz Gal and working out the past sequence of events more accurately.

He knew someone who *could* do that analysis work for him, of course. Then, if they worked in parallel they might get to the point of understanding faster. With a resigned smile, he rang her.

'Yep? Need me yet?'

'Sad to say, yes, probably. But first I'm going to scan some papers and send them over for you to read and try to make sense of. Let me know what you think?'

'OK. Well, it'll be tomorrow. I have to get an essay in tonight. But I'll start reading your scans straight after that. OK?'

'Sure. Look out for them.'

'I will. By the way, your D.C. mate's protection seems to have evaporated.'

Calum straightened his back. 'What? Why?'

'I called him, he said there was a lot of staff leave coming up and a few big events … couldn't spare the guy who'd been watching me anymore.'

Calum rubbed his chin and pressed his eyes closed.

'OK. OK. I guess you'd better come over here then, at least I'll be able to keep an eye on you. Get a cheap flight, let me know when you're arriving and I'll get a room sorted for you.'

'Sure Calum, if you're OK with that. That's great, thanks. I'll text the flight number.'

Calum just knew she was grinning and punching the air.

# Watching Aliz's eyes

Calum decided he would visit Aliz Gal personally at the Hotel Cristal. He wanted to observe her eyes and body language when he asked some difficult questions.

He made no appointment and just walked into the lobby. Aliz wasn't at reception so he asked the girl at the desk if he could speak with the manageress.

She went to find her and returned with Aliz at her back. Aliz introduced herself and whisked him through into the back office.

'Coffee?'

'No thanks. I hope I won't take up much of your time, Mrs Gal.'

'Miss.'

Calum rolled his eyes without moving them.

'Sorry.'

He composed himself. 'I just wanted to go over the things we talked about on the phone the other day.'

She shrugged her shoulders. 'OK. But I don't think I can tell you anything else really.'

She looked at the floor then back up, making a point of holding his gaze.

'Well, I do have a further question or two. Simply put … I rang the taxi firm you said Sarah had used following the meeting with Mr Kovacs. They said they have no record of it.'

He let that sink in, determined to say nothing more until she answered.

Calum noticed her breathing quicken slightly before she answered. Her eyes darted sideways, then back again.

'I can't understand that,' she said, shaking her head. 'They must have made a mess of the records, you know what taxi drivers are like, maybe just forgot.'

Some classic physical lying signals there. Especially the rapid sideways eye movements. 'Mmm, maybe … but they record bookings and journey starts and ends at the switch, and it's computerised. The car doesn't get dispatched without it. So it's a bit odd that it's missing. If it got dispatched, that is.'

She shifted her eyes left. He'd noticed she was left-handed when she picked up a pen and started playing with it, twisting it around her fingers. Another leak of her lying. If she was going to lie, it might be difficult to get much further right now. Maybe better to retreat and observe her from a distance.

She returned her gaze to him. 'Well, that's a mystery then.'

'It seems so. Maybe I need to ask them to recheck. Anyway, the other thing I wanted to understand was … why was Sarah seeing Mr Kovacs … do you know?'

The old woman hesitated before she spoke again.

'No. I have no idea. I am … I mean *was* Mr Kovacs's manageress. I was not party to his personal life. Well, not so much anyway.'

'Umm, OK. Look then, I suppose there's not much else. Let me know if you can shed any more light on the taxi mystery, though? Here's my card … I'm staying at the Grand Danubius, please call me if you remember anything?'

She nodded frostily. He got up and left, knowing not to expect a call anytime soon.

\*

Jenna's flight got in that evening and Calum met her in the small bar for a drink once she'd settled herself in her room. They sat cradling glasses of white wine.

'Actually, Jen, I feel a bit lost out here. It's a different culture, different language … and this Arrow Cross thing is bound up with a dirty past. Not the sort of thing anyone really wants to talk about. It's hard to get an opening or a handle on anything.'

'That's where I come in, Calum-o!'

He smiled. In an avuncular sort of way.

'How exactly, though?' He wasn't expecting anything concrete from her quite just yet.

'I read the papers you sent over last night. Interesting. I didn't realise this all happened in the war in Budapest. Not that I would. But you can imagine how someone might get touchy if Sarah was prodding around in old war wounds?'

He dipped his head. 'Yes, you can. I can. That's what it felt like when I visited Aliz Gal.' He filled her in on the details of his interview with Gal earlier in the day.

'So, you think she's hiding something?'

'Hiding? Don't know about that. But I think she's lying about the taxi. So there's something not right.'

'And how do we find out what that is?'

Calum looked at her askance and laughed. 'Well, that's easy, Watson.'

'How?'

'Haven't a bloody clue, that's how.'

Jenna feigned throwing her wine at him. Enough to make him flinch.

'Well, have *you* got any bright ideas?'

Jenna pondered for a moment. 'So you say this Marton guy lived in the hotel?'

Calum knew her next sentence would bring something interesting into play.

'Maybe we need to look inside his room or rooms. Find what we can. Don't you think?'

Calum leant back on the low sofa and screwed his face into a tight smile. 'Really? And since I can hardly go poking my nose around in the hotel now I've made myself known to the manager, who would do that?'

He still hadn't learnt that with Jenna, asking rhetorical questions didn't always give him the outcome he really wanted.

'That's right. Me.'

'Err, I don't like that idea. First, you don't speak Hungarian, second, we don't know where his rooms are. Third, we don't have a way of getting into his rooms. How do we solve all that? Plus, it isn't your job. You do research.'

That *really* made her mad. Being mad was good for the brain, though. It made it process faster. At least that's how hers seemed to work.

'It's simple. Here's how.'

Ten minutes later, after Calum had finished picking holes in her plan, he decided it was good enough to go with.

'OK. I'll start looking for a hotel cleaner to approach first thing tomorrow. When I visited Aliz I noticed a couple of them arriving in uniform, so they shouldn't be hard to spot. So let's finish this wine now, eh? Then I've got an appointment with a pork pie. I'm getting fed up with schnitzel already.'

'Checked your cholesterol lately, boss?'

'Shut up and drink your wine.'

He was happy being her boss again. Not so pleased to be reminded about his cholesterol levels. He *did* need to watch them, she was right, family history and all that.

'Anyway, what's going on with Gregor? I heard you two were talking again?'

'Heard the same about you and Cassie.'

Jenna looked like she instantly regretted saying that. 'Sorry. I shouldn't pry. Gregor and I have talked yeah. After the funeral and everything. But that's about it. Nothing's changed really. I don't know if it will or not. Anyway ...'

'No, that's OK. Obviously, Cassie and I had things to sort out. That's it really. Well, hope you and Gregor fix things ... don't forget, now you've moved to Inverness, I still have to see his unhappy mug in Plockton most days. He needs something to cheer him up!'

She smiled. 'Not sure I can help. We'll see. Can we get another bottle? Nice stuff that.'

Calum sighed but signalled the waitress over. 'Another bottle of this wine for my drunkard friend here.'

Jenna managed a direct hit on Calum's nose with a couple of peanuts.

'If the wine wasn't so good I'd leave you to your bad humour right now. As it is, I guess I'll have to suffer *in vino.*'

He laughed aloud. He realised he'd needed it. They trudged up the stairs an hour later, much the worse the wear for the alcohol.

'Night, boss,' she slurred as she clicked through into her room.

# 2 WEEKS EARLIER

## Burton sees an opportunity

---

For some reason, the only regular newspaper the prisoners in Barlinnie jail could get at the moment was the Evening Times. Not the best read as far as Alan Burton was concerned, but anything was better than staring into space or having to converse with the less intelligent of the prison population. He grabbed it just before another of the inmates pounced on it.

'I was gonna read the sports there, buddy.'

'I'll make sure you're next, mate. No worries.'

His competitor glowered at him, then thought better of a confrontation and retreated to the TV corner at the other end of the lino-floored recreation area.

Burton sat down on a hard chair, nothing more comfortable left.

The day's headlines didn't catch his attention so he turned past the first couple of pages and started to catch up with the Scottish news.

Riddled throughout those pages were reports of various crimes and minor misdemeanours. It was a game he played with himself, trying to match these wrongdoings with his known criminal network. Sometimes he recognised the type of crime, other times he was just plain guessing. The style of the reporting these days, though, meant the sort of detail that would really help him wasn't there. Occasionally a follow-up report of a trial outcome proved him right. It made him feel connected with the outside world. A bit more alive.

The university researcher from Inverness who'd gone missing in Budapest, though, that wasn't likely to be one of his associates or anyone known to him. That was a foreign job, for sure. Hard to say what made someone disappear … could be a number of things. Petty theft gone wrong. A date that had soured. Not one for him to work out. He passed on.

The next felony reported was a car-jacking and valuables grab. Now that one … that one could be the work of a number of people he knew. As well as the up-comers, of course … there were always a few young lads who fancied themselves as pros. Some would succeed. But this one … he'd take a bet on Gaz Worth. Gaz was an old hand, he'd been done for it once to his knowledge. He was the kind of guy who didn't know when to stop doing something that had probably run out of track for him. He made a mental note to check on the outcome of that one.

He worked his shoulders around, relaxing them and letting them drop. He was enjoying this and leafed through the next couple of pages, searching for his next case. A good, clean murder would be just perfect.

It amused him to see a case reported over time when he just knew who had done it and yet the police were making no headway into solving it. He remembered one just like that and dropped his head back, had a little internal giggle to himself. To his irritation, Neuman and Strick entered his thoughts once more, just as he was getting nice and relaxed. It was like an insect bite, itching every now and then when you thought you were over it. Now it was needling him again. The investigator, his assistant, the banes of his life.

His mind dawdled around the word investigator for no good reason for a moment … until he made the connection with his earlier read. The brain doodling had spawned an idea. The more he thought about it, it became a really neat idea. A way to take some revenge, away from the home spotlight. It could prove to be the balm to his itch.

# Aliz is overwhelmed

As far as Aliz knew, she was the only person who knew about *all* the things that Marton and Alfred had done. Well, of course, a handful of their old colleagues did in 1945. But they were dead now. All of them. And she was determined to keep the secret. Otherwise, both men would be under potential threat of discovery … and the judicial bodies didn't seem to care about peoples' ages when dealing out justice for these sorts of crimes. It was all about ensuring the murky deeds of war were seen to be abhorred without exception. Not that it mattered to poor Marton now, but then there was the link to herself through the party … and Katalin. Katalin might be aware Aliz had been involved in hiding her, she couldn't be sure.

No, it was all too much: she needed this to remain a secret forever. She wondered what she could do about Mr Neuman. She thought about it for a long time. The answer to her question was staring her in the face, though.

Peter Kovacs would be coming to see her soon. He'd been left a note by his father, telling him about Katalin and asking him to resolve her future.

From the tone of their discussion when he rang her this morning, he wasn't decided. But it was clear he was thinking only of himself, not Katalin. She knew he wasn't the most moral of people … and that might be an understatement. His involvement in a new, underground Arrow Cross wasn't without an element of thuggery … and she knew he had the contacts to leverage the criminal fraternity. Maybe he'd be interested in determining the future of Mr Calum Neuman too.

She returned her attention to the lunch she'd had one of the kitchen staff bring in. Some cold chicken and pickles. She forked a piece of chicken and chewed slowly. As she relaxed, she turned back to the city newspaper and settled down for a break from the office tedium.

Ten minutes later, she sat bolt upright. At her age, the obituary column was something she read. There was always a friend that might be close to a column inch or two. Today it wasn't a friend, though. It was Alfred Nemeth. She looked at the date. The day after Marton died. One hell of a coincidence. Or was it? Her brain went into overdrive and she started to tremble.

She knew Marton had left something with Alfred for Peter to retrieve when his father died. But Peter didn't say much about it when he rang this morning, just that he'd been to the solicitor and he now knew about Katalin. All the pieces of information assembled in her mind in the space of five seconds. Peter must have had something to do with his death.

She scanned the rest of the paper. Sure enough, there it was. Inside the front page.

*"Jeweller's death investigated - police treating as murder."*
'Oh my God.'


She blew her cheeks out and most of her mouthful of chicken.

Her mind scrambled through the implications. Peter might be a murderer. On the other hand, there was now one person less who knew about the war-time deceit. What's more, if he *was* the culprit, it underlined his credentials to deal with Neuman. But where would the killing end? Katalin had done nothing, other than ask a few ill-timed questions eight years ago. And as for the other girl … she hadn't actually found out anything, had she? Had Peter killed Alfred just because he had learned about Katalin? It seemed hard to believe.

She started talking to herself. And her father.

'This is just too hard. Dad, if you were here … what would you do? How much is a life worth? My reputation? My freedom? What if it's actually three lives in the end?'

Her father couldn't hear his daughter anymore. He would have been glad.

'I think you would want to protect me, wouldn't you? But would you forgive me if I protected myself?'

Aliz's long-dead dad would be even more relieved he didn't have to answer. Human emotions had never been his strength. When Aliz was small she was always strong-willed but showed a sensitive side that he could never empathise with. He admired her for it somehow, though. Aliz had eventually grown up from being a tough, spirited tomboy into a fiercely determined woman, never more so than when protecting the legacy of Arrow Cross. He would know that trait would be the one to prevail now.

**217**

Aliz knew it too. She decided to leave Peter to his own devices.

The trouble was … there was another girl in there now. One who was actively being searched for. And the lie about the taxi taking her back to her own hotel hadn't washed with Calum Neuman, she knew that. She hadn't had the nerve to mention the new girl to Peter. And the truth was, maybe it would be better for herself if she pretended she didn't know anything else.

# JANUARY 1945

## A cold night

---

The winter had been harsh in Budapest. Piles of dirty snow lined the streets and the Danube carried a steady stream of slush along its banks. The air held a constant freezing damp and every day seemed to bring dark skies. They underlined the mood of the city. It was gripped in terror.

Arrow Cross thugs were running riot in the streets, aiding the dying remnants of Nazi influence. Germany was losing the war, that was clear. Everyone knew the Russians were advancing on the city. But for now, there was no other choice for Ferenc Szalasi and his party, but to cling to power. As the outcome of the war became inevitable, their actions became more extreme. Desperate talons clawing at survival.

The Arrow Cross gangs had become erratically violent. In theory, they were helping control and guard the Jewish ghetto in District VII. But the most deluded ones just wanted revenge. Revenge for their failures. Revenge on the Jews who were surviving the war and would be saved by the Russians. Some groups went hunting in the early hours of the morning, surprising people in their beds.

And, mostly, those little packs of men were very, very young. Barely men at all, except for the experiences they'd endured.

Marton Kovacs and Alfred Nemeth were part of one group that night.

Their target had been singled out during the day by Marton. A butcher. A man that Marton had actually known. He had never liked him. When his father used to send him to the butcher's shop for bags of meat scraps, he always got given the fatty ones and was scolded by his father for not paying attention and asking for better meat. He never understood why his father didn't go himself. Laziness probably.

It was pure chance he'd seen his name on the list of ghetto inhabitants the other day. He knew then he would grab himself some payback. For being a butcher who cheated him … and for being a Jew. All he had been able to think about since then, had been how to do it.

He had a small group. They were just boys really, boys that were all making attempts at fledgeling moustaches. He knew he could persuade them to do what he asked. Some of the senior officers had fled the city, fearing apprehension by the Russians when they inevitably entered and took control. They knew they would be targeted.

But Marton was a corporal who'd stayed and assumed more power. The other boys were too scared to question him now. Many of them had lost their parents. They were living a visceral life. Eating, drinking, trembling, running, shooting. Often crying. Everyone was on the edge of a terrifying kind of darkness.

Two of them were at the ghetto sentry post when he arrived at midnight. They were sheltering under a lean-to, with scant uniform for a bone-chilling night, just a grey standard issue greatcoat over their own threadbare clothes. By the time they'd been recruited, helmets and boots had run short.

'Tamas … Mor.'

They nodded back at him, with cautious eyes.

'Did you see Medard or Alfred?'

Tamas spoke. He had always been a bit more confident than some of the others.

'Yes, I saw them together at the cafe not long ago. They were eating stew.'

Stew. And thin with it. All they could get right now. Better than nothing in this cold, though. He'd give them fifteen minutes. He was a little early, after all.

A white sheet of light froze them all like statues, capturing their paste-white faces and grimy skin, stippled with the first curls of facial hair. Then another one, followed by the rumble and blast of detonating shells. They were getting ever closer, more intense.

Fuck the Russians, fuck the war. He would kill the butcher and it would feel good.

He pulled out a couple of bottles of home-made palinka from his canvas satchel. It was the strong stuff, over fifty per cent. It would warm them up and make them courageous too. He worried sometimes, with one or two of them, whether they would bottle it at the last minute. Or worse.

Once, one of his group had tipped off a policeman with their plan for one night, when he decided he couldn't face carrying out the job. It was just an incredible piece of good fortune that the policeman was killed in a shooting incident that same day. When the boy didn't turn up on their mission that night, Marton found out why. And he made sure it couldn't happen again.

They all took large swigs and passed the first bottle around. After a little while, Medard and Alfred showed up. They'd clearly started drinking already. Alfred took the second bottle and glugged a large mouthful before handing it on to Medard. He was a big boy, Alfred. He'd need plenty of alcohol to get him in the mood.

It was only after another forty-five minutes of steady drinking that Marton gave them the nod to move into the ghetto.

Marton and Alfred were armed with pistols they'd recovered from an officer's corpse the previous week. Better than the knives they'd used last time out. Marton tapped his weapon again to check it was still there, as they moved off through a gap in the ghetto wall torn out by Soviet artillery.

The main danger was the police. They'd started to protect the ghetto against the party. They knew how it would all end and were probably lining themselves up on the winning side. Whatever the reason, they were a problem and would throw them out of the ghetto if they spotted them.

Marton led them through a couple of short streets, then stopped on the corner of a large open square, breath rasping out in an icy cloud in front of him. The sole inhabitants of the dank, frosted space were two police officers, hulking Danuvia 39M sub-machine guns and a couple of very bright lanterns.

No way through. Marton rethought the route and figured out a way to backtrack and work around the square without encountering another similar space. It took them fifteen minutes to trace that out but then they were on the far side of the square and only a few minutes away from the house they were heading for.

Marton turned to his group and stared at them all, slowly, one by one. He was assessing their mood and their courage. He'd learnt a lot very quickly about leading men, even at such a young age.

He saw fear and excitement in all of them. They were on edge. The sort of edginess a hunter might have cornering a bear with a hunting bow. You know you have the advantage … but a wrong move and it could end badly. Medard and Alfred looked rather drunk. He needed to make sure they took on board what he needed of them.

He whispered to them. Their senses were on full beam despite the palinka and they drank in every word with clarity.

'So, now we move around this corner and down this street, the house is on the left. Number 16. We will go down the side passage to the back door and windows. We'll find a way in there, with no noise if we can. We must surprise them in their beds. Medard, Alfred, you must find the children's room and keep them in there after they're woken. Keep them quiet somehow. The rest of us, we'll go into the butcher's room. We'll kill him and his bitch wife. At the same time. We need to have no screams. Understand?'

They all nodded. Alfred more slowly than the rest. He wasn't feeling good right now, too much drink and the surge in adrenaline had created a bubbling mixture in his belly. The stew hadn't tasted quite right either. It was making him drowsy and sick. He just wanted to get this over with now.

Marton turned away from them, checked around the corner and motioned for them to follow him. They stepped lightly down the street, cautious of any figures they might see in the distance in case they were police. They got to number 16 without seeing a soul. The side passage was black dark. Once Marton had stepped into it, they followed on trust rather than sight. It was short, though, and in the back yard of the house, there was a little light from a thin sliver of moon.

The cobbled yard stank of blood and meat. Marton looked around. There was a small outhouse behind them. Probably some meat storage in there or maybe he cut the meat up inside it. Either way, it was worth a look afterwards, to see if there was anything worth pilfering.

The solid wooden door to the house was locked, predictably. A window at the side of it looked like it could be easily forced. Marton slipped a large knife in between the casement and frame, levering it open with hardly a sound. It was weak and came open easily.

At Marton's signal, they all climbed in through the opening as carefully as their cold and inebriated limbs would allow. They stood in a small parlour room, breathing fast, breath condensing into a rising column as they stood facing each other in a tight circle.

'OK. So we will run up the stairs as fast as we can, but try to be as quiet as possible. Take off your boots. The stairs might creak so best not go slowly. We must surprise them.'

They all removed their footwear. They too smelt of old blood now. The yard must have been smeared with the stuff.

'And remember who is dealing with the children. We will see who is in each room quickly, move to the right room if you find yourself in the wrong place. We must be quick.'

Alfred frowned, wondering why they just didn't get assigned to rooms and save confusion. He guessed Marton wanted to be the one to kill the butcher. He was Marton's target, after all.

'On my signal, we move. I will be doing the killing. You two just hold the wife down while I get the butcher first.'

Alfred thought Tamas and Mor looked a little disappointed at that. They said nothing, though.

Marton took out his pistol. It had a silencer fitted to it, unlike Alfred's. He held it aloft briefly, scanning everyone's faces to make sure they were watching. He knew they were pretty drunk. He'd need to be clear. He motioned them all to move to the foot of the wooden stairs, which led up between flaking plaster walls to a small landing, flanked by two bedroom doors.

He dropped his arm briskly and skipped up the narrow staircase. There was a split-second delay, then the others all piled clumsily in behind him, jostling each other softly to get onto the stairs. At the top, Marton went right, the others followed according to the plan.

As soon as Marton swore gently, they all knew they were in the wrong rooms, and started to move across the landing, bumping into each other and nearly pushing Mor back down the staircase.

Even though only a few seconds of scuffling noises had passed, it was long and loud enough to have started to rouse the family.

The butcher's wife sat bolt upright in bed, moaning something about a noise, trying to focus her eyes into the darkness around her. She could make out smudges of contrast where the bodies moving towards her were outlined by the faint moonlight in the room.

As her senses came to, she understood what was happening and screamed loud. The pitch went higher before it was stopped by a hand clamped across her mouth and she was pushed hard down onto the bed, bumping against her husband who was wakening a lot more slowly.

His lack of speed cost him his life. Marton levelled the pistol at him and pulled the trigger quickly, three times. The flashes illuminated the butcher's face as he stared at Marton, his expression twisted into a mask of confusion.

He was dead instantly, his skull splintered all over the pillow and bedstead, grey brain matter slapped against his wife's cheek.

She gawked upwards, in no particular direction, blinded by the muzzle fire and with her eyeballs wildly gyrating, bursting out of their sockets.

Marton lowered the muzzle and pressed it into her throat. Mor released his grip on her as her body stiffened against the hot steel. Tamas slapped her face and spat into it.

Then there was a scream. From the *other* room. Marton half turned but kept the barrel pressed against the woman. 'What the fuck is going on … Mor go and help them.'

Alfred and Medard had found two children, after struggling to see anything for a moment, in a room less illuminated by moonlight than the butcher's bedroom. They had woken quickly.

One of them jumped sideways out of the bed, with the astonishing litheness of an eight-year-old boy. His ten-year-old sister jumped the other way and the two teenagers were momentarily caught off guard and behind the pace.

Medard threw his hands out towards the boy and grasped at him wildly. He was lucky, in the darkness, the boy somehow fell into his hands and he closed his arms around him like a tight vice. The boy croaked and tried to shout but Medard had a strong hold on him and he couldn't make much of a noise.

The girl slipped past Alfred in the dark, heading for her parents' room in a blind panic as she realised the bodies moving in her room weren't friendly. Alfred felt her move by him and swung around, grabbing at thin air, then leaping forward and clutching again. This time he caught some hair, a ponytail, and yanked it back hard. The girl screamed and threw herself back against him and clung to his leg, trying to pull him down.

He was too heavy for that. So she bit him, in his calf, as if it was the first piece of beefsteak she'd seen for a year.

Alfred felt the nausea rise in him again and he vomited, spraying the girl with his sickness. He staggered back a step and kicked at her with his free foot. His mind was whirling, caught in a current of drunkenness and panic. He fell flat on his back, discharging his pistol with the impact. She screamed again. He rolled onto his side and vomited twice more.

By now, Mor was in the children's room with Alfred, but the girl had somehow by-passed him onto the landing and he heard her second scream behind him. That was the signal for Marton.

He pulled himself away from the butcher's wife and turned into the landing. He shouted back at Tamas, pointing at the woman. 'Kill her! Now!'

He heard the result of his instruction as he entered the landing.

The girl started to scream and scream again. It was too much. The neighbours would be alerted if they hadn't been already. He pointed the pistol again, picking out the girl's shape in the light from the room behind him.

He pulled the trigger once more. There was a brief flash, catching a dancing ponytail flying in the air as she fell backwards, her face shattered by a hot bullet. Then silence.

Marton thought quickly. No one could really see what had happened just then. He took a deep breath before he spoke.

'Alfred for fuck's sake, you killed the girl! We need to get out of here. You may as well kill the boy too. We can't leave him to scream.'

Medard suddenly spoke up. He still had the boy clamped under his forearms. 'No, no we can't do that. I can deal with him.' He felt for Marton's face and whispered into his ear.

Marton nodded.

Medard dragged the boy onto his bed and told him in a surprisingly kind way to be still, that his life depended on it. The boy did as he was told and lay perfectly motionless. Medard lay a pillow softly across his face. Amazingly the boy still didn't move. He pushed his knife against the boy's throat gently.

'Move and you're dead. If you keep quiet I might let you go in ten minutes.'

Laying a nearly empty palinka bottle against the knife handle and wedging it up against the pillow, he managed to create a little pressure on the knife tip. Then he carefully stood up and motioned for the others to go.

By now they were all seeing better in the dark and made their way downstairs, out through the window into the yard. Medard followed, as quietly as he could, leaving the boy assuming his assailant still held the knife against his throat.

The smell of blood in the yard reminded Marton of the meat. He crossed the greasy stone flags to the outhouse and pushed against the door. Locked with a heavy padlock. There was a large window around the side, though. With a jacket to muffle the noise, he broke it and scanned the shelves and refrigeration unit for meat. There wasn't a lot and it looked and smelt poor: supplies had dried up badly, especially in the last year. But in a couple of minutes, he had cleared out enough meat to feed them all for a few days. *Double payback, butcher man.* They were soon out of sight of the house, dissipating and stealing home quickly.

The boy, on the other hand, lay on his bed for a very long time before he dared to move.

*

Marton rose wearily from his bed the next morning with only one thought in his head. It had kept him awake through a freezing cold night despite the weight of palinka in his head.

He needed to make sure the death of the child wasn't attributed to them. Especially to him. He'd blurred the trail to himself, hadn't he? That was quick thinking, suggesting in the dark that Alfred had done it. But for some reason, Alfred hadn't even reacted to his lie.

He liked Alfred. He was solid, always stuck to the group and did what was needed of him. Now the effects of the alcohol had worn off, Marton was beginning to feel a sense of guilt pulling away at his cover story.

He made some coffee from leftover grounds, nasty bitter stuff but it was all he could get now. There was some bread from yesterday. A bit stale but it would have to do. Then he remembered the meat he'd stolen and suddenly he gathered some enthusiasm for a hot beef sandwich. As he began to fry some small strips of meat, he came up with an idea to help deepen the deceit and cover them both a bit further. He took the first bite from the sandwich and sighed, feeling a bit happier.

He sat thinking about it, chewing away on the tough meat. It could work. Not a guarantee but another layer for the authorities to unravel. There was the rest of the group, of course. But they hadn't talked about the girl afterwards, either … they were probably all too shocked. And they were all in it together, actually. They couldn't really have seen what happened in the dark … could they? Anyway, odds were some or all of them might not be alive when the war was finished. Nothing was certain in Marton's world anymore.

He nodded to himself. It wasn't foolproof by any means, but it was good enough. He'd go and see Alfred now.

*

He found Alfred at his house, or what was left of it. His sister was in the small downstairs room with him, eating some bread and meat straight off the tabletop.

'I had some too, for breakfast. Great eh?'

Alfred nodded.

'I need to speak, Alfred … alone.'

Alfred motioned for his sister to leave and she jumped up and skipped upstairs without a word.

Marton smiled. 'Well trained, Alfred!'

'She's just scared … of anyone.'

Marton raised his eyebrows by way of a resigned understanding.

'Look, Alfred, about last night. I know you were drunk, I know you didn't mean to do it. The girl I mean. I want to help protect you. And, I have a plan.'

Alfred cocked his head to one side, inviting him to continue.

'We will swap our names, our identities from now on. I am your corporal and I was the most senior member of the party at the house that night. It will confuse anyone who investigates this. If they ever do. Both sets of our parents are dead, so we can cover this.'

Alfred looked at the floor, confused for a moment, then raised his head.

'I see.' He shook his head.

'It will be fine Alfred, it will work. Don't worry, I've thought about it a lot in the night.'

Alfred wanted to believe Marton. He'd spent the whole night awake. The thought he had killed a little girl was haunting him. His sister was a similar age … full of life, innocence.

'But why? How will it help?'

'Look. Some of the others saw it was you. If anyone ever tries to trace the incident after the war, it will lead to me, because we have changed names. That's if there's anyone left to ask. Then, anyone asked to verify it was me, well … when they are asked to identify me face to face, they will see me and say I am *not* that same face that killed the girl. So then the trail will end.'

Alfred listened as hard as his tired mind would let him. He sat silent, thinking it over for a moment.

'But won't that witness remember your *real* name? Then it would all look suspicious, wouldn't it?'

Marton, in his hasty attempt to cover up his crime, hadn't thought of that possibility. He hesitated a little, then spoke with a manufactured confidence.

'Well, firstly, if it was one of the group of us from last night, I don't think they would mention that was not my real name. I'm their officer. I don't think they'd want to contradict me or deepen any investigation. In a way we are all in this, so they would all be worried about being blamed for a part of it. Anyway, who is going to give anyone a lead to us in the first place? Our group will stay quiet. There is only the boy we left.'

Alfred nodded.

'Well, maybe it would work. If you really want to. But what about my sister? She has the same family name?'

'Change hers too. Needs to be the same. After this damn war ends, everything will be confused, I'm sure. Lots of people lose their birth certificates and stuff in a war like this. We just need to tell the same story and we have a chance. Anyway we can swap birth certificates if we have them?'

'Yeah, I have mine. We could. But why do we need to? We can just keep quiet about it, can't we? Anyway, I can't understand how it happened. I fell backwards and my gun went off. I don't get how she got hit. I heard other shots too. It was all a blur.'

'I know. But never mind now, it did happen, we can't change that. And if people do try to track it down because they get to hear about it from someone in the group or something, they might look at photos. You know, the official party ones. If we've changed names it will be harder for them to identify us.'

Alfred nodded slowly, the persistence of Marton's argument starting to convince him of its worth.

'OK. Let me think about it. But when would it start to happen?'

Marton hadn't considered that. Too early and it would be obvious.

'Good point. I guess we can swap the certificates now and start using the new names ... well, when the Russians get in. It won't be too long by the sounds of it. Straight away at that point makes sense, eh? We'll probably all be split up then and no one will notice it?'

Alfred looked up at the ceiling. 'OK, I'll tell you next time I see you. Tomorrow night?'

Marton decided that was good enough. He thought he'd convinced him, he just needed to let him get his own mind over the line now. His head hurt with the complexity of it. He wasn't *sure* if anyone in the group had seen him shoot the girl, though. This was the only insurance he could think of for now. He'd speak to the others, too, about what they saw, find a way to understand that without interrogating them. He might have to take some other action depending on what they said. One step at a time, though.

'OK. Tomorrow then. And ... of course, not a word to the others.'

Marton smiled and left the house with a wave.

Alfred nodded his agreement to meet again. Not that he needed to. He'd already decided that he would be called Marton for the rest of his life, however long, or short, that turned out to be.

# NOVEMBER 2018

## Peter decides what to do

---

Peter Kovacs had thought long and hard about how to deal with the girl. At least, he pretended to himself he had. Hovering above his contemplation had been the dark cloud of the fate of Alfred Nemeth. He'd left him seemingly dying and he knew there was probably little doubt how that had turned out.

Peter was a selfish man. Always had been. A single child, always given everything his parents could afford, did well at school without trying too much, even found his medical training easier than most did. He had never had to work too hard for anything and somehow, perversely, as a result, looked after himself first. Always. He knew right from the start he would end up choosing to kill her, ever since he'd read the note left by his father with Alfred. In truth, this false debate with himself was just helping subdue his nervousness in carrying it out.

The tricky question was how. There was a complication too. Aliz knew about the girl. Aliz was an Arrow Cross sympathiser, for sure. But would she agree with his intentions towards Katalin? If not, then the choices would become even more difficult.

Maybe he could just get into the room and kill her. Then leave her to rot in there. What motive could anyone pin on him, when she was eventually found, so long as he left no trail back to himself? But he needed to be sure about Aliz and her silence on the whole sorry history of this girl. There was an obvious way to be sure, of course. He wondered if he had the nerve for that too. He'd already probably killed Alfred, even if unintentionally.

This was all getting out of hand. But now he'd started, it seemed hard to see any other way but to finish it. Cleanly. Once and for all. The first thing he needed to do was visit Aliz and see the room. Then he could think about finalising his plan.

*

Peter strode into Aliz's office the next day, trying to create an image of self-assurance and confidence, to mask his own tension.

She was sat at her desk. She greeted him cordially. Nothing more.

'Have a seat, Peter.'

'No, I'll stand, thank you.'

'Look, Peter, I know this must have been a big shock to you.'

'Shock is a bit of an understatement, Aliz.'

Peter looked around the office, wary of flapping ears and lowered his voice to a murmur. He placed his hands on her desk.

**235**

'He imprisons someone against their will … and keeps them *here*? What the hell had this girl done that was so bad?'

'She found something out, Peter.'

He narrowed his eyes and edged his face a bit closer to Aliz's.

'Exactly what? I always knew he had some sort of dark past from the war. He never went into it, though, and well … it seemed best left alone. But what the hell was so bad he had to do this?'

'He killed a child, Peter. He killed a child.'

Peter more or less collapsed onto the chair he'd been offered earlier.

'Really? I can't … believe that … he's a kind man. *Was* a kind man. Why would he have done that, Aliz? Why?'

Aliz shook her head gently from side to side, in an *I don't know* kind of way.

'I think … no, I'm sure, it was a mistake. He killed her, in a dark house one night. The situation was confused, I think, and he was quite drunk too. This is what he told me, Peter.'

'And this girl found out?'

'It seems so. Or at least she was digging to find out more about these types of atrocities.'

'And he had to keep her here? What was she going to do?'

'I don't know, Marton didn't know. He kept her to give himself time to think. Then he realised he didn't know what to do.

What would she do if he freed her? Because he'd kept her for a while, probably she would now be more hostile than if he had let her go straight away. It just got harder to decide. So she stayed here. It's been eight years now Peter. I know …'

'Eight years!' he shouted from the other side of the desk. 'Eight fucking years?'

'I know, I know, it was a mistake to keep her at all. Your father knew that. But it's done … and we have to sort it out.'

She looked up at him. Her eyes were soft. She was pleading.

'I don't know what to do. But I want this to end, Peter. I'm old now too. I can't live like this anymore.'

He leaned back, cradling his head with his hands and shook it.

'Eight years. My God. And she's OK?'

Peter noticed the old woman was trembling now.

'Yes, she's OK. But, it's more complicated now.' She paused, but Peter didn't fill the gap. He just stared expectantly at her.

Aliz sighed. 'I should just say it. There's another girl in the room with her now. Only just recently. Someone else who was poking around his past. I think an academic. So now we have two people to decide about.'

Peter's mouth dropped open. He still couldn't manage to say anything.

'There is one more thing. Then you know everything. It will be hard to understand … but your father is not Marton.'

Now he snapped into focus.

'What the fuck? *What?* What do you mean? Of course, he's my father!'

'Sorry. Yes, he is your father. I didn't mean that, it came out all wrong. I mean … your father is not really called Marton. That is not his real name. It's Alfred.'

Peter's mind spun at a dizzying rate. Alfred. He'd just left someone called Alfred in a bad way in his office. What was she saying?

He let out a strange choking noise. 'Alfred … Alfred who … and why Marton then?'

'Alfred Nemeth. The jeweller. They swapped names. After the girl was killed, to try to stop anyone from tracing them properly. It worked, Peter, it worked, they escaped prosecution. The killing of the child was a mistake anyway, so, well, it's OK, I think. And you always knew him as Marton. It's just a name, Peter, just a name.'

'So Marton is Alfred and Alfred is Marton?'

She nodded.

But Peter soon stopped worrying about the name. He realised there were more concerning things to deal with.

'Why did you kill Alfred, Peter? Well, the man you knew as Alfred?'

Peter recoiled, shrank from her a little and sighed.

'Shit. He … he fell. It was an accident. I left him alive … I didn't know he'd died, Aliz. Really, I didn't. How do you know anyway?'

She handed him a folded newspaper, her finger indicating the article.

He read the column and placed the newspaper down on the desk.

'This was a horrible accident. He did try to keep father's note from me, though, Aliz, if he'd given me it, this wouldn't have happened.'

Aliz nodded her agreement. There was a silence before Peter spoke again.

'So didn't anyone come looking for this Katalin? And who is the other girl and how long has she been there?'

'No, no one came looking for Katalin. Not that I know of anyway. Maybe strange, but maybe no one knew she was here? The police did visit, but they didn't get anywhere. The other girl is Scottish, I think. She's only been here a few days Peter. I'm worried someone will come looking more closely for her.'

Peter considered that. 'Yes. Someone might. So we had better be ready.'

'Actually, someone has already been asking, Peter.'

He cocked a quivering brow, still dazed by the developments.

'An investigator, a private one. Looking for her. I think her mother has hired him. He has been here to talk to me. I told him the young woman had been to see Marton and then left. Nothing more. But I think he is suspicious.'

'Christ, why tell him she was here?'

'He already knew. I don't know how exactly. But I don't think he believes she left.'

Peter got up and started pacing the room, fast-paging through the implications.

'So, if he thinks she didn't leave … he's going to start poking around more. He might try and come into the hotel and look for himself. Does he know Marton's room number?'

She thought briefly. 'No.'

'Name? Where's he staying, do you know?'

Aliz picked up Calum's card and held it aloft. Peter plucked it from her hand. He took a quick look.

'OK. I need to deal with him. Leave it to me.'

'I was hoping you'd say that, Peter. Be my guest. What about the girls, though? They're being fed, of course. But what do you plan to do?'

'I'm not sure yet, Aliz. I need time to think! Keep them healthy for now. I'll work it out soon, you can be sure.'

He got up to leave. 'I'll be back soon. I need to see Marton's room. Maybe I'll eat first then come back later today. There's a funny smell in here, by the way. Smells like gas?'

Aliz leaned back in her chair. 'Yes, I smelt it recently too. One or two of the guests did as well. We have reported it to the utility company. They're fixing it, I think.'

'Good. We don't want to asphyxiate the guests, do we? Or the prisoners.'

He grimaced and left.

*

Back in his hotel, Peter sat down in the small armchair in the corner of his room, two fingers propping up each of his temples. He felt overwhelmed by all the surprises and secrets. Killing an old man, intended or not, was choking him with guilt. He was a doctor and proud of it. So proud of it. His altruism weighed heavily on him, but the analytical side of his brain was telling him to act. He remembered he always thought through things better by writing them down. So he summarised the whole mess to himself on a hotel notepad, in as simple a set of words as he could muster.

In the end, it *was* simple. He must murder four people. Murder four people. He repeated it over and over to himself. Finally out loud, softly. It sounded dreadful. The investigator, the two girls in the room … and Aliz. Aliz just knew too much. It would make five if he included Alfred. Who was really Marton. Not that he counted that as a murder really, more of an unfortunate accident.

What's more, three of these people were in the Hotel Cristal. Maybe he could find a way to entice the private investigator to be there? But he needed a method … a way to kill them all. For that, he'd probably need some help from the old network. Or his doctor's bag. Or both. Yes, that needed to be his focus now. He opened a bottle of water from the dressing table and slaked his thirst, driven by the effects of the adrenaline surging around his body.

His ever-present logic had won the battle with his heart and was the thing driving him now. He turned the page of the notepad and started to scribble. He needed to work fast. Two girls together in that room was a risk in more ways than one would be. Sure, they were in the same room. But together they might be more able to work out a way to make their presence known. And now there were two people who had an insight into Marton's past, two people who could blow his world apart. He couldn't let this state exist for much longer. Not much longer at all.

As he sat back in his chair, he wondered what his poor, dead mother would have made of all of this. And did she know anything about the Arrow Cross trail?

As he thought about her, he remembered her gentle kindness and found it hard to believe that she could know, yet still be a loyal wife to his father. Those memories kicked his emotional side into play. He couldn't kill these people without trying some other way. But it needed to be swift.

# Hanna helps

Hanna Elek was feeling a bit brighter today. Money was a struggle. Always. This morning had started on a bright note, though. An Englishman had stopped her on the way into work. She hadn't understood him very well at first. Her English was pretty basic, mostly phrases about room cleaning and the usual greetings. But she got it in the end after he pulled out a couple of ten-thousand forint notes and suggested she could help him.

He was tall. Not bad looking, nice smile. Quite charming really. It wasn't too hard to agree to help him. The money was the clincher, of course. She wasn't going to do even this *little* thing, without some reward.

All she had needed to do was leave Mr Kovacs' old room door open at 7 p.m. Just a little ajar, that's all. She was working the late shift. It didn't seem a risk; she thought anything valuable would have already been removed ... and anyone could leave a door open by mistake. The money would pay for Lili's gym class for the next term ... and more.

She decided to give the room another dust, just for an excuse to have entered it. It was eerie, being in there, with Mr Kovacs dead. Some items were definitely gone from the room and it just seemed, well, a place in decay, like poor Mr Kovacs had been. She dusted quickly and made her retreat, leaving the door open but pushed close to the frame, so there was no light. Harder to spot if another staff member came past.

She was interested in what was going to happen. The man had said a lady friend of his would come to the room. Something in her inner curiosity made Hanna want to see this woman. So she busied herself around the cleaning store cupboard at the end of the floor. She could see the door entrance from here. Far enough away not to be conspicuous.

At exactly 7 p.m. a pretty girl appeared out of the lifts and walked towards the room. Younger than she was expecting. Much younger. If she was really his lady friend he was either lucky or very rich. She winced at the thought of it being the latter … maybe she hadn't asked for enough money to help him out.

The girl looked briefly up at the room number screwed onto the door and pushed it, moving quickly inside and shutting the door behind her. The deal was she'd be out in thirty minutes. She'd wait around in case someone else arrived to get into the room. Not much she could do if it was Miss Gal. But she could talk the other cleaners away easily enough. She sat down on the edge of her mop bucket and kept watch.

*

Jenna spotted the cleaner at the end of the corridor immediately. She didn't betray anything though and went straight into Room 41, breathing a sigh of relief as the door gave way to her gentle push.

It smelt fusty, with a chemical edge. She clicked the door shut carefully and took in the room in one big sweep. It looked a bit sparse somehow, still lots of furniture but not much in terms of ornaments. Probably been partly emptied by now. It reminded her of an uninhabited lecturer's study in an ancient place. How she imagined Oxford University, or somewhere like that.

She needed to work swiftly. She looked around for a place to start. A bookcase looked promising. It was glass-fronted. She pulled at the handle. Locked. Break in or look for the key? She went for the latter and started rifling through the drawers of a large wooden writing desk. There *was* a key ... but little else. It looked like it had been cleared out, just some scraps of paper and loose paperclips and biro pens left.

She slotted the key into the bookcase lock and turned it. It worked. She pulled the doors open and scanned the spines. Not so many. Pretty much all in Hungarian, so that wasn't much help. She did have the words for "Arrow Cross" in Hungarian in her head though. After a few minutes rummaging around, she found one tome with those words in the title. She stuffed that into her rucksack. The few titles in English were about American baseball. She made a mental note of that and left them in place.

She looked around the room again. There were two large wardrobes on the far side near the windows. She opened the first. Some coats and shoes. She poked between them and found nothing else.

The second wardrobe was partly shelved, stacked with underwear, socks and men's toiletries. And some cardboard boxes. The boxes held nothing of interest. However, behind them, there was a rucksack, pushed hard against the back of the shelf and hidden by the boxes and some more socks until she pulled them out.

She reached in and grabbed it. It was grey. The top zipper was open. Inside was a blue notebook and an iPad.

Hadn't Eszter told her Sarah had a grey rucksack? That together with a blue notebook and an iPad, it was missing from Sarah's hotel room? She would check her notes … but she was sure. Like when you wonder if you've locked the back door when you're sitting in the airport-bound taxi. You know you have … but your mind wants to needle you with doubt.

For now, though, she was trusting her recall. Which meant that either Aliz was lying or very dozy about her recollection of Sarah leaving in a taxi. Aliz Gal didn't strike Jenna as a dozy woman from what Calum had said about her. But Calum could make his own mind up about that, now she had some semblance of proof. Proof of what exactly, she wasn't sure. But a very old man doesn't keep these kinds of things belonging to a missing young girl in his room for no reason. And she could think of no reason why Sarah would have left them here.

She rifled through the rest of the wardrobe but found nothing more. She looked around the room again. A small wooden door set into an inside wall, which looked like it rolled up rather than opened outward. She walked over and pulled the door up. Just an empty space with a wooden box that seemed separate from the cupboard frame and was supported by a thick rope attached to a large metal loop on its top. It looked like one of those serving hatches they used in some restaurants.

Then she noticed the pair of pushbuttons set in a dull steel panel next to the hatch.

She mused on whether he had all of his food delivered this way. It was unusual to find one of these in a normal guest room. Wasn't it? Maybe things were different in Hungary, in an old hotel. Whatever the reason, it looked well used and reeked of spilt food.

She wrinkled her nose in distaste and turned to face back into the room.

Just the bathroom left. Pretty empty on the face of it. She opened the bathroom cabinet. Cleaned out.

She turned around and as she did her foot touched the side of the bath. A small panel moved slightly. There was a gap and she prised the panel away to discover a small cupboard. She opened it and found a safe inside.

The safe was locked. She pondered on that. Marton Kovacs had been dead a good few days. So … so nothing. Too many possible options around why it was locked. She made another mental note. Back in the sitting room, she couldn't think of anything else to look at.

She glanced down at the floor. A large rug covered most of the floor space in the open area of the room. She checked her phone. She had a couple of minutes left still. With an expectation of finding nothing, she rolled the rug back slowly. It was thick and heavy. It smelt of coffee and old smoke.

She only had to roll it about eighteen inches before she found a circular metal ring set in one of the floorboards. It had a glass disk recessed inside. She stooped down further and peered into the glass. A spyhole.

The field of vision was fairly large. There was a room below, lit by electric light, which struck her as odd in the middle of the day. Everything was static. A carpeted floor, the edge of a bed, some tables … then her eyes snapped back to the bed.

There was a leg poking into view at one end. A leg encased in denim. Bare feet. The leg looked slender, a woman's probably. It was circling, idly. Was it Sarah's? She looked for a few moments. Nothing changed. She couldn't hear anything either.

She looked again at her phone. Time's up. She reluctantly rolled the carpet back into place and grabbed the grey rucksack with its contents. Pushing it into her own backpack, she left the room as quietly as possible.

The cleaner had gone. Must have got impatient or had something to do. She walked to the end of the corridor and paused for thought. Why would Kovacs have been spying on the room below? Just a voyeur? Or something else? She could ask at reception who was in that room … but she didn't want to arouse suspicion, so maybe there was a different way to find out?

As she wondered how best to do that, a movement down the corridor caught her eye. A man had appeared from the lift lobby and was walking down the corridor towards her. She looked down at her phone, pretending to be typing a message.

The man turned and stopped at Room 41 and used a key to open it and move inside. Jenna breathed relief at the close call. She noticed he had a long scar on his left cheek. It made him look sinister. And she wondered what this man was going to do in an empty room.

# In Marton's room

Peter returned to the Hotel Cristal in the early evening. He looked behind reception for Aliz. Not there. So using the manager's pass he'd agreed with Aliz he might need, he retrieved a key for Room 41 and took the lift upstairs.

There was a girl at the end of the corridor, not far from Marton's room. For some reason it made him feel guilty. He straightened his back and told himself he had no need to be. It was his father's room, after all. What's more, it would be his hotel too, once the estate was sorted out.

That thought reminded him how much he needed to fix the issues in Room 31. Without a clean start, it would be nigh on impossible to enjoy the fruits of his inheritance. He could hardly think of selling it with *"two captive women included"* on the sales brochure.

He shut the room door behind him and leant back against it. The room had a smell of old tobacco and bathroom cleaner. Most of all it looked empty. Not of things, as such, but empty of his father's presence.

It was still and silent and there was an intangible vacuum that confirmed his father was dead. A vacuum that would linger for a while. Weeks, maybe months. And then one day someone else would be in this room and the vacuum would disappear, moving on somewhere with Marton's spirit. For all he'd learnt about his father in recent days, he had loved the old bull and still did.

He snapped himself back out of his contemplation and took a look around the rooms. One big lounge, a bedroom and a bathroom. Some wardrobes and cupboards, chests of drawers. But not really much to show for a long life. It crossed his mind that maybe Marton had some things in storage somewhere, maybe in the hotel. He made a note to ask Aliz.

He rummaged through all the drawers and shelves he could see. There was nothing of interest other than his father's own stuff. He looked down at the floor. Aliz had mentioned there was a spyhole.

He rolled back the loosely-laid carpet and found it, a cylindrical piece set into the floorboards. He moved in close, his eye right up to the metal ring at the end of the lens.

The view startled him. He hadn't expected to see their faces staring back up at him, side by side, smiling. Laughing now. Laughing at him? Surely they couldn't see him?

They looked young, especially the dark-haired one. He supposed she was the Scots girl. For a moment his heart softened and he thought maybe he should think of another way. It was a fleeting thought, though, one cut short by the reality of the situation. He tightened his resolve and brought himself back to his plan. It was the only way.

He watched their faces for a few moments. Their smiles turned into laughs and then morphed into strains as they seemed to be exerting themselves somehow. He couldn't see past their waistlines, but they looked like they were enjoying it, whatever it was. It was strangely attractive watching them. Then they pulled their heads up, rolled themselves forward and they were gone.

He dropped the carpet back down. Better he didn't look again. He couldn't afford to get interested in them, in any way at all … and a few stirrings of ideas were already circling in his head. He shook himself, wriggling his mind free of them. No, he needed to treat them as two problems … and nothing more.

He stood up. There was nothing more to see here. Nothing to find, it seemed. Being in this room was helping him, though. Helping him think through the way to do it. He found himself sweating and pulled a cotton handkerchief from his jacket pocket. He held it to his forehead, soaking up the droplets, closing his eyes for a moment, beginning to visualise the way it would happen. There were bits he couldn't quite see yet. But there was an idea forming that he could develop, one that could work. He just needed to lie in his room and think some more.

He locked the door on the way out. Something made him look to the end of the corridor, where the girl had been standing earlier. She was gone and any thoughts he had about her left him.

He strode down the stairs to reception rather than wait for the lift and walked up to the desk. 'As you know, I'm Peter Kovacs. I've been staying in a hotel nearby since I came to Budapest. I'd like to take a room here now, to sort out my father's affairs. Can you find me one at the end of a corridor, a nice room, please? I'll probably be here a while.'

The young man on reception was eager to please and shuffled reservations around in double quick time to free up a corner room. He was obviously aware that the man in front of him might be his future employer.

'Room 21, Mr Kovacs. It's a large room. Hope you like it, come and tell me if it isn't suitable?'

Peter nodded and took the key from him. He realised that, by chance, the room he'd been allocated was directly underneath the girls' room. He would move in tonight.

# Brainstorming

Calum knocked on Jenna's room door.

'Entrez.'

You're Scottish and you're in Hungary, think you're getting the language confused.'

She rolled her eyes and motioned towards the rucksack on her bed.

'Really, my girl, speaking French to a gentleman, now suggesting bed at 8 p.m., I'll have to speak to your mother when we're home.'

They'd lived side-by-side in their small Scottish village, growing up knowing each other very well. It let them say things without any inhibitions, in a way they wouldn't to others.

'Calum, just shut up a minute. The rucksack. With a blue notepad and iPad inside it. Sarah's, from what Eszter told me.'

Calum sat down and pulled his serious face back on. 'Where from?'

'Marton Kovacs' room.'

'Really? What else?'

'A spyhole in the floor, under a rug. Looks down into a room below. I saw part of a leg, dangling over the edge of a bed, I think.'

'Jesus. You think it could have been Sarah?'

She shrugged. 'Maybe. The leg looked slim-ish, but I couldn't see more than the lower part. The description and photo set of Sarah we have says not too tall, medium build. So maybe not. I can't be sure.'

'Let's have a look at the notebook and iPad then. You take the iPad … I'll stick to the old technology. By the way, I bought us a chimney cake while you were out spying. It's in the paper bag. Have some … cinnamon sugared, it's good.'

She got up, broke off a big chunk of the cylindrical bread-cake and stuffed a piece into her mouth. Delicious. He was good at finding tasty food, it was one of his pluses.

She pulled the notebook and iPad out of the rucksack and handed the notebook to him. She clicked the iPad on. She was pressing buttons, sighing.

'What's up?'

Calum had his eyes down, leafing through the notebook.

'Password protected. We might not get anything from this.'

'Let's hope the boring old technology helps, then. No password on this book, Jen.'

She threw him a withering smile. 'You're a Luddite, Neuman. And annoying with it.'

'Wrong. The Luddites tried to prevent progress. I'm actually making it here. Seems she'd been to visit Marton twice … and was actually invited back the second time.'

He read a bit further, then jumped to the last page of notes.

He read the last few lines out aloud.

*Marton Kovacs 12 Nov.*
*Invited back to complete questions.*
*Asked about Arrow Cross personal involvement 1944-45. Seemed*
*nervous. Not sure how to progress without provoking resistance.*

'That's it?'

'That's it. She didn't write anything else. Which makes you think … doesn't it?'

They stared at each other.

'You know what,' Calum said, 'I'm going to go back and talk to the librarian again, Beata Sandor. Eszter mentioned she'd been helping them personally, which I thought a bit unusual. We know Sarah visited Marton in pursuit of some research threads or the like. I just wonder if Beata knows anything about Marton Kovacs?'

'Why don't I go? Get a different perspective? She hasn't met me so a fresh angle might work?'

'No, I'll do it, I think continuity is better on this one. I'm sure you can find more notes and research leads from the notebook to pursue tomorrow?'

Jenna grimaced but buttoned her lip and grunted in the affirmative.

'Let's crack on then. Catch you in the bar later?'

After he left the room, she growled to herself. It was true there were more papers to sift through and she needed to hack the iPad password somehow. But she wondered if there was a more Jenna-like contribution she could make. It was what made her get excited about this job, after all. She started leafing through some remaining research papers, whilst simultaneously imagining likely passwords Sarah may have used.

Then she remembered she knew someone from university who had used an algorithm thing that came up with lists of possible passwords based on personal information about a person. So she created a list as long as she could, all the basics they captured on a new case plus mother's and friends' names, any pets (none that she knew of) boyfriends (none again) and interests. Some of the last category would ironically probably be on the iPad once she was in. She sent the list with a plea for quick help to the guy from Inverness and silently wished him good luck.

In the event, he didn't need it. He sent her a link back to his algorithm immediately and suggested she could feed the information in herself. She sighed with a kind of resigned understanding and started the process of typing the data in.

\*

The evening meeting in the hotel bar had already become a ritual. Calum ordered more of their, now favourite, white wine. It was a new waitress who brought it over to their table. She set two glasses down next to the wine bottle, thanked Calum, then looked across at Jenna and smiled. A second longer than Jenna might have expected.

They both sank a glass quickly then refilled. Thirty minutes later they were staring at an empty bottle. The downside of a slow day at the office. Or bright spot, depending on how you looked at it.

'I'm trying with the iPad data but it's hard going. Maybe tomorrow I'll have something. I might need to ask her mother a few questions about personal data to help me. How did you get the cleaner to help us, by the way?'

Calum rubbed the thumb and first finger of his right hand together as if rolling a cigarette.

'Everyone has their price, Jen. And for a cleaner, it isn't too high.' He looked a little sad.

Calum waved the waitress over again. A tall girl, slim with long dark hair tied back into a ponytail. Thirty-ish probably. She took the repeat order, smiled at Jenna again, just that bit longer than most people feel comfortable with. She returned quickly, bringing them peanuts, too.

As she walked away. Calum turned to Jenna.

'Think she fancies you. Free peanuts for miss.'

Jenna flushed, which encouraged him. 'Oh, you too eh?'

An elbow in his ribs made him gasp with a squeaky laugh, causing some of the other guests to take a look at them both. They fell silent for a moment, as they felt their age difference come under scrutiny.

They went for the bottle at the same time and giggled again, as Calum finally wrestled the bottle away from Jenna and filled their glasses. By the time they'd drained the last of that bottle, the other guests were a fuzzy haze.

'OK. Calum, you're a *baad fluence.* I'm off to bed.'

\*

Jenna carefully rose to her feet and half-waved to Calum as she meandered to the lift. The lights inside it were bright and she screwed up her eyes until she got out and walked to her door.

She sat down on her bed and wondered about the waitress. Her name badge had announced her as Izabella. She liked the name … or was that some kind of halo effect? And why was she smiling at her?

Was it because she was so much younger than Calum and Izabella had assumed he was her lover? Or something else? She looked at herself in the wardrobe mirror. Did she look gay? Could you even look lesbian anyway?

Too hard. She pulled her clothes off, hit the light switch and fell asleep with her toothbrush standing unwanted in the bathroom.

# Jenna & Izabella

Calum and Jenna met back at the hotel later the next day. Izabella was serving them again, this time from behind the bar counter. Smiling as ever. But longer and deeper when she spoke to Jenna. Jenna was sure she wasn't imagining it now.

'Sooo, Calum-O, I have some more information. I got into the iPad! And I found out some useful stuff, besides a load of personal information.'

'Ah, good stuff. Tell me. Then I'll tell you about Beata Sandor.'

That sounded like *tell me yours and I'll better it* ... but she pressed on.

'Well, from notes on the iPad it's clear Eszter found some lists potentially implicating Marton Kovacs in war crimes. So that explains a bit about the notepad scrawl that you found yesterday. Also, there was a book referred to that they couldn't find, so they stopped there. I guess that may have been part of what she was asking him about.'

Calum scratched his chin stubble.

'OK. So clearly the meeting she had with Marton could have been a bit tense. Or worse. Not sure about the relevance of the book. We're trying to find Sarah McTeer here, after all, not investigate war crimes. Although, I don't believe Sarah was either, in terms of what you told me about her research scope?'

Jenna nodded and stored her annoyance at his shut down on the war crimes. Maybe true, but there was something about it that was nagging at her.

Calum turned and looked at her directly. 'Beata Sandor then.'

He waited for Jenna to signal she was ready to hear.

'So I asked her why she'd been helping Sarah and Eszter. Put it to her that it might be seen as unusual.'

'And?'

'She, well, she said she was always helpful, especially to visitors. But I did wonder how she did that, you know, does she have a foreign visitor scanner in the lobby?'

Jenna smirked.

'So, no, she doesn't yeah? So that didn't stack up and she offered no other explanation. Also, I pressed her on Marton Kovacs. She said she didn't know of him. But her eyes and body language told me different. She wouldn't be pushed on it, but there is something wrong there, I can smell it.'

'I trust your sixth sense, Calum. So what next? We can't talk to Marton, he's dead. And the hotel manager Aliz seems shifty too but won't talk anymore. So what do we do?'

Calum shook his head wearily.

'You're right. We need a new angle … or a lever on Aliz Gal. We need to sleep on that one. Problem too, is that in Scotland I'd ask my police buddies to help with background and swap details. I'm hamstrung here, don't know the police or the lingo. Makes it harder, eh?'

He took another draw on his glass and drained the last drop, stood up and pulled a tired scowl across his face.

'Well, we made some good progress today eh? I've had enough of this second-rate booze. I'm off to my bed. See you bright and early, Jen.' He waved a half-hearted goodbye and ambled off to the lifts.

Jenna threw a limp wave and smile back, thinking about what that new angle might be. She swivelled her gaze back to the bar. She had a feeling about what would meet her now. She was right.

'Another drink? Jenna isn't it, I think I heard? Sorry, I wasn't meaning to listen in!'

Izabella was smiling and peering into her face expectantly.

'Err … yes OK. A small beer please.' She smiled back at her. A bit longer than she normally would, she thought. Or was it? She wasn't really sure what was going through her mind … or heart … but there was a dimension in this simple conversation that was more than a bar chat … and not something she'd felt before.

Izabella turned and looked for a beer glass, bending down to a low shelf for a small one.

Jenna realised she was staring at the girl. More than staring. Admiring. Admiring her shape. She swallowed, hard. Something else was building as well, and it was surprising her. Almost shocking her. Almost … were it not for the fact that it wasn't the first time she'd felt like this.

She peered down into her empty glass. She was lusting, that was what it was. Jenna smiled to herself and thought of Gregor. When she did the feeling changed … not into a bad thing … but into something distinctly different … but similar.

'Here you are.' Izabella slipped a paper mat under the beer glass, slopping a tiny amount before setting it down.

'Thanks.'

'A beer here too, please,' came from further along the bar. Jenna turned. A stranger. Izabella went to serve him.

Jenna relaxed a little and sipped her beer, watching the interaction further down the counter. Friendly. But no more than that. Not from Izabella anyway.

She opened her phone and started to type a message to Gregor. She'd found herself thinking about him quite often over the days since Ellie's wake. She knew he'd be doing the same, of course. But for once he'd been restrained in showing it. Jenna wondered if tactics ever entered his thinking and then chastised herself for thinking that way. Of course he might … and wouldn't that mean he *really* wanted them to be together and was trying to find a way? Not that she'd ever really doubted it.

She settled on no more than 'how are you … what's up?' as an opener, then clicked send. It was difficult to know how friendly to be, given how hard it'd been to leave him behind in Plockton when she finally took the delayed plunge to study in Inverness. She really, really didn't want to mislead him. Right now, though, she wasn't sure where she was leading herself. Or who was leading her. Or where. Maybe she'd texted him out of guilt.

Another couple of small beers followed. She was getting tired now, but didn't want to leave the bar counter … and Izabella's increasing attention. She had to draw a line at some point, though … and Calum would expect her to be ready by nine in the morning.

'Can I get the bill to sign please?'

Her waitress nodded. She looked disappointed but got on with it.

She placed the receipt on a plate with a pen and edged it towards Jenna.

Jenna picked up the pen and scribbled her signature across it. Her hand was strangely wobbly.

'Thanks.' Izabella put one hand on the plate, sliding it away, as she put the other briefly on Jenna's hand on the bar counter.

'Goodnight. Hope to see you tomorrow, Jenna.' Jenna looked down, moved away then glanced back at the bar.

'Goodnight. Yes, tomorrow. Izabella.'

'Everyone calls me Iza.'

'OK.'

Jenna squeezed a little smile out as she turned away again, feeling her face flush warm. Suddenly, her bedroom couldn't come fast enough.

\*

Jenna flopped down on the mattress and turned onto her back, sighing, rolling her eyes in the dark. She felt her heart beating fast. She was excited … and confused. She searched for some kind of answer to the multitude of questions circling in her head.

The only thing she kept coming back to, in the long time before she fell asleep, was why she'd always wanted to peck the girls, rather than the boys when they played kiss-chase at primary school. And she didn't have an answer. Not only that, there was the thing with Caroline Meredith. That caused a stir at school and in a tiny, parochial place like Plockton, everyone knew about it. She wondered if it had all been forgotten or whether people still eyed her with two minds. Gregor had never mentioned it. Too scared to probably, she smiled to herself. For a fleeting moment, she felt sad for him.

With some difficulty, she pushed those thoughts to the back of her mind, to try and concentrate on what was exciting her more about the next day. *What could she do to get the case moved further on?* The only thing she came up with, was something she'd proved herself good at in previous cases. Casing a joint. And getting in illegally if needed, to see what she could find. But she needed an address first.

# The book thief

Jenna and Calum met for breakfast at eight-thirty the following morning. Calum was picking over the buffet for low-fat items as usual.

'Maybe they'll do you an egg white omelette?'

'Maybe. I didn't ask so far, just had toast and some smoked fish.'

'Bacon looks great, though, doesn't it? Think I'll slip a couple of rashers into some hot buttery toast.' She loved teasing him.

'Your arteries can start clogging up from the day you're born, you know,' he said dourly, grabbing some more toast and heading off for the omelette station.

Once they'd sat down with some calories in front of them, Calum declared he would take a walk along the river for some inspiration. It seemed sleeping on the problem of the next step had just buried it deeper. He asked Jenna if she could continue with Sarah's research papers while he was gone.

'Got enough to keep you going still?'

'Yup. Looking forward to it.'

He gave her a mock sour look and downed the last of his coffee. 'You're good at it. Later then.'

Jenna looked down at the remaining half of a bacon sandwich, picked it up and chewed it lovingly, as she thought through her day's work. It didn't include too much time sitting going through the research papers, though. The first thing on her agenda was the address.

*

It turned out to be easier than she had thought. Beata Sandor was listed in the phone directory together with her address. She just needed to check the librarian was at work then go for broke.

'Yes, I want to speak to Ms Sandor, sorry my Hungarian is not good, well, I don't speak the language at all.'

She was put through after a short delay.

'Hello, this is Beata Sandor. How can I help?'

Jenna dropped the call. Good, the coast was clear.

*

The address necessitated a metro ride up north of the city centre to Ujpest, then a few streets walk. She was soon there. The house stood on a quiet street, full of similar houses. Post-war build, faded paintwork, a motley collection of broken, rusty railings and scrubland between the closely-built dwellings. There seemed to be no garage nearby that she could see, but there was space enough between the houses to walk down and round the back of the ones adjacent to number 306.

The issue was, it was broad daylight. So she needed to be really careful about neighbours.

She walked slowly down the right-hand side of the house, trying to look casually around, searching for windows overlooking her and the house.

A high wall extended straight down from the side of the main house and ran for thirty yards or so. She got to the end of it and turned left along a back wall, where there was a gate a few yards up.

There was little by way of vantage points of her from the neighbouring houses, only a bathroom on the side of one, and the bedroom windows looking down at the back. Mostly low risk in the daytime, she thought, so she tried the gate. It gave a little but seemed stuck. She slipped her hand over, stood on her tiptoes and with her fingertips managed to feel a bolt at the top. She slid it across and moved smartly into the back garden of the house.

She crouched down immediately.

There were large windows on the ground floor looking out onto the garden. No signs of life … but she had no idea if Beata had any family living with her. So, approaching the house was a risk. She scuttled to a back corner of the garden, near to a swing, and then worked slowly up the side wall to the corner of the house. She dared a couple of glances through the back windows before walking up the side to a back door. Locked, of course.

Jenna was good at finding handy tips on YouTube, though. A simple old-fashioned rim lock wasn't going to be a problem and she had some makeshift tools to get her in. It took her a couple of minutes or so, but then the lock slipped back and she quietly opened the door. No alarm so far … and no sign of a dog, in the kitchen at least.

She moved carefully through the house, making no noise, but it was soon clear it was empty … and she found the room she was looking for … a study lined with books from floor to ceiling along the whole of the back wall, behind an imposing old desk, then more texts along one of the side walls, facing the garden window.

She looked at the literary leviathan in front of her and sighed. This could take some time. Whilst she had the Hungarian title she was looking for written down on a scrap of paper, there were a lot of spines to look through, not all the same way up, either, so she was going to get neck ache and light-headed if she didn't find it quickly.

After ten minutes of looking, she rubbed her neck and resigned herself to a long haul. She'd only done twenty per cent of the titles she reckoned: the language recognition, or lack of it, was slowing her down; it would have been faster if they were English titles.

It was only late morning, though, she should have plenty of time still.

But a different clock had begun ticking. And it was running faster than hers.

\*

Next door, Aron Kis had been settling down, finally, to some college work. It had been a struggle to get out of bed today. His mother had brought him some tea before she left at seven-thirty, but he'd gone back to sleep after she'd gone for the day.

For some reason, he could only sleep properly in the morning, the night time just didn't quite work for him. His mother told him it was his age and he would grow out of it, but that he'd better get some decent grades or else he'd get no more cups of tea in bed. At least that was one person who loved him.

As he got out of bed and stretched and yawned, he caught sight of a pretty girl he'd not seen before. She was in the garden next door, walking slowly up towards the house. Nice. He could go for her. He suddenly realised he was staring out of the window naked and pulled back a little, then she disappeared from his view. Hey, he'd keep a look out for her again, though. Maybe Mrs Sandor had a new lodger, as she did sometimes.

He moved to the bathroom to clean his teeth. Through the frosted glass, he could make out the girl's shape at next door's back entrance. There was a scratching noise going on. Sounded like her key didn't fit, but he couldn't make her out properly through the opaque glass. Shame, he'd have liked another look at her.

When she was still there after he'd finished his teeth, though, he started to wonder why she hadn't got in the house yet. With that thought, he heard a click, then her blurred image was gone from view.

It was after a leisurely breakfast and two cups of coffee that he decided to sit out in the garden and read something for college. He grabbed an economics textbook, more as a style statement than a firm intent to work and sauntered outside, pulling up an old folding chair by the back door. In that sheltered spot, it was warm enough to sit out in the sunshine with a jumper on and he preferred the fresh air.

Thirty minutes later, he'd stared at the same page a few times and begun to read it but somehow he kept drifting back to the start of the page to re-read what he'd already forgotten. It was so hard to get started in the mornings. He put the book on the ground by the side of the chair, with some relief that he'd decided it wasn't for now. He stood up, shoving his hands in his jeans pockets and breathed deeply, surveying the garden.

Out of the corner of his eye, a movement flicked past. He turned and saw the girl from earlier in the study room next door, pulling books from the shelves. She was facing away from him and his gaze was drawn to her pert bottom. He stole forward for a slightly closer look. He got to the fence and rested both his forearms along its top, leaning forward and enjoying his view.

She turned quite suddenly to put a book on the desk behind her and as she did so she had obviously caught sight of him.

A sharp step back and up from the desk was followed by an even quicker withdrawal from his line of sight. She was up to something. He knew Mrs Sandor quite well, she'd always been kind to him when he was little, giving him biscuits, that kind of thing. Especially after her daughter had disappeared, so he felt obliged to investigate.

He went up the garden to a wooden crate stood by the fence and used it to hop up and over into next door's drive.

He tried the back door … open. He walked into the kitchen quietly, peering through the kitchen door into the hallway, which led to the study. He couldn't see all the way into that room, so he stepped slowly through into the hall and leant around the study door.

He was startled to see a pile of books on the desk and an open window. He dived at the window and fell out through it, scampering back up to his feet and running up the drive to the road.

He could see the back of the girl, sprinting away from him, holding a backpack under her arm. Making an instant decision, he ran hard after her.

*

It had been a boring but nervy task looking through all the spines, so there was a guarded euphoria when she found one with a similar title to the one she'd been looking for. Similar, but not quite right.

Jenna turned to put it down on the desk to have a good look through it. It was then that she saw the boy … and he was looking straight at her. When he moved at speed up the garden, she knew he was coming after her. She whacked the book shut, shoved it into her rucksack and thought quickly. There would be no time to get out the front door, he'd cut her off. She looked at the window, Just a simple latch. She opened it with a quiet smoothness, worried about making any noise that might trigger him to run around to the window rather than the back door.

She hopped out after a quick look and ran down the garden, looking over her shoulder for a sight of him. She sped through the gate, hanging a right, pirouetting on the right-hand gate frame and shot across the back of three adjacent houses before cutting back up to the road.

She ran, harder than she had ever done in her life. She almost fell down the steps of the metro station. It was only then that she dared a glance backwards … her heart sank when she saw him twenty yards back up the steps, eyes fixed directly on her.

# The shoes

Calum walked slowly along the side of the Danube for a couple of hours after breakfast. He was lost in thought around the case, intertwined with flashes of his daughter's funeral. It was like a stream of black water that kept burbling up and touching him with its chill. As he walked with his head down, he saw a pair of shoes just ahead of him. Then another pair. He stopped and looked up. There were scores of them along the side of the river. He realised they weren't real, but made from some type of metal. Iron.

There was a signboard nearby, so he went over to read it.

TO THE MEMORY OF THE VICTIMS

SHOT INTO THE DANUBE

BY ARROW CROSS MILITIAMEN

IN 1944-45.

Arrow Cross. Wasn't that what Sarah McTeer was researching? It made him imagine what study into that kind of thing could lead to. Especially if she was digging where secrets were buried.

It led him to wonder … to wonder about Aliz Gal and Beata Sandor. Too young for the war, of course … but the daughters of members? Hiding something close to their families or hearts in some way? There was a line of investigation there. But he wasn't sure, even if he found some link, that it would help him right now. Still, best not pre-judge the outcome. His thoughts turned to getting Jenna involved in that when his mobile rang.

Cassie. His heart sank when he remembered he hadn't answered her last text. It had been a few days now.

He grabbed his first instinct, which was to run away, wrestled it to submission and pressed the answer button.

'Hey.'

'Hey back.'

'Yeah, sorry I didn't text you back, Cass. Been busy, I'm in Budapest right now, missing person.' He cursed himself straight away for being defensive. But he *hadn't* got back to her, had he?

'Ah OK. Well, was just catching up, wondering how you were. Like I said, it was so good to have you with me at the wake, sad as it was … is … and, well, you know. That you stayed.'

There was an awkward pause.

'Yeah, it was. And it is. God, Cassie, I've been thinking about her so much this week since I've been away. I just realised that. Is that good or not?'

'I don't know. It's all I can think of. And you. Sorry, I mean that just came out, I don't know what I meant by that. But I miss her so much, Calum.'

**273**

He could hear the tears starting down the phone line and it made him well up too.

But this wasn't what he wanted right now. He wanted to pull away from all that sadness, those thoughts of his daughter's death. Cassie too if he was honest. But he had to ease her away softly and that was feeling tricky.

'So, how've you been this week? Did you go back to work yet?'

'Not yet, no. Don't feel up to it, I think I'll take the rest of this week then I'll see.'

'Might be better to get back there next week, yeah. Give you something else to think about, eh?'

'Huh. Don't think work will stop me thinking about our daughter's death, will it? Maybe you can block it out but I can't, Calum. I just can't.'

Wrong words from him. More tears. Now he was stuck in a verbal corner and didn't know how to move. He took the easy option as usual.

'Ah, got a call on another line, Cass, sorry, I'll need to take this one. Budapest police. I'll call you end of the week, see how you are?'

A disbelieving pause and frustrated exhalation of breath.

'OK.'

He clicked the call off sharply and sat down on the concrete bench near the iron shoes. Stared at the river, then turned his head upstream towards the cathedral-like parliament buildings. He looked at them but wasn't seeing.

He rubbed his chin. Hadn't shaved this morning. He felt tired now, conversations like that drained him instantly. Made him feel nervous inside. He turned his mind away from it, to seek an escape. Was that so bad? He knew he could be insular, push his emotions into the background without too much thought. Maybe *too* easily. But he wasn't a bad *person* for that, was he? He just dealt with it in his own way.

He stood up wearily to go back to the hotel and freshen up, get a coffee, lie down and think about how to identify any Arrow Cross ties for the two women who clearly weren't telling him everything.

He had the feeling that it might be risky. Anyone with links to that kind of hated organisation would be protective … of themselves and each other. So, talking to one may well be just the same as talking to all of them: because they'd all hear about it. He'd talk it over with Jenna when she came back.

Then his phone rang and sent his thoughts in another direction.

*

Jenna cursed as she realised there wasn't a big crowd of people to get lost amongst in the metro foyer. She risked not stamping her ticket and ran onto the platform. There was a toilet just farther up, so she bolted to the ladies' and ran into a cubicle without stopping, bolting its door shut with a bang which shook the cubicle sides. There was a grunt from the next stall and what sounded like an angry expletive.

'Sorry.'

More expletives. Probably blaming her for being a tourist.

She listened for the boy. Nothing. He was probably wondering whether to come in. He might do that if he saw someone leave and no one else come in. Or he might call the police. She'd run away, hadn't she? He wouldn't have any doubt that she was doing something *wrong* ... so why wouldn't he call the cops?

She looked behind her. Her heart soared, then fell a little. There was a window, partly open. It was small but doable. It looked like there was some daylight behind it, probably up a chute: though the Metro wasn't at all deep, just one flight of stairs, they were still underground.

She stood on the toilet and pushed her rucksack through the opening ahead of her, then eased her body up towards it. That was when she heard the woman next door leave. She held her breath. The door to the toilets opened and a man's voice rang out, loudly, in Hungarian.

She pressed forwards in panic. Her hips stuck a little but she managed to wriggle through the frame. There was a short flat stretch of about four feet then the shaft she was in turned upwards to daylight. It was a struggle to get up round the bend but she was soon pushing her head through a flimsy wire grill which flopped out onto a bank of grass outside the station. She clawed at the grass as she struggled to her feet and sped away, thinking she'd work out where she was after she'd run at least a couple of blocks and having turned a good few corners.

Completely out of breath, she came to a halt at a tiny square off the side of a main street, with a couple of benches and a solitary tree, shorn of most of its summer leaves. She sat heavily down on the bench and let out a huge burst of air.

She seemed to have shaken him off. She had a book, which she needed to get checked out. But what was she going to tell Calum?

*

Calum wasn't in a position to be told anything. He'd shaved, then fallen asleep on the hotel bed for half an hour. When he woke up, he felt worse than he had before the nap. He flicked the coffee machine on and made himself a strong brew.

By the time late afternoon came around, he was feeling more awake but no further with a way to get at Aliz and Beata.

He texted Jenna looking for an early dinner arrangement and found her back at the hotel. They arranged to sit out under a gas heater at a small restaurant by the river they'd spotted on an earlier sortie.

They ordered bowls of goulash stew. Something to warm them through … despite the gas heaters, their legs were already feeling the chill of the early evening November air.

'You know, after what I saw on the riverside, those iron shoes of people pushed … murdered, into the Danube … well, I think anything Sarah did in her research that dug into that organisation could have triggered some strong feelings. These types of things have a way of lingering. Sometimes resurfacing. Like the neo-Nazi groups around Europe, you know?'

Jenna nodded. 'I do, I agree.'

'So, I guess my point is, we need to be careful, for our own sakes. We need to look for any links at all that Aliz Gal or Beata Sandor may have had with the old organisation or any new form of it. Maybe something you can help with? It might be just as useful as any more time spent on Sarah's notes. Anyway, how far did you get with those today? Must be pretty much done?'

'I didn't actually go through them, Cal. I did something else.'

As soon as she used his name's diminutive, he knew she was in an apologetic stance. He sat back and waited for it to pour out.

'There's good news and bad news.'

He laughed softly. 'Go on, then.'

'Well, the good news is … I got hold of a book that Eszter alluded to. What's more, I took it over to Eszter's place and we had a very quick scan of it.'

'Uh-uh.' She had his interest now.

'Err, well, the bad news is that it isn't the *right* book. It just had a similar title.'

'Great. Bit of a waste of a day then? And where did you get this book?'

'Well, Beata's house.' She gulped some air before the next admission. 'There's more bad news. I got caught taking it by a neighbour and so Beata may … *will* get to know about it.'

'Oh Jesus! OK, so what the hell do we do, Jen? He doesn't know who you are. Neither does Beata if he describes you. So odds are you won't get traced. But she'll hear about it when she gets home I guess, so then she'll be on high alert.'

'I don't know. Maybe we lie low for a day or so, carry on with quiet probing, you know …'

'Well, I think you'd better get on with it, then, don't you? Make up for the cock-up.'

*

Jenna left the restaurant in appropriately feigned disgrace. But she knew exactly what they should do next. Beata would find out about the house intrusion tonight for sure. That's if she hadn't been contacted already. So it was important that she acted straight away. If the book wasn't in Beata's house, then her office was the obvious alternative. She needed to get into the library early tonight.

# The night library

It wasn't too hard to pin down the location of Beata's office after she'd got a tourist pass for the library. Luckily it stayed open very late. She needed to find somewhere to hide for a while. The obvious place was the toilets and then to hope for a poor security sweep. She sat with her feet up on the toilet seat for quite a while after the scheduled closing time, but still, no one came and looked under cubicle doors or checked them. It was an hour before she felt brave enough to approach the office. Her legs were stiff with squatting by then.

She'd chosen toilets close by, so she had a clear line of sight of the office door from the toilets' entrance. The light that had filtered from under the office door earlier, was now extinguished. Time to move.

She expected to need her lock-picking skills for the office door but it was an old, simple lock of the sort you'd normally find on a garden shed … what's more, it was open.

She guessed they didn't get much call for security internally in a library after hours. But if there *was* something to find here, then wasn't Beata being slack?

She shut the door behind her. No light from anywhere, pitch black. She used the torch on her iPhone to scan the room. There were a number of open shelves behind Beata's desk, probably no more than fifty books amongst files and other office paraphernalia. She glanced at them quickly. No sight of the book she wanted.

She looked around again. She tried a chest of drawers. They were open, but no books in them. Same for the three small drawers under one side of the desk. On the left side of the office, there was a large cupboard set into the wall. She walked over and opened the wooden doors, to be met by the reflection of her torch.

Glass doors on an inset cabinet, holding a small number of books. Somehow, this had to be where Beata Sandor might keep something which was not in its normal place. She tried the lock and found it tricky to pick. In the end, she had to force it. Not ideal, but the means justify the ends and all that, and she'd already spotted the title she wanted behind the dazzling reflection of her flashlight.

She pushed the book inside her jacket and closed everything up. The cabinet door now had a broken lock, but it would only be discovered when someone tried to unlock it. She hoped that might not be for a while.

She moved to shut the office door behind her and then realised that she hadn't exactly planned her escape with any real thought. She'd probably have to spend the night in the loo and wait for library opening time.

Before she reached the door handle, though, she stopped dead in her tracks as she heard a noise behind her.

Her heart raced and she turned as slowly as she could. Nothing as far as she could see. The only area she hadn't explored were the full-length curtains at the windows. She felt like her heart couldn't beat any faster but she summoned the nerve to move towards them.

She got to within a foot and reached a hand towards the edge of one of the curtains, hoping to find nothing.

She didn't get the chance to see what was behind.

The curtain exploded at her, hitting her face and draping itself over her as she fell, barged over by a heavy force. A man, judging by the strength of the shove. She flailed backwards, the curtain falling away from her. She turned her head just in time to see a man's form disappearing through the office door, faintly illuminated by the iPhone torch which was pointing at the ceiling.

She flopped back on the floor. Not library security, for sure, they wouldn't hide behind a curtain, would they? So who? She sat up slowly, rubbing the back of her head. Whatever. She'd better get out of this room fast in case the man triggered some other action. She scrambled to her feet and headed back to the ladies.

\*

The following morning brought with it a ridiculous game of hide and seek with the early cleaners who, luckily for Jenna, had propped the door open with a bucket while they grabbed some other equipment to wash the floors down.

She managed to move around the building keeping ahead of them before the doors finally opened at nine. She left it a little longer before she dared to go down the stairs to the exit barriers and head off to Eszter's place to decipher her stolen tome.

Calum had left her a couple of texts since late the previous evening. She had made only one reply.

*I'm fine, don't worry, I'll catch you tomorrow morning probably.*

He'd no doubt wring his hands about *that* message too … but it seemed the best option in the circumstances.

\*

'So it's clear Marton Kovacs was implicated in murders? Including children?'

'I'm afraid it seems so. This book is clear about the report at the time. Of course, I can't verify the truth of it right now. Maybe I wouldn't be able to anyway. But that's what it says, yes.'

Jenna twisted her mouth into a grimace and scrunched her eyes up with the awfulness of what she'd just heard. The implications for Sarah were clear too, if she'd been sniffing anywhere near these events, accidentally or otherwise.

'Well, thanks. Really not what I wanted to hear, but it's useful to have the background … now Marton is dead, it is hard to see how to progress, though.'

'What will you do next?'

'Maybe we need to make the information available to the police.'

Eszter nodded. 'Yes, maybe. But whatever you do, please keep me informed, Jenna … I got to really like Sarah while we worked together, she is a nice girl. I'm so worried for her now.'

Jenna left her with a hug, and headed back to the hotel, wondering how the next conversation with Calum would go.

*

Calum was feeling pretty edgy about the conversation too. She could see it in his eyes as he opened the door to his room and let her in.

'Sorry I didn't answer your call last night. I was busy. But productive though. Very productive in fact.'

'Uhuh.' He rubbed his chin. She'd noticed he often did that when he was a bit stressed about something.

'Go on, then.'

'Well, I found the book. The missing text. What's more, I got Eszter to look at it and it confirms Marton Kovacs was in the group that killed a family one night in their beds. One of them was a child.'

She looked for his reaction, before deciding whether to offer anything about where she found the book and the encounter with a stranger.

'OK. I guess that tells us for certain what we suspected: that Sarah was delving into dangerous territory. But not much else, really. We have no clear link between Sarah's disappearance and this book. We just know Aliz Gal was probably lying about Sarah leaving the hotel after her second visit and that Beata Sandor wasn't actually as helpful as she seemed in the library. After that, we're stuck.'

'Yes. You're right. We need to find a firmer link between some or all of them to move on.'

'If there *is* one, Jen. This might be a red herring. But I think there's only one way to get closer to this.'

She looked at him expectantly. It felt like one of his light-bulb-on moments coming up.

'You should check into the Hotel Cristal. They don't know you there. Snoop around, see what you can find. Maybe get in Kovacs' room again. We don't know what there is to find until we try, eh?'

She was excited by his suggestion … it felt like the right step.

'Sure, sure. Today then?'

'No time like the present, as my mum used to say when she was trying to get me out of bed on Saturdays to clean my dad's car.'

She smiled and nodded. She remembered Calum's father. He'd been a bit of a grumpy man, always on the bottle. Luckily Calum hadn't turned out the same way.

'I'll go pack my things then and, well, report back in the morning?'

'Yeah. Do it. I'll see if I can get closer to Beata Sandor, now we know she likely isn't all that she appears to be. But not so fast, though. Firstly, easy on the room service there, it looks expensive. Secondly … where did you find the book?'

'The library. Beata Sandor's office.'

He nodded slowly. Knowingly.

'Of course. The obvious place after her house.'

His face spread into a wide grin. 'Meet any scary monsters while you were there?'

Jenna's face went from shock to wild amusement in a flash. She laughed out loud.

'You! It was you!'

'Great minds think alike. Only I thought faster. Shame it was only by a bit, else I'd have been gone before you got there. The toilets weren't too comfy though, were they?'

'Err?'

'Heard you go in. I was in the gents. At least I could take a pee when I needed.'

Calum dissolved into laughter and stood up. He grabbed a couple of plastic cups from the side of the bed.

'Think this calls for a Talisker toast.'

She smiled. 'But ... why didn't you find it?'

'Well, I could say you were a better looker than me ... true in one way,' he winked.

'But truth was, Jen, the scary monster arrived, so I hid.'

Jenna rolled her eyes.

'Anyway, there is some other news I hadn't mentioned. Peter Kovacs called me yesterday afternoon. Told me he'd heard I'd been asking at the hotel about Sarah McTeer. Told me that whatever I thought I knew, she must have left the Cristal after seeing his father and has never been seen since. What's more, since the family are in mourning over Marton's death, and busy with the funeral and estate, he asked that we respect their privacy now.'

'I see. So ... do you think that's genuine? Should we back off?'

'No. No, on both counts. I don't believe Sarah ever left that hotel. We need to stick to the plan. I'm on Beata Sandor's trail first and foremost.'

# Checking in

Jenna felt nervous as she arrived at the Hotel Cristal. True, no one should know her here, but there had been the cleaner who had seen her briefly when she'd first snooped in Marton Kovacs' room. She told herself that the cleaner probably saw hundreds of different people for fleeting moments each week and remembered only a tiny fraction of their faces, if that. On the other hand, she'd watched Jenna enter the room for a reason.

She was allocated room number 314 and filled out the reception paperwork with her head down and as little verbal or eye contact as she could manage without appearing odd. She didn't want them to remember her.

Once unpacked, she set out on what felt like a good first step. Scout the whole hotel. Just to see what was there.

Around an hour later, she returned to her room, none the wiser. The restaurant, lobby, small poorly-equipped gym, and reception didn't offer any surprises or clues.

Not that she'd expected that on first sight. But Marton Kovacs had lived here and had been the manager-owner. If he was in any way connected to Sarah's disappearance, she had to find out more about his daily routine and so on, especially around the time of her disappearance. Maybe reception could help in some way, but she'd need to be subtle.

As she walked back to her room from the lift, she peered ahead without purpose, to the end of the corridor. A strip of old-fashioned carpet lay between her and a tall sash window, letting in a grey light from the miserable day outside.

Something looked odd about the scene ahead of her. There was an imbalance of some sort. She felt it rather than saw it.

She took a step back and refocused her thoughts just on the corridor. Then she got it straight away. On her side of the corridor, there were more doors. On the left-hand side, there was more blank wall.

She walked up the corridor slowly, checking the room numbers as she went. Her room 314 was opposite 34. Her next-door neighbour, 313, was opposite 33. Room 312 and room 311 … were opposite a blank wall. She stared at it, then looked back down the corridor. Maybe room 33 was a suite or something. Odd that the number didn't start at 31 though? Or maybe it had been created after the hotel was built, to cater to more affluent guests. Something to check out maybe? And wouldn't a room 31 or 32 be under room 41, where she'd found the spy-hole?

She paced back to her room and sat down, looked at the phone next to her bed … and had an idea.

She checked out the room-to-room prefix from the small card next to the phone and dialled room 31. Just a continuous drone. Line unavailable. Same for 32. She paused and thought again. Then she dialled room 33. A phone rang. It rang for a long time but no one answered it. She shrugged her shoulders and flopped back down on the bed, wondering what her next move to get closer to Marton Kovacs' recent activities might be. And also to get into room 31.

As her thoughts drifted, they returned to the subject of Izabella. Now she'd moved hotels, she wasn't in her face anymore. That felt like a good thing … and also a bad thing.

She found herself missing the anticipation of seeing Izabella in the bar each day. She hadn't told her she was leaving either … well, why would she if she wasn't sure she wanted anything to come of it. The trouble was … perhaps she did. Maybe she'd pop over to the bar tonight and see if she was there. Then play it by ear. Whatever that meant.

# Calum digs deeper

It took Calum only a few hours of detailed web searching before he managed to track down two activist groups that had some sort of ideological link to Arrow Cross. Not in name, or by direct reference, but with strong sympathies to the sorts of regime and nationalist policies that Arrow Cross had adopted.

One of them had a more open presence on social media and he quickly tracked down some meetings that were held in the capital, and beyond. By a large slice of luck, there was one in Budapest tonight.

He wondered whether to go further with this. It was still a fairly weak route of investigation. Even if Beata Sandor or Aliz Gal had any kind of ties with these groups, it didn't mean it had anything to do with Sarah McTeer's disappearance. But it *might*, and *might* often had to be enough, especially when there was no other promising line of investigation at the moment.

There was a registration process to go through before the location of the meeting could be revealed. Even with using Google translate he was worried that his lack of Hungarian might trip him up or alert the organisers to his credibility. So he asked Eszter to help.

She wasn't too keen at first, but finally, she allowed him to use her address as a reference and guided him through the few questions. He had no intention of attending: his lack of Hungarian would mean he'd be rumbled immediately. The rest of the registration process was smooth and he was sent an address. Now he needed to find somewhere to watch proceedings from.

\*

Calum rented a small car, with tinted glass, so he could watch in relative obscurity. As the light faded before the appointed time, though, the darkened glass turned into a hindrance and he cursed himself for his faux cleverness.

The address was a little north of the city centre and he parked twenty yards away; it was a quiet street with a few cars parked along its length, so he didn't stand out. Around twenty minutes before the scheduled start, he saw the first person ring the bell and be admitted. He couldn't see inside the house from his line of sight and the door wasn't opened wide, so he wasn't able to make out the host.

He counted about twenty or so people filtering into the small house. He noticed there was quite a range of ages, though most were men. There were a couple of women: a youngish girl, dressed in casual clothes that thousands of her generation would wear and a much older … in fact elderly, woman, who was much more smartly dressed.

She stood out by virtue of her sartorial elegance. The thing was, though, he thought he recognised her. Even though he couldn't quite place her in the twilight and from a side angle, she was familiar to him.

She was the last person to be admitted. No Beata Sandor then. But that nagging familiarity made him stay and wait for the attendees to leave. He fired the ignition and moved the car ten yards closer. He needed a better look.

It was two long hours later, punctuated only by a risky stroll up the street to find a dark place to pee, that he saw figures emerge from the house. He snapped to attention and watched for the woman carefully. Most of those he'd seen enter, left. A few late stragglers dribbled out. Then, there she was.

As she passed over the threshold and moved a yard or so down the path, she turned to bid goodbye to someone. Her host maybe. It was another woman who started down the path to give her a brief hug and kiss on the cheek. As the elderly woman turned to the house, the light from within illuminated her face. Of course. It was Aliz Gal.

# A final plan

Peter awoke very early the next morning, finding himself unable to go back to sleep. He was filled with a strange mixture of nerves, excitement and a desire to plan it all out and get on with it. He'd always been a doer, eager to act. His grandmother had called him her clockwork boy, because, she said, he always seemed to be wound up and buzzing around. Right now, he needed the emotionless intent of a coil-sprung alligator.

He'd *tried,* hadn't he, to settle this more peacefully, he'd *asked* the investigator to back off? Then Aliz called him late last night to say she'd spotted the Scotsman having a pee near a house hosting a meeting she was attending. Saw him from an upstairs room when she'd opened a window to smoke a cigarette. Hardly a coincidence and it had really riled his temper to hear the investigator hadn't played ball with his request to stay away.

So it was back to plan A. He needed to murder them all.

He had a way in to the investigator. He'd been looking for the Scots girl, after all. So it would be perfectly reasonable to invite him back to the hotel, with the enticement of more information, wouldn't it?

As for Aliz, well, he had a little false drama worked out that would require her attention. It would cause her demise too. Which was a shame ... he quite liked her old-fashioned ways and stiffness. She reminded him of his mother in some ways. He pushed that thought firmly away.

He would leave it for a day, work his plans through. Then he'd deal with Aliz. Once he'd resolved the situation with her, he could concentrate on the last part of the jigsaw. She'd called him Neuman. It sounded German but Aliz had said he was Scottish. He found himself curiously interested in meeting him before he dealt with the threat this man posed.

Somehow, the idea of murdering all these people had started to seem less difficult to countenance than it had at first. He'd begun to immunise himself against the *wrongness* of it all. He knew there was a paradox here. He was a doctor, trained to keep people well. Yet here he was, contemplating ending lives, deliberately ... and in numbers.

Maybe it was all his experiences of people's illnesses ... and deaths ... over the years, which had lent him an emotional shield of some sort, a way to deal with human suffering day in, day out. One way or another, he had begun to deal with the prospect ahead of him. He couldn't see another way, without losing everything and everyone dear to him.

His heart knew very well, though, that he wouldn't be feeling quite so detached when the killing began.

# Peter entices Aliz

Peter called Aliz from his room.

'Hello, Peter. Do you need something? You can call the front desk if you do.'

Peter felt somewhat insulted by her brevity.

'Of course, Aliz. I know that. But this is not something for the front desk. It is about our secret. Our *secrets*.'

Now he had her full attention. 'What is it, Peter?'

He could hear her apprehension ... he had to deal with that. He needed her to be calm and do what he asked of her.

'Aliz, I heard some things going on in the room above me. Our secrets' room. It's odd.'

Aliz looked around the office. She was alone.

'What's odd? I'm surprised you can hear anything, the ceiling between your room and the one above is very heavily soundproofed.'

'Yes, but there's thumping, very low, like a big object being banged on the floor. But it's not random banging. They're banging SOS … you know, in Morse code. Three short, three long, three short pauses. It's faint … very faint, but I can hear it. Also, because of this, I went upstairs to check their return food tray. There was a note on it.'

Peter could almost hear her dread over the line.

'What did it say?'

'I'll read it out to you.'

*The new girl is sick. I think she keeps choking on food and her neck looks puffed up. She has a nose bleed too. She doesn't know why. She needs some help in case it is serious.'*

Peter paused and waited for Aliz to respond.

'I don't know, Peter. Do we let her suffer? I don't want to, but, well it depends on what you are going to do about them. I mean … is it worth helping her?'

Peter hadn't anticipated this line of thought.

'Ah, I don't know for sure yet Aliz. But I think maybe we should take a look at her. I mean, well, we don't want to limit our options if she is really ill, do we? Has there ever been a doctor called here to the first girl?'

'Once. Early on. We had to spike the girl's food to make her sleep so we could get in and look at her without her being aware of the doors blocked up behind the wardrobe. It was an old AC doctor who came. He was sympathetic to the cause, of course. But I think he's dead now.'

'OK. So maybe we should take a look. I just think we should check them both out. It might be useful to see them for a number of reasons. I want you to come and pretend to help examine the girl, she will be more relaxed with a woman present. I know you're thinking that I'm a doctor, but they don't know that, do they? Anyway, I think we can do this without drugging them this time, well, maybe a little to make them less likely to be aggressive. I'll give them some Lorazepam crushed up in their next meal. Then we can go in, OK?'

'Peter, no, I can't rush this.' He could hear the panic in her voice. 'I really don't think it's a good idea to go in there with two of them. Not at all. You must think what else to do. Anyway, I'm sorry I'm busy, I need to go now.'

She put the phone down on him. It wasn't something that happened to Peter very often and it pushed up his anger level. He knew he needed to stay calm … calm but insistent. Insistent in a *worried* way, so she would believe he was concerned about the girl. He'd need to try with Aliz again later, once she'd got used to the possibility of going into the room to investigate.

For now, he'd wait, and sharpen his hook for the Scotsman.

# Aliz agrees

After a few hours of reflection, Aliz didn't need any more persuading.

It was just an overwhelming resurgence of the guilt she'd held for so long. Guilt at the knowledge that an innocent girl had been imprisoned. Guilt that the reason for her imprisonment was all based on what Marton had done so many, many years ago. Now there was someone else suffering the same injustice ... and she was ill.

She knew she had to help, but she was nervous about how she could do that, really worried it would go wrong and that these young women would turn on her. She was no spring chicken, not strong physically. She needed to be sure she would be safe. The other thing, of course, was her *shame*. The shame she would feel when she looked in their eyes and they saw a *captor*. She didn't want to see how that looked. But she knew she needed to find a way to deal with it ... and the only way was to brave it through. She called Peter in his room. To her relief, it seemed he'd thought it through.

'Yes, but as soon as we can in case it is something serious, Aliz. So this evening when you go off shift?'

'OK. So seven, then?'

'Let's make it eight. Time for the Lorazepam to have worked from their evening meal at six. Come to my room Aliz, we'll go together from here.'

*

As Peter and Aliz walked out of the lift close to eight o'clock, Peter's brain was whirring at high speed. But it was operating in a different universe to Aliz's. One where he would eradicate this threat to his inheritance and family name forever. He felt almost positive; weird and nervous … but positive.

As they paced slowly up the carpet, a girl came out of a room ahead of them. She turned towards them, heading for the lift. Peter looked at her, then did a double-take. He'd seen her before, he couldn't pin where from, though. The girl dropped her face down and scurried past them. He thought about turning his head to look back at her … but didn't. He didn't want to be remembered himself, walking with Aliz towards this room at eight p.m. He pressed on and quickened his pace to the door of room 33. Aliz put on a spurt and caught up with him at the door. He moved his doctor's bag to his left hand and opened the door with a key.

He held the door open for Aliz. She looked at him, then stepped through the threshold.

The first thing Peter did was to push the heavy wardrobe that blocked the plastered up doors to room 31, away from the wall. It was on castors, just as well as it contained an immense amount of heavy, sound-deadening material, designed to make sure the boarded over doors weren't a noise weak spot. That was duplicated on the other side of the wall, as was the thin layer of plaster over the original double doors between the rooms.

Peter pulled a short metal pick out of his doctor's bag and started to pull the plaster away from the wall. It crumbled easily and it wasn't long before he had the old doors completely exposed. He reached for the handle and turned it. It moved with a rusty scrape in its barrel, the mechanism clogged with old plaster dust.

Peter held his breath.

# The other side ...

They'd been watching television at the specified time after
dinner and they'd both wolfed down the bowls of goulash, even
though for Katalin it had been a daily staple of her diet for the
past eight years. There had been some fruit too, just apples, but
the crisp, juicy tang of those little spheres had refreshed their
senses, like a walk in the fresh air changes your mood after a day
indoors. The coffee helped too. Katalin felt *very* relaxed tonight for
some reason. It was her favourite time, though it normally led to a
steep drop in her mood when the television slot ended. It was
then that she started to anticipate a long, image-less night, broken
only ten to twelve hours later when daylight allowed her to peer
out through the crack.

Since Sarah had arrived, though, things had been different.

Firstly, she didn't feel the need to peer out through the
crack each morning at daybreak. Just the distraction of Sarah
snoring or simply breathing made her smile; made her feel alive.
She had some company and her mood had changed a great deal.

The times watching the television had become more interesting. She talked to Sarah about what they were watching. They laughed together at sub-titled shows that were in English and she enjoyed telling her about those that were in Hungarian, which Sarah couldn't understand. After the first few days, they had even leant against each other on the bed as they relaxed into the viewing.

'Need a pee,' Sarah said, as the television switched itself off for the night.

As she walked towards the bathroom, she stopped, turned her head toward the wardrobe.

'Listen,' she said.

Katalin heard it, like a rustling sound coming from inside the wardrobe. She got up from the bed and walked over to the wardrobe, stooped down a little and listened.

'Yes, I hear. Maybe it's a mouse. I saw one before, a few months ago. Not in the wardrobe, by the hatch. It ran through to the bathroom and then I didn't see it again.'

Sarah was already on the bed, huddled up with her feet drawn in close, clutching her toes protectively in her hands.

'Just have a look then, Katalin. Quickly. Tell me when you've caught it, I can't stand mice.'

Katalin squeaked a clip of amusement as she saw her roommate looking terrified on the bed. She wondered if all Scottish people were soft like this.

'OK. I do this. Watch out, Sarah!'

She grabbed the wardrobe door handle and pulled it open with a theatrical flourish, watching for Sarah's reaction, grinning as her new friend scooted up the bed.

'Quick! Catch it! Before it escapes!'

Katalin turned to look inside. The floor of the wardrobe was littered with a pair of old shoes and some bits of toiletries she rarely used. There was no mouse that she could see. But the sound was still there ... intermittent but still there. It wasn't louder, though, and that seemed odd, something didn't compute between the sound and what she saw.

'Well?' Sarah asked.

'No mouse,' Katalin said. She stood back up and peered around the side of the wardrobe. She could see no little creature scratching away. But still, the noise persisted.

She went back to the open door and knelt down in front of it, leaning completely inside.

'Be careful!' Sarah squeaked.

The sound stopped. So did Katalin, dead still, listening for the creature's next move. Then there was a scraping sound ... then nothing again.

Katalin stopped her breathing, to listen harder.

An almighty bang thundered against the rear of the wardrobe. It felt like it had exploded and the impact threw her body sideways, banging her head. She rolled, reeling backwards into the room, to the sound of Sarah screaming.

# Visitors

Jenna took a glance back as she passed Peter in the corridor. What she saw intrigued her, especially after her discovery of the lack of a room numbered 31.

She'd been over to Calum's hotel to see if Izabella was around. She was disappointed to not find her behind the bar that evening, so she'd made her way back to the Hotel Cristal early.

The man and a woman stopped at room 33 and opened the door to it. The old woman she had seen down at reception, behind the desk. So she was staff, she supposed. The man, she'd seen him entering Marton Kovacs' room just after she'd scouted it: she recognised him by the scar down his left cheek.

She slipped through her own door and watched through the small gap she left. They just moved quickly into room 33 and shut the door.

She shut the door and sat down on the bed. She only took a moment, before paying a quick visit to the loo then re-entering the corridor. She looked both ways. No one around, as usual: it didn't seem too busy in the hotel right now.

She walked quietly up to room 33's threshold and listened carefully, stilling her breathing to get more chance of picking up whatever was going on inside the room.

There was nothing at first, then she heard something being dragged or moved, followed by a regular light tapping, like a hammer being struck gently on a picture hook: except it carried on for a few minutes.

Then some scraping before the tapping re-started but this time with a much louder, urgent tone. It lasted only thirty seconds or so until it finished with a splintering and a large crack and thump. Then she heard the screaming.

# Peter & Aliz enter room 31

Katalin dived sideways, in time for her torso to escape the falling piece of furniture, but it landed on her legs and made her scream out loudly. There was a fibrous snap as Sarah watched on in horror. She felt slow to react, as if in a dream.

Sarah screamed again, as she saw what lay beyond where the wardrobe had stood. A gaping hole the size of two doors, a massive bellow of dust puffing out from the space, and out of the centre two people stepped, looking like fantastical ashen dervishes.

A man and an old woman. Sarah recognised the woman from her first visit to see Marton Kovacs. She was the hotel manager. The woman hung back slightly, looking around and taking in the scene, her hand over her mouth. The man coughed the dust out a few times, then held a hand up.

'Sssh. Be quiet. We're not here to hurt you. Please be calm.'

Sarah was too shocked to move … but Katalin was in pain and moaned softly from the floor.

The man moved into the room and picked up the wardrobe, slowly, it was clearly heavy.

'Give me a hand.'

Sarah was woken from her inertia and stood up to grab a corner, watching the man closely. She also felt strangely slowed but managed to help push the furniture back up to the wall. Katalin moaned louder as the pressure was released from her leg.

'Let's have a look at your leg.'

Katalin looked wide-eyed at the man as he knelt down to her: but he appeared to be trying to help.

'It's OK, I'm a doctor. Aliz, pass my bag please.'

The old woman passed his bag over and opened it for him. He felt Katalin's leg. She shouted out as he pressed it.

'Broken maybe, I can't be sure. I'll give you a painkiller before we do anything else, OK?'

She nodded.

He took a phial from his bag, sucked the contents into a syringe, then plunged the needle into Katalin with barely a pause. Katalin had little chance to object.

'Lay still … pass me a pillow someone.'

Sarah grabbed a pillow from the bed and handed it to him. He looked at her. There was no warmth in his eyes, just the cold reflection of someone going through a process. Whether that was him just treating his patient or something else, she wasn't sure, but the mechanicality of it spooked her.

The man stood up. He addressed them all, in a vague sort of way, head bowed, avoiding eye contact.

'OK, that should help. I'll give this thirty minutes and see how the leg changes. If it swells a lot, we may have to think about an X-ray.'

'What are you doing here? Who are you?' Sarah ventured, with a great degree of nervousness. 'Can we get out of here now?'

'Well, I need to get something else to help your friend, I'll be back in a moment. We can talk about that then. I'll be two minutes.'

He turned and walked back to the doors. As he passed through the doorframe, the old woman shouted after him, 'So shall I ask the other girl what her problems are?'

'Yes, why don't you examine her while I'm outside the room, Aliz?'

The word *examine* registered sharply with Sarah and she leapt towards the man as the door was closing.

'What do you mean? Examine?'

He didn't answer. He pushed the doors shut as she thought about resisting and then it was too late. The scrape of the wardrobe on the far side of the doors as it was moved back into place didn't sound very encouraging.

The old woman dashed to the doors and hammered on them.

'Peter, what are you doing? Open the doors please!'

There was no reply. She hammered again, less aggressively this time. Another plea. Another round of banging. Then an exhausted silence.

'Damn, damn ... damn that man.' The old woman looked at Sarah, 'So, I suppose you haven't been sick or had any bleeding, Sarah?'

'What? No ... what do you mean?'

The woman looked pitiful. 'Never mind. I think we are now three in here.' She sat down on a chair opposite the bed and started to cry.

# Jenna listens in

Jenna kept listening at the door of room 33. After the screams, it went very quiet for a while, there were some muted voices if she strained to hear, but little other noise. Then there was a cacophony of door slamming, heavy scraping, banging and yelling, before she heard footsteps approach the room door from the inside.

She stepped away sharply and skipped back to her room, just in time to close the door to a thread and observe the man come out. Only this time without the woman from reception.

She waited until he'd called the lift and disappeared before listening again at the door. She couldn't hear anything.

She sat back down in her room and thought about the facts. Screams … so some fear. Two in and one out … might not be anything for her to be concerned with. But she could ask for the woman at the desk and check that out tomorrow. For now, sitting watching the door of room 33 wasn't a particularly appealing exercise.

She decided to go to the bar at Calum's hotel.

*

Peter Kovacs was feeling smug about how easy that capture had been. Nothing to it, though he had to admit the girl being injured took a lot of pressure off him, made his withdrawal from the room a bit easier to pass off as natural.

But the harder bit was yet to come. To get the damned investigator in there with them. Now he had three of them there, he needed to move fast. Aliz would be missed very soon and he didn't fancy the idea of feeding the three of them alone. Ideally, they needed to be alive when Neuman was brought in, so he'd better spring that particular trap now.

# Making moves

Jenna was relaxing with her third gin and tonic. Time off, a bit of downtime with Facebook and Snapchat. She'd had a brief catch up with Calum, but now he was holed up in his room, pleading he wanted a night in to watch the football on the television. Sometimes that was a cover for him doing something he didn't want her involved in. Whatever. It suited her tonight, despite her annoyance when he did that. She couldn't quite get over to him her concern over rooms 33 and 31. Sometimes he listened better in the mornings.

Izabella was serving again … and paying her a lot of attention as usual. She knew that was the reason she was sat in the bar … and why she was sipping slowly and sticking around, despite her Facebook feed having been read three times over.

It had crept towards midnight slowly and Jenna had begun to wonder why she was there when Izabella marched over with some purpose.

'We are closing now as there are no more guests in the bar … unless you want another?' She smiled with intent.

Jenna was stuck for what to say, but Izabella helped her out.

'Or if you do want another, we could take a bottle of wine … to your room?'

Jenna shrank at the boldness but suddenly felt excited. No mistaking this … she'd been thinking of Izabella a lot since they first exchanged those lingering glances. She'd wanted her to say something like this, she hadn't had the nerve herself somehow. Maybe because of Greg, whatever … it was hard to do. Now, something might happen and the thought of it was making Jenna buzz.

'OK. Yep, that would be nice. But I'm at the Hotel Cristal now. Room 314. It's not far … a ten-minute walk?'

She said it with her eyes partially averted, as if to not quite take responsibility for the decision. She kicked herself for such a boring response.

'Nice. Yes, I think it will be nice, Jenna.' She laughed, gaily and swept up Jenna's empty glass. 'Fifteen minutes, OK? And white is OK?'

'Great. Yes, white is good.'

'You go back. I'll come to your room.'

Funny how fifteen minutes can be very short or very long depending on your circumstances. Jenna felt like she aged a year in the next ten minutes. When Izabella brought the bottle up to her room and said "Here I am", it released her from a hell in which her rear was stuck immovably to her bed and her heartrate was making a pounding loud thump in her head.

Jenna showed her in. They both came into the centre of the room, starting to giggle with nerves.

There was a bed and a chair. Jenna took the chair out of indecision. Izabella stopped and looked at her, then unscrewed the wine bottle top. She looked around for glasses …

'In the bathroom, some glasses there.'

Izabella nodded and went to get them. She returned with the glasses full and the bottle half drained.

'Cheers. That's what you say, eh? In Scotland?'

'Yes, it is.'

Izabella made a gesture with her mouth, a signal of a proposition.

'Want some coke?'

'Coke? We're having wine, aren't we … oh, err no, I don't, thanks.'

'OK, that's cool.'

Jenna was a bit disappointed by that. She didn't approve of hard drugs. She'd also became vaguely aware that, as far as she could recall, she'd not mentioned she was Scottish. But maybe everyone could tell a Scottish accent, not just Brits. She'd noticed that Izabella had turned the dimmer switch down a notch or two as she came out of the bathroom … and there was a nice scent about her. She seemed to have freshened up before she came over to the hotel. Jenna sipped her wine slowly, as she chatted to Izabella, who was perched predator-like on the edge of the bed. She kept leaning sharply towards Jenna as she spoke, smiling and laughing.

Then the conversation stopped. One of those awkward silences, when you could try to find something else to say … or just go physical.

Izabella made her choice and leaned forward, sliding her open palm warmly down Jenna's forearm. It sent tingles of excitement into Jenna. She looked down at the sliding hand then up at Izabella's eyes. They were large, dark brown … her pupils dilated with anticipation.

Jenna's phone rang.

Gregor.

It could have been one of those phone calls you click off at a tricky moment. But this time, it triggered guilt in Jenna. She couldn't not answer it. So she did.

'Hey.'

'Hey, you too.'

Izabella stood up and shrugged her shoulders, arms and palms outstretched.

'Just a min, Greg.'

She flattened her hand over the phone's mouthpiece. 'Sorry, Izabella. I need to talk to my friend, sorry.'

Izabella nodded … but stayed put.

Jenna pressed her lips together, a feeling of regret spreading through her. But it was an excuse to delay what was to happen with Izabella, an excuse she suddenly found herself wanting to take. She let her hand fall from the phone.

'Sorry, Greg. Just talking to someone. How are you … ?'

It was twenty minutes of small talk, punctuated with Greg's good humour that finally started to send her to sleep. She was tired and struggled to concentrate on not giving him any wrong signals. But the guilt was still there and she couldn't understand why.

Fifteen minutes in, Izabella's face clouded fast and she harrumphed softly around the bed for a moment before grabbing her handbag and display-marching out of the room. Over her shoulder … 'OK, OK, another day then.'

Jenna looked up at her and tightened her eyes and mouth into a hurt-plead-sorry message.

'Who was that, Jen?'

'Someone in the bar, saying goodnight to someone. I'm a bit tired myself to be honest.'

Greg didn't take the hint. He never was very good at that. Eventually, she said goodnight rather arbitrarily and went to the bathroom, throwing the rest of the wine down the sink. She fell asleep slowly, thinking all sorts of erotic things, involving a twisting pattern of male and female lovers. She knew she was confused, but this was silly.

*

Izabella went home to her apartment. Now she was worried. Worried that the man who was paying her would start to get impatient. She could try again the same way maybe. But it was finding the opportunity. It wasn't always the case she came into the bar in the evening. The pressure wasn't nice, but she needed the money. Perhaps she had to find another way. Spiking her drink was a simple way to get her compliant. Then she could do the rest easily. She could be more direct, of course, but she wasn't sure her own strength was enough if the girl was fully alert. But maybe she'd need to risk it if she couldn't snare her into a room again. She texted the man, telling him she was close. That it would be soon.

# A headache

Jenna's alarm repeated itself at least half a dozen times before it developed into a long persistent tone that finally woke her up. She raised her head a tad from the pillow to peer at the time and found her head weighed about the same as a small car.

She rolled onto her back and exhaled through slack lips. She felt nauseous and tried to count how many drinks she'd had the night before. Two, three … maybe four gin & tonics? She didn't have much wine before Greg rang and Izabella left. She'd thrown the rest away. But right now it felt like she'd had the whole bottle.

It was late, there were only twenty minutes left before breakfast closed in Calum's hotel, so she turned and launched herself into a sitting position on the edge of her bed. That just made it worse and a sudden urge to vomit sent her careering into the bathroom.

Just bile. She needed some food probably. She threw some water over her face, did the minimum to make herself presentable and staggered into the lift, ready for a bracing walk.

Calum was waiting in the breakfast room of his hotel, with a cup of coffee and his plate showing the evidence of a devoured hot grill platter.

'Late night or lazy morning?'

She sat down and glared wearily at him.

'Sorry. I feel really bad this morning, didn't have a lot to drink but … God I feel crap. Maybe the food, I don't know.'

'Well, your "not a lot" might be another person's "loads"?'

'Get lost,' she snapped back.

She thought better of that straight away. 'Sorry, Calum, sorry, I really do feel rubbish. I need some food.'

'Leave it to me,' he said, heading over to the buffet and returning a minute later with sausage and eggs. He poured her a coffee and sat back.

'Come on, enjoy, get some calories into to you.'

The smells of the hot food didn't turn her off like food poisoning would normally do. She ate it slowly, but with increasing relish.

'So, while you're eating. I cased a neo-Arrow Cross meet last night. North of here. The thing is … I saw Aliz Gal leave the place. So that's concerning … especially as she lied about the taxi from the hotel. I'd say that implicates her 70-80% in some way that we don't understand yet.'

Jenna nodded. She was chewing a bite of sausage and looking at the various bits of paper Calum had by his place setting: he'd evidently been scribbling notes whilst waiting for her to appear. One scrap of paper had caught her eye.

'Where'd you say the meeting was?'

'At a house, up near the end of the tram line. Not far from Ujpest's stadium as it happens.'

'Ujpest?'

'Sorry. The football club. Keep forgetting you're not a believer.' He winked.

'Never mind that … is this it?'

She'd grabbed the scrap of paper from his pile of papers.

'What? The meeting house? Yes.'

Jenna grimaced.

'This is Beata Sandor's address.'

Calum swallowed his mouthful of coffee with a little gasp.

'Wow. Well, that bumps the percentages up, eh? Now you mention that, there *was* a woman saying goodbye to Aliz after the meeting, but I didn't get to see her face. I guess that was her.

So … they are both probably sympathetic to Arrow Cross. Aliz lied about the taxi. Beata tried to "help" Sarah's research … but what were her real motives? And then Sarah disappears, with her last known sighting at the hotel room of an ex-Arrow Cross party member. An ex-member who is now dead.'

Jenna was silently agreeing, but struggling to overcome her body state. Analytical thinking wasn't top of her skills list right now.

'Next move?'

'Your move, Calum. I'm too tired to think.'

'OK. We have a choice now. This is something we could go to the police with. Not hard evidence … but enough to make them think and look into it, I reckon.'

'Or?'

'Or … follow it up ourselves. Or both. But what our next steps might be, I'm not sure. Beata is sure to be on high alert due to the book theft. Aliz knows I'm suspicious of her story. They *know* each other so may have swapped these pieces of information. They'll certainly have their radar out on me, for sure.'

318

'Jenna to the rescue again, then?' Her thought processes weren't *that* slow. 'But … which option?'

Calum settled back in his chair, looked like he was deliberating.

'Get over your headache this morning. I'll talk to the Budapest police. If I can. Maybe decide what we do depending on my reception there.'

# Mars bars

Burton's next message was what he wanted to hear. It was a difficult delivery. After the last drone was spotted by the warders, he'd gone to considerable lengths to ensure that the risk of them being in the delivery area was minimal. He'd ensured some distractions and that any unintended line of sight would be poor anyway. It worked. He got the drop at the expected time. There was a pre-planned, seemingly random, pattern of delivery that *he* knew, but that would be extremely hard for the prison staff to guess, except from observation over a very long period.

He unrolled the paper note.

*We've made good progress. The mother took our bribe. Turned out she was pretty skint, husband cleaned her out a few years ago, so not a hard sell. N took the case and the girl's joined him in Budapest. We've some unusual bait for her there … we think we found a little weak spot to try. It's getting her attention, which makes the job easier. So much neater outside the U.K., much harder to link us to it.*

*Either way, I'll update when all done. You want N too? It will be easy to add him now he's there. For a price of course. Discount for the second one. Not quite BOGOF, but another 50? Let me know if you do. Just text '50', as they say. Hehe. :)*

Burton looked at the note with a wry smile. Better news. It was costing him, costing him more than he'd planned, but it would be worth it to see Neuman's grief. It was that particular thought that made him decide not to text his man for the optional extra. He would enjoy Neuman's agony, just like he'd suffered himself with Glenda's death. It was all Neuman and Strick's fault.

The bonus items in the delivery bag this week were a new SIM card and two king-size Mars bars. He could call his contact now to understand the attempt timing, then tip off D.I. Gregg a little too late. He grinned, wider than he had for some time.

He unwrapped one of the Mars bars and took a large bite, letting the melting chocolate fill his mouth.

# The police palace

Calum wasn't expecting the meeting with the Budapest police to go particularly smoothly and was spot on with that instinct. He'd made an appointment to see an officer from the Redorseg at the police headquarters in Budapest ... known locally as the "police palace". Booking the appointment had been a labour and he got the distinct impression that private investigator wasn't a favoured profession in this country.

He jumped off the tram across the street from the headquarters, looked up at the massive steel-blue tinted-glass edifice and decided its local title had been badly assigned. Not the elegant old building he'd been expecting. He entered the lobby and asked for detective Nagy.

The meeting was even more disappointing.

He was met by the detective at the lobby security gate and escorted to a small office on the ground floor. His host was a small, weedy and very pale man, who looked like he needed to get out from behind his desk more often.

'So, you want to tell me something?' No welcome, no handshake, no offer of a drink. Just a transaction. Carried out with an impassive stare from a man who looked distinctly uninterested.

'Well, yes I do. I know you've investigated the case of Sarah McTeer, and I've some more information. I'm helping her mother look for her. So, if it helps you, then great … and if you want me to work alongside you so we don't trip each other up, that will be fine too.'

Nagy nodded, indicating he should carry on.

Calum went through the Beata Sandor-Aliz Gal-Arrow Cross-Marton Kovacs links as he saw them. He described Beata and Aliz's lack of honesty. He expected at least some raised eyebrows. But he got no visible reaction at all. Not a scrap. Nagy appeared to be making *some* notes, but he was either very good at shorthand or he was just box-ticking.

He was made to feel like a foreigner. He was, of course, but it was the feeling that because of that, his information was somehow less pertinent, that really hacked him off. The interchange was stilted due to the Hungarian officer's poor command of English and getting through the detail that Calum wanted to share took a painfully long time.

'OK. Thank you, Mr … err, Neuman. Thank you for telling the police this. I will consider this information. Now I must go, thank you.'

*Yeah, thanks for nothing, you won't be doing anything with that, will you?*

They exchanged contact details … and that was pretty much that. He left, expecting no further interaction, whether or not the police followed up the lead. A request for him to be kept informed by the investigating team in case of any progress was met with a very grudging assent. Maybe they had other priorities: that was the best spin he could put on the whole process.

The one positive thing that came out of it, was that it clarified his own position. He needed to get to the bottom of the whole affair himself. He couldn't rely on any help from the police. At all.

In the event, help eventually came from an unexpected source.

\*

Back at his hotel, Calum rang Jenna's room at the Cristal. 'How's the head?'

'It's better laid flat. But go on, what did the police say?'

'Not a lot. Think we're on our own, I'd say, so it's time for us to really get our thinking caps on. If you can put yours on lying down?'

Jenna groaned at his joke. 'I'll be down in Cafe Zanta, it's a couple of hundred yards from your hotel, in fifteen minutes, OK?'

'Hang on, whereabouts is it?'

'I think the phrase is "Google it".'

'Humph. OK.'

\*

'So look, Jen, the way I see it is this. No way are Gal or Sandor going to tell us any more than they have *if* they're covering something up. I think they are, but how do we uncover it? If we confront them, they'll lie again. Even if we get them rattled, there's little we can do unless they come completely clean: I suspect that isn't going to happen, it feels there are deeper interests at work here. This Arrow Cross thing must drive strong feelings either way. So …'

'Uhuh?'

'What we really need are witnesses. Witnesses to what happened to Sarah after she went into Marton's room, what happened when she came out of it. Assuming she did.'

'Well, she's not there now, I can vouch for that, I searched the room so she did come out one way or the other.'

'True. So who could have seen her leave?'

'The staff, of course. Well, at least they're the prime candidates.'

'Exactly, Jen. We need to talk to them. The ones that were there that day. And maybe the days after.'

'Well, Aliz Gal wasn't too friendly last time out, was she? How are we going to get the staffing list?'

'Needs to be me, Jen. I'll at least *try* to persuade her. I don't want to break your cover at the moment. You can be more useful observing unnoticed. I'll get to her first thing in the morning.'

'Yep, sounds right to start with. Want me to do anything?'

'No just go back to your room, but keep browsing the hotel, see what might take your interest. Keep sniffing around room 33 as well. You may see me in an hour or two. I might try and look around and talk to staff myself if Ms Gal isn't around in the evening. She can't be there all the time, can she?'

'I guess not. She was there later last night though, it was around eight I saw her with Peter Kovacs,' she reminded him.

'True. I'll be careful. Anyway, right now, I'm hungry. And I've run out of the pork pies I brought from home. So some late lunch here: want to stay for some?'

'Ha. If it's not work, it's eating, with you. Don't you ever think of anything else?'

'That would be too much information for you, Jen.'

Jenna blushed and buried her face in a handily placed menu.

# Nagy deliberates

Officer Ervin Nagy flumped down on the sofa in his family's two-bedroomed apartment and switched on the television. Ferencvarosi were playing tonight and he couldn't get to the game in time, so he thought he might watch some of it on the screen. Assuming they weren't 0-3 down by then, in which case he might help his son with some maths problems he had. He'd always been good at maths. Maybe that's why he was good at solving crimes. The analytical side of him seemed to excel. Not so good with people, maybe, but sifting through lots of information and structuring it, together with his thoughts on how to use it, that was his forte.

So, as he watched the first passage of play, his mind rumbled over what the Englishman ... no, Scotsman had told him.

It sort of matched with what he already had, but extended it to make a more complete picture. Not a whole one by any means, not one with which he could involve a prosecutor and make an arrest. But ... enough to dig deeper.

What's more, he believed the man. Just something in his eyes and manner: the sort of instant sizing up of a person you did as a police officer. They taught you that stuff in the Budapest police college.

He didn't want to encourage him, though, to think he could work directly with him. His management would frown on that. Too proud of their own ability to solve everything, without much help from the underworld or anyone else. But he could try to take it a bit further himself and maybe only go back to the Scotsman if he really needed to.

His instinct was to home in on Aliz Gal. She worked at the hotel, had for a long while as he recalled. If she'd lied about a taxi taking Sarah McTeer from the hotel after meeting Kovacs, well, that needed harder questioning. He'd start with her and maybe extend it to interview the rest of the staff that were there that day, to see who or what could corroborate her story. He needed to put her under pressure too, to read her eyes when she was stressed. He'd do it tomorrow.

'Hey, Dad, they're losing. Again.'

He turned his head and looked at his son. 'You're supposed to be doing homework, Tamas. No sneaking in here to watch the game!'

Tamas pouted at him. 'I bet your dad let you watch sometimes.'

'We didn't have a television, Tamas. So no, he didn't. But you can watch the rest of the first half, then we look at those maths problems together, OK?'

'Deal, Dad.'

Tamas dropped down on the sofa by his father and slapped him on the leg.

'We just need to score now!'

His father nodded and smiled. 'Let's hope we can Tamas.'

Nagy was wondering what he'd do if the match was tense and he wanted to watch the second-half himself.

*

Officer Nagy had a mildly fuzzy head the next morning as he briefed his junior detective on the plan for the day. Tamas had become too good at manipulating him over the football and three beers and a second-half later he'd had to ditch the idea of maths homework. Next time he'd insist they did that first.

'Get a car, we'll go first thing, maybe talk to the staff after interviewing Gal, if we feel the need. Let's go, Jan.'

The two officers arrived at the Hotel Cristal thirty minutes later, the short journey drawn out by the heavy morning traffic.

Nagy spoke to the single duty receptionist. The response from the girl was rather surprising.

'What do you mean you don't know where she is?'

'Sorry, officer, but just that. Someone in the office rang her home phone this morning and she has also had a mobile phone recently but no reply from that either. She hasn't been seen since yesterday and she hasn't been in touch with us. She's normally in work by eight-thirty.'

Nagy checked his watch. It was nearly ten-thirty. He thought for a moment.

'At what time did she leave yesterday?'

'I'm afraid I can't be sure, I was on duty, but I left at six p.m. and didn't see Miss Gal when I left. She usually leaves about then too if there's nothing major happening. Maybe someone else will know.'

'So you didn't see her leave before six?'

'No.'

'And you were on the desk all the time till six?'

'Yes, yes I was. I would normally see her go past if she left before me, I mean it's a small lobby and she usually goes out through this reception, from the office behind.'

Nagy nodded.

'So who is managing the hotel if she isn't here?'

'Well, there is normally a duty manager. Miss Gal is the manager, of course, but she isn't here all the time. But we don't have one right now, no one has arranged it, I think.'

'But who would? I mean who's in charge?'

The girl paused for a moment.

'I suppose Mr Kovacs was, but now he's dead. So, his son is, I suppose, though we haven't seen much of him.'

'Where does he live?'

'I think normally in Bucharest, but now he is living here since his father died.'

'Here, in Budapest?'

'No … well, yes I mean, in Budapest. But also here, in the hotel.'

Nagy glanced at his junior, Jan.

'I think we need to see Mr Kovacs. Can you call his room and ask him to come down please?'

\*

Peter Kovacs sat opposite the two detectives in the lobby area, in a corner away from the rest of the armchairs that the guests used. He joined his hands and laid his forearms across his knees as he leant forward over the low coffee table that sat between them. It helped stop them trembling.

He'd already been spooked by the phone call to his room, asking him to meet two police officers. Now they were asking him difficult questions.

'So, in the absence of any first-hand knowledge by yourself of the events around Miss McTeer's disappearance and the fact this Miss Gal is apparently temporarily missing … then I think we need a list of all staff that were on duty the day Miss McTeer supposedly left here in a taxi, so we can interview them. Can you arrange that for us now please, Mr Kovacs?'

'Err, well, I think so … yes, I suppose there will be rotas, I hope they are kept. Of course, I didn't run the hotel, I've been thrown into this by my father's death. So, please be patient, but I will try to find out what you need.'

'OK. We understand. We'll stay here until you see what you have. In the meantime … where can we get a coffee please?'

Peter looked relieved there was something easy he could do to please his interrogators.

'I'll have some brought over to you. I'll try to be back shortly, officers.' He walked over to the reception desk.

Nagy turned to Jan. 'Eh?'

'Looks nervous. We should check him out a *lot* more.'

'That's what I thought.'

*

Peter did manage to find the staffing list for the day in question. He took a look down it, whilst still in the reception back office. He didn't recognise all the names yet, but it looked a normal staffing day and there was no one on the list he would have concerns about on the face of it. So he took it back to the officers, expecting it would provide a dead end for them.

He handed them the list. The older one took it and scanned down it. Thirty or so names.

'OK. We'll make a start today. Please arrange for all staff who are in today to see us, we will be here, it would be good if you can arrange them to arrive to sit here and talk with us one by one. Any not in today, we will return tomorrow morning to see them all. They must be here, no question. OK?'

Peter didn't think there was a choice of responses available to him. He started the process of gathering staff together to see the detectives and had one of the front desk team finish the arrangements. He decided to go back to his room and keep well away from it all. He wasn't here at the time, after all, so there was nothing he'd be able to add.

# Salad days

The afternoon they decided to re-scout the Hotel Cristal proved fruitless for both Jenna and Calum. Jenna tried to casually engage a couple of cleaning staff in a conversation about Sarah's disappearance but found their lack of English language skills to be a barrier. She concluded if Calum succeeded in being allowed to interview any staff, for many he would need an interpreter.

Calum wasn't any more successful either, especially as he tried to avoid being in direct view of the reception desk. Funnily enough, he didn't spot Aliz Gal all day.

So they resorted to plan B and turned up at the Cristal together the following morning. They delayed the visit until after the morning checkout rush, hoping to get some time with Aliz. They decided Jenna would hang back at first until there seemed a reason to break her cover.

Once at the desk, Calum was met with some surprising news.

'What do you mean you don't know when she will be here?'

'I'm afraid I can't tell you more sir. There's a detective here interviewing people and he asked me the same, maybe he will find out?'

Calum flashed a concerned glance behind him, in the general direction of Jenna, who was sat on a sofa in the lobby.

'Where is he?'

'On the back side of the lobby, over there, round the corner. But I think Mr Kovacs, the new owner, might be with him, so perhaps he will not be free.'

'OK, thanks.'

He turned and walked across the lobby. Jenna started to walk vaguely alongside him as he got clear of the reception desk. As they reached the left turn into the far corner, Calum pulled Jenna by the arm.

'A second.'

Calum took a couple more steps forward and peered into the alcove, where he saw a pair of detectives talking to a young girl. Presumably, a member of the domestic staff judging by her overall.

He knew they were definitely detectives because he recognised one of them. The surly officer Nagy was, rather unbelievably, right there. The detective looked up, saw him, then turned his attention back to the girl without any discernible change in his face. Calum was sure he'd have been recognised, though. He took a couple of paces back and dragged Jenna away from the area.

'So the detective I thought was disinterested: seems he likes to use other people's information and not give them any credit.'

'Eh?'

'He's round there talking to one of the staff. Like we want to. So he's a step ahead, which I don't mind, assuming he helps find Sarah and lets us or her mother know.'

'Shall we wait and talk to him?'

'Yes. Let's grab a coffee and wait.'

\*

Peter Kovacs was becoming increasingly on edge. He saw the couple drinking coffee in the lounge on his way to reception as he popped out to talk to a member of the front desk staff. The girl he knew he'd seen before in the hotel. And the man who, on questioning the reception staff, turned out to be the private investigator. Neuman. And so, unless they were having a casual chat, they must know each other.

He looked at the current list of guests and homed in on any English sounding names. He soon found a possible match for the girl: British passport. They didn't get many British guests in this hotel, according to his father. The new addition to room 31 was Scottish, wasn't she? His mind jumped to Neuman and he searched for him on the internet. As soon as he saw the entry for Calum Neuman, private investigator, operating from a town in Scotland he'd never heard of, he realised the girl he'd seen in the hotel must be linked to Neuman: she *had* to be helping him. What the hell was he going to do about *her*?

His troubled mind was fearing the worst of everything now. He could only see this as a threat. A big threat. He made his excuses with a conversation at the front desk and went up to his room.

It was early … too early, but he poured himself a whisky. He sank a large slug before exhaling some tension and dropping into an armchair. He felt like he might sink completely through the bottom of it if he didn't conclude all of this.

He was really feeling the pressure now. He knew it and he reached for his bag. Beta-blockers would smooth this excited dizziness, help his heart tick along steadily. He popped a tab of propranolol and washed it down with another sip of whisky. He knew he had to stay calm. The worst was to come.

*

Calum and Jenna had two rounds of coffee, then decided they'd start to float from their seats if they had any more. The detectives were still interviewing a steady stream of staff, with no obvious end in sight, so they walked down the street to a cafe and bought themselves an early lunch.

'I need a salad,' Calum said, 'I know it's not warm outside, in fact it's downright chilly, but I need a salad. Too many carbs and fats, eating at the hotel.'

'For once I agree with you, Calum. I'll do the same. Did you finish all the pork pies you brought with you?'

'Eh? I didn't bring many this time.'

'Oh yeah. And what about the *mini*-pork pies?'

He smiled. 'Well, they're a different thing, of course. Yeah, all four gone. Just as well.'

He tapped his Apple watch and checked his heart alerts. All good. A little reassurance maybe. He knew that wasn't entirely true, of course … but it was a positive of sorts. Good enough for today.

The waitress bought them chicken paprika sliced on a bed of salad. Calum picked up his fork with a distinct lack of interest.

Some people passing by the large cafe window caught Jenna's attention. 'Isn't that the pair of detectives?'

Calum looked sharply out of the window. 'Yes, it is.'

He stood up and moved towards the door. 'You stay here, guard the salads. They're valuable. Won't be long.' With a wink, he was out onto the street and scrambling to catch up with the two men.

'Detective!'

Nagy and his junior wheeled round in perfect unison, a well-drilled reaction to someone approaching them from behind.

'Ah. Mr Neuman, I think.' Nagy's face was as impassive as when he'd first met him.

'Yes, sir. It is. And we were in the hotel just now, we saw you interviewing some staff. We were hoping to do the same. Especially Aliz Gal. Did you track her down today?'

Nagy stared at him, obviously deciding what to share.

'Ms Gal seems not to be in work. No one has heard from her today, even though she was due in. The rest of the staff … well, not so much. Except for maybe one cleaner. She thought she may have heard some kind of screaming that day, the day Miss McTeer supposedly left the hotel in a taxi. But, well, she was quite vague.'

Calum cocked his head into a quizzical pose.

'You'll follow it up though, right?'

'Yes, of course. We need to ask Ms Gal about it. Peter Kovacs wasn't living here then. So it's a thin lead but … yes, of course, we will check it out.'

'Uhuh, so, what was the name of the cleaner? Maybe we can try to talk to her too, you know, try a different set of questions?'

Nagy considered for a moment.

'No, I'm sorry I can't do that. This is a police investigation. But if I need your help, Mr Neuman, I will call you. Sorry, but we have another appointment.'

'OK. Thanks then.'

Nagy turned on his heel, his junior shadowing his movement perfectly. His figure skating partner. They were gone.

Calum returned to his appointment with a salad. Jenna had eaten half of hers.

'Any luck Calum-O?'

'Not much. They don't know where Aliz Gal is. One cleaner mentioned something about hearing some screams that day. Nothing else … well, nothing they wanted to share anyway.'

'A cleaner?'

'Yeah, they didn't seem too concerned about a quick follow-up. Maybe I'm misreading them, it's hard to tell behind those blank faces.'

'Well, we know one cleaner there. The one you bribed. Maybe you could talk to her again? See if she knows which cleaner it was?'

'Yep, good thinking, I should. I'll try and see if she leaves the hotel later … sounds like another afternoon drinking tea, looking out of a cafe window, waiting for an unknown moment that you miss when you finally give in and go to the loo.'

'Ha, you chose this job. I'll sit with you awhile.'

'No need, go shop. Buy Greg something.'

That was a barb too far. She stood up.

'Thanks for the salad, it was lovely. Catch you later. Might go for a swim.'

# Calum follows up with Hanna

Calum's favourite cleaner stepped from the hotel's rear entrance at five minutes past four.

He startled her when he tapped her on the shoulder. 'Remember me?'

'Yes, sir, I do.'

'I have a few questions for you. Can you stop for a few minutes?'

'You pay me for questions?'

Calum nodded. 'Of course.'

Hanna suddenly looked very interested.

'OK.' She beckoned him on to walk a short distance and turn past the corner of the hotel, where there were a couple of benches. She sat down and motioned for him to do the same.

'Sorry to stop you when you are leaving work … but I know the detectives talked to all the staff today and I wanted to ask you … it's all about the Scottish girl who disappeared in Budapest recently. I think you heard all about her? Did the detectives talk to you too?'

She smiled. 'Yes, he talked to me.'

'Ah good. And did you hear that one person told him that she heard some screaming on that day?'

'Yes, I did, sir.'

Calum beamed. 'And do you know who that was? Would she be able to talk to me, do you think?'

'Yes, of course, sir. Because it is me!' She threw him a crafty looking smile, which wasn't entirely attractive. It made Calum suspicious.

Nonetheless, if she was telling the truth, Calum couldn't believe his luck. He felt he'd earned it, not much else had broken in their favour. This could be a real bright spot.

'Fantastic. So I think I'd like to know more about when this happened and exactly where. Can you show me?'

'Maybe sir. How much you give me?'

Calum did a swift calculation. 'Ten thousand.'

She smirked back at that. 'Twenty-five thousand. You are lucky to find me.'

Calum's rough check on that amount into pounds sterling gave him a high and cheeky figure ... but one he'd pay. 'OK.'

'I need to pick up my daughter from school now. Come meet me in hotel tomorrow. I start at two in afternoon tomorrow. Meet me on fourth floor at two-thirty. I tell you everything then. And you pay me first, OK?'

Calum smiled. 'I'd better go to the bank then.'

# The temperature rises …

Nagy sat down at his desk with a coffee and wrote up his notes on the interviews at the Hotel Cristal. He'd sent Jan away to do some digging on Peter Kovacs. Right now, he'd need to wait for Aliz Gal to resurface before he took his next steps. He thought a joint interview with Gal and the cleaner who had heard some faint screams might be a way of surfacing anything Gal had to hide. Trouble was, he didn't know where Gal was. He'd tried to call and visit her after the interviews and had drawn a blank. He'd give it twelve hours before he started looking at hospital lists.

Jan was at his desk fifteen minutes later, with the edgy impatience he always had when he had some useful news to tell his boss. Nagy knew he just wanted to impress his superior, it made him chuckle inside.

'Go on then, what did you find?'

'Peter Kovacs is a doctor living in Bucharest normally. No police record, but he *is* on a list of suspected neo-Nazi sympathisers. Interestingly, so was his father, Marton, who died recently. What's more surprising, is that Aliz Gal is also on the list.'

Nagy raised an eyebrow and twisted his mouth simultaneously. 'And that list contains, what, people linked with far-right organisations like MNA, other Jobbik satellites?'

'Yes, sir. Especially MNA. And we know that Marton Kovacs was part of the original Arrow Cross, at least that's what our database tells us.'

'And this Scottish girl, McTeer, she was researching Arrow Cross right?'

'Yep.'

Their eyes met and acknowledged their joint conclusion. Jan waited for Nagy to suggest it, though, acting the dutiful junior.

'We need to search the hotel, preferably without any warning. Can you arrange the numbers, Jan? We'll need the chief of police onside with this, I'll sort that out, just start getting us ready please.'

# Izabella homes in on Jenna

Izabella was standing behind the bar, polishing a glass. She hadn't seen Jenna for a day or so. Her paymaster had been chasing her this morning and it seemed she would have to take the hard route now. She needed the money, sooner rather than later. Her habit was getting more expensive to feed. It was just a habit, though, she knew she *could* stop if she needed to. She just didn't want to.

It would have to be a surprise … a sharp knife in a quiet place. She couldn't risk a struggle. At least she knew where Jenna's room was. She'd somehow have to stake out the corridor for a night and hope for an opportunity. She took a deep breath. It would need to be tomorrow, she couldn't put this off any longer. It wasn't the first time, not at all. But it felt like this *every* time. She wasn't cut out for it, she just did it, hated it, took the money and moved on. She had never felt she would get caught, though … she wondered if other criminals had that sense of invincibility.

She put the glass back on the shelf and caught the reflection of herself in it, distorted by its curved surface. Even through that stretched and twisted image, she recognised the tension in her face.

Shame. What started as a feigned interest in Jenna had caught her by surprise. It had kindled her own sexual ambivalence … not for the first time. Jenna would actually have been a pleasing prospect.

She shook her head and turned to a customer who was trying to get her attention. Suddenly her thoughts were snapped back to real-time and she started to draw a large glass of pilsner for a man in a grey business suit.

'And what's your name?'

'Izabella.' She smiled weakly, hoping not to encourage him. Usually, that didn't work, though. Usually, it took a while for them to get the message, especially after a few beers. But this was his first. She could feel a conversation of attrition coming on. She had the tactics ready. A feigned loo break. Filling the peanut barrels around the other side of the bar. That sort of thing. Eventually, they lost interest or started annoying someone else.

She gave him the room tab chit to sign, then looked for another customer to serve before he could develop his attempts at conversation.

# The trio

The three women looked at each other warily. Aliz was sprawled on the floor, head propped against the bed. Katalin was at the other end of the bed, legs dangling over the edge, facing Sarah, who was sat in a chair on the other side of the room. Outside a tram passed and the floor vibrated weakly with the rhythm of its wheels.

Ever since Peter had shut the door on the three of them, Aliz had thought only about two things. Firstly, she was sure Peter intended to kill them all. He wouldn't be able to keep them all fed and healthy without arousing suspicions somehow. He would have worked that out already. He had that hardness in him too, the mentality needed to kill people, she knew it. They had to find a way out of room 31 before that happened.

The other thing was what to say to these two, what to admit she knew, how to explain it ... explain *anything* about this whole mess. Maybe she would play dumb: after all, Peter had shut her in, so she could pretend she was innocent of any complicity in all of this.

Sarah asked the question that had been strangling Aliz's mind during the evening before and right through a sleep-deprived night.

'So, is he going to kill us?'

Aliz let out a soft gasp. 'I do believe so, my dear.'

'Then we need to escape, right? How do we get out of here? You know the hotel. How can we get out or get a message or signal to someone?'

Aliz shook her head. 'Not easy. Katalin has been here for eight years, so you have to consider that. Everything is soundproofed. Everyone thinks this is a room reserved for management use. The extra food supplied to Katalin was not hard to hide. For three of us, it will be. That's if we get any.'

'We got breakfast,' Katalin offered, by way of evidence.

'Yes, we did. But I'm not sure he can keep doing that without making the kitchen staff suspicious. For one thing, they will know I am missing. I expect the food to stop soon. And he will kill us then. Or I suppose he could just leave us to starve to death.'

Her words threw a dead hush over them all for a few moments.

Sarah broke the silence.

'But why would he kill us? Why?'

Katalin looked at Aliz for the lead. She took it.

She threw her head back on the edge of the mattress and then forward, steeling herself to start.

'Lots of reasons, I'm afraid. First, you both know about his father's implication in some things that Arrow Cross did in the war. He is afraid you might talk to many people about that.

**347**

Second, if it became public, then the hotel might somehow be threatened … I don't know how exactly but I think he is worried it will be seized or something. You have to remember it is his inheritance. Of course, there is also the shame this could bring on him and his family. He is a well-respected doctor. One of his sons is still quite young, he had him later in life. I suppose the other thing is that he can't think of a better way to stop all these threats to him and his reputation.'

Katalin and Sarah sat silently, absorbing the implications of all of this. Then Katalin threw out a question.

'So, why are you here? Did you learn about Marton's activities with Arrow Cross too?'

Aliz had been ready for this question very soon after she realised she had been imprisoned with the two young women. She'd decided not to tell the truth … at least not all of it.

'Yes, I did, not long after you were put in this room, Sarah. I learnt then that both of you were here. I told Peter Kovacs soon after Marton died. I didn't know what to do about it before then. I tried talking to Marton about releasing you both but he wouldn't listen. I think he couldn't cope with the thought of it, as he was so ill then. Peter was horrified, of course, but, well, then he started to think about the implications, as we just talked about. He must have decided that since I knew about you, that I was a risk too.'

'So he just threw you in here too?' Sarah asked, 'And he's a doctor? Would a doctor really kill us all? I mean is he a madman or something, is he a bad person? That's just crazy, you can't just kill people because of your reputation! Well, not unless you're a drug lord or something.'

Aliz let out a heavy sigh. 'Well, I think he will. He is in a corner. Also, I have heard some … bad … things about Peter over recent years. I think he is associated with some neo-Nazi groups and I think he is not always, well … I mean there are rumours he has done some criminal things. I don't know if these rumours are true. But I think he is not a purely good person, no, I don't think so.'

'So much for the fucking Hippocratic oath then!' Sarah spat.

Aliz looked bemused by the language.

Katalin was shaking her head, in disbelief. 'I didn't know Marton died. When was this?'

'Just a few days ago, my dear.'

Aliz was surprised to see some sadness in Katalin's face.

Contemplation hung over all of them. Sarah broke the stillness again. 'Look, we need to get out, that's the main thing. We can worry about Peter Kovacs' intentions but that won't help us. Maybe we can do something about the door. It was plastered over before. Now it isn't.'

'Mmm, maybe,' Aliz said, 'it's worth a look. He will have locked it and blocked it behind with a wardrobe I expect, maybe more than that. But it's worth a try.'

Sarah and Aliz stood up. Sarah tried the doors.

'Well, it's locked, of course.' Sarah looked through the cracks around the edges of the doors, to see if she could see anything in the room beyond.

'It's all dark through there but it looks like some fabric is pushed up against the doors. Stripy.'

'What colour?'

'Green and white, I think.'

'Hotel mattresses then. They're all that colour. He must have pushed them up against the door for sound-proofing now the plaster's gone; between the doors and the wardrobe in the far room. Not that it will make much difference, either way, these rooms are at the end of the corridor. There aren't many people in a position to hear us.

Katalin coughed. The other two turned around. It was the kind of a cough you made when you wanted to say something.

'We could start a fire?'

Aliz was taken aback by the suggestion of fire when they were trapped in a room.

'But how would that work? Anyway, how would you start it, do you have matches or a lighter?'

'No. But there is the gas fire. I could light a piece of paper from it. But it will only work if there is a smoke alarm in the next room. There isn't one in here.'

Aliz was suddenly interested. 'Actually, there is one in the next room, yes.'

'Has it been tested recently?' Sarah asked. 'Do we know it works? I mean, if it doesn't, by the time the fire has gotten into the corridor, it could be too late for us, it will be burning in here too, or the smoke will have killed us!'

They all considered this. In the end, it was Katalin that recognised the truth of their situation.

'Look. Aliz thinks Peter may kill us. Or let us starve. Either we take a chance or we stay here and are a simple target. What you want to do, eh?'

Neither Aliz nor Sarah had an easy answer to that.

Aliz stood up and walked over to the dumb waiter, lifted the hatch.

'Actually, lunch is late.'

The implication of that darkened Katalin and Sarah's glum faces. It just made Aliz more certain of their fate.

She remembered what had happened that night in 1945. She remembered Marton imprisoning both of the women and how he fed them in room 31. She knew more than she had spoken about Peter Kovacs' murky character. She knew everything. She told herself she should know what to expect.

Over the years, though, there had always been one thing that Marton *hadn't* told her.

*Because he didn't know of it himself.*

# Last meal

Peter peeled back the rug in room 41 and peered through the spy-glass. He could see some part of two of the women below. He could see Aliz's face staring upwards, almost as if she were looking directly at him. She probably knew about the spy-hole but he knew she wouldn't be able to see him. There was a leg too, he couldn't tell who that belonged to.

It was at that point, that he realised he knew the best way.

Of course, this spy-hole was under his control. It was up to him what he did with it. Or what he *put* through it.

Putting something through it seemed almost, well, poetic. A resonance with the past.

To gas them.

He knew he shouldn't have that thought. He knew the *new* right-wing wouldn't profess that they should follow those old ways. But how many of them thought it? Maybe a few. Maybe more than that. He was searching for some shred of justification for what he was thinking, for what he was about to actually do.

But what gas? Carbon monoxide would be easy: he just needed a cylinder of the stuff, to pump through the hole. He'd already been researching the step after that.

Human composting was something that he knew was viable. He needed the clothes out of the room, so he could dispose of them, remove their rings, lever out any metallic teeth fillings. He'd have to hope there were no metal hip or knee replacements. The only one he wasn't sure about was Neuman but he was probably way too young for that. Anyway, he could always sift the compost afterwards, if he was worried. Not the nicest of jobs.

And then, well, mix the bodies with some other dry composting materials and seal it all up so there would be no seeping odour. A couple of months later and he should be able to remove it unnoticed … and it would be unrecognisable as anything remotely linked to a murder.

Murders.

He got up from the floor and sat on a dining chair, staring at the spy-hole. His mind seemed to split into two, arguing whether to do it, each side glaring at the other: hostility, surprise and embarrassment all mixed in the exchanges. They were fighting for control, but one was destined to lose. Over all of the cerebral functions, a more basic instinct was watching and waiting, determined as ever to drive his actions. Personal survival was going to win. He made a phone call.

\*

Peter personally prepared the final meal that Katalin, Sarah and Aliz would eat. He collected most of it from the kitchens then added some bits from the lounge cafe.

**353**

No one questioned him when he asked for things. It was weird being the boss, everyone running at the snap of his fingers. Best not to get too overbearing with it, though, he needed the staff to be neutral to him, to be low profile. If he made enemies, then any mistake he made that exposed itself to the staff might be pounced upon. People with grudges were dangerous.

He looked down at the two trays he was going to send down the dumb waiter.

Spiced chicken soup. They would eat that first. That's why he put the tranquilisers in there. They'd take a little while to kick in, but when they did they'd be subdued for at least the rest of the day.

Some cold beef salad. Then some patisserie as a treat. Raspberry tarts and sacha torte. Coffee too, though by the time they got to that the caffeine would be in vain. Chocolates to finish. It was what he would like *himself* as a last meal.

It was three in the afternoon. They'd be hungry. Ready to scoff the soup.

He placed the trays onto the shelves in the lift and pressed the start button. Then he pushed the bell to warn the other end it was coming. Not that it was really needed, the noise of the motor would be enough.

As the trays disappeared from view, his doorbell rang.

He walked over briskly and opened the door. He stared blankly at the man who was stood there. Not who he was expecting.

Though he did have something with him that eased Peter's sudden tension. Tucked under his arm was a slim metal cylinder. He'd come in the trade entrance with the security code Peter had provided and brought the cylinder up in the service lift, to avoid arousing reception's suspicions.

'Not Toth then?'

The man frowned. 'No. Mr Toth is unable to come. He sends his apologies and asked me to deliver these to you.'

Peter took the cylinder from him and threw him a quizzical look.

'And the other item?'

The man dropped his head in a short nod and fished a small bundle from inside his overalls. He passed it to Peter with a gentleness that wasn't worthy of the item inside the wrap of cloth.

Peter unrolled the material and smelled the gun oil. This was his insurance policy. 'Nice. Thank you. That's all then. Here's your recompense.' He pushed a large envelope into the man's hand.

'Count it.'

The man raised his eyes until they were boring into Peter's. 'No, no need, sir. Mr Toth will ask me to come back if it's not correct.'

He turned on his heel and left, leaving Peter wondering if he ought to have checked the banknotes total for a third time.

He sat on the bed and picked up his phone. He started to write a text. To Calum Neuman. Teasing him with the possibility of information. Inviting him to be snared in his widening web in room 31. He knew he wouldn't be able to resist.

He assumed he would bring the girl he thought was assisting him. The one he'd seen talking to him in the hotel lounge yesterday. If not, it might get messy. Hard to imagine how much more of a mess it could really become.

# Calum receives an invite

Calum was getting a little irritated as Jenna regaled him with tales of how relaxing the thermal spa baths at Gellert had been this afternoon.

His phone saved him with a text. A local mobile number ... he clicked it open.

*Mr Neuman, I have some information for you about the missing Scottish girl. I can discuss with you this evening if you come to the hotel at say ten? I am rather busy but just come up to room 21 ... no need to call at reception. I hope I can help you. Let me know if this is OK, please. Peter Kovacs.*

Calum stared at the message a moment, then looked up at Jenna. He turned his phone towards her and raised it so she could read the message.

'Hmm. Good break ... or sounds a bit spooky?'

'Exactly what I was thinking. Why now? What happened?'

'On the other hand ...'

'If we don't go, we'll not find out.'

'Exactly.'

Calum tightened his lips and then took a deep breath.

'But we should be careful. It's a shame I'm not meeting that chambermaid until tomorrow morning … it would have been useful to hear what she said first. I suggest we don't arrive together, just a few moments apart maybe. Maybe you go to your room first. I meet him, then you follow a little later.'

Jenna nodded, slowly at first, then more enthusiastically.

'OK. Let's get some food first then. I need hot food tonight, something hearty if we're out on the case later, I had a salad already today.'

Calum smiled. 'Suits me. Always will.'

# Nagy gets ready to move in

A secretary from the pool brought Nagy the permit from the Chief of Police to enter Hotel Cristal en masse. He called Jan into his office.

'We have the go-ahead to search Kovacs' hotel. Are we ready?'

'More or less, we can go after eight p.m., sir.'

Nagy dipped his head. 'Good enough. We'll inform Mr Kovacs on arrival. We need to search quickly with as many men in parallel as possible. How many do we have?'

'Twelve, sir.'

'OK, that's good.'

'What are we looking for, other than the obvious?'

'Well, yes, the Scottish woman. But maybe Aliz Gal too. We need to look for all the rooms not used by guests first. The public areas are obvious, so are things like the kitchens but also any other rooms not necessarily obvious to us. So we need to enlist the help of a receptionist to help us with that, not Kovacs.'

'Clothing, sir?'

Nagy looked surprised.

'We're maybe dealing with a neo-Nazi organisation. If they *have* taken two women, then we can expect it may be a difficult task, depending on the level of surprise we manage. We should expect the worst. Full protective gear … I assume you included a couple of marksmen?'

'I did, sir. And OK, I'll get the gear arranged now. So when?'

'Let's go at ten-thirty when things are quieter with the guests. Don't want to scare too many of them, huh?' He cast an evil smile at Jan. He was going to enjoy this.

As Jan left the room, he pulled out a pack of unfiltered French cigarettes.

Nagy shouted after him. 'Next one of those cancer sticks will be with a beer. Maybe we'll have something to celebrate eh?'

# Calum & Jenna at the Cristal

Calum walked up the steps to the Hotel Cristal at five minutes to ten. As he walked through the entrance, he cast his eyes around the lobby. Almost deserted. He walked on through to the lifts, jumped in one that was waiting and pressed the second-floor button. Jenna was hanging back in her room for a few minutes, as planned. He was sweating slightly, despite the cold weather outside. He shook his head to settle himself and stepped out as the lift doors opened on the second floor.

He walked up to room 21 and knocked on the door.

*

Peter Kovacs was at the limit of his ability to cope.

He picked up his insurance policy and slid it into the back of his trouser belt, under his suit jacket. He'd seen that move on T.V.: seemed like a good place to hide it from view. He felt like leaving his jacket off, he was sweating more than normal, but he needed the gun to be concealed.

He opened the door.

'Hello, Mr Neuman.'

Calum dipped his head.

'I have some information for you, but it's best we go upstairs, where we can discuss with Sarah McTeer in person.'

*

Calum felt a surge of tension rise within him.

'She's here?'

'Yes. If we go upstairs, you can meet her and you can discuss the situation with her.'

Calum hesitated, alarm bells ringing.

'Your assistant,' Kovacs went on, 'I think I saw you together in the hotel before. She isn't coming?'

'Ah, yes she is, she's been held up by something, she'll be here in a while. Let's start to talk to Sarah, though, that's fine.'

It was Kovacs' turn to hesitate. Calum thought he noticed something in his eyes, betraying his apparent calmness.

'Hmm, well OK, I'm sure we can unless you'd prefer to wait?'

'Nope, let's start, Jenna isn't necessary for anything, she just helps me.' Calum hoped Kovacs wouldn't repeat that in any shape or form to Jenna later.

Peter nodded and stepped forward, closing his room door behind him.

'This way then.' They walked together and took the stairs to the third floor.

As they passed room 314, Calum gave a mental nod to Jenna, waiting inside.

Kovacs pulled a small set of keys out of his pocket and opened the door to room 33. Calum noticed the lock seemed stiff as if it wasn't used too much.

'After you.'

# Another capture

Calum walked into room 33 and looked around. Peter had shut the door behind him and was moving past him to the other end of the room.

'Through here.' He pointed to a pair of doors. They'd been cleared of the mattress and old wardrobe camouflage.

Again, he turned the key in what seemed a stiff lock. He motioned Calum forwards, again with the same words.

'After you.'

Calum noticed the doorframe looked dusty and the plaster around it fragmented. He walked slowly through the doors as they were opened by Peter. As he lifted his eyes and peered around the scene in front of him, he knew this was all wrong. He turned back to look at Peter but was beaten to it by a sharp prod in his back with something hard, which jerked him forwards a couple of yards into the room. He stumbled, then recovered, to find Peter pointing a revolver at him.

'What's this? Who are all these women?' he asked, knowing one of them well enough: Aliz Gal was slumped on the sofa, seemingly asleep. So too was a dark-haired girl, pale in complexion. He assumed this was Sarah. There was another woman, on the bed, who he didn't recognise. She had her eyes open, though she looked subdued.

'Phone please.'

Calum thought briefly about the alternatives but decided quickly to do as he was ordered. He passed his mobile slowly into Kovacs' outstretched left hand. He felt nervous, but those nerves were giving way to fast-boiling anger.

'What the hell's got into you?'

He watched Kovacs back slowly to the doors.

'Please ... please let us out of here, sir.'

Calum turned his head to find the half-awake girl had sat up a little.

Peter stopped for a fleeting moment then carried on out through the doors. As he pushed them shut, he spoke quietly through the narrowing crack.

'I can't. I'm sorry ... but I can't.'

*

Peter locked room 31 and retreated into the corridor, securing 33 as well. He pushed a couple of mattresses into place across the double doors into 31 before he left, to minimise any noise Neuman might make before he returned with the Scotsman's assistant. *If* he could find her. He might try her room, he knew where she was at night: in room 314. Question was, was she there now or on the way to the hotel? All he could do was try her room door and see.

# Jenna opens the door

Jenna was in her room, waiting on the bed for the right time to join Calum at Peter Kovacs' room. She was anxious, nervous for her boss. Since she'd heard noises of distress when she saw Kovacs and Aliz Gal enter room 33 the other night, she'd had a sense of doom gathering around her. She hadn't let it get to her when she was with Calum, but right now she was scared.

When a sharp knock rapped on the door, it vibrated her nervous system and set her panicking. Who the hell could that be? She didn't need any interruptions right now.

She debated whether to let it go, then remembered the peep-hole. She crept swiftly to the hole and pushed her eye up to it.

There was another sharp rap on the wood which nearly threw her off balance. She pressed her head forward again and saw an outline, then a face, partially in shadow from the bright corridor lights.

Izabella!

It was perhaps no surprise she was here, she hadn't seen her since their aborted tryst the other day. She felt bad about that. It drove her to open the door, to make amends at least.

'Hi.' Izabella looked a bit sheepish. Jenna *felt* a bit sheepish.

She dismissed that thought instantly and smiled. 'Hey. Come in.'

'I brought vodka. I just thought …'

She held up a plastic bag.

'Yeah, sorry about the other night, it was … err awkward. Old boyfriend. Heh.'

'Oh? I thought … well, you know …'

Jenna grimaced at the awkwardness.

'Just not sure what I'm doing, Iza, sorry, look, please sit down, let's have a drink.'

'Sure, that's good.'

Izabella visibly relaxed and sat on the bed, close to Jenna. She ripped the seal off the half bottle of vodka she'd brought with her and poured into two plastic cups, together with some orange juice she pulled out of the same bag.

'Cheers!'

'Yeah, cheers, Iza.'

They both sank a good slug.

Iza moved a little closer to Jenna, testing the water. Jenna swayed away, almost imperceptibly.

Iza twisted her mouth into a warm smile. 'Sorry. I shouldn't assume.'

'No, no, it's OK, let's just have a drink, eh?'

Jenna knew she didn't have time to do this. She had to get Izabella out of the room and soon. It would be a second rebuff but she had no choice. Then there was a loud knock at the door and it all became easier … and harder, in one breath.

'Jesus, not again, is the boyfriend actually here this time? This is a plant, eh?'

Jenna let out a nervous laugh. 'No! He's in Scotland. Just a minute.'

She hopped over to the door and peered through the peep-hole.

Peter Kovacs.

Why the hell was he here, he should be with Calum right now. She wasn't going to open the door to him. She turned to Izabella, pursed her lips and gave her the universal *sshh* sign. Iza nodded back, albeit with a sceptical scowl. She felt the inside of her sock, where she'd concealed a knife.

Jenna waited in silence. The doorknob rattled. Lucky she always snicked the catch when she shut the door.

Then she saw Peter move away. Another minute or so and nothing.

Now her mind was in turmoil. Something felt wrong. She needed to excuse herself and find Calum.

\*

Peter Kovacs walked away from room 314, wishing he'd availed himself of a master key before he came upstairs this evening.

He decided against returning straight away to Ms Strick's room. He'd wait a little, see if she turned up to room 21 as planned. If not, he might have to start his dirty work. He was wary of Neuman helping the women find some way of escape ... from the personal profile on his website he looked like a bright man.

For a little while, at least, he felt calmer in his room, readying himself to take the next, terrible step.

# Peter begins…

He'd waited thirty minutes and Ms Strick hadn't turned up at his door. Now his vital signs were all pushing their boundaries, bullying him into taking some action for relief.

He slipped the CO cylinder into a large plastic bag, together with a hose and some tape. He left his room and headed off upstairs to room 41, his father's old apartment.

Once in the room, he rolled back the rug and peered through the spy-hole once more.

He could see the top of Neuman's head. Slightly thinning. Moving gently, as if he was talking to one of the others. The rest he had no sight of.

He lay down near the hole and rolled the cylinder close, so he could attach the hose. Then the tricky part. He had to unscrew the spy-hole. He'd rather they didn't notice, so he was trying to be very quiet, though in truth it really didn't matter if they spotted him or not.

He remembered about the extra light that would shine down through the hole from his room and went back to switch off the main light, leaving only the torch on his phone switched on.

He grasped the eye-piece with his thumb and index finger and turned it slowly anti-clockwise. It soon came free from its housing, which was set into the floorboards. He placed it down and looked again. He saw a couple of flakes of plaster, floating down towards Neuman's crown. They seemed to take an eternity to reach him, then they settled very gently on his hair.

Not gently enough though.

*

Calum felt a tickle on his head, like an insect alighting and brushed at it, only to see a couple of white flakes fall off. He instinctively looked up.

He'd not noticed the small metal ring in the ceiling in his brief stay in the room. He motioned to Katalin, who was the only one of the three women somewhat awake. She nodded.

'Yes, I don't know what this is. It never did anything before. In eight years. But it looks different tonight.'

Calum felt his blood freeze. 'Eight years?! You mean you've been here eight years?'

Katalin bowed her head and left it hung down, unable to meet his gaze.

Calum looked up again, gazed steadily at the hole, thought he detected a change in the colour of the opening. He held his index finger to his lips and looked at Katalin.

They both looked up at the ring and listened.

There was a faint scraping sound, then a darkening of the hole inside the ring. A couple more flakes of loose plaster floated down, so slowly they felt the world had suddenly slowed to half speed.

Their breathing quickened in contradiction. Time slowed even more. Then, the sound of a nightmare began.

# The chamber

Peter watched as the plaster snowflake fell onto Calum
and made him look upwards, directly into the spy-hole. He shrank
back automatically, then thought the movement might have been
seen. But it didn't matter now, did it? They were moribund, all
four of them. Five if he could get the missing assistant into there
later. For now, four would have to do.

He pulled the flexi tube end towards him and lowered it to
the hole. It fit pretty well without any padding or adjustment. He
pushed it in a couple of inches so it was nice and tight. Now he
was all ready.

He turned his head sideways and stared at the cylinder
head. There was the standard red hand wheel on the top. He
reached for it, let his fingers curl slowly around the curves of cold
metal.

He held his breath for a few seconds, then turned the
wheel anti-clockwise. It was hard to turn it, so it moved with a
slight jerk, releasing an initial hiss which then subsided to a steady,
hushed breath of gas.

He held his ear to the floor next to the hole listening for sounds from the helpless people below but could hear nothing over the deadly shushing of the gas. He stood up, left room 41 and went back to his own room. He might be a monster but he couldn't watch.

*

Calum heard the gas hiss first. Katalin heard it too, looking up at the hole in the ceiling.

The other two women were rousing themselves a little and Calum could see them sensing his own panic. Aliz hitched herself into a sitting position and mouthed 'What's happening?'

Calum pointed upwards. 'Gas. He's gassing us. Well, I assume it's Peter.'

Aliz recoiled and clasped her hands to her cheeks.

'I don't know what it is or how long it will take, but we need to do something quickly, or I suspect we'll be dead pretty soon. I can't *smell* anything. Any idea, Miss Gal?'

Aliz shook her head. 'No, no idea. But why don't we try lighting the mattress through the door like we said, just maybe the fire alarm will save us?'

'First I've heard of that … but yeah, we can try it. Right now, I can't think of anything else.'

Katalin nodded at Calum, got up and tore a few scraps of paper out of a book on the shelf above her bed. She screwed them into long thin tapers and switched on the gas fire. 'Here, I'll light them, you push through the door crack and against the mattress.'

Calum grabbed the first one and did as he was asked. Then another, then another until he had pushed around ten lit tapers through the crack between the double doors. His forehead was covered with a nervous sweat by the time he was done.

'OK, push some blankets or something against the doors now, or else we'll get killed by the smoke.' Katalin grabbed some large towels out of her wardrobe and bathroom, doused them in the sink and then pressed them against the doors with Calum's help.

By now, Sarah was fully awake and aware of what was going on too.

The three women moved closer together, some sort of protective reaction … Katalin put her arms around the other two, squeezing them.

'I'm praying this works.'

Calum stared at them, unable to move at that moment, his mind frantically circling for more ideas … and the gas hiss continued, quietly, unabated. He felt himself become a little light-headed.

'Can we get something to stand on and push a wet cloth against the hole?'

'Of course, why didn't we think of that already?' squawked Katalin.

Then the hotel fire alarm sounded.

# Alarm

As the alarm bells started to ring, Peter sprang up and called reception. One of the more senior members of staff answered.

'Yes, Mr Kovacs, it's appeared on the fire alarm display panel. We think on the third floor. Maybe. Some lights on the second floor are showing too but sometimes it's not accurate, I think.'

Peter shook his head at the seeming nonsense of an inaccurate fire alarm circuit but pressed on.

'So the fire service is called automatically?'

'Yes, sir.'

'OK, have we started the evacuation process?'

'Of course.'

'OK, good. I'll meet you all outside at the assembly point. It's behind the hotel, isn't it?'

'Yes, sir, next to the Italian restaurant.'

He replaced the phone. Then he sat and thought about the process he'd just started in the room above him. He walked over to the window and stared out, wondering what to do next. He looked down the street and spotted a few guests running away from the hotel towards the fire assembly point.

*

Jenna knew she'd been taking too long, trying to excuse herself politely (again) from Izabella, when the fire alarms exploded into life.

Izabella looked at her, frowned as if it had been orchestrated to get her to leave.

'I think you are trying to avoid me!'

Jenna half-smiled. 'Come on, we need to get out, grab your bag, here …'

Jenna saw Izabella flinch as she picked the bag up and handed it to her. Something worrying flashed across her mind, then disappeared again as the alarm continued its insistent shrieking. She gently pushed Izabella towards the door as she opened it with her other hand.

As they crossed the threshold together, they both noticed a faint drift of smoke in the corridor.

'OK, it's for real!' gasped Izabella, with a heavy dose of panic across her face.

Jenna nodded vigorously.

'Look, I need to check on my colleague, he's just along the corridor. You go downstairs and get out, I'll catch up with you.'

Again, there was a flinch in Izabella's response. Again, Jenna ignored it and pushed her away from the door and towards the entrance to the stairwell.

'*GO.*'

She did … still there was a reluctance to her movement that was now pricking at Jenna's conscious thought … but she needed to find Calum right now.

'See you downstairs.' She turned up the corridor towards room 33 and saw there was a thicker haze of smoke around the doorframe. She ran up to the door and banged hard. No response. She banged again until her hands pulsed with the pain of bruising.

She pressed her head sideways against the door, listening for any responses inside. The smoke was beginning to get thicker and was making her eyes tear.

Was there someone else banging? She hammered at the door again and listened. Yes, there it was, muffled, but someone was returning her drumbeat. She *knew* Calum was in there still. Her mind flared wide and tried to think about how to open the door. A key. That was the only answer. She wasn't strong enough to force it. She turned to race down to reception.

# Hanna's message

On her way home, Hanna Elek looked inside the paper bag she had stuck into her shoulder carry-all. One of the kitchen guys had slipped it to her before leaving work. There were a few bread rolls inside. She was thinking she'd prefer the guy to the rolls, but rolls were good anyway, nice and fresh and Lili would enjoy them filled with meat and cheese for supper.

The thing was, when he slipped her the bread rolls, he'd slipped a note in the paper bag too. She hadn't seen it at first, but when she took the last roll out at home, there it was. Addressed to her, folded up into a neat rectangle. She opened it while she was making supper.

*Why don't you pop back to the hotel around ten? I'm off shift then and we can go for a drink for an hour if you like?'*

Her heart rate blipped upwards and she smiled at the chopping board.

*Hmm, maybe I could if I get Lili to sleep by nine. It's just a short tram ride, and the neighbour will probably look over Lili for an hour or two. I knew he fancied me. Yeah, maybe I will.*

\*

Around nine-fifteen, Hanna fluttered her fingers in a wave to her neighbour who was perched on the sofa. 'Promise I'll be home by eleven-thirty.' Her neighbour smiled.

Hanna set off towards the tram stop, smelling of the new perfume one of her friends had given her for her birthday last week. She felt good, light of step and gently excited. It had been a *while*.

She arrived early and sat on a bench near the rear entrance, waiting for him. Robert was his name. A little younger than her. Round face, stocky build, her sort really. And always kind to her.

She looked at her watch. Actually, there was no need to wait ten minutes out here. She could wait in the kitchens, why should that matter? She punched her code into the entrance security pad and wandered slowly into the staff restroom, just next to the main kitchens.

Robert came out pretty much on time into the staff room, to get rid of his kitchen overalls and collect his things. His face beamed out a broad smile when he saw her. It made her glow.

'I would have texted but I didn't have your number, hope you didn't mind the note.'

'No, of course not, it was quite nice to get a real note.'

'Well, shall we go? There are a few bars close to save time … mind if I have a quick cigarette first outside?'

Something about his smile overcame Hanna's natural disapproval of smoking. She nodded her head vigorously.

'Sure, of course. I only have an hour or so, my daughter has a babysitter who might be like Cinderella. You know, goes poof at midnight? It smells of gas in here anyway, I thought they were supposed to have fixed that?'

'Yeah. Dunno. I smelled it today too, even with my sense of smell. A cook with a dumb nose eh? I'll never make the grade.'

Robert held the door open for her and touched her shoulder gently as she passed through it. Hanna smiled inside again. A good start.

As they turned into the street, there was an almighty screech as the main fire alarms in the hotel started up. They looked at each other.

'Let's just wait here. If it's real they might need us to help.' He left the door ajar, to listen.

They stood a yard from the door, as Robert pulled out a packet of filters and slid one between his fingers, sparking it with a cheap plastic lighter. He sucked in fiercely, like he needed it, then exhaled as if he had all the time in the world.

A few more languid puffs, while he chatted to her through the sirens' wail, then he dropped the tab to the floor and squidged it with his heel, kicking it aimlessly away. It skidded through the doorframe into the corridor to the kitchen.

'OK, let's go then. We've waited enough I reckon. And you don't have long ...'

Hanna didn't get a chance to respond. The cigarette butt travelled far enough into the corridor to seek out an invisible swirl of the gas, leaking from the cracked pipe under the kitchen flooring.

It wasn't much of a leak ... but it was enough.

# Apocalypse

Peter felt it first in his ears and a fraction later in his legs. A slug of compressed air thumped into his back with brutal force.

His head whacked into the window as the booming filled his senses, cracking his nose, spurting blood against the pane, smearing a thin red veneer down it as his legs felt like they'd given way. He fell vertically, surrounded by a curtain of shattered glass, through what had been the floor of his room, down through a cavernous space, edged with splintered floorboards, shreds of carpet and gushing water. He saw the pavement outside the hotel for a fraction of a second, before it slapped into him with the force of an articulated truck.

In an instant, all of his worries about his captives and the future of the hotel were gone. He expired with two last, rasping breaths as dozens of faces in the street were turning towards him, eyes and mouths wide, witnessing the disaster that was happening in real-time in front of them.

\*

Two teenage girls fell backwards against a nearby shop front, banging against the glass, screaming together. It echoed down the street, triggering the panic response in others, who started yelling without understanding what was happening. Until they turned and looked at the facade of the Hotel Cristal. Most of the front of the hotel at the eastern end was missing, collecting itself into a storm of debris and dust on the road in front of the entrance … which wasn't an entrance anymore. It was more like the cutaway view on the front of a doll house.

Except this one had dead dolls. Littered inside it, hanging from its open timbers, scattered in front of it.

People started running in all directions, randomly towards and away from the hotel, caught between fear and the animal compulsion to help their own species.

High above them, a series of connected dramas were just unfolding.

# The void

Rooms 31 and 33 were unrecognisable.

Most of their fabric had completely vanished. It was now lying in hundreds of pieces, three floors below on the pavement and road outside the hotel. There was a terrible wailing noise emanating from the pile of masonry piled around a waiting taxi, the driver trapped inside his flattened sardine can of a car, dying slowly, in horrible pain.

The first two or three minutes after the explosion were painted by the emotion of the humanity around the hotel. A great outburst of yelling and wailing, then quickly an eerie quiet, punctuated only by the cries of the dying, as people began to comprehend what had happened. After a little while, new sirens started to wail, as the emergency services wound their way through the Budapest traffic.

Bystanders gathered together, pointing at people injured, bits of the hotel that looked precarious. A girl dressed in her infant school uniform held her mother's hand, asking her what was happening, with all the matter-of-factness of childhood.

Two teenage boys broke away from their self-absorbed world to run towards a man lying on the pavement screaming in front of them, pulling their earphones out, with no idea how to help. An elderly couple, wrapped up in thick layers against the cold, stood side-by-side, arms around each other's waist, hoping there were no children injured.

High above them, some of the inhabitants of room 31 were pressing themselves against the inner wall of what remained of the room, standing on a tattered ledge of floorboards no more than six feet wide. The ones that gathered together trying to plug Peter Kovacs' gas hole had been lucky, they'd been near the inside wall when the explosion struck. Aliz Gal, however, hadn't been so fortunate. She'd sat down to watch while the other three tried to plug the hole. Her chair was near the window ... a window that no longer existed. Its wooden frame lay twisted on the road, underneath Aliz's equally distorted body, looking like some ghastly 3D wall hanging.

Calum felt a brisk breeze push against his jacket lapel, cooling his sweat. He found himself looking out at the void to his right, his body drawn by the space. The evening lights of the city sprawled out in front of him for miles, the sky covered with low clouds which took on a dull orange hue from the flames licking out from the hotel. He looked in front of himself, at Katalin. She was backed against the wall, staring out at the dark void in front of them, her legs shuffling frantically around in small edgy movements, going nowhere, but unable to keep still.

He shouted to her and caught her eye.

'Stay still, Katalin! Lean with your side to the wall.' He put his own hand to the wall to steady himself and saw it was sheathed in blood. He turned it over … there was no wound. The blood extended a way up his forearm. He turned his head slowly and peered behind him.

No Aliz. Sarah was laid on the ledge. One leg dangling freely into space. Her other leg was missing below the knee. In its place was a pool of blood. Probably the blood that was all over his arm. She was crying, little faint whimpers, her only movement her lips gently pursing open to let the sound out.

His eyes returned to the pool of blood. Sarah's leg had been torn off about an inch below the knee, torn being the right description. Muscle and sinew were frilled around the splintered white bone in a dark red curtain. Blood was pulsing out into the glossy puddle, which was now spilling over the edge of the ledge. He knew she needed skilled treatment … and fast. He looked back to the void and turned his eyes down towards the street, snatching as much of a glance as his vertigo would allow before snapping his attention back to Sarah.

The sirens had been wailing for a few minutes now and there were emergency vehicles down there and the sound of equipment being moved, but he daren't trust his balance to any more glances down. He turned to Katalin and nodded his head towards the ground.

'They are coming. Stay still, they'll get us out.' She shook her head up and down in a weird staccato figure of eight, trembling with fear.

They'd have to wait … and hope time didn't run out for Sarah. By now, the spasms from her severed leg had started to register with her brain. As the pain burned, the shock her body was in prevented her from any visual reaction. Her face was pale, going grey fast.

*

When the fire engine platform finally levelled itself up to the third floor, Calum was beginning to think it was too late. Sarah's face was ashen and the screaming had ceased. There was only a shallow motion across her chest now.

The fire crew looked at the scene and immediately moved her onto the platform, motioning for the other two to stay put. It did strike Calum that they really couldn't do much else. Maybe some might jump out of panic … there were a few flames down and to the left, but it didn't feel like they were in danger of being burnt alive. Then things changed.

A rushing sound welled up from beneath them, followed by another explosion. Not so big as the first one, but it threw a small fireball up the side of the building, scorching Calum's eyebrows and the remains of his jacket. What was left of Room 31 was now punctuated by little islands of flame. He caught a blur of movement in his peripheral vision and turned … Katalin was stumbling towards him, wide-eyed and with her tee-shirt alight.

She fell at him and he anticipated just early enough to avoid being knocked off balance. He pulled her to him, beating at the flames on her back until they were gone. She was heaving with sobs and difficult to hold still.

'Sssh … sssh, they'll be back for us … in a moment.'

He knew that was about as long as they had.

# Smoke

Jenna stared at the ceiling for a moment, blinking rapidly, flicking dust from her eyes and regaining a sense of where the hell she was.

She remembered and jerked her head up, saw the door to room 33 with puffs of smoke and dust escaping around its edges.

She jumped up, then staggered back, her body aching. She must have been thrown by the explosion, it'd left her bruised and slow to move. She lurched forward and hammered on the door again. This time, it gave way at the lock, part of the door falling away as it swung open, weakened by the blast.

Smoke billowed out, causing her to step sideways and let some of it pass into the corridor. She peered around room 33's doorframe and saw right across the room, through the broken jambs of the door to number 31, right out into fresh air and the lights of the buildings opposite the hotel. She sucked in a deep breath and steadied herself against a sudden giddy wobble.

She could see a thin, dark-haired girl, pressed to a wall, pushing herself away from the edge of the floor, which had fallen away to nothing. Calum was beyond her, his interest focused on a different woman. She looked like the pictures of Sarah McTeer they'd been given.

Her mind whirled with what to do next. That decision was taken from her by another explosion, which cut through part of room 33 and sent her back down to the floor again.

She recovered and got to her feet, but flames had taken hold of the carpet in front of her and pushed her back out through the door into the corridor. She turned and ran, finding the stairs and scampering down them as fast as her battered legs would let her.

Getting help for Calum was her only focus.

*

Robert had walked away from the hotel slightly before Hanna. As a consequence, her body took a lot of the force of the blast from the back door, but he still hit the ground hard and lost consciousness for a few moments. He came around with Hanna's body draped across his own.

He struggled to turn onto his back, holding her left arm to stop her rolling off him and bumping the floor.

He looked at her face. It was clear of injury and she was breathing. A bit shallow, though. He pulled himself further sideways until he could lower her to the ground. He turned and put his hand under her head, cradling it like a baby's.

'Hanna, Hanna, are you OK … speak to me. Speak to me please.'

She didn't reply. She didn't open her eyes either. He laid her head back down and pulled his hand away. It was covered with blood from the back of her head.

Robert looked around him and saw people running everywhere. He suddenly tuned in to the sound of emergency sirens and got up clumsily, turned towards the end of the building and ran for help.

# Crucifixion

As Izabella ran down the stairs, her mind was warmed by the thought that if Jenna acted the hero too recklessly, then her task for the night might well be done for her. It almost made her smile her very last smile.

When she reached the ground floor, she was flung sideways by a thunderous gust of air and heat that hammered against her body, spinning her like a clockwork mouse across the lobby floor.

A few seconds later, she was up and lurching out of the hotel, as the fire and smoke began to encroach into the lobby's open space.

Once through the front door, she went a yard or so further and looked up. No reason really, she wanted to see where the explosion had come from, or just some natural instinct to cover all threats. A couple of the front desk staff had scrambled to near where she stood, fleeing their posts. They moved even closer to her, some instinct around safety in numbers perhaps, and looked up with her.

One of the staff screamed. She only just had time. She didn't get the chance to pull in another breath to replace the air expelled by her yell. A huge lump of masonry from the hotel facade hit her square on, driving her skull down through her body like a stone through a glass of raspberry milk.

The chunk of stonework was long. It spanned a few feet both sides of the woman. Crushed either side of her, like the thieves crucified next to Christ, were the head concierge and Izabella.

All around them people fell away in horror, driven by the spray of fragments and dust still falling around the block and the pools of blood already spreading from the pile of crushed corpses.

Their wails were backed by the vehicle sirens around them … a symphony of scorched souls.

Jenna sprinted out of the front entrance, past the crucified trio to the other side of the street, almost accosting a fireman to ask for help, before she realised that's exactly what he was trying to do. She looked up.

High above the street, flames punctuated the night sky, lighting up the faces of a few people still in their rooms, trapped by fires. She could just make out Calum's face, peering into the scene of two firemen gently easing a girl onto the hydraulic fire platform, taking a lot of care with their movements. The other woman was clinging to Calum, her face dead, still, no expression, shock frozen onto a skin canvas.

The firemen stood up and Calum waved at them as if to hurry them away. He stood there, the other woman draped around his shoulder and looked down. Jenna shouted and waved at him. He didn't notice her.

The platform was down on the ground quickly and the girl ferried off to a waiting ambulance. The firemen were riding back up the building before the girl reached the ambulance doors.

Calum and the other woman were bracing their bodies, as close to the edge as they dared, wincing and wilting from the heat of the flames creeping behind them, cutting them off from the precarious route back to room 33.

They pretty much fell onto the rescue platform as the small gate on it swung open, Katalin's hair smouldering with glowing pieces of ash.

One of the firemen swatted the embers out of her hair as they descended. Twenty feet from the ground, the leaking gas gave its final shout and blew out the first-floor windows ten feet below them. The platform lurched backwards then steadied itself, before rolling the other way and crashing into the front of the burning building.

Jenna's eyes were owl-wide, not wanting to believe the catastrophe unravelling in front of her.

# War zone

Jenna ran towards the rescue platform as fast as her bruised body would let her, but a fireman motioned for her to move down the street to safety.

As she turned to head left, she caught sight of a pair of trainers, on the end of legs trapped under a huge piece of masonry. She recognised them and hesitated a moment. The fireman waved wildly at her again to move on, so she turned and ran. Her brain was processing the image of the trainers ... and it didn't take long to place them. Izabella had been wearing the same bright pink trainers ... or at least a very close match. She felt cold sweat tingle across her forehead. Now she did stop and peer back. She couldn't see the spot, because of a stream of people running along behind her. She'd need to work her way around back up the street and have a look from the other side.

By the time she managed to do that, the hydraulic platform was empty and the area around Izabella's body shut off by police. She ran back toward the safety cordon where the ambulances were lined up, but was stopped by a number of police officers who refused to let her through.

One of them was detective Nagy. She recognised him, but of course, she'd not made herself known to him in the hotel so she had no real leverage with him. She mentioned Calum's name, but Nagy was having none of it.

'Wait here. I'll go and talk to him once he's been seen by the ambulance crew. You can't cross the tape until I say it's OK. It looks like he's had a lucky escape.'

\*

Robert had finally managed to grab the attention of a paramedic to follow him back to where Hanna was. The medic examined her.

'She needs a stretcher. Don't move her while I'm gone. She has some neck and head injuries and bleeding. I can't tell how serious it is, we need to get her to hospital.'

Robert mouthed an 'OK' and slumped down to the ground by Hanna, taking her hand in his own and stroking it. He remembered she'd said she had a babysitter for her daughter. But he didn't know where she lived or any home number. The hotel might have it but no one was going to be able to get that right now. Until she came around, there was little he could do. And somewhere in Budapest, a little girl would be waiting for her mummy to come home.

## Beata recognises...

Beata had felt the impact of the explosion in her library office. She'd been working very late again, on a new book collection project. Her eyes rose up from her computer screen and she listened. After a moment, she carried on with her work until the sound of sirens started to fill the neighbourhood. A member of building security ran in a few minutes later to tell her it was at a hotel a few blocks away. He had heard it may have been the Hotel Cristal. Marton's hotel.

Somehow she felt obliged to go and see what was happening. Marton had been good to her. Helped her in the house when he was younger, after her husband had left her. Lent her money when he could, when he was still building his own hotel business. She'd taken from him over the years, even though he had never really understood why. She rolled back her desk chair and picked up an overcoat from the rack peg behind her.

She passed the security guard on the way out.

'Won't be long. Just going to see what the commotion is all about.' He nodded.

She pulled up the faux fur collar around her neck and set off at a brisk pace. It wasn't far to walk. The streets near the library were quiet now, but as she approached the environs of the hotel, the density of people increased, in tandem with the noise from the emergency services. As if that wasn't enough of a signal, the amber wash in the sky above where the hotel stood could be seen from the start of her brief walk. Then a second explosive blast sent a shock wave through the air that she actually felt.

She quickened her step until she turned a corner and saw the Cristal. She gasped at the sight.

The hotel ablaze. Building rubble scattered all across the street in front of a large hole in the hotel facade. Bodies thrown amongst the fallen stonework and medical teams stretchering casualties away from the immediate shadow of the hotel to safety … to ambulances, all lined up neatly, like boxes on a shelf of the last shop standing in a war-torn street.

She knew people at the hotel. Aliz. She'd met Peter before, knew some of the staff a little. She walked towards the area of carnage but soon hit the police barrier tapes that had been hastily stretched between temporary posts.

She looked around for another way. There was a man with a mobile stand selling coffee. She wondered whether it had already been there or he'd been quick to spot an opportunity.

She bought a double espresso then wandered back towards the row of ambulances. She raised the small paper cup to her lips and started to sip.

Then a young woman's face caught her eyes and something slowly registered. It was slow because … she wasn't sure who it was. Not *just* who it was, but whether she actually *knew* that face. It was a fair distance away and hard to make out in the dark.

It was familiar, yet not. Someone she knew … but had somehow forgotten.

There was a man with her. A tall man, stooped over her, as she sat on the steps at the back of the ambulance, being examined by a medic in a green jacket. She frowned, wondering who he was. He was older. Maybe just a concerned co-victim.

She took a few steps closer, straining her sight to focus on the girl.

Then she remembered. Remembered it all, in one sudden heart-lurching rush that made her press her hand to her mouth and force a gasp of disbelief through her fingers. All of the years of joy, chased by an eternal nightmare. She dropped her coffee cup and ran towards the ambulance.

A police officer at the tape grabbed her shoulder, asked her to stop. She whispered something in his ear and pointed to the ambulance. He shook his head, released his grip on her shoulder and let her run on.

As she approached the three of them, huddled together, all focusing on the girl's arm, she stopped.

They must have noticed her halting. They looked up together, stared blankly at her. Only the *girl's* face changed as a result. It changed a great deal, creasing her eye sockets and pursing her lips, before she leapt upwards and towards Beata, pushing the two men aside.

She stopped short of her mother. Then she ran at her, arms grasping for the comfort of her embrace. Beata caught her, grabbing her tightly, pushed Katalin back a little, taking a look at her through eyes curtained with tears.

'It's really you! But, but … why are you here? Were you walking past the hotel? So, so … why have you not talked to me for eight years? *Eight years* Katalin! Where have you *been*?'

**397**

Katalin couldn't speak. She was crying and words couldn't come right now.

Beata gently motioned for her daughter to sit back down, keeping her arms around her.

'Are you alright? Are you hurt?'

Katalin sucked in some air and cleared her throat twice.

'Just some scratches … some little burns.'

Beata looked at the paramedic and the tall man for an explanation.

It was the man who spoke first, just as the paramedic was opening his mouth.

'Katalin got the injuries in one of the rooms that were caught by the explosion. We, well I was with her and we were pulled out of the room by the fire platform. I'm Calum, by the way.'

'*You* were with her? What were you doing here?'

'I was looking for another girl, and I ended up being held prisoner in the same room as that girl and Katalin. Your daughter I'm assuming?'

'Prisoner? What do you mean prisoner?' Beata looked at Katalin for an explanation but she seemed to be in shock, the paramedic trying to calm her down.

Calum spoke again.

'Your daughter … I'm assuming that … she's been held in this hotel for eight years … by the owner, Marton Kovacs. And since he died, by his son Peter. Peter also tricked me into the same room where Katalin has been held all this time.'

Beata's face froze as he spoke, then she gasped in a lungful of air and wailed, a piercing, singing howl.

Calum waited a moment before he continued.

'The other girl was there too … she's badly injured.'

Beata stopped her keening abruptly. 'But why, why? Why has he kept you all here?'

'Because of Arrow Cross, I think. Because of something Marton did in the war.'

Beata shook her head repeatedly and started to howl again.

'Dear God, this has gone on too long … it's not fair … it's *so* unfair …'

Calum narrowed his eyes at her. 'What do you mean? So long?'

Beata looked at her daughter. 'Katalin knows. I told her it was a long time ago, that they were young, it was the war and things just happened that didn't exactly get planned. But now it has led to this. It's just so stupid, just damn … stupid. I'm so sorry for it, but I don't know why … I … just want the past to be gone, it's too long ago now. And now I'm told he kept you there for *eight years*? It's just so damn, damn *pointless.*'

She shrieked again, a short, frenzied burst that ended with her grasping her daughter to her again.

She pulled Katalin's head towards her own and touched their foreheads together.

'I'm so sorry, Katalin, sorry this all happened. I've missed you so much. And to think you were held by that man. It's … too much to bear.'

'But didn't you come looking for me at Marton's?'

'Of course, of course, I did. I asked him if you had been there. He said yes, but that you had left after talking to him about the book. How could I know he had you here, at this place? I had trusted him. The police went to see him too after I'd reported you as missing. I really had no suspicion about him. Never.'

For a moment, Katalin had nothing to say. The paramedic gently took her arm. 'Let's finish off this bandage. Then we'll need to get those burns dressed at the hospital.' He glanced at Beata for approval. She nodded.

Katalin sat up, peeling herself away from her mother and allowed herself to be attended to. As she sat there, another medic approached from the direction of the ambulance line, with a member of the fire platform crew trailing just behind her.

'Sir, you were with the girl we took down from the platform weren't you?'

Calum nodded.

'Are you her father, sir?'

'No, I'm someone who was looking for her … she had been held prisoner here, well, me too. Her parents are in Scotland. Why? What have you to tell me?'

'I need their details, sir. I need to speak to them, well the police will. It sounds like we need to get a police officer to talk to you about what happened here too, given what you just said.'

'Yeah, we need to speak to them. Detective Nagy is aware of me, so if we can talk to him? Anyway … how is Sarah?'

The medic lowered her eyes, then looked up again. 'Well, sir, since you were with her, I should tell you … she has died from her injuries, just now. We were treating her in the ambulance but we just couldn't stop the blood loss fast enough. I'm so sorry, sir.'

## Susan McTeer gets a visit

Susan McTeer was eating a toasted bacon sandwich for lunch. She had her feet up on the worn leather stool, watching daytime TV. Another game show, another set of rules for her to learn. She'd been watching TV a lot recently. Ever since she'd taken the money, she needed something, anything, to try and distract her thoughts from wandering around the question again and again. *What were they going to do to Calum Neuman?* It was spoiling everything, seeping into all she did, dulling her pleasures. Even this bacon sandwich.

The doorbell rang, making her start and choke softly on a morsel of toasted crust. She looked out the window, twisting her head around so she could see her driveway. There was police livery on the BMW parked across the end of it. Her heart was pounding to bursting point by the time she'd got to the door and opened it. She looked at the two male officers in front of her, furiously trying to work out which one of two topics they were going to talk to her about. Either one was going to be bad news, but one of them would be heart-breaking.

'Can we come in please?' asked one of the two, politely, once they'd established her identity.

She nodded curtly and led them through the short hallway into the lounge. She motioned for them to sit down.

Once they were all perched on the edges of their seats, the one who appeared to be taking the lead spoke. Susan sensed from the way their eyes didn't lock steadily with her own gaze, that this was bad news. She knew why they were here now.

'I'm afraid your daughter has been killed in an accident in Budapest. We were informed by the Hungarian police an hour ago. It seems there was an explosion in a hotel where she was staying. There seems to be some suspicion she may have been held there against her will, Mrs McTeer. We're very sorry. We don't have any more details at this stage, I'm afraid. My colleague here will be able to support you through this.' He turned to the other officer. 'PC James.'

Susan gasped, the shock, though not entirely unexpected, howled its way down into her guts and reverberated around her entire nervous system. She caught her breath, then started to sob.

As she held her head in her hands, despite her grief, the instinct of self-preservation surfaced and she wondered if they were going to say anything more. About a different thing. Now she felt ashamed at even worrying about that … but it had seemed money for nothing really. It might have helped Sarah get found, it might not have. Either way, she got some much-needed cash. Her former husband had a lot to answer for, for the financial mess he'd left her in.

She sat very still, waiting for the second storm to come.
It never did.

PC James talked her through what details might emerge and how they might get Sarah home. It wasn't sinking in, though. Not heard at all.

'Sure you don't need us to ring a friend? Or we can stay a while longer?'

Susan shook her head. 'Nope. I'm OK, thank you very much. I want to be alone now please.'

She showed them out, took a card from PC James and gently closed the front door. She sat back down on the sofa.

She burst into tears again and cried hard and long. As the grief welled out of her, the darkness inside intensified as she wondered what had happened to Calum Neuman. Now she hoped he was safe. She had the money so that was that, wasn't it?

A horrible, stomach-churning thought occurred to her. What if they came to get it back? Especially if Neuman had survived whatever they were planning in luring him to Budapest.

So for a very long time, every morning when Susan McTeer woke up, and often it was early, her first two, depressing, thoughts were Sarah … and the money. Breakfast didn't taste the same for almost a year.

\*

Alan Burton was feeling *very* stormy. He'd had another note dropped via the unofficial drone prison delivery service. Another failed attempt and some pathetic excuse about a gas explosion was enough to send him into such a bad temper that later that day he punched an inmate after a squabble over a pack of cigarettes and ended up in solitary for twenty-four hours as a result.

As he sat in the cell alone, he could only think of Batman and Robin, the bastardly duo. He could see them laughing through their fucking masks. One day, he pledged to himself, the Joker would be on *them*.

He'd paid the money upfront as well. Now it seemed they were reluctant to pay it back. Natural disasters and all that. And they'd handed over the cash to the mother too. Anyone would think it was a legitimate business they were in, to see their mutterings.

He'd need to see about putting them right. It didn't do to be weak. Too many people got to hear about it. Then you were nothing again. They'd failed him, for the second time, and that was the *only* point.

He stood up, punched his arms out long and hard, before closing his eyes and beginning to plot. Again.

# Homeward bound

Calum tried to stretch his legs out under the seat in front. His knees were jammed against the seat back and left him in a slightly uncomfortable position. He angled his thighs outward to allow them to relax a bit.

'Should have let Peter Kovacs cut you down to size.'

'Ha bloody ha. These damn budget airlines don't cater for normal-sized human beings. Well, not *this* airline or *this* human being anyway.'

'Oh, you *are* one of our race, then? Anyway, you're a bit taller than most, Calum.'

He grimaced at Jenna. He'd missed their banter in her time away from his office and enjoyed it in Budapest. He was wondering how to keep her semi-employed after he got back to base … and her to Inverness. If he could afford it.

'So I guess I'll call Susan McTeer when we're back, now we know the police have informed her. Mission not accomplished this time. Bit of a blot on the CV, eh? Damn awful though, just a random gas leak, could have been any, or all, of us.'

'I know you're not worried about your CV, but you don't seem too upset by her dying. Just saying.'

'Yeah. Maybe that's right. Maybe because someone more important to me died.' He looked away from her.

Jenna flushed and grabbed his arm. She was suddenly glad that she hadn't mentioned Izabella had died too.

'Calum, I'm so sorry. I … I didn't forget about Ellie … it's just, being away here, it makes you further away from home thoughts?'

He turned to her and smiled.

'You're right, Jen, don't worry. I've been a bit detached myself. Like you say, out of sight … well, not out of mind at all really, but maybe a bit fuzzier somehow. I don't know, I can't explain it.'

'Yeah, I get that. How's Cass bearing up? Sorry, I know you don't chat all the time, just thought maybe …'

'Maybe what? Maybe we'd be closer because Ellie died?'

Jenna looked at him sharply. 'No, no of course not, just thought maybe you'd been, well, supporting each other a bit.'

'Yeah. Sorry. You're right. We should do. Well, we have. A bit anyway. It's not easy, though. Not easy to *not* get the wrong end of the stick. Anyway, I'll try and get over and see her this week I guess. See how she's doing.' *No, I won't. Really bad idea.*

Jenna turned to him again and squeezed his arm. 'I'll pop some flowers down by her stone in the next few days.'

'Put some there for me too?'

'Sure.'

'Thanks, Jen. Anyway, what about you and Greg? He texted me the other day. Before I was captured. Asked how this job was going. I guess he was asking how you were too but didn't. He doesn't normally text me and I didn't get a chance to answer before Kovacs took my phone. Which reminds me, I need to get a new one pronto.'

'Well, he texted me too. Said he had no response from you. I said all was good. To be honest, I'm not sure, Cal. Not sure. Something happened in Budapest, made me feel like I needed to have a bit more life before, well, definitely before I think seriously about getting back with Greg. It's not fair on him, if I'm not sure, you know?'

'Yeah. I know.' He did know. That statement was too close to home and made him feel uncomfortable.

He squeezed her hand. The warmth of her skin briefly led him to wish he was twenty years younger. Then he pressed the call button, hoping beyond reality that they might just have some Talisker miniatures on board. It made him think of Plockton. The little harbour shoreline, with an odd sailboat out on the water and the fishing skiffs farther along, parked up after bringing in the early morning catch. The faint smell of salt in the air. It would be good to be home.

# Beata & Katalin start again

Beata drove the last mile to her house slowly, consciously delaying the moment.

The moment when she would bring her daughter back from the hospital and into their home again.

She felt it was a barrier. It had to be negotiated, it wasn't some small thing. Katalin had left because of what she had uncovered. Not with the intent of staying away for eight years admittedly, but she was *mad* with her mother. And her mother didn't blame her for that.

Beata turned the key in the front door and pushed it open. She held her daughter's arm as she stepped gingerly over the threshold into her old home.

\*

Katalin stopped a yard or so inside, taking in the smell ... lavender, home cooking. She inhaled deeply.

'I made a stew. Your favourite. To feed you up. Come on, let's sit you down and get some coffee.'

Katalin smiled wryly but did as she was told. She sat on a kitchen chair and watched her mother fiddle with the coffee grounds. She was remembering a night eight years ago, a conversation in this kitchen that had spawned all of this awful time. She was feeling good to be *home*. But living with her mother … that was different. She had kept the stories about Marton's war crimes from her. He had been a monster and killed a child.

Beata brought the cups of coffee to the table and placed them on straw coasters, together with some tiny sweet biscuits.

'Here we are, sweetheart. You can relax now. You are home. Now you will be safe, forever. I promise.'

Katalin smiled dutifully and picked up her cup.

Beata sat down next to her, perched on the edge of her chair. She looked worried, like she had some bad news to deliver.

'Katalin … this has been such a terrible ordeal for you. And me also. But we need to live our lives better now. We have to build from this. It was just so awful being without you.'

Katalin looked at her mother with a cold understanding, which forgave little for now.

Beata leant towards her and wrapped an arm around her shoulders, drawing her into her embrace.

'And there is something that makes it much, much worse, my dear Katalin.'

Katalin tried to pull away gently, to listen better, but her mother held her firmly.

'Katalin, I … I'll just say it. Marton had been holding his own daughter prisoner for eight years.'

Katlin burst free from her mother's embrace and glared at her.

**409**

'What? Don't be stupid! My father disappeared a long time ago!'

'Yes, Katalin. I did tell you that. But Marton … he was your father. Your father has been keeping you imprisoned all this time. It is so … I can't say what, it hurts *so* much to know this.'

Katalin winced. She leaked a fresh spurt of tears and blurted at her mother.

'But, Mother, why would he do that? To his own daughter?'

Beata pulled her daughter gently into her bosom and whispered over her shoulder.

'My dear. He never knew he had a little girl. I never told him. That's why.'

Katalin opened her eyes wide, despite the tears and pulled her head up.

'Mother? What … why, I mean … what were you thinking by not telling him? He was visiting our house sometimes. And he was my *father*.'

'Be … because it was a mistake, that's all. It was just once. The man who I married, he wasn't your father. He left me for another reason altogether. I'm so sorry. But I just didn't want Marton to know, in case my husband found out. Huh … in the end it didn't matter to him since he left us, but at the time … '

Katalin was overwhelmed by the news. Her mind was spinning trying to process it all, spawning a torrent of new questions.

After all the hurt of being kept captive by a man who was her mother's friend … now he was her father on top of all that? Sure, he didn't know it, but she knew it now. Who would want a child murderer for a father? And her mother kept *that* from her.

She shook her head and stood up, walked over to the window. The swing was moving in the breeze. It reminded her of that fateful day eight years ago, when she'd sat there, wondering what to make of the book she had just found.

Now, she wondered about how to re-start her life. That would include deciding whether she could live with her mother … in both senses of the word. As of two minutes ago, she wasn't sure she could do that.

# In a graveyard

Jenna was wrapped up well against the early-December chill, as she made her way down the gravel path that ran through the centre of the graveyard on the outskirts of Inverness.

She carried a small bunch of roses in front of her, together with some carnations that Calum had asked her to bring. Not much for a young life.

She slowed as she approached Ellie's grave, sensing an aura of sadness shrouding the headstone. She stopped in front of the plot, read the inscription on the stone and started to cry gently.

She hadn't known Ellie that well, she'd moved away from Plockton with her mother Cassie after she'd split up with Calum. It was a few years back now, but she remembered her as a small child playing on the village harbour with her friend after school. It made her think of home herself, what she'd left behind there in Plockton. The peaceful, loch-side village … and Gregor.

Stooping to slip the flowers into the metal holder, she became aware of footsteps. She didn't look to see, didn't want to invade anyone else's private moments.

But the steps came closer and then she felt a hand on her shoulder.

'So nice to see you here, Jenna.'

She turned to face the voice.

'Oh. It's you, Cassie. Hi.'

'Hello. It's lovely when I see someone else at her grave. Feel less alone with it, you know?'

'Yeah, I guess so, Cass.'

Cassie pressed her lips together. She looked at what Jenna was holding in her hands.

'Nice flowers.'

Jenna wasn't sure what to say. She hesitated before confessing.

'Yes, they are, the carnations are from Calum, he asked me to bring some for him. He's a bit busy this week.'

'Uhuh?'

Jenna shrugged her shoulders. Somewhat apologetically.

'That's Calum. Distances himself from messy emotional things, eh?'

Jenna smiled and nodded.

'How is he anyway?'

*Loaded question. Not answering that one.*

'Talk about Ellie much?'

Jenna shook her head. 'Not a lot, no.'

'Hmm. Talk about me? At all?'

Jenna looked up at her. She spoke slowly and kindly. 'Not really, Cass, no.'

Cassie sighed a long sigh. Her breath warmed the chill air in front of her and turned to mist.

'That's that then, I guess.'

# List of Characters

### Calum Neuman

Scottish private investigator residing in Plockton, a small village on the west coast of Scotland.

### Cassie Neuman

Calum Neuman's former wife.

### Ellie Neuman

Daughter of Calum and Cassie Neuman.

### Jenna Strick

Calum's former assistant, now at university in Inverness, Scotland.

### Gregor Macleod

Jenna Strick's former boyfriend in her home town village of Plockton.

### Sarah McTeer

Scottish Masters student, researching in Budapest.

### Susan McTeer

Sarah McTeer's mother. Resides in Inverness, Scotland.

## Aliz Gal

The manageress of the Hotel Cristal, Budapest, Hungary.

## Katalin Sandor

A young woman from Budapest. Daughter of Beata Sandor.

## Beata Sandor

Head librarian at the Ervin Szabo central library, Budapest, Hungary

## Marton Kovacs

The elderly owner of the Hotel Cristal, Budapest, Hungary.

## Peter Kovacs

Marton Kovacs' son, practising as a doctor in Bucharest, Romania.

## Alfred Nemeth

A friend and former colleague of Marton Kovacs, owner of a jeweller's shop in Budapest.

**David Pasztor**

Marton Kovacs' solicitor.

**Eszter Borbely**

Hungarian academic, assisting Sarah McTeer in her research in Budapest.

**Izabella**

A barmaid at the Grand Danubius hotel.

**Niamh Sampson**

The flatmate of Sarah McTeer in Inverness.

**Alan Burton**

An inmate at Barlinnie jail, Glasgow, Scotland. Jailed for a previous attempt on Calum Neuman's life. Had also been incarcerated due to evidence from Calum Neuman in an earlier case.

**Hanna Elek**

A cleaner at the Hotel Cristal, Budapest.

**D.I. John Gregg**

A Scottish police detective, based in Glasgow.

**Ervin Nagy**

A police detective in Budapest.

# ACKNOWLEDGEMENTS

Thanks are due to:

Jill for her reviews and support

Max for proof reading

Dan for the hotel illustration

John Hudspith, for being my editor

Cover design: Jane Dixon-Smith.

## ALSO BY THIS AUTHOR IN THE CALUM NEUMAN SERIES

**Search** (available in paperback and Kindle). Buy from Amazon direct or through www.dkbohlman.com

If you liked this story, please leave me a review on Amazon it helps so much. Only a paragraph is necessary!
Many thanks, D.K.Bohlman

Printed in Great Britain
by Amazon